MOTHERSHIP

MOTHERSHIP

BOOK ONE
OF THE
EVER-EXPANDING
UNIVERSE

MARTIN LEICHT
AND ISLA NEAL

SAGA PRESS

LONDON SYDNEY **NEW YORK** TORONTO NEW DELHI

AN IMPRINT OF SIMON & SCHUSTER, INC.

1230 AVENUE OF THE AMERICAS, NEW YORK, NEW YORK 10020

This book is a work of fiction. Any references to historical events, real people, or real places are used fictitiously. Other names, characters, places, and events are products of the author's imagination, and any resemblance to actual events or places or persons, living or dead, is entirely coincidental.

Text copyright © 2012 by Lisa Graff and Martin Leicht

Cover illustration copyright © 2016 by Tim O'Brien

All rights reserved, including the right to reproduce this book or portions thereof in any form whatsoever. For information address Saga Press Subsidiary Rights Department, 1230 Avenue of the Americas, New York, NY 10020.

SAGA PRESS and colophon are trademarks of Simon & Schuster, Inc.

For information about special discounts for bulk purchases, please contact Simon & Schuster Special Sales at 1-866-506-1949 or business@simonandschuster.com.

The Simon & Schuster Speakers Bureau can bring authors to your live event. For more information or to book an event, contact the Simon & Schuster Speakers Bureau at 1-866-248-3049 or visit our website at www.simonspeakers.com.

Also available in a SIMON & SCHUSTER hardcover edition

The text for this book is set in Electra LT.

Manufactured in the United States of America

First Saga Press paperback edition January 2016

2 4 6 8 10 9 7 5 3

The Library of Congress has cataloged the hardcover edition as follows:

Leicht, Martin.

Mothership / Martin Leicht and Isla Neal. — 1st ed.

p. cm. — (The ever-expanding universe ; bk. 1)

Summary: In 2074, while attending the Hanover School for Expecting Teen Mothers, set aboard an earth-orbiting spaceship, sixteen-year-old Elvie finds herself in the middle of an alien race war and makes a startling discovery about her pregnancy.

ISBN 978-1-4424-2960-4 (hc)

[1. Human-alien encounters—Fiction. 2. Pregnancy—Fiction. 3. War—Fiction. 4. Science fiction.] I. Neal, Isla. II. Title.

PZ7.L53283Mo 2012

[Fic]—dc23 2011026283

ISBN 978-1-4814-4286-2 (mass market pbk)

ISBN 978-1-4424-2962-8 (eBook)

To Stephen and Joanna, who were there from the beginning
—I. N.
To my parents, who were there even earlier
—M. L.

CHAPTER ONE

IN WHICH OUR HEROINE FALLS ON HER ASS, LIKE, A LOT

As far as scientists have been able to determine, the primary function of the human coccyx, or tailbone, is to remind us that once upon a time we were all monkeys or something. But I happen to know that it can still serve a useful purpose. Say, for example, that a pregnant teenager three weeks from her due date, who weighs, oh, approximately 145 pounds (lay off, all right? The baby loves ice cream), were shoved down force-fully on a Treadtrack in gym class by a bitchy cheerleader. This so-called vestigial growth would most definitely act as a shock absorber, preventing serious damage to the rest of said pregnant chick's body.

Basically what I'm trying to say is that evolution saved my ass. Well, evolution and the fact that when you're orbiting the planet this high up, the artificial gravity is bound to be a little more forgiving. But that's not nearly as poetic.

I guess I should be thanking my lucky stars, seeing as I'm still in one piece, but instead I'm furiously scrambling to yank my pregnant keister off the Treadtrack and away from Britta McVicker.

"Need some help?" she sneers in a tone that I'm sure is supposed to sound sincere. Britta is the aforementioned bitchy cheerleader. We go way back, Britta and me—too far, if you ask me. She doesn't remember, but I've known the girl since she first mocked my Hercules lunch box in second grade. We are the only two students at the Hanover School who knew each other before the school year began. Because apparently the universe is not through punishing me just yet.

I scramble to my feet quickly so that I don't roll with the Treadtrack all the way into the wall. Balance is not my strongest trait at this point in my pregnancy, but I still have the maturity and poise to flip Britta the bird without stumbling again.

Britta snorts. "Jeez, tubbo," she says, beginning what I am already positive is going to be one of her classic McVicker slams, "how'd you ever trick anyone into pity screwing you?"

That's when one of Britta's innies comes over to take in the scene. She's this girl who glommed on to Britta the second we launched into orbit and who spends so much time stroking Britta's ego that in my head I only ever think to call her Other Cheerleader.

"Pity screw or not," Other Cheerleader says, jerking her head in my direction, "the guy must've been blind *and* deaf." And I have to admit, that one stings a little, until she decides to take it a step further. "And had, like, no sense of smell," she adds. "And he also didn't have—what's the other one? Touch. Yeah, he was touchless."

I bite the inside of my cheek as I yank my sweat shorts down at the hem. I avoid making eye contact with Britta. Would she be so smug if she knew that . . . ? No, I decide, staring at my shoes. I'm not going to go there. Britta McVicker is not nearly worth it.

But I guess I should've gone *somewhere,* because before I even notice what's happening, Other Cheerleader has punched the Treadtrack control, jacking up the speed to max. I topple over again as the exercise track flies under my feet, and I crash into a girl running behind me. She falls on top of me, and together we slam into the wall, the track still running underneath us. The thing damn near burns a hole right through my ugly running shorts.

"Turn off the track!" comes a cry from the far side of the gym. It's Dr. Marsden, Hanover's school physician, rushing over to us past the station of Japanese fit-bots, with our PE teacher, Mr. Zaino. Other Cheerleader shuts the track down and tries to put a concerned look on her face. Although, if you ask me, it just looks like she's eaten too many beans and is holding in a nasty moon rocket. When Dr. Marsden reaches us, he looks down at me with concern. "That was quite a spill, Elvie," he says kindly, helping me to my feet. "You all right?"

Even though he's my school doctor and all, I blush a little bit when he takes my hand. I am *not* into the whole May–December-romance thing, but you'd have to be from another planet not to think Dr. Marsden is one damn fine specimen of a man, standing nearly two meters tall with broad shoulders and just enough stubble to let you know that he's sophisticated but still a little dangerous. But I try to play it off cool. "It's not the last time I'll fall on my butt," I say with a shrug.

Zaino is more accusatory than inquisitive. "What happened?" he asks. Zaino's a pretty good-looking guy himself, although he's a little too rah-rah about dodgeball to seriously crush on.

Britta gives me this look like, *You better not rat me out*, and while nothing would give me more satisfaction than watching her and her doppelganger lackey run laps for the next hour, I know I won't say anything.

"I just misjudged the speed," I lie, dusting myself off. I turn to the girl who toppled over behind me on the Treadtrack. It's this chick from my trig class who is, like, *always* chewing on her hair. She's currently looking at me like I'm the world's biggest doof—although, hello, she's the one with an entire braid crammed into her mouth. "Sorry," I tell her.

She mumbles something in reply, although who can tell what through all that hair?

"Are you sure you're not hurt?" Dr. Marsden asks again. I look at Britta and smirk a little.

"Well, I *am* kinda sore, but I'll survive," I say with as much earnest reluctance as I can fake. "I'm mostly just worried about the baby." I place my hands under my swollen belly and put on my most concerned frown.

The doc nods. "Why don't you go back to your quarters and lie down for a bit? I'll give you a pass to skip yoga next period, and we'll see how you're feeling at your checkup this afternoon."

Game and match. I'm pretty sure there's not one girl on this ship who wouldn't give her right arm to get out of a single day of underwater prenatal yoga.

Chewie spits the braid out of her mouth. "Uh, maybe I should lie down too," she says.

"Just run it off, Sanderson," Mr. Zaino replies.

On my way out of the gym, I offer Britta and her friend my smuggest grin. "Enjoy yoga, ladies," I tell them.

"I can see your fat ass through the hole in your pants," Britta shoots back.

I want to ask her if when her baby's born she's going to cut the horns off right away, or wait until the kid is older. But I'm a civil sort of gal, and civil sorts of gals don't say things like that.

Did I not mention earlier that Britta McVicker—former cheerleading captain and most popular girl at Lower Merion— is now simply another knocked-up teenager at the Hanover School for Expecting Teen Mothers, just like me? Due to pop any day now too.

Okay, so it's not like I actually *wanted* to end up preggers in outer space or anything. If you'd told me a year ago that I'd be here on this ship, and with Britta McFreakingVicker to boot, I'd've told you to check the dosage on your Phezalin prescription. But, you know, shit happens.

I guess, if you want to be specific about it, the first shitty thing that happened was that I got the hots for Cole Archer, which was the perfect example of what my dad would call "one's loins speaking more loudly than one's brain." My dad finally stopped using that expression when I told him that saying the word "loins" was the most psychologically damaging thing a parent could do to a child. But maybe I should have let him stick with it, because when it came to Cole Archer, my brain didn't stand much of a chance. His eyes were this unearthly blue-green-blue-again that could, like, make you melt or something. And that part wouldn't have been so bad — the getting the hots and melting, I mean. But somehow that single, solitary time we got steamy, I — hello, biology class! — got knocked up. And then Cole totally bailed, leaving me with one bun and no baker. Which, you know, sucks and stuff.

The second shitty thing that happened was that I was forcibly enrolled at the Hanover School for Expecting Teen Mothers. Since I'm a member of Hanover's inaugural class, they don't have a motto yet, but if they ever decide to get one, my vote will be for "Catapulting Troubled Young Ladies into Outer Space Since 2074." Well, technically we're in low Earth orbit, but that's not as catchy. I've been here for three full months now, and even though my baby is due to pop fairly soon — the week before Christmas, like someone's idea of a gag gift — I'll be spending the rest of my junior year here with all the other Hanover girls. I mean, it's not like they can just land the whole ship for winter break or anything. I can't decide if life on board the *Echidna* will be better or worse after the baby is born. As meticulously scheduled as my every second is now, I get the feeling that once the Goober arrives and I hand it off to the adoptive services coordinator, I'm going to have a redonk amount of free periods. Which, given the bafflingly terrible connection speeds and limited flat pic library up here, could actually be more of a curse than a blessing.

As I travel the ten levels on the lift from the Health and

Wellness Center up to the living quarters, I decide that a bruised coccyx is a steep but acceptable price to pay for an hour's respite from the inane chattering of my classmates. I'm only a few steps from the door to my stateroom when I feel a buzz in my back pocket. I yank out my phone and check it. A blink from Ducky. Smiling, I tap the screen while the phone's still vibrating.

check it out found britta's online dating profile.

I tap the link and shut the door, and then flop down onto my bed in my holey gym shorts while the new site is buffering. It'll take, like, nine hundred years. Shit takes *forever* in space. Which totally blows, because my blinks with Ducky are the only thing keeping me from going completely bonkers at Hanover.

When I finally get to the site, it's not a dating profile. It's a vid of a baby elephant peeing. Like, this fire-hydrant torrent of pee.

I snort so loud, a little snot comes out my nose. I shift my phone around until I get a good angle against my belly, and I blink back to Ducky.

britta's never been that hot in her life. flippn skank just tried to take me out in gym. :(

I told Ducky once that Britta McVicker was my arch-nemesis, and he told me she was more like my arch-nematode. Which really just goes to show that while I was busy getting knocked up, Ducky was actually paying attention in life science. But nerd king status notwithstanding, he was right. Britta McVicker is a genuine grade-A worm. The lowest form of life on the planet—and now, God help me, in space, too.

I mean, really, I know that I'm not exactly a saint, but I swear that in my former life I must have been a claims adjuster or something, because there is no other way to explain why fate decided that Britta McVicker should *follow me into the cosmos*. If only I'd gotten a screen cap of my face three months ago on launch day, when Britta showed up with two trunks, eight garment bags, three totes, and a big-ass baby bump of her own. Up until that point I thought the worst thing I'd have to deal with until my love child popped out was suffering through morning sickness in zero grav. I didn't even know the girl had gotten herself storked. But she had, of course. She trumps my due date by two whole weeks. Which made sense, once I did the math. But I don't care to think about that particular math very often.

I'm guessing the surprise wasn't a pleasant one for Britta, either. As soon as she saw me, she got a look on her face like she'd just accidentally used the wrong hair smoother. I think maybe I deal better with shock than some other people.

I feel a rumble on top of my bump. Another blink from Ducky.

:(heres something to cheer u up, E-fab.

I tap the link, and twenty thousand years later it opens. Ducky's gone and bought me another poster. I smile. Damn you, Ducky. Way to make me cheer up just when I'm getting a really good funk on. I aim the phone at the last square of remaining white space on my wall, tap IMPRINT, and *snap*! The image is pasted on my wall next to the last poster he sent me, of *The Godfather*. Ducky knows I have a thing for classic flat pics, so lately whenever I've been feeling particularly gruesome, he goes and buys me a poster of one of my faves. So far I have *The Princess Bride*, *Transformers 5* (totally the best of the series, no matter how hard Ducky argues for number 7), *Rebel Without a Cause* (Mom was really into James Dean, Dad tells me), and now, the crown jewel, *Mega Shark Versus Giant Octopus: The Musical*. Call me a sap, but I eat up that tortured unrequited love stuff with a spoon.

As I'm rummaging through my closet for a change of clothes, I set a hand on my belly and feel around for the Goober—that's what I've decided to call the mini Cole who up and ruined my life. Sure enough, the little bugger's lodged itself lengthwise in my uterus. It's weird to be able to feel a tiny *thing* inside you. That's something they never mention in health class, that you can actually feel it, especially when they get bigger. Head here, over there an elbow, foot poking into what used to be your gallbladder. It's a little gross if you think about it too hard, being a human hotel room for some kid you've never even met before. So I try not to think about it very often. Instead I try the trick Dr. Marsden taught me, rubbing my belly in tight little circles, slow and steady. Dr. Marsden says this calms the kid down, lets it know you care about it. I told Dr. Marsden that all I cared about was the little bastard not kicking me in the bladder anymore, and he just handed me my vitamins and told me the rubbing would probably work for that, too.

After I'm changed into my "favorite" pair of maternity stretch pants, I check my clock. Almost an hour until my physical, and not a thing to do.

Thank you, Dr. Marsden.

The trauma of gym class has left me famished, so I decide to make a trip upstairs to see what grub I can rustle up. I grab my phone as I head for the door, just in case Ducky decides to send me any other choice Britta vids, and make my way down the corridor toward the elevator.

The Hanover School is actually an old recommissioned low-orbit luxury cruise liner. The kind that folks my dad's age used to travel on for tacky ooh-look-we're-playing-shuffleboard-in-space style vacations back in the fifties and sixties, when being in orbit was still sort of a novel experience. These days, of course, you can't throw a rock out the viewport without hitting a vacant ship or orbital station that's floating aimlessly through the void. Most of them have been empty for decades, or are home to some less than desirable characters, but in recent years there's been a real push to refit them as residential, commercial, and educational estates. "Ozone re-gentrification" my dad derisively calls it. The L.O.C. *Echidna* is supposedly pretty small by space cruiser standards, but the first time I set my swollen feet on board, I have to admit I sucked in my breath at how freaking huge it is. It's pretty kitsch, honestly, but it's not all bad.

My cabin is on deck eighteen, same as the other girls. There are more than a thousand rooms on board, but the place is mostly empty. There's just forty-six of us girls, and about half that many teachers and counselors. Apparently hundreds of applicants were turned down for matriculation. I guess I should feel honored that I have such a desirable set of ovaries, but mostly I just feel how deserted and lonely this place is. The faculty all sleep on the next floor up, deck nineteen. Kate Mueller once told me that the faculty's rooms are much bigger, although how she came across *that* information is probably more interesting than the square footage. There are twenty-five decks total, ten for staterooms, one each for the mess hall, auditorium, and the athletic courts. There's a big honking hangar for shuttles that runs nearly half the length of the deck, and it's situated in the lower fore section of the ship. Leading off of that is the entry parlor, the game rooms, and the Health and Wellness Center. The HWC houses all the medical suites, in addition to the fitness center and the understandably (given the condition of most of the school's residents) underutilized sauna. The lido deck has the big lap pool and "sunbathing area," which reflects sunlight through a system of adjustable mirrors so that people can work on their melanoma even in space. I'm heading for the uppermost level of the ship, the observation deck, where the snack kiosks are.

I'm steps away from the elevator when I run into someone barreling around the corner. For the third time this morning, I find myself flat on my ass. Although to spice things up, this time I'm covered with dozens of tiny, hard, and stinky round objects.

Brussels sprouts. I'm covered in brussels sprouts.

"Good grief, Miss Nara. Would it really hurt to look where you're going?"

I look up at my brussels sprout attacker. It's none other than Fred, Hanover's "chef." I'm no gourmand or anything, but even I know that someone who serves up succotash more than three times a week needs to think about returning to culinary school.

"Sorry," I mumble, flipping over to my hands and knees before grabbing a handful of the vile little veggies to toss back into Fred's crate. I shouldn't be apologizing. Fred was the one who wasn't looking where he was going. And what the heck is he even doing walking around the girls' living quarters carrying a crate of brussels sprouts, anyway? But I'm not going to argue with a dude who holds my gastrointestinal fate in his hands.

He just growls at me, ever the picture of friendliness. "Shouldn't you be in *class*?"

"I have a pass from Dr. M," I tell him.

Fred harrumphs like he doesn't believe me, but I guess playing truant officer is low on his list of priorities at the moment, because all he says to me is, "Try to stay out of trouble, will you?"

"I'll do that." I plop the last sprout into the box and shuffle as quickly as I can to the elevator.

When the lift doors open on the observation deck, I find the floor totally deserted. This is my favorite deck—completely encircled by curved, six-meter-high windows, permanently bathed in Earth light. The first few weeks after launch, anytime we didn't have class or yoga or some other mandatory project, you could always find all the girls up here, faces plastered against the windows, staring at Earth as it shifted down below us. It takes a little less than two hours to make a full orbit around the globe, and for those first few weeks, just watching that sucker sweep by was like tweaking out in geography class. "Look, there's Japan!" "Holy crap, it's the Nile!" "Guys, check it. I can cover up Greenland with my thumb." But once they'd seen Earth go by a few times, they seemed to get over it. Now the observation deck stays pretty much empty around the clock.

The only reason most girls head to the observation deck these days is for the snack area. It's basically just an alcove filled with vending machines. Junk food, juices, and some sort of dehydrated dessert called Astronaut's Delight, which I think is someone's idea of a joke. That corner of the spaceship is a pregnant lady's neon-lit paradise. But there's one machine that is calling to me more than any other—the one stuffed with pint-size cartons of Midnight Craving. Yes, the flavors and ad campaign that are specifically targeted at pregnant women border on the offensively stereotypical, but damn, sometimes you *do* just want to dive into a pint of Double Cheese'N'Chocolate Pretzel Swirl.

The vending machines on board the *Echidna* work on the HONOR System—Honest Operations Necessitating Objective Reward. You do something the faculty thinks is pro, they give you points for vended nachos. I slap the button for my ice cream and hold my HONOR bracelet up to the scanner. The scanner beeps and flashes red, and then the robotic voice I'm beginning to loathe informs me: "You currently have *zero* HONOR points. Request for *Cherry Marsala* denied."

It's not like I'm shocked that I'm out of HONOR points, since for some reason the Hanover faculty doesn't seem to condone my ditching Mandarin class, or napping during study hour. Still, I could really go for some craving cream right now. I take a step back and stare at the vending machine for a minute, the scanner blinking its infuriating red eye at me in this, like, Morse code, which I am *positive* means "No-ice-cream-for-you-no-ice-cream-for-you." But I do my best to ignore it, and focus instead on what my dad likes to call the "thinking behind the machinery."

I was six years old the first time my dad strapped a tool belt on me and took me out to the garage for what he liked to call lessons in self-sufficiency. "Elvie," he told me seriously, "no matter how advanced a machine is, there's a brain behind its creation. A human brain. And *you*"—he tapped my skull—"you have a human brain too. Right?" I shrugged. I was pissed because I wanted to be inside playing Jetman online with Ducky, not in the garage with my dad staring at a broken toaster. "You do," he told me. "You have a brain. A good one. Which means that no machine is a match for you. Now"—he plopped the busted gizmo on the worktable in front of me and yanked a screwdriver out of my tool belt, wrapping my six-year-old fingers around it— "you can come back inside when you've fixed the toaster."

"But I don't even *like* toast!" I hollered at my dad as he shut the garage door behind him. It took me five hours to fix the damn thing. And to this day Ducky still totally kicks my ass at Jetman.

Looking back, it probably would've been better if my dad had taught me how to survive hunky boys and bitchy cheerleaders, but at least now I know I can defeat this vending machine in three minutes tops.

First I unhook my Swiss Army knife from my belt and

use the mini screwdriver to pop the top panel off the vending machine's scanner, exposing the vid card and laser reader. Then I take my dad's lucky old five-dollar coin from my pocket and slip the sucker between the card and the magnetic strip at the bottom of the panel. After a few seconds I swipe my bracelet again, and *BEEP!*—"You have *one million* HONOR points. Request for *Cherry Marsala* accepted. Your remaining balance is *one million* HONOR points."

Child's play.

I peel off the top of the ice cream carton and pop out the tiny spoon underneath. Then I settle myself into one of the observation chairs, staring down at Earth while the ice cream melts into smaller and smaller ovals on my tongue.

I lean forward in my chair and study Earth below. Having passed over the western coast of Africa, we're now directly above the Canary Islands, with the Atlantic Ocean stretching out in front of us. When I was a kid, I used to spend hours poring over my mom's giant book of maps, running my fingers over the lines of rivers she'd planned to raft down, or cliffs she wanted to climb, or valleys she wanted to hike. I'd study the careful curve of her letters in all the spots where she'd written *Can't wait!* or *Won't this be fun?* All the places she would've gotten to if she hadn't had me and then died, like, a nanosecond later. I must've memorized the whole world through that book. And even though I never really officially met the lady, every time I'm up on this deck, I feel like maybe I know my mom a little bit better—staring down at her book of maps blown up life-size.

Just as I notice the East Coast of North America coming

into view, I get a pang in my belly that at first I think means I have to pee but that I soon recognize as homesickness. Honestly, I'd rather need to use the toilet. I sigh and flop back into my chair, doing my best *not* to squint at the continent to pinpoint which blobby part is Ardmore, Pennsylvania. I miss my dad. I miss Ducky. I even miss that goddamn high school.

You'd think that life two hundred and fifty kilometers above Earth's surface would be totally different from life in the suburbs of Philadelphia. But it turns out it's almost exactly the same. I still spend more time doodling in English than diagramming sentences. I still talk to Ducky more than anyone else. And I still have to deal with mega-skank Britta McVicker. I can't even believe cheerleaders are allowed to breed.

From my ice cream container I hear a dull *thunk*. My spoon has hit the bottom of the pint without me realizing it. I'm just debating how much my hips will hate me if I go back for another pint, when from behind me comes a soft, quick rumble, and the ship rocks under my feet. It's over almost as soon as it began, but if there's one thing I know about orbiting the planet, it's that bumps are bad. As I'm heading to the window to see if maybe we collided with some debris or something, there's another thud, and my jacked-up center of gravity lands me ass-down on my ice cream carton, bringing the grand total to four pratfalls in one afternoon. The intercom from the far-up corner of the observation deck crackles to life, but all that I can make out is static.

I hoist myself up onto my feet, and I'm sure I have flecks of cherry, butterscotch, and mushroom smeared on the butt of my maternity stretch pants, but at the moment I'm slightly more concerned about the ship. The lights above me start flickering, dimming and sparking back to life. In and out, light and dark. The displays by the door are glitching too, and now I'm starting to freak just a little bit. I'm trying to remember the Survival Checklist for Emergencies in Space my dad made me memorize before launch, but all I can get through is "Oxygen? Check!" before my feet roll out from under me again.

Okay, this is starting to get old.

And now the Goober is at it too, kicking me in the bladder.

"Listen, bud!" I shout, flat on my back, my right elbow wedged under a chair. "Stop kicking me! I do not want to *pee* right now!"

I manage to right myself again, and I make it to the window as the intercom sputters back to life. Someone is saying something over the static, I can tell that much, but I can't make out what it is. Whoever it is certainly isn't speaking English. The sounds are deep, creaky, guttural. Like no language I've ever heard.

I press my body against the full-length window, so close to it that the Goober can probably see out too, and together we examine the length of the ship. We have a full 360-degree view from here, but I'm so busy looking for debris that it's several seconds before I spot the obvious.

Protruding from the starboard side of the *Echidna*, like a giant tumor, is another ship.

Another ship?

I race to the door, ignoring the Goober kicking me the whole way, and I'm just about to fly down the main staircase when something passing by the foot of the stairwell makes me reconsider that course of action.

Dudes in helmets. With guns.

Da-*fuh*?

I duck behind the door and try to hide the best someone can with a fetus jutting out her front end. I don't know who these dudes are, and I can't see their faces, but I know for a fact that they weren't on board ten minutes ago. The faculty doesn't pack heat. They usually stick with demerits. Which means that the L.O.C. *Echidna* is under attack.

Lights flickering, intercom crackling, I suddenly realize: Everyone else is on the lido deck doing underwater prenatal yoga *except me*.

And that's when I think something else. Probably the most real, true thought I've ever had.

Oh, shit.

CHAPTER TWO

IN WHICH WE PAUSE FOR A
BRIEF FLASHBACK

"No guns allowed," Ducky says, reaching his scrawny arm across my face to dip a deep-fried pickle chip into the peanut butter jar. "The whole point is to think of nonviolent forms of torture."

I push his hand away and grab for my phone to flip the channel on the TV, finally stopping on an infomercial for the Food Atomizer 9000. *"Turn those greasy, fatty snacks into a light, refreshing mist!"*

"Whatever, Gandhi," I say. "I'm not going to *shoot* her. I'm going to make her *think* I'll shoot her so she wets herself in front of the French club."

Ducky ponders this as he crunches down on my newest hormone-inspired concoction. It took several failed efforts, and we lost three bottles of peanut oil, two jars of gherkins, and a few patches of skin in the attempt to get the frying process down, but now every taste bud on my tongue is grateful we persevered. Pickles and peanut butter washed down with butterscotch milk shakes must taste disgusting to anyone who isn't incubating a fetus, but Ducky insists on eating whatever I do, as part of some solidarity thing.

"Nope," he says after he licks the peanut butter off his bottom lip. "No guns."

We've been playing Most Ingenious Ways to Destroy Britta McVicker, the game that Ducky invented this afternoon to cheer me up. I have to say it's working pretty well, although my ideas keep leaning toward physical pain and/or public humiliation, whereas Ducky seems intent on working on a strictly psychological level. Like sneaking into Britta's house every morning to swap out her bra with a series of nearly identical brassieres with infinitesimally larger cup sizes, causing her to believe that her boobs are shrinking. I had no idea what an evil mastermind Ducky was until he busted that one out.

Playing the game with Ducky, I can almost forget that Britta's been trying to destroy *me* for the past two and a half months. Or that she's coming pretty close to succeeding. She's always been a bit of an ogre to anyone unfortunate enough to cross her path—she even made Miss Langhoff cry back in second grade with her point by point criticism of her slingbacks—and I've had the bad luck to be in her path a *lot*. (I'm pretty sure that whatever schedule-bots have assigned our teachers for the past eight years have been downloaded with a virus specifically designed to make Elvie's life miserable, because Britta and I *always* have at least four classes together.) But lately she's been particularly gruesome. It's like, now that she doesn't have a boyfriend at her beck and call, she's hell-bent on making the entire human population as unhappy as she is, and I'm the closest victim. Her latest pièce de résistance was having my likeness superimposed as the "before" example in a poster for poor hygiene awareness that was then snapped all over the school. The posters were so effective that the principal is beginning a policy on mandatory showers after gym.

I swear that pic was taken during my bout with food poisoning last year.

I sigh as I reach for another pickle chip, and Ducky raises a concerned eyebrow.

"Yes?" he asks me.

I shake my head. "I'm just glad it's almost summer, that's all." There's only one more week of sophomore year left, but honest to God I'm not sure I'm going to make it. "It'll be nice to be Britta-free for a few months."

He thinks on that. "Do you think she's been more evil lately because she"—he glances down at my stomach—"*knows*?"

"Nah," I say quickly, popping the pickle into my mouth. I've put on a couple pounds, sure, but I'm not showing yet. I haven't even reached the end of the first trimester. And Britta's not exactly Sherlock Holmes. Although, God help me if she ever *does* find out about this baby. And the father.

I swallow and return my focus to watching TV.

"So," Ducky says after we've been watching the infomercial for a while, and I can tell by his forced-casual tone that he's been thinking pretty hard about what he wants to say next. "How's your urine flow?"

I cough so hard, a glob of pickle shoots across the room

and sticks just below the TV screen. "Excuse me?"

"I've been checking out that new site I told you about," Ducky says. He tosses another chip into his mouth while he says it, as though talking about my pee is what we always do with our after-school time. "They said you're supposed to document how much you go, every day of the first trimester. I signed you up for a free online account so you can track it."

I didn't want to tell Ducky I was pregnant. I did *not*. But I was starting to get hormonal and teary at, like, everything—big things like Cole skipping town, obvi, but also not-so-big things like accidentally oversteeping my tea. I guess what finally tipped him off was the unfortunate incident at my sixteenth birthday dinner, where Dad lopped the head off my panda cake and I cried for well over an hour. I was able to pass it off as normal girl hormones to my Dad, but Ducky was not so easily deceived. He wrung the truth out of me that night, and since then he's quickly earned Best Bud of the Millennia status with how awesome and supportive he's been. He comes with me to doctors' appointments and spends time researching alternative birthing practices and prenatal nutrition. I'm really hoping he'll go and get E. coli soon so I can donate my kidney and make it up to him, but so far he seems totally healthy. Which if you ask me is just being selfish.

"Gee, thanks, a pee diary," I say, grabbing a handful of pickle chips. I forgo the peanut butter, letting the tangy brine tickle my tongue.

Ducky seems to have missed the I-don't-really-want-to-talk-about-my-pregnancy tone in my voice. "Did you check out those vitamins I told you about? They're chewy. You like chewy."

"I can't get them without a prescription, and I can't get a prescription without parental consent." I reach for my milk shake to wash down my snack, but before I can get to it, Ducky puts his hand on top of mine.

"You have to tell him, you know." He's giving me that sweet, deeply concerned look—the one that makes me want to punch him right in his sweet, deeply concerned face.

I pull my hand away from Ducky's and grab my phone, aiming it at the TV. "Wait, this is the best part," I say, and turn up the volume.

As the woman in the infomercial sprays atomized chili cheese fries onto the tongues of ten kilted Scotsmen, who spontaneously break into the world's worst bagpipe rendition of the classic tune "Funky Cold Medina," Ducky pokes me in the knee with his big toe, trying to get me to look at him. But I ignore him so long that he finally gives up.

Ducky's right, of course. Sooner or later I need to tell my dad about this thing in my uterus. Because he's a pretty smart guy, and I'm thinking he just might notice when a baby blows out my girl parts six and a half months from now. But—call me crazy—I'm not exactly superstoked to tell my father that his only darling daughter went and got herself fertilized a week before her PSAT.

The infomercial finally comes to an end, only to start all over again. And as I'm double-barreling the straws of my milk shake, giving myself serious brain freeze, that's when I notice Ducky—pressing his finger into the bottom of the pickle bowl with this total puppy-dog look of concern as he studies the coffee table. It's obvious that while I've been zoning out on junk TV, he's been busy worrying about me.

I know I shouldn't think this, but part of me seriously wishes it were Ducky's baby I was having, instead of Cole's. Not because I'd want to, ew, *do* it with Ducky (Ducky is ruling the Friend Zone with an iron fist), but because I know he'd actually be cool about it. He definitely wouldn't bail on me the second I told him he'd knocked me up, for one thing. He'd, like, squeeze me up in a hug and kiss my forehead and tell me we'd figure it out together. All the things Cole Archer was too busy packing up his suitcase to have the time to do. If it were Ducky's baby, maybe I'd actually want to keep the thing. Because Ducky would make a hell of a dad. He might even be amenable to sticking around, going to PTA meetings while I'm off colonizing planets—assuming this little detour hasn't nixed that plan. And because I wouldn't mind having a miniature Ducky around all the time, with the same shaggy black curls, goofy brown eyes, and long pointy elbows (seriously, they could, like, cut paper). But it turns out that the kind of guy you want to raise a baby with isn't always the kind you want to make one with in the first place.

"Ducky?" I say. He looks up, his pointer finger still covered in brine bits. I give him a soft smile. "Don't worry about me so much, all right? I'll be okay, I swear."

He bites his bottom lip. "But you don't have a *plan*," he says.

The guy is starting to sound just a little bit like my dad, which is seriously making me rethink donating my kidney to him. But I fight the urge to sock him with a couch pillow. "A plan?" I say. "I've got a plan." He raises an eyebrow at me. "Seriously. Check it out. I'm going to rock the bump for six-and-whatever more months, Lamaze it out in, like, an hour, and some infertile rich couple will adopt the crap out of it. Then next year I'll get accepted early admission into the honors program at Penn State and spend all of senior year chillaxing while you're stressing about your SATs. See? A plan." I've been gunning for an engineering scholarship to the Honors College since the president first proposed the Ares Project as part of his Solar Colonization Initiative when I was still in middle school. How could I not want to be a part of that? An actual colony on Mars—the first ever terraforming attempt on another planet. Sure, there are a few small domed colonies on the moon, like New Houston, but that's child's play compared to what they're planning now. Of course, the program is still in its infancy, at least ten years off—which will give me plenty of time to ace my way through college, get into a top space engineering grad program, and then hopefully qualify for one of the eight NASA postdoc fellowships to prepare engineers for Ares. I've had the itch for this forever, and before now there'd never been anything keeping me from scratching it.

Ducky does not look convinced. "But what if you decide you want to—"

"Dude, Duck." I give him a look, one usually reserved for sitcom actors dealing with *serious moments*. "I have an entire book full of stuff my mom didn't get to experience because she had me." I point upstairs to my room, where he knows very well my mother's book of maps is propped up on my bookshelf. "I'm not gonna let some boneheaded mistake ruin my chances of actually doing something myself."

"I get it," Ducky says. "But don't you want to *think* about other—"

My death glare silences him. "I'm going to the library next week to look up adoption agencies," I say.

Ducky is silent for a while, scratching his mop of messy black curls. "What about Britta?" he asks at last.

"You think she wants it? 'Cause she doesn't really seem like the maternal type."

Ducky rolls his eyes at me. "If you think she's bad now, how brutal do you think she'll be when she finds out the father of your baby is—"

I sock him in the arm. "Not worth mentioning?"

"Obviously," he says as he rubs the bruise. "But still . . ."

"No one has to know," I tell Ducky, and now it's his turn to give me a look. "I'll wear muumuus. Or, like, a neon fruit hat. You know, draw the eye away from my problem areas."

"*El*-vie. You—"

Suddenly Ducky's eyes snap to the TV. I follow his gaze to the screen, where an ad has popped up featuring a muscular caveman in a hairy loincloth, carrying an axe hoisted over his shoulder. The man lumbers toward us, snarling, and just as he looks like he's going to reach through the screen and grab me, a lithe little dude with a jetpack zooms in and punches the barbarian in his baby-making area.

"*Jetman: Time Wars! Upgrade your game client today!*"

Ducky's face is glazed over with little-boy glee as he watches the images of martians and mastodons flashing across the screen. "Dude, how did *this* come on?" I say, jumping at the chance to change the subject. "I *told* you, you gotta stop using your phone to change channels at my house. It effs with my profile settings, and I get stuck with all these nerdy ads."

"How do you know it wasn't your dad?" Ducky asks weakly, wrenching his eyes away from the TV as the commercial ends.

"Dad doesn't MMO, nerdlinger."

"Then leave your phone out here next time," he says with a laugh. "You were in the bathroom for, like, an hour. Watching soap operas without female company shrivels my man parts. PS, I can see your midriffass."

Instinctively I tug down the back of my shirt to cover the exposed skin just above the top of my jeans, then reach over and grab his phone off the coffee table. "At least clear your memory first," I say, and I toss the phone clear across the room, where it wedges itself behind a wilted fern.

The door to the kitchen creaks open then, and Ducky cranes his head around the top of the couch. "Hey, Mr. Nara!" he calls out. "What's crackin'?"

"Hello, Donald," my dad replies, walking over to peer into the living room. "Elvie. How was school?"

I don't even bother to look up. "Endlessly diverting," I tell him, flipping through the TV channels again. "I'm thinking of writing a musical about it."

Ducky kicks me in the leg. He hates when I'm sarcastic to my dad. Probably because my dad is way cooler than his stepfather, Zeke. Zeke is some bigwig stuffed suit over at OmniNews, and his idea of a good time is collecting porcelain hippos. Ducky practically lives at our house, which is fine by me. I'll take as much Ducky as I can get, and my dad doesn't seem to mind either. Sometimes when Ducky's over—scarfing down multiple helpings of tuna casserole, or working on his lit homework, or even futilely arguing the merits of 3-D films versus flat pics—my dad gets this look on his face, a sort of wrinkled wistfulness, and I can just tell he's thinking that if my mom hadn't passed away, maybe they could have ended up with a son like Ducky.

"What've you got there, Mr. Nara?" Ducky asks. "More plans?"

"Yep," Dad replies. "This new solar deck should reduce our heating and cooling costs by four percent."

I turn around and see that, sure enough, my dad is holding a stack of blue-tinted transparent LED readouts, all flashing with various schematics for yet *another* remodel on the house. "Dad," I say, rolling my eyes, "haven't you Winchestered the place enough?"

Our house was built in 2042, when fusion tech was still a little wonky, so unlike at Ducky's place, where everything runs smoothly all the time, our house is full of gremlins. You never know when there's going to be a brownout, or a surge that'll send the washing machine spurting suds into your face. And just try taking a shower that doesn't either freeze your hair into a shampoo-cicle or steam you like a dumpling.

To tell the truth, I think Dad likes the challenge. He's always renovating *something*—drafting new plans, getting estimates, designing, gutting, hammering, welding—and I'm constantly enlisted to help. School vacations are especially bad. While Ducky spent his eighth-grade winter vacation skiing with his mom and Zeke, I helped my dad jackhammer up the uneven floor in the basement and lay new concrete foam. While Ducky sent me letters from summer camp about solar gliding, I was running new wiring through the walls for a state-of-the-art alarm system. And any sunny afternoon has the danger of turning into gutter cleaning day. Not to get all Psych 101 or anything, but I have a sinking suspicion that Dad's constant need to refurbish our home might have something to do with missing my mom. It's sort of an unwritten rule in the Nara household that we don't talk about her, ever. I learned at a very early age that any mention of Olivia Nara would lead to hours of stony silent distracted Dad. There are very few pictures of her, and Dad can't even bring himself to display them. Even her book of maps is something we don't discuss. He just walked into my room one day when I was six, handed it to me with a "Your mother would have wanted you to have this," and walked out without another word. So I think that, in some way, Dad keeps himself busy so he won't have time to think too much.

"For your information, young lady," my dad informs me, walking over to the couch, "this new addition is essential." He plops the plans onto the coffee table, nearly knocking over the peanut butter jar. I rescue my snack and take a gander at the schematics.

"Dad!" I cry. "This deck is attached to my room!"

"Yes, and?" He has, as usual, totally missed the point.

"You're going to tear out my whole wall!" I jab a finger at the plans, in which a fourth of my bedroom has been replaced by an enormous window that looks out onto the semi-wraparound deck. "That pervy little Richie Phillips next door will be able to see straight into my business."

Ducky starts poking me in the ribs. "Elvie, can I see your phone for a second?" he whispers, but I ignore him.

"Honey," Dad says, "we need to reduce our energy output. It's just smart thinking. And this way we can stockpile more of our own energy in the well in case of brownouts. You remember last summer?"

"*Elvie . . .*" Ducky's whispering is more insistent, as is the prodding I'm getting, but I'm still too annoyed to pay him any mind.

"Where am I supposed to sleep while the construction's going on?" Ducky's prodding is becoming too much to ignore. I round on him. "Dude, Ducky, what's your problem?"

Ducky is trying to grab my phone from under my leg, which is, hello, so not cool. I'm about to give him a good wallop, when I notice that my dad has this, like, utterly perplexed look on his face. And he's not looking at us.

He's looking at the TV.

I turn to the screen and immediately suck in my breath.

"*From the makers of Bumpy Roads cocoa butter, Face Your Baby acne cream is strong enough to attack even the fiercest of pimples but also pH-balanced to nurture your growing baby.*" On the screen a round-as-a-globe thirtysomething chick is smoothing goop onto her smiling face. "*Now with your recommended daily dose of folic acid!*"

Adorable, lovable nitwit Ducky's been using his phone to look up baby things for me . . . and to change channels. All without bothering to clear his search history first. Guess who's *not* getting a spare kidney for his birthday.

"Elvie?" my dad says. He's staring at me, forehead wrinkled.

I try to play it innocent. "Uh, yeah?" I reply.

My father smoothes the front of his pants. "Is there a reason that our television seems to think you might be interested in advertisements for" — he clears his throat — "maternity products?"

For a split second I think that maybe Ducky has done this all on purpose, to force my hand with Dad. I'm ready to pounce on him, but one look tells me he feels awful enough already. I sigh. I might as well do this now. "Dad?" I say. He's gonna blow a gasket, but he might as well blow it now, while I still have some mobility to duck. "I'm pregnant. Two and a half months."

My dad does not blow any gaskets. He doesn't blow any anything.

"Dad?" I say. He hasn't fainted, or screamed, or stormed out of the room, which I'm pretty sure are, like, the only options the parenting handbook gives you when your barely-sixteen-year-old daughter tells you she's knocked up.

He sucks in a deep breath through his nose, nods quickly, and, without saying a word, turns and walks across the room to his desk.

Dad is riffling through the bottom drawer of his antique gray filing cabinet. He's had that old rusty thing for years, but I never thought there was anything *in* it. As I head over to see what's up, Ducky hot on my heels, I see that it's filled with all kinds of LED readouts and even old papers. My father must be the only person on earth who doesn't simply upload everything to his lap-pad or phone.

"Uh, Dad?" I say. "What are you doing?" He doesn't answer, just continues rummaging, and I raise my eyebrows at Ducky, who shrugs. I'm starting to wonder if there's any chance that instead of telling my dad I was pregnant, I accidentally told him I needed Great-Grandmom's old meatloaf recipe.

"Found it!" he shouts, straightening up to his full height. He is gripping a thick green folder bursting with papers. Ducky and I lean in to stare as he slaps it onto the desk. The plastic tab on the top of the folder reads TEENAGE CRISES.

Inside the larger hanging folder are many thinner beige folders, each full of papers of their own. They all have labels of potential teen disasters—TRIAXOCIL OVERDOSE, AUTO ACCIDENT, FLUNKS HIGH SCHOOL, JOINS A CULT. Dad thumbs past each one until he finds the one he's looking for—PREGNANCY. He grins and hands it to me. "Here's everything we're going to need."

I pinch the bridge of my nose. "So glad I could help fulfill your dream of solving a crisis, Dad," I tell him.

He's definitely not listening. He's so proud of his own preparedness, he's practically giddy. "Look, I've got a scenario for every option." He opens it up, and a storm of pages and LEDs tumble out onto the desk. For Christ's sake, he's even got notes scribbled on *cocktail napkins*. "Can't say I was expecting to need any of these, but, well, that's why you have a crisis folder in the first place, right?"

He looks up at Ducky then, as though noticing him for the first time. "Is it yours, son?"

It takes a second for Ducky to grasp what my father is asking him. When it finally does dawn on him, he goes completely bug-eyed. "Mine? Mine?" he sputters. "Oh, no. I mean, no sir, Mr. Nara. I wouldn't—I mean, not that I wouldn't, I mean not that I *would*—We haven't . . ."

"You don't know the guy, Dad," I say.

Dad rubs his chin. "Do I want to?" he asks, and I shake my head. "I see," he replies. "Then I'm assuming we won't need this." He points to an LED with a listing of local chapels.

I fight off the brain nova I'm getting from the idea of my dad trying to marry me off to either Ducky or Cole, and put a hand on his shoulder. "Dad," I say, "I really appreciate that you've gone to all this work and everything, but I've already figured it out. I'm going to look up adoption agencies all on my own, so you don't have to—"

"*Are you an expecting teen mother?*"

The voice is coming from the television.

We all turn to the screen. A tall, strong-jawed dude walks down a long corridor, carrying a baby and talking to the camera.

"*Teen pregnancy can be a confusing time, and research has shown that the comfort and support of kindred spirits can greatly improve the health not only of the developing child, but of the mother as well. The Hanover School is a brand-new safe haven for confused young mothers-to-be. Our mission is to give otherwise unprepared young ladies the tools they'll need to raise a child in today's fast-paced world.*"

The dude is giving the camera the ol' smoldering eyes routine, with just the right amount of sexy stubble accentuating his chiseled jawline.

"*At the Hanover School we'll provide you with a plethora of options. You'll have access to our world-class infant care preparation courses, day care facility database, and even adoption agency networks, all right at your fingertips.*" Now the studly mister is joined by a whole team of similarly steamy men. The whole thing is so cornball that I think it must be a joke. I'm just waiting for one of them to pull out a wrench and ask if my pipes need cleaning. They're all holding babies, though, which is kinda ruining the vibe.

"The Hanover School for Expecting Teen Mothers. Come and experience a learned faculty, a supportive staff, and most important, new friends. Not to mention views that are out of this world!" The camera pulls back and out of a window, and suddenly it's clear that the hottie brigade is on the deck of a huge spaceship or something, waving out at the stars. Now I *know* this is a movie.

As the ad ends and turns into a promo for a new sitcom starring two robots and a superchimp called *Two Robots and a Superchimp*, I let out a snort. "Pregnant space school? Puh-leeze. And why was everyone in that commercial a mega-hottie? Aren't there any uggos at the Hanover School?"

My dad has an unsettling twinkle in his eye. "A low-Earth-orbit cruise liner. A *school* on a low-Earth-orbit cruise liner . . ."

"You can't be serious," I say, but my dad is already punching up the info on his phone.

"I'm going to download an application now," he says. "Want to make sure you get in before all the spots fill up!"

"Dad, you're kidding, right?" I look to Ducky for backup, but instead he bites his bottom lip and avoids looking me in the eye, which I know means exactly one thing.

"Ducky!" I poke him in the shoulder. "No way. No way do you *agree* with him. Space school for pregnant girls?"

He looks me in the eyes then, and I almost wish he didn't. Because the shitbird looks more busted up than I've ever seen him. "You can't go back to school next year, Elvie. You know you can't. Britta will murder you *and* that baby. Besides, you're always talking about going out into space one day."

"How much do you think I'll actually see floating in circles in a rusty tin can?" I say weakly. But even as the words are leaving my mouth, it's already hit me. Ducky is right. My dad is right. A new school is probably my best option. And you can't get much farther away from Britta without a passport to the moon.

"But . . ." I'm close to tears now too, and I hate Ducky for making me cry. I *hate* him. "A whole year?" My cheeks begin to quiver, and I know I'm a goner. "How am I going to . . ."

Ducky squeezes me up in a hug and kisses my forehead. "We'll figure it out together," he says softly.

"Go to hell," I tell him. But I hug him back, hard.

It's a hazy late August afternoon, near the end of my second trimester, that finds Ducky stuffing my suitcases into the trunk of my dad's car. I told him I could pack it myself. I may look like the prizewinning pumpkin at the state fair, but I'm not crippled, for Jiminy's sake. It's getting harder to hide my bump now, and the farther my belly sticks out, the less likely it is that either my dad or Ducky will let me do anything on my own. I'm almost relieved to be going away to school, because if I stick around here, in two weeks I won't be allowed to brush my own teeth.

Ducky grips my hand through the open window, so tight I think he might be trying to take my fingers as souvenirs. It's been a good summer—lazy and relaxed, with very little to mar it except for the occasional leg cramp and the fact that I'm now so ginormous that I basically need a series of pulleys and levers just to get out of bed. But I'd gain thirty more pounds if it meant one more day at home.

"Send me pics," he says. "Every day. I want to know what everything looks like up there. And take caps of any hot spots you think might be choice places to hit up on our trip after graduation next year."

"Of course I will," I tell him. "And blink me. Like, every day. I'm going to be so bored without you."

"No, you won't," he argues. We've had this conversation about a billion times in the past three months, but now, knowing this is the last time we'll have it, it's almost sweet. Familiar. One more thing I'll have to miss. "You'll be too busy having adventures."

"Adventures, my ass," I say, and pull him halfway into the car for a killer hug. "At least in space no one can hear your water break, right?"

Ducky laughs into my shoulder. "You'd better hope Hanover has a better physics teacher than Ms. Schneider."

"Every day, you hear me?" I tell him, tugging on his ear. "You'll blink me *every day*?"

He tugs my ear right back. "I promise," he says. And I know he will.

Watching Ducky wave from my driveway while my dad pulls onto the street, I figure I now know what it must feel like to have your arm yanked out of its socket. I'm about to up and geyser all over my scoop neck, when my dad interrupts my reverie.

"Did I tell you that the L.O.C. *Echidna* is one of the

original orbiters?" he says. "Commissioned in 2046. Can you believe that?"

Nonemotional Elvie would roll her eyes at her father right now. Nonemotional Elvie would tell her dad, *Hello, you've been totally blabbering about how much you love these old ships for, like, months now, poring over floor plans at the dinner table, spouting anecdotes and factoids, and making me memorize the locations of all the emergency pods, and telling me four thousand times not to use the toilet during a Yeomen's Curve. And PS, if you really think your daughter might get sucked into the crapper because of a sudden vacuum, maybe you shouldn't shoot her off into space to begin with.* But nonemotional Elvie checked out about the time her stretch marks got to be the size of the Mississippi River, and now it's just me. Miss Sappy Pants.

Dad's still going on and on about the push to recommission old space cruisers as commercial real estate, seeing as they're all stuck up there in orbit anyways, and I'm trying *not* to think about what I'm leaving behind—when I notice that Dad's voice seems to be getting more distant. I turn to see what's up.

Leaning fiercely to the left, my father is driving with his head completely stuck out his window, still chatting away as if he did this sort of thing every day.

"Dad! What the balls are you doing?"

"Sorry?" He sticks his head back inside the car. My eyes must be as bugged out as beach balls. "Just practicing. You know, in case the hood pops up one of these days while I'm driving and I can't see out the front. Be prepared for any situation, Elvie."

Maybe pregnancy hormones make you mental or something, I don't know, but for some reason this strikes me as the funniest thing I've ever heard. I let out a guffaw so loud that I nearly upchuck the pancake sundae Ducky made me for breakfast.

Dad looks over at me then, and I think he's going to lecture me more about preparedness, but he doesn't. He gets this sort of sad, crooked smile on his face, and he tells me, "I'm going to miss having you around, dearheart."

Talk about sniffle territory. I try to swallow down the lump in my throat, but no luck. "I'll miss you, too," I tell him.

It's at that moment that my phone buzzes in the pocket of my stretch-waist maternity jeans, and I smile, thinking how very Ducky it is to be sticking to his one-blink-a-day promise already.

But when I flip the phone open, I see that the blink isn't from Ducky.

It's from Cole.

i <3 u more thn the starz

I stare at the phone for a good three miles' worth of highway. Cole Archer? He can't even *speak* to me for five months after I tell him I'm carrying his love child, but as soon as I'm about to blast off into space, he suddenly <3s me? My heart skips so many beats, I'm pretty sure either me or the baby is going to pass out soon.

"Elvie?" My dad slows the car to a stop. "We're here." I look up from my phone. Sure enough, we've arrived. It's a relatively small shuttleport with only three launch pads. Right now there's just the one shuttle, prepped and ready to shoot us into orbit, casting a long shadow over the entire parking lot. "You okay, kid?"

I don't even stop to think. I delete the message. And then, thumbs whipping through the menu tabs, I delete Cole, too.

"I'm just great," I say, stuffing the phone back into my pocket. And I step out of the car.

CHAPTER THREE

WHEREIN THE BENEFITS OF DITCHING YOGA CLASS BECOME ABUNDANTLY CLEAR

So, um, invaders. That's new.

The first thing that happens, of course, after processing that our ship is being attacked by dudes toting guns and wearing space helmets, is that I feel an overwhelming desire to crap myself. But I refuse to be captured with soiled Underoos. Dear God, how embarrassing would *that* be?

Once I take a few deep breaths to calm myself, I do what my dad would tell me to do if he were here: assess the situation.

Poking my head out just a smidge from the top of the stairwell, I see that my helmet-wearing friends are still lurking in the halls. There are five of them, dressed in dark fatigues that are sooo five years ago. If we were on better terms, I'd inform them that they might want to, you know, invest in some plaid or something. But the guns make me think maybe they're not here to discuss fashion.

One thing's for sure—I can't stay where I am. If anyone decided to hike up this stairwell, I'd be screwed. There's not a single good hiding place on the observation deck, and it doesn't take a math genius to figure out that BIG OPEN AREA + SPACE INVADERS = BYE-BYE, ELVIE. So it looks like I'm going down the back stairway.

Slinking, soft-footed, across the length of the deck, I make my way past the vending machines, past the elevator, and slowly open the door to the emergency stairwell. The door opens with a soft *ka-chunk*, but I hold my breath and don't hear footsteps following me, so I push it open farther and squeeze myself through. My yoga class is in the pool on the lido deck, just two floors down. I figure my best bet is to get there so we can all work through this ship-under-attack dilemma together. Safety in numbers, right?

I book it down the two flights, one hand on the railing, one hand under my belly, and I thank my lucky stars that I decided to go on my ice cream crusade with my most sensible yellow flats on. I'm running so fast, I could be the star of my own cardio workout vid—*Get Chased With Elvie!*—but when I crash into the exit, the door doesn't budge.

Locked shut.

The sudden jolt of ramming shoulder-first into the door sends the Goober careening into my uterine wall. *Shit.* How can an emergency exit door be locked? If my dad were here, he'd already be halfway into a letter to the Federal Bureau of Public Safety. Not cool, Hanover School. So not cool. I turn around on my heel and charge my way back up the stairs until, gasping, I reach the sports deck one level up. Thankfully this door opens, and I practically tumble out of the stairwell. The Goober is still kicking me like the kid's trying to place in the Olympic freestyle, so I wrap my right arm as tight around my belly as I can, until I'm, like, choke-holding my own stomach, and I tell the thing, "When you get out of there, bub, the two of us are going to have *words*." Then I straighten myself up and head down the length of the hallway.

Thanks to all the time my dad spent poring over the floor plans of the ship with me, I had the layout of every deck pretty much memorized before I even set foot on board. So I know for a fact that if I can make it down this hallway and across the basketball courts, then the main staircase at the other end will land me directly in front of the lido pool on the floor beneath. I'm just tiptoeing past the locker room, sneaking glances over my shoulder for space intruders, when from around the corner behind me I suddenly hear a *crunch-crunch-crunch* that can only be a group of gunmen. Without thinking twice, I dart into the locker room and push shut the heavy green door behind me.

As soon as I'm there, of course, I realize this is one of the worst places I could have stuck myself. If the baddies come after me, what do I think I'm going to do—shove them into the steam room and turn the heat up to high? I should've run. I should've booked it to the pool at all costs. I should've—

"You having an aneurysm or something?"

"Huh?" I whirl around, and there, straddling the locker room bench, a thin, brown cigarette lodged between her fingers, is one of my classmates, Ramona Knudsen.

Ramona takes a deep suck on the clove cigarette and exhales all the smoke in one long puff. "Don't tell me your water broke. An aneurysm would be way more interesting."

"I'm not . . ." I shake my head. "You realize we're under attack, right?" I say, pointing toward the hallway. "There are, like, these dudes with guns—"

"You have ice cream on your ass," she tells me.

Ramona Knudsen and I have never really conversed before. Mostly she keeps to herself, doing wholesome things like scratching dirty limericks onto her desk, so it's not like we've ever had time to bond during knitting class or share a box of tissues while crying over *The Martian Diaries*. But I can respect the chick. She has that bad-girl thing going for her— torn gray tank, faux-leather skirt that she can still almost rock because she's only five months in yet, and a streak of purple in her jet-black hair. Not to mention that when Britta tried to give Ramona crap about her eating habits last month, Ramona unloaded her entire bowl of stroganoff onto Britta's head. The pasta was hells hot, and Britta had blisters on her scalp for a week. It was pretty much the most glorious thing I'd ever seen.

But now is not really the time for a stroll down memory lane.

"Invaders," I tell her. "With *guns*. Outside. Didn't you feel that jolt?"

"For serious?" Ramona says, and for the first time she looks mildly interested. "I thought that was a drill or something."

"Not a drill," I reply. "We need to get down to the pool."

She squints her brown eyes at me. She's wearing so much mascara, I think it might be more effective to just glue the bottle to her eyelashes. "Eve, right?"

It takes me a second to realize she's asking about my name.

"Elvie," I correct her. I place my hand back on the doorknob. "We have to go. *Now.*" Ramona might be on my good list, but that doesn't mean I'm going to sit around shooting the shit with her when there are lunatics out there waiting to shoot the shit out of me.

Ramona shrugs as if to say *Why not?* then snuffs the clove cigarette out on the bench and tosses the butt to the floor. I'm just cracking the door open to scope out our escape route, when Ramona says—way too loudly for a girl who's trying to evade a group of freaky gunmen—"Should we bring the Gnat?"

I pinch the door closed again and whirl around. "What part of 'We're under attack by armed invaders' did you not understand?"

Ramona swings her leg slowly over the bench and rises, almost reluctantly. You'd think she was being asked to come to the front of the class to diagram the Krebs cycle or something. "The Gnat," she repeats. "She's in the shower."

I let out a huff of breath and stomp over to the showers. The second shower stall from the far wall has the curtain drawn in front of it, and sure enough I can hear a hissing sound coming from it. It's not the sound of water running, but softer, like a sustained whisper. And the smell is foul. I whip back the curtain.

Squatting on the floor of the shower, furiously attacking a beach-ball-and-chicken-wire contraption with a can of beige spray paint, is Hanover's resident weirdo, Natalia Ferrera. If anyone truly belongs in outer space, it's Natty. At the moment she's surrounded by what I can only imagine must be art supplies—paste, glass beads, and a lot of those little fuzzy pipe cleaner thingies. Her long, kinky brown hair is spewing over her shoulders, the ends approaching what appears to have once, long ago, been a braid. Her bare feet are covered in spray paint, her fingernails are chipped and grimy, and she smells musty, which is sort of an accomplishment in space. She doesn't even notice me either, because she's plugged into her headphones, rocking out to God knows what sort of music as she continues to "work."

"Natty!" I whisper-shout at her. "*Natty!*" Still no response. I turn around to look at Ramona, who just laughs and lights up another clove. "Hey, *Gnat!*" I rip the headphones out of the girl's ears, and she finally looks up.

"Oh, hey, Elvie," she says, totally blasé. She loosens her grip on the spray nozzle for a split second and gives the can a good shake. "What's up?"

"What's *up?*" I say. I look again at Ramona, who is absolutely no help. "What's up is that the ship is under attack, and the three of us"—I point to Natty, Ramona, and myself—"need to get down to the pool, ASAP."

Natty's eyes go bug-round, and her chin drops. "The ship is under *attack?*" she says.

"Yeah," I say. I hold out a hand to hoist her up. "Come on. We have to get going."

"Oh, but . . . oh. I . . . oh." I would never have thought that the Gnat could look even more frazzled than before, but there it is. "*Attack?*" she says again.

"*Yes,*" I repeat. I'm starting to think the paint fumes have damaged her brain cells. "Now let's *go.*" Even Ramona looks ready to book it.

"But what about my baby?" Natty asks.

"It's kind of attached," I tell her. "Two-for-one combo meal."

"No, I mean"—she holds up the desecrated beach ball contraption in her hands—"my *baby*."

I can't believe I'm trying to save this nut bar.

"It's not . . . ," Nat continues. "It's . . . Well, I mean, it's not finished yet, but it's going to be a swollen tonsil. You know"—she looks up at me, eyes wet—"as, like, a representation of the lightness and darkness of man."

"Natty," I say, and I try to make my voice steady. I can only imagine that her getting pregnant in the first place must have been part of some elaborate performance piece. "We gotta go."

That's when we hear the scream. It's a girl, definitely, and piercing—the kind of scream a girl doesn't even know she has in her until she absolutely needs it. It's definitely muffled, so I can't be sure where it came from—our floor? another deck?—but I know exactly what it means.

I'm racing back toward the locker room door, and this time Natty doesn't argue. Ramona's ditched her cigarette and is hot on my heels too. I wedge the door open a few centimeters and put an eyeball up to the crack. No invaders to the left or the right—at least not as far as I can see.

"Looks like the coast is clear," I whisper over my shoulder. "On three." The girls nod. "One. Two." I push the door open as quietly as I can. *"Three!"*

We're scuttling down the hallway, toward the basketball courts, and I keep shooting glances backward to see if we're being followed, but it looks like no one is on our trail. But it's on one of these glances that I notice something else.

"Natty!" I growl. "What the hell is wrong with you?"

"It's *art*," she insists, still carrying the giant tonsil as we careen toward the door to the courts.

"I'm telling you, freak," Ramona calls back, well ahead of both of us. She's making excellent time for someone wearing chunky-heeled boots. "That is not art. It is—"

"*Shit*," I wheeze.

"Hey!" Natty hollers. "You know, guys, when you say things like that about my work, it really—"

"No," I tell her, one hand tucked between my belly and my pelvis. God, it's hard to run for your life with a fetus inside you. "I meant"—I point down the length of the hall behind us, where Natty's bare feet have left beige-colored tracks to our exact location—"*shit*."

"Ohhhhhhh," Natty says, eyes buggy again. "Shit."

Ramona agrees.

At least we are almost to the basketball courts now. With any luck the invaders won't find our trail. With any luck they are all off on other floors, terrorizing other girls. With any luck we'll be—

"There they are!" comes a deep, booming voice behind us. "Sir, this way!"

"*SHIT!*" Together Ramona, Natty, and I run like we have never run before, and within seconds we have reached the doors leading to the courts. We throw them open and race inside.

The basketball courts are sunk a half level deep into the sports deck, and we've come in right at the top of the bleachers. We start plunking down the bleacher steps as fast as three pregnant teens can go, but still there's no way we can make it to the court-level entrance at the far end before those freaks behind us catch up. That is just the sad physics of pregnancy.

We race down the bleachers, the entire court echoing as we skip-crash-thud onto every step. Ramona is almost to the bottom row, but I'm only halfway down. My belly is jolting up so hard with every jump that I'm starting to wonder why they don't make support bras for baby bumps. But even I'm outpacing Natty, who—at seven-and-something months—has quite the belly of her own to support.

Not to mention that goddamn tonsil.

I narrowly miss wiping out on one of the bleacher steps, when I get an idea. "Ramona!" I holler down at her, just as she hops down to the second-to-last step. "The bleachers! Close the bleachers!" She makes it to the bottom and spins to give me a look like I'm nuts. "Punch the goddamn button!" I holler again.

Ramona runs to the wall and whips open the plastic cover over the button that will automatically collapse the bleachers into the wall. She looks up at me, and I can see what she's thinking. As soon as she punches that button, the bleachers are going to start rapid-fire closing, top to bottom—and with me and the Gnat only halfway down, there's a good chance we'll be squished like termites. But then we hear the *stomp-stomp-stomp* of boots from the doorway behind us. Clearly there's not a second to waste.

Ramona punches the button.

Just like that, the bleachers creak to life. *Shuck-AH! Shuck-AH! Shuck-AH!* Every split second another step slams into the row behind it. And if I thought hopping my pregnant ass down the steps was hard before, it's a nightmare when the whole thing's *moving*. With each jump I make, the distance between the steps grows slimmer and slimmer, and I have to react lightning quick to make sure my foot lands square. Twice I misjudge and almost bite it, but I manage to right myself.

I land at the bottom, squeaking on the waxed court floor, and look behind me to see that Natty is still struggling. "You can make it!" I shout at her.

Ramona is less encouraging. "Bitch, drop the beach ball!"

Natty is picking up speed, but not enough. All the steps are closed now but the bottom ten, and those are moving fast— she's going to get squashed. I'm reaching for the button when Ramona grabs my hand and points to the top of the bleachers.

Invaders. Five of them, looming ten meters above us in the doorway.

Shit.

"Natty!" Ramona and I bellow together. She's seven steps from the bottom now. She could jump across them all and probably make it, but the slamming and shifting is clearly upsetting her balance, and she looks freaked. "Jump!" I scream at her. "Jump the rest of the way!"

She looks at me, and she nods, and she swings her arms wildly and makes the leap, straight for me and Ramona.

And she almost makes it.

Her foot catches one step from the bottom, just as the bleachers are slamming shut around her. She falls to her knees and tries to get up, but it's not fast enough. I can't watch. The bleacher is going to catch her right below the knee. She's going to lose that leg, all because of my brilliant idea.

And then the bleacher stops. Natty skids forward and falls awkwardly down on top of me and Ramona, all of us landing with a thud on the court. I look back at the last row of bleachers, still ajar, the motor whirring in distress, to where Natty's severed leg should be.

"It's *ruined!*" Natty wails as she stares at the mangled corpse of her art project, mashed between the bottom two steps of the bleachers.

I grab her by the elbow. "We're going," I say, my eyes darting up to the gunmen in the doorway. "*Now.*"

"But . . . ," Natty begins. She is clearly hysterical. "But—"

That's when Ramona slaps her across the face. "One more word," she tells her, "and I will *cut* you."

And that pretty much does the trick.

We're booking it across the gym floor when from behind us we hear several soft thuds, and when we whirl around, we see that—holy mother of God—the gunmen have jumped the ten meters down from the top of the bleachers. They're tucking and rolling and popping back up to their feet like freaking ninjas—except for one bozo who twists his ankle and stumbles to his knees as he lands, shouting, "Mother-*humper!*"

So apparently even ninja space invaders can eff up.

I don't exactly have the time to contemplate this, though, because at the moment I am busy screaming at the top of my lungs as I race for my life to the end of the basketball court.

Natty and Ramona and I bust out of the doors at the far end, and we're rushing, rushing, rushing down the length of the deck, when from behind me I hear a deep voice bark, "Elvie, wait!"

Da-*fuh?*

That's when Nat and Ramona both shriek. And I see it. Up ahead. More invaders. Three of them.

Seriously, can't a pregnant girl in space catch a break these days?

We come to a screeching halt, of course, because that's what you do when you're pinned between gun-toting baddies. You stop running. It's, like, common sense. You stop, and you huff to try to catch your breath, and then you wait for them to just get it over with and shoot you already.

Only they don't.

We've come to a halt on top of the glass floor that looks down onto the main pool below—the very pool we've been trying so hard to get down to. Our lit teacher, Mr. Wilks, would probably point out the element of tragedy in our predicament— that we can literally see our goal and yet are still so far from it.

I knew there was a reason I always hated English class.

"You gonna shoot us or what?" Ramona says, cocking her head to the side. She may look sassy, but I'm thinking that the eight dudes with guns could still take her out. "Is that what you guys do for kicks? You got some sort of pregnant-lady fetish?"

I elbow her in the side. But just as I think she's gearing up to say something even worse, Natty shrieks again and slaps her hand over her mouth.

"What now?" I say. Seriously, if she's broken her favorite paintbrush or something, I'll—

She points down at the glass floor. I've always thought that whoever designed this particular area of the ship was a little pervy. It's like the *purpose* is for creepy guys to stare down women's cleavage while they swim. Not to mention that anyone engaging in water-related activity can tilt their head toward the ceiling and see all up your business. But if I thought *that* was demented, it's nothing compared to what's going on below us at the moment.

At first the scene is hard to make out, because it's all splashing and chaotic and confusing, but slowly I take it in. There are teachers down below in the water with the girls. About a dozen or so, more than half the faculty. No camo-wearing gunmen in sight. But do they seem happy about that? No. Not in the slightest. Because the teachers—our teachers, the instructors we've been living side by side with for three months now—are *drowning the girls in the pool*. I blink once, twice, to make sure my eyes aren't playing tricks on me, but it's clear that what I'm seeing is real. There's Mr. Wilks now, his strong arms forcing one of the girls under the water while she flails and gulps for air.

From my right I hear one of the invaders boom out a confused "Sir?" I snap my head up. It's the dude who bit it coming off the bleachers. And he's looking at the guy beside him, a fellow I'm assuming must be the Head Space Invader in Charge. "*Sir?*" Ninja Klutz asks again, more frantically. But his boss isn't looking at him. He's taking aim at the glass.

He pulls the trigger.

In a mass of light and sparks, the floor crackles beneath us, and there is a brief moment—just a nanosecond, really—where I think, *Hey, the floor is going to hold. Right-O.* But then there's a massive CRACK! and a shatter, and the floor crumbles into a million tiny pieces of glass. And we tilt and topple and fall.

Straight.

Into.

The.

Pool.

SPLASH!

Okay, so there are a lot of things going on in my mind as I fumble around under the water, trying to figure out which way is up so I can, hello, get some oxygen into my lungs. I'm wondering, for one thing, why my teachers have decided to go all schizoid, and who these camo guys are, for another. And I'm wondering who it was who said my name up there on the sports deck, and how these people know who I am, and, like, what *else* do they know about me, and why, of all things, would they find it necessary to shoot themselves into a pool?

But all of that falls away in a flash, because as I'm still flailing and kicking, trying to get my head above the water, I see something that would've sucked all the breath out of me had there been any left to suck.

The girl who always chews on her hair is being shoved under the water right in front of my face, two beefy arms forcing down her shoulders. Her eyes are bulging, and she's doing her best to rip the hands away from her, but she's clearly no match for the dude. She sees me looking at her, bubbles escaping from her mouth, but she doesn't scream out. She blinks at me, and I know it's, like, this totally panicked SOS. I reach out for her, but in that moment something strong grabs me from behind and yanks me backward. I try to twist free, but the grip is too strong. I'm gulping for air as I struggle with my captor, but I'm less concerned with the grip on my shirt than

53

with what's going on in front of me. I have to get to that girl, I just *have* to. The hands push her deeper, and her cheeks are bulging and her eyes are rolling back into her head, and even as I struggle to free myself, I'm thinking, *That's it. I'm going to watch this girl die.* But just as I know it's over, just when I'm sure I've lost her, the beefy hands that have been gripping her so tightly go suddenly limp and let go of their grasp, and Chewie gathers enough strength to kick her way free and swim to the surface. And as Mr. Wilks sinks down into the water, a deep red stain inking out of his body, I realize that he's been shot from somewhere up above.

Which doesn't totally make me want to come to the surface—you know, the whole people-shooting-other-people thing—but whoever has me from behind tugs harder, and I am pulled up. Eyes stinging, my head pops above the water, and just as I'm gulping in the best bit of oxygen I've ever tasted, I see that it's one of the space invaders who has a hold of me. He scoops me up under the armpits and plops me, rag-doll-style, onto the edge of the pool. I'm trying to talk and breathe, both at once, but I can't get anything out. He drags me to the wall behind a row of lounge chairs and lets go.

"Stay here. You'll be safe," he booms.

I blink the fuzz out of my eyes and look up at his gun.

"No offense," I force out, the trembling in my voice undercutting my biting wit. "But I'd feel a whole lot better if you pointed that thing somewhere else."

He looks down and realizes he's got his gun trained right at me, and for a split second I detect just the slightest slump in his shoulders.

"Just stay low," he says, and then he turns back to the fray, leaving me a wet shivering heap in the corner.

It seems that these camo guys really have a bone to pick with the Hanover faculty. That's the gist I'm getting from the way they're shooting them in the face and all. The guns they're using don't fire bullets, as far as I can see. Instead when the trigger's pushed, there's a low hum and a circle of sparks seems to whirl around the barrel. But however they work, they're effective, because the teachers are dropping like wet teen-murdering flies, their chests or—ewww—*faces* exploding as they get hit. Without even registering what I'm doing, I barf up every last bit of my ice cream.

Now more teachers are coming in from the outside, and they have guns of their own, which make a distinct popping sound as they fire—but again, no bullets. So my teachers are shooting at space invaders with what amount to ray guns, and that's insane. I mean, not exactly what you'd expect for the wrap-up of an underwater prenatal yoga lesson. The teachers seem to have given up on drowning the girls, who are now scrambling in every direction, some trying to escape the cross fire, while others just splash about uselessly.

That's when I see something that you'd think would be, like, my ultimate escapist fantasy—Britta and Other Cheerleader being dragged out of the pool by two teachers, writhing and wailing for dear life. The teachers are hauling them toward the back doors, for God knows what purpose, and in all the commotion it appears that the invaders haven't even noticed. There's a part of me that wants to order a monster-size soda and a tub of popcorn and just watch the whole scene play out, but in the moment . . .

"Goddammit," I spit as I slither out of my hiding spot toward the two biggest bitches I've never wanted to rescue. Staying crouched (like that's going to stop a ray gun from slicing through my brain—real smart, Elvie), I scamper across the slick tile floor, snatching a stray pool skimmer off the ground as I go.

The guy with the death grip on Britta is Mr. Zaino, the phys ed teacher. He's almost to the door when I reach out with the skimmer and hook the net around his raised foot.

"Hey, dirtbag!" I holler, giving the skimmer a sharp tug.

Mr. Z's feet fly out from under him, and as he stumbles, he loses his grip on Britta and smacks his face into the tile. Blood and teeth fall out of his mouth as he tries to rise back up. Britta wails and slumps into a ball, crying. *Holy cripes*, I want to shout at her. *Could you be more useless?*

Mr. Sandinsky, our French professor, is giving me the old hairy eyeball, making me think he might drop Other Cheerleader and attempt to tackle me. But Mr. Z., still splayed out on the floor, gestures weakly at the door and squeaks out something that sounds like a foreign language. I don't think it's French, although in my defense, it's sort of hard to understand someone with no front teeth. Mr. Sandinsky seems to get it, though. He gives up on the whole sinister-glare-at-Elvie thing and turns back toward the door, Other Cheerleader in tow.

Unfortunately for Monsieur Sandinsky, that's when he comes face-to-face with Ramona, water running in rivulets off her leather skirt. She is one pissed-off *mademoiselle*. She looks down at the ruined pack of clove cigarettes in her hand and squeezes the water out of them, forming a fist.

"Conjugate this, asshole," she tells him, then socks him square in the jaw.

As tough as Ramona is, Mr. Sandinsky has a good half meter on her, not to mention that he's built like a truck. Her right hook has left him surprised but still standing, and his grip on Other Cheerleader doesn't seem to be loosening anytime soon. He's about to give Ramona the tit for her tat, arm cocked in striking position, when there's a sizzling sound, and before my very eyes a hole burns right through his chest and he collapses to the ground.

Zapped, good and dead.

Toothless Mr. Z, still doing his best jack-o'-lantern impression on the tile floor, turns just in time to see the shot that kills him. Britta, of course, is still a helpless mess. She's just sitting there, eyes squeezed shut, squealing like a toddler who's wet her pants.

Man, how great would it be if she pissed herself?

I'm not sure how long the rest of the fight lasts, because, you know, time flies when you're dodging lasers. But it does end eventually, and there isn't a single faculty member left standing. The invaders are starting to pull the girls out of the pool, and Ramona and I jump back in as well to help. I fight the urge to tell the weepers what helpless snots they're being. *Some* of us were chased through kingdom come before falling through a broken ceiling, for crying out loud. As the remaining girls are retrieved from the pool, the invaders usher them toward the chairs so Mr. In Charge can take a head count. I've pulled three girls out of the pool so far, and reach to grab the last one left. She's just floating on her back, staring at the shattered ceiling, all, like, catatonic or something. She doesn't even move when I tug on her arm.

"Come on, Linda," I say, in this sort of harsh voice because, sorry, it's been a rough morning. "Or Lindsey. Or whatever the hell your name is. Paddle party's over."

I tug again, and the water around Linda—or Lindsey, or whatever—turns cloudy and red.

There's a bitter taste rising in my throat as I slowly turn her over in the water.

Burn marks.

There are two of them, one on either side of her spine. All of her innards are oozing out into the pool.

"Linda!" I cry. "Lindsey!" I shake her, hard, which I know won't do any good. She's dead. But I can't stop. And suddenly I'm shaking too. The harder I shake her, the darker the water grows.

I feel hands on my shoulders, warm and strong and holding firm.

"It's okay, Elvie."

It's the gunman with the busted ankle, the one who pulled me out of the pool and stashed me behind the chairs. Gently he removes my hands from the body and turns me toward the edge of the pool. Then he lifts me out in one fluid motion, as if I didn't weigh anything at all, and leads me back to the mess of chairs, where the other girls are huddled. I sit down next to Ramona, who looks at me out of the corner of her eye, clearly as unsure about what to do as I am.

"So, to hell with midterms, huh?" she says.

The dude taking the head count walks over and points his

finger at me. "You," he says. "Are you injured?"

"No, I don't think so. I—"

But he's moved away before I can finish, barking into a little walkie-talkie-looking thing that he's whipped out of his pocket.

"Alpha Leader, this is Tango Squad. We have neutralized all hostiles and secured the yoga class. Copy?"

There is a long crackle-gargling noise, and then, at last, a voice. *"Copy that, Tango Leader. Casualties?"*

The Tango Leader dude looks over to the pool where Lindsey—no, I think it was Linda after all—is still floating.

"Minimal," he replies, and he says it so matter-of-factly that I kinda want to shove one of those ray guns up his ass.

"Good work, Tango Leader. We've secured the package on our end and are heading back ourselves."

"The package?" I whisper to Ramona. I'm doing my best to wipe the tears and chlorine and snot off my face, and I'm pretty sure I look like a drain clog right now. But no one else here would really win Miss Universe at the moment either, so I guess it's not really an issue.

Ramona wrings about three liters of pool water out of her hair—right onto my yellow flats, I might add, which would most certainly piss me off if they weren't already long past saving. "Must be the girls in On Your Own," she tells me. "Over in the atrium. We were supposed to get our flour babies today. Didn't exactly feel like showing up for *that*."

I nod knowingly. If anyone can ever find a way to explain to me how carrying around a sack of flour with a diaper on it is supposed to prepare you for motherhood, I will personally bake that person a chocolate cake with my practice baby's insides.

The walkie in Head Count's hand is still crackling. *"Perform a final sweep for surviving hostiles and rendezvous at the extraction point. Copy?"*

"I copy," the butt munch replies, and he flicks off his communicator. He looks like he's ready to bark out some orders, but I am totally over this being-kept-in-the-dark-while-people-shoot-me-with-ray-guns bullshit.

Plus, that idiot with the busted ankle is lazily aiming his ray gun in my direction. Again.

"What the hell is going on?" I ask him, swatting the barrel away. "Who are you guys? What do you want with us? Why were our teachers drowning the shit out of people?"

Ninja Klutz turns his head toward the pool, where two of his buddies are busy pulling Mr. Wilks's limp body out of the water. "Your teachers?" he asks. I nod. "They weren't really teachers."

"What?" Natty squeaks, before I can get the word out myself. She's been silent up until now, probably brooding over her ruined masterpiece some more.

Ninja Klutz brings his visored face close to ours. "They were aliens," he tells us.

Suddenly Mr. Head Count is interested in us again. "That's enough!" he snaps, jerking his head in the other camo's direction. "Fall in line!" And our friend the ankle buster harrumphs and stands up straighter.

Aliens? For serious?

I peer over to where the two camos are squatted over Mr.

Wilks's bloody corpse, checking for a pulse. He looks pretty human to me. Even pretty attractive, in a dead older hippie sort of way. I shiver. All I can think about is studying *The Adventures of Huckleberry Finn*, and the way Mr. Wilks's face lit up as he talked about the symbolism found in Huck and Jim's journey down the Mississippi. It was the one time in an English class that I felt like paying attention, instead of literally staring into space. It's hard for me to grasp that the whole time he was someone who'd be capable of murder.

But an alien? No way.

Next to me Ramona gives up on her quest to light up a soggy clove and finally tosses it into the pool. "No wonder I was failing lit," she says.

After bellowing a bit at the guys checking out the pool area, Head Count turns his attention to Britta and Other Cheerleader. "You two!" he shouts at them, and Other Cheerleader cowers a bit at his tone, while Britta is too busy sobbing her poor pathetic guts out to do much of anything. "They weren't trying to kill you," he says, waving a hand in the general direction of our slaughtered teachers. Just by the way he spits his words out, I can tell that he thinks not being a target for murder is worse than cheating on your driver's test. "In fact," he continues, "it looked like they were trying to get you out of here." Other Cheerleader manages a weak nod, not seeming to understand. "So tell me, then." He takes a step closer to them. "What makes you two so special?"

"Bet you anything they're aliens too," I say. I mean, right? It makes sense. They're way too evil to be human. But all I get are a couple of weird looks.

Just then one of the other camo guys shouts, "Captain!" and waves his boss over. Head Count goes off in his direction, leaving the rest of us alone with the klutz.

Who, by the way, seems to be totally staring at me. I mean, I can't *quite* tell because of the visor on his helmet, but I swear that his head has not turned from my direction in the past several minutes. Which is a little bit freaky, if you ask me.

"What do you think you're looking at?" I finally ask him, hands on my hips—like *that's* going to be threatening to a dude with a ray gun. "What's your problem, anyway?"

And that's when he takes off his helmet. Just whips it off, the last dribbles of pool water cascading down his uniform.

And out of all the freaky moments I have had today, this one is by far the freakiest.

Dark brown hair. Perfectly sculpted eyebrows. The constellation of freckles beneath his left eye.

No shit, the klutz with the ray gun is Cole Freaking Archer.

CHAPTER FOUR

IN WHICH LIFE IN ARDMORE BECOMES SLIGHTLY MORE COMPLICATED

"So what does 'alien' mean in this context? Elvie?"

I snap my eyes away from what I've been staring at, which is the back of Cole Archer's head—namely, the soft V of hairs that forms at the nape of his neck—and turn my attention to Mrs. Kwan. "Huh?" I say.

Mrs. Kwan lets out a quiet sigh and does that thing where she pinches her nose right at the corners of her eyes. "Line sixty-seven," she tells me. "Second to last stanza."

I nod and flip to "Ode to a Nightingale," which is hidden three windows deep on my lap-pad. Wow, long-winded much? If you ask me, this John Keats guy should have stopped sitting at home pining over some stupid songbird and gone out for, like, some soft serve once in a while. Who puts this stuff in the curriculum?

"Ummmm." I read the line Mrs. Kwan is talking about.

She stood in tears amid the alien corn. "I don't know," I say. "Like, weird or, um, foreign?"

Mrs. Kwan offers me a tight smile, like she's not sure if she should be delighted that I answered the way I did or disappointed that I don't answer like that more often. Whatevs. Poetry isn't gonna get me to Mars. "Exactly," she says, then moves on to brain-probe someone else.

"John Keats is talking about Ruth here," Mrs. Kwan continues, as though a single one of us is actually paying attention. "From the Old Testament. She's homesick and in a foreign place, but she hears the song of the nightingale and it cheers her. The song finds a path through her sad heart, as Keats puts it." I pinch myself, realizing I'm back to staring at Cole's neck again. I turn my eyes to my lap-pad and start doodling a hamburger–hot dog wedding ceremony to distract myself. "This bird, the very symbol of beauty and immortality, has the power to charm people, to make them almost drunk with happiness. But it brings sadness, too, since it reminds us that we ourselves are mortal." She clears her throat, which is what she does when she wants us to know that what she's about to say is, like, superdeep. "It's ironic that Keats would take this theme so much to heart, actually, since he died at the tender age of twenty-five." She stops talking momentarily, and then: "Cole?"

I snap my head up again, and catch Cole in the act of tossing a handball to one of his football buddies across the room. With the teacher's eyes on him, he rights himself in his seat, and even though I can only see the back of his head, I just know he's giving her one of his I'm-so-adorable-how-can-you-hate-me smiles.

"Yeah?" he says, leaning back in his chair so far that I have to jerk back to avoid being nailed in the forehead. He settles his hands over that soft patch of neck hair. "What up, Mrs. K?"

Mrs. Kwan smiles despite herself. But then she quickly returns to her strict teacher persona. "What do you think the poem is about, Cole? What is Keats trying to say here?"

Cole Archer has only been at Lower Merion for two months or so, but already he thinks he owns the place. Like, just because he has beautiful eyes and lips with exactly the right amount of pucker and, okay, every time he wears shorts I get goose bumps from looking at his Michelangelo-sculpted calves, that does not mean he's all that, you know? God, talk about being full of yourself. The guy is a *goon*.

"I don't know," Cole tells Mrs. Kwan. "Keats is way too moody for me." The poem's not even up on his lap-pad. He's been watching epic fail vids of would-be martial artists for the past half hour. "I think he just likes to hear the sound of his own voice."

If I were the one to give this answer, it'd be Elvie in detention time for sure. But Cole's hot, so he gets away with it. Even the teachers aren't immune. It makes me want to upchuck, really. The one time he actually spoke to me was when my phys ed class was running laps past the boys warming up for varsity jai alai, and he asked me if I had any gum. Really. Because everyone keeps gum tabs in their gym shorts.

When Mrs. Kwan finally turns her attention back to the nerd section of the classroom—the kids who actually have a chance at caring about bird poetry—there is a quiet *psst!* from my left. I look to the side, and see Britta McVicker holding out a vanilla frosted cupcake with a grin so toothy she could

65

be the "after" shot in an orthodontist's ad. But when she sees me looking at her, the grin turns quickly into a sneer. "Not for *you*, chunky," she tells me. And really, I should probably feel flattered that she even deigned to acknowledge my presence. Britta is queen of the innies, and if you listened to them, you'd never know they went to school with twelve hundred other kids. She rolls her eyes at me with an exasperated "God," only to flip the charm on again when Cole leans back to take the cupcake. "A sweet for my sweet," she tells him.

Oh, yeah—the final reason that Cole Archer is dumber than a sliced banana? He's dating Britta McVicker. Talk about vomit in my mouth. If he can't see that Britta McVicker is the spawn of Satan, he should be checked for functioning brain waves. But Britta and Cole were LM's "it" couple almost the instant Cole arrived.

"Thanks," Cole says as he takes the cupcake. Then he sees me glaring at him and winks. "Hey, Elvs."

Elvs? For serious?

"*Douchetard*," I cough. Still, my heart skips a beat. Cole knows my name.

Well, part of it.

Cole raises an eyebrow before turning around and taking a massive bite out of the frosting while from my left Britta squeals with happiness. And they continue their bite-squeal-bite flirtation, all through Mrs. Kwan's boring-ass lecture about symbolic birds and my general wonderment about how one might go about committing suicide with nothing but a lap-pad and a bottle of hand sanitizer, until Cole finally finishes the damn cupcake. That's when the back of his neck—which, okay, yeah,

I was staring at again—turns as purple as an overripe plum.

I'm shifting my way forward in my seat—because I think he might be choking to death on cupcake crumbs, and I'm wondering if Britta could possibly get a life sentence for that— when I see it. Scrawled on the inside of the cupcake foil is a note from Britta.

Want to do it in the handicapped bathroom after gym?

Who said pod people can't be romantic?

"God, talk about a gag-fest," I tell Ducky as we walk home from school that afternoon. "You should have seen it."

"I feel like I have," Ducky replies. "You've told me the story in painstaking detail about, oh, nine hundred times now. You've painted me quite the mental picture."

I kick a pebble over in his direction. "Stop being so dramatic," I say. "I didn't tell you *everything* yet. I didn't tell you about what kind of cup—"

"Chocolate with vanilla frosting." Ducky kicks the pebble back to me. "And rainbow sprinkles."

I bite my bottom lip. Okay, so maybe I've been obsessing just a smidge.

"Look," he says as a car zooms by on the road beside us. "Britta McSicker is evil. We know that. Let's move on."

I laugh. "I think you mean Britta McPricker," I tell him.

"Britta McLicker."

Ducky and I have been walking to and from school together since we were eleven, after our month-long campaign to convince my dad that we would be safe from international terrorists and/or wild beasts on the bucolic streets of Ardmore. No matter what happens in school—and usually because of it— my walk with Ducky is always my favorite part of the day. I mean, sure, Ducky spends almost all his time at my house anyways, but the walk is special. Like how he insists on buying me an iced tea from Louie's Pizza Palace almost every day, or how, when we cut through the old graveyard, he makes up life histories for all the people whose gravestones we pass over. I'm almost—*almost*— not looking forward to getting my license this year, because if my dad ever actually lets me borrow the car, I'm afraid I'll end up playing designated driver for all of our friends, and I'll lose that time with Ducky for good. Luckily I don't turn sixteen for a month and a half, so I have plenty of time for walking.

"All I'm saying is," Ducky tells me after a good five minutes of excellent Britta puns, "you spend a whole lot of time talking about someone you claim to hate."

I scrunch my eyebrows together. "Are you saying I'm secretly in love with Shitta McFlicker?"

Ducky scratches his head. "No. Not with Britta."

I flick him right in the forehead for thinking such putrid thoughts. "*Um, gross,*" I say. "As if."

"As if," he replies, rubbing his forehead. "I can't think of a conversation in recent memory that *hasn't* turned to Cole." He clasps his hands to his chest, in what I'm pretty sure is supposed to be an impression of me, and he makes his voice all high and girly. "'Who cuts their *hair* like that?' 'Where did he *come* from, anyway?' 'I didn't even know they *made* cologne that smells like a spring morning.'"

While Ducky may have a remarkably awesome falsetto, the fella's seriously asking for a beat-down. Laughing, I flick him again in the forehead, then the arm, then his puny-boy chest, his arms grasping to catch me before I can get the flicks out, but I'm too quick for him. "Uncle?" I say. *Flick, flick, flick!*

"Never!"

Flick!

He doesn't give in until I flick the tip of his nose. "I didn't say that thing about the cologne," I tell him as he rubs the red out of his pores.

Ducky laughs. "I apologize," he says. "You are clearly *not* obsessed with the guy. My mistake."

"Thank you." I stick my hands into my pockets, and we walk for a while in silence, until I remember what I've been meaning to ask him. "So," I say, "Spring Fling is next week."

"Yeah?" Ducky perks his head up.

"I'm thinking Molly Ringwald marathon?" Every school dance, Ducky and I hole up at my house and watch old flat pics together. Last month it was British gangster flicks, and before that there was an unfortunate period when I was pretty into vampires. The movie marathons are our miniature rebellion against the mindless drones at school preening in off-the-rack evening wear. When you've got popcorn, nachos, and a four-liter of GuzzPop, who needs dresses and mirror balls?

"Oh," Ducky says, and I don't have to have been best friends with the guy for eleven years to know that he hates the idea. "Yeah. Molly Ringwald. That sounds good."

"I thought you liked all the Ringwalds." My good ol' buddy Donald Hunter Pence IV actually got the nickname Ducky from a Molly Ringwald flick—*Pretty in Pink*—way back in kindergarten, the year we officially became PIP: Peas in a Pod. Up until that point he'd always gone by Donald, which he hated, or Donald Duck, which some of the more creatively-challenged five-year-olds in our school thought was hilarious. So when we were watching the flat pic one afternoon at my house and Molly's totally awesome partner in crime, Duckie, showed up on-screen—with his funky, floppy hair and his funny round little glasses—well, it seemed like an obvious transition. I decreed then and there that all best friends should be named after waterfowl. And my Duckie has been Ducky ever since (as a five-year-old I felt little need to check the spelling). I asked him once if it bugged him having everyone in school call him that, and he looked at me, deathly serious, and replied, "Anything's better than Donald."

"I *do* like them," Ducky says with a sigh. "It's just . . ." But he trails off.

"Would you rather catch up on some old episodes of *Martian Law*? We haven't watched any in a while. It doesn't have to be Molly Ringwald."

"No, that's fine," Ducky says. "Really."

"Hey, stealth spaz," I say. "Spill."

"It's just . . . ," he says again, then shrugs. "I was thinking we could, maybe, you know, *go* to the dance this time."

As soon as Ducky says it, I get this feeling in my stomach like I've swallowed a fossilized hair ball or something. "Why would we do that?" I ask slowly.

"Well, the whole crew is going," Ducky says. But he's kicking a rock while he says it. He won't even look at me. "Jennie and Leo and Greg and Malikah . . ." He counts them off on his fingers. In my head I'm pairing them off in the most logical combinations. Why all our friends suddenly feel the need to mingle with the innies and dance in circles with their hands on one another's waists is beyond me, but I'm not on board.

"So who'd be your 'date' in this madding crowd? Malikah?"

Ducky clears his throat. "Uh, no," he says.

Okay, I swear I'm not operating on dial-up here. I know that boy plus girl plus spending lots of time together can sometimes lead to one or more of the involved parties falling for the other one. And I think—I've thought it for a couple months now, actually, ever since I caught Ducky watching me in the mirror while I brushed my hair—that maybe that whole falling thing has happened to Ducky. And that sort of sucks. Because I don't want to date Ducky. I don't want to date anyone. I went on one date, once, with Ricky Goldfarb back in seventh, and he tried to kiss me on the mouth, and I bit his lip so hard it bled. Maybe when we're, like, forty, Ducky and I can fall for each other. Until then I wish we could just keep watching flat pics, playing Jetman, and having contests to see who can launch the foulest moon rockets.

Ducky stops walking and looks at me, and I think for a second that he might say it—an awkward, stumbling declaration of love that up and ruins our whole friendship.

"It's just that I found the perfect dress," he says, flicking an imaginary lock of hair over his shoulder in his best Britta impersonation. Seriously, he ought to take that falsetto on the road. He could make a fortune. "But on second thought I don't think I have the hips for it. So Molly Ringwald it is."

I laugh. "Good," I tell him.

That's when we hear the noise behind us, the sound that's a cross between an old-fashioned kazoo and a pygmy elephant in heat. We turn and look, and wouldn't you know it's Cole and Britta, driving along with shit-eating grins like they're the god-damn prom king and queen, revving the engine of his classic red '55 Kia Metric convertible. Beside me Ducky lets out a groan.

Cole spots us and waves, and then—seriously, what the hell?—pulls over to the curb to say hey.

"Hey," he says.

I can sense Ducky's entire body go stiff. So I do what any good PIP would do in such a situation.

"Bite me," I tell Cole.

Britta, who looks like she'd rather be swallowing live scorpions than conversing with Ducky and me on the side of the road, flips me the bird. "What's your problem, pugly?" she says.

I ignore her and instead inspect the length of the car.

"Pretty sweet, right?" Cole asks with a grin.

I snort. "Sure," I tell him. "Just makes me wonder what you're making up for, is all."

My dad has always had a thing for classic cars—any anti-quated trip-dub machinery, really, but cars especially—so I've spent my fair share of time around automobiles, my head ducked under the hood of an old classic or tinkering with the motherboard of the more contemporary models. And I know for a fact that the Kia Metric is a penis-mobile, pure and simple. It has a two-cylinder hydrogen-injected engine, but Cole's tricked it out with a newer set of magnetic spheres, the ones with the insta-gel traction system, which are really useful, you know, if you're a race car driver or need to make a detour up the side of a building. But for the 'burbs, it's a bit much. That confused puppy look crosses Cole's face, the same one he gets whenever Mr. Fipps asks him to solve a proof in Algebra 2. "Huh?" he says.

Ducky pulls on my arm. "Come on, Elvie," he tells me. "Let's go."

"You want a ride?" Cole asks. A small self-assured smile creeps around the edges of his mouth. "I can drive you guys home if you want."

"*Excuse* me?" Britta trills. Her eyes have become swirly orbs of fury.

"We're good," Ducky says coolly. "We enjoy the exercise."

"But it's really no prob—," Cole starts, but I cut him off.

"Where exactly are we supposed to sit?" I say. The Metric's "backseat" is barely big enough for a full set of toenail clippings, let alone two human beings. Cole looks in the back, finally understanding, and starts sputtering like a dying goldfish. I roll my eyes. "Thanks for the offer," I tell him, and wave him on his way. Britta turns around to shoot me the stink eye as they roll off down the road.

"God, that guy is so dumb," I tell Ducky when the prom putzes are finally out of sight. "Did you know that he's flunking, like, every subject? The dude couldn't pass a class if he swallowed it first."

"Funny," Ducky says. "I thought we were done with this particular topic of conversation."

I bite at the skin around my thumbnail and dart my eyes down to my feet. Ducky moves on to the subject of his new Jetman strategy.

And I'm actually into it, talking about power-packs and the secret underwater cave world Ducky recently discovered, and for the next fifteen minutes or so, Cole Archer and Britta McVicker are the very last thing on my mind. . . . Until we turn the corner.

There's the penis-mobile, pulled off to the side of the road again, hazards blinking. Cole is peering under the hood, doing his best impression of someone who actually knows what he's looking at, while Britta is sitting up on the back of the car, pissed as hell, furiously jabbing at her phone.

We can't avoid the scene—we have to walk right by them. But while I'm passing with blinders on, Ducky heaves a deep sigh and stops walking.

"Do you guys need help?" he asks. He says it the way you would ask someone if they wanted you to jump into a sandpit filled with bat guano, but he still asks it.

"You're a better man than I, Gunga Din," I mutter.

Britta screeches into the phone and then throws it into her purse. "My mom's at rock aerobics," she hollers to Cole. "And no one else can pick me up."

Cole pulls his head out from under the hood, brandishing a blue-stained rod. "It's fine," he says. "I've totally got it. It's the Kuiper bonding. To conduct the current properly, it should be clear."

"That's so true," I say, and Cole nods, unaware of what a freaking dimwit he is. "Except that's the wiper fluid."

"Oh," he says.

Ducky sighs again. "Elvie, why don't you take a look?"

I'm not sure who looks more surprised at that, me or Cole,

but Ducky just pushes me toward the Kia. "She's really pro with cars," he explains.

"Uh, thanks," Cole replies, scooching over.

"Whatever," I tell the dumbass in distress. *I'm not doing this for Cole*, I tell myself. *It's just the nice thing to do. It's just NICE.*

"First of all," I say, lacing my voice with as much conde-scension as I can muster, "you're looking in the wrong place." I slam the hood shut, barely missing Cole's perfect nose, and open the driver side door to slide inside. While Cole stands around blank-faced and Britta vies for the Scoffer of the Year Award, I punch up the diagnostic program on the console display.

It doesn't take me two seconds to see what the problem is. It's not a hardware problem; it's the software. When Cole tricked out the car with the new mag spheres, he must have decided to upgrade his primary CPU at the same time. Too bad he chose one with an architecture that conflicts with the original engine systems around it. Without the right emula-tion software installed, it's no wonder the POS glitches. This is one reason my dad hates mixing and matching different-generation auto components—if you're going to drive a classic car, you've got to use classic parts. Dur.

I upload the correct emulators to my phone, sync to the console, and three minutes later I've got the coupe purring again. "That'll get you home," I tell Cole, slamming the door as I get out. "But you really need to get some native routers put in."

"Thanks," Cole tells me, and I can't help thinking as he says it how gratitude really makes his eyes sparkle. And God, how have I not ever noticed those cheekbones before? And that utterly adorable constellation of freckles just below his left eye? "You're a lifesaver, seriously. I don't know what I would've done without you, Elvie."

"Yeah," Britta says, leaning out of the car to grip Cole's arm. She gives it a protective squeeze, and smiles at me. "It's so awesome to know that ugly girls can be good at stuff too."

In my mind I am already lunging at her throat, mountain-lion-style, when Ducky grabs my arms from behind to stop me. Cole hops into the car and looks at Britta pointedly. "Elvs hasn't had an ugly day in her life," he tells her, and the way Britta's face falls is enough to make me stop wanting to rip her jugular out. After putting his now revived automobile into gear, Cole pulls away from the curb, then turns back to me and winks.

And my stomach flips a somersault.

The next morning there is a surprise at the bottom of my locker—a cupcake with chocolate frosting. No sprinkles. I stare at it for a moment, then peel off the wrapper without bothering to eat the thing.

There, written in the handwriting that I know so very well from gazing over his shoulder in lit class, is a message:

You really rev me up.

(Thanks, Elvs.)

—Cole

CHAPTER FIVE

IN WHICH OUR LITTLE
REUNION TURNS DEADLY

"*Cole?*" I screech, looking my former almost-boyfriend straight in his blue-green-blue eyes. Yep, there's no denying it. It's him. "What the—?" There aren't enough synapses in my brain to process what's going on right now. I can handle being attacked by space commandos. I can handle that our teachers were evil (heck, I already kinda suspected that). I even think that I'm handling the whole your-teachers-might-be-aliens thing pretty well. But when my estranged baby daddy turns up as one of said commandos, well, that's just one cherry too many for Elvie's drama sundae.

"Uh, hey, Elvie," Cole replies, and he actually sounds sheepish. You know, the way you might sound if you *totally bailed on the girl you knocked up and then ran into her in outer space three weeks before her due date.* "How've you been?"

Oh, this goon is going *down.* If anyone were in line for an Elvie beat-down special, it'd be Cole Archer.

"Hey," I reply.

It's a really *cutting* "hey."

Ramona steps over to my side. "You know this haircut?" she asks, clearly unimpressed with Cole. Which makes me heart her just a little bit. She rounds on him, unfazed by the ray gun he's been swinging all over the place. "Who the hell are you?" she asks.

Cole opens his mouth to answer, but looks at me instead, as if he needs my permission to lay out our whole sordid history.

"Cole is . . . ," I begin to tell Ramona, and then realize that the English language doesn't have the right word for what Cole is. Boyfriend? No. Ex? It's hard to be an ex if you were never a boyfriend. Raging douchetard from planet Ass Hat? Closer. "Cole is the Picasso of Lower Merion High School," I tell Ramona. I point to my baby bump. "Behold, *Guernica*."

"*Aaahhh*," she says, nodding in Cole's direction. "Well, it's nice to meet the artist in his prime."

"Look, Elvs . . . ," he begins.

"Nice job biting it on the bleachers, by the way," Ramona adds. "With moves like that, I'm thinking . . . Olympic long jumper."

I'm just about to tell Cole where he can stuff that ray gun, when from behind me I hear, *"Baaaaaay-bee!"* And Britta, still surprisingly agile for an about-to-burst cheerleader, elbow-smashes past my face and leaps into his arms. "Oh, my God!" she cries, kissing him all over—mouth, neck, hairline, shoulders. "I can't believe you're *here*! I haven't seen you since . . . Why did you ever . . . How did you know I'd be . . . Oh, Coley, I've *missed* you!"

I cross my arms and scowl. Much as I might not need some asshole like Cole Archer sucking up my oxygen, I can't help being jealous at the sight of him sucking someone else's. He plops Britta down onto her feet and runs his hand across her belly while she giggles. "The little guy's doing all right?" he asks. And, okay, it's not like I didn't know before that Britta and I had the same baby daddy, but just now, at this moment, is the first time it's occurred to me that our kids are going to be *siblings*.

They should have put that in the posters for the Abstinence Club at school:

Sex: Don't Do It
(Or your baby might be related to Britta McVicker)

Just then the captain comes back our way, and when he sees Cole with his helmet off, palm to Britta's maternity swimsuit, he goes ballistic.

"Soldier!" he barks at Cole, whipping his own helmet off—to yell with greater clarity, I guess. "What exactly do you think you're doing?"

Cole straightens up, stiff-as-a-plank, but Britta just scowls. "God, loosen your jockstrap," she says. "We're having a reunion here."

Ramona nudges me in the side, gesturing toward Captain Freak-Out, and says, "Damn, are all these commandos smoking hotties?"

Seriously. Even as the captain's ears start spewing steam, I can't help noticing that they are pretty handsome ears. He's got a pretty handsome everything, actually. Cropped black hair, smooth dark skin, no trace of stubble. He's kinda like an olive-skinned Cole. Stick a pout and a squint on him, and he could be an underwear model, easy mode.

But maybe now is not the time to inform him that he rates billboard status.

"Archer!" he hollers as Natty and Other Cheerleader wander over our way to find out what all the commotion is about. Apparently no one has ever told him that shouting is bad for your blood pressure, because the guy has one volume, and it's Loud. "You're acquainted with one of the targets?" *Targets?* I scratch my nose and play tennis spectator between Captain Whatshisname, who's so mad he's spitting, and Cole, whose face is absorbing the majority of said spittle. "Do you have any idea what a serious breach of protocol this is?"

"I didn't know she'd—uh, be here," Cole stammers back. But Big Boss Man doesn't seem to be biting.

"You were given intel on all forty-six students at briefing, just like everyone else. If you knew this girl, you should have said something."

Cole looks ready to piss himself, but he does his best to squeak out an answer. "Yes—I— Sir, I know that, sir, but . . ." For once his dreamy good looks don't seem to be enough to get by with. He straightens up and clears his throat. "But I hadn't seen her since—"

"And why would it matter *when* the last time you saw her was?" the captain bellows. Seriously, dude needs to check his spittle situation. I might as well go dunk myself back in the pool.

Britta is glaring daggers at the captain. "For your *information*," she tells him, "Cole is my boyfriend."

"*Your* boyfriend?" Ramona says, a curious smile creeping across her face. "But I thought—" That's when I give her a *Please, please, no, don't bring it up* look. Now is not exactly the time for Britta to learn about the whole maybe-sort-of-sleeping-with-her-boyfriend-behind-her-back-and-getting-knocked-up-in-the-process debacle. That's really the kind of thing you need at least two minutes for.

Thank God Ramona speaks eyebrow, 'cause she keeps her trap shut.

"Archer!" Captain Loud barks at Cole. "Are you purposefully trying to jeopardize this mission, or are you just a *complete* moron?"

Ramona folds her arms across her pregnant-lady rack. "This is better than Soap Net," she says.

"Are all our boyfriends here?" Chewie pipes up.

Britta is still plastering Cole with wet kisses. "You're *so* heroic!" she gushes. "Rushing in here and saving us from these creeps!"

"Saving us?" comes a voice from behind me. "The teachers didn't go all psycho until these guys showed up in the first place. What's the deal? Who are you guys?"

But it seems that Captain Spaz Attack doesn't really feel like chatting. The vein on his forehead is getting the workout of a lifetime. Pretty soon he'll be able to bench press with it. Rather than deal with all our baby mama drama, he decides to pull Cole aside—well, "yank" is probably a better verb—to yell at him in private. Still, he isn't exactly mayor of Shushville, and the pool room is made for echoes, so we get the gist of things. A little bit of "If I even THOUGHT that you MANIPULATED your way onto this strike force . . ." with a generous helping of ". . . COMPLETELY disregarded the basic PRINCIPLES . . ." and a chorus of ". . . SUCH an idiot!"

Honestly, part of me feels sorry for Cole. The guy looks like he wants to drop a smoke bomb and ninja vanish. Still, I'm not really in a forgive-and-forget frame of mind at the moment. He actually thinks he can just knock me up, totally ditch town, and then show up a couple months later to rescue me from murderous aliens, only to start sucking face with his "real" girlfriend right in front of me? Beefcake, *puh-leez*.

While Cole practices his ghost impression—paper white, shaking, boo-hoo-hooing—one of the other commandos distributes towels and tells the girls still in their swimsuits to dart into the changing room to put on some real clothes. My sopping black V-neck and stretch jeans are sticking to my body, but my only change of clothes is back in my room, and now doesn't really seem like the time to ask for a hall pass. It looks like I'll be spending the rest of the day looking like a drowned marmot.

The plan, the commando tells us after Ramona digs it out of him, is to rendezvous with the other girls and commandos from the On Your Own class, then jettison out of here on the ship they rode in on, leaving the Hanover School for good and returning safely to our homes. I join two of the commandos in their attempt to check for survivors while waiting for the girls to change. I do my best not to look at Linda's—or Lindsey's—floating body, the bile once again rising in the back of my throat. I try not to think about how they'll tell her parents. How her folks will react to the news. Actually, it's pretty easy not to think about things like that, what with Natty trailing behind me, yapping in my ear.

"Do you really think they're going to take us home?" Natty asks, apparently oblivious to the dead teacher I've just uncovered smushed behind a lounge chair. I close my eyes for a moment, squeezing them hard so that it's only pinpricks of light I see behind my eyelids. When I open them again, the dead teacher's still there, but I swallow down the awfulness, make a mental note to tell the commandos about him, and move on down the length of the wall.

"Sure, Natty," I tell her, although I don't really know what to think. Obviously there's a lot that Cole and the rest of these commando guys aren't telling us. And yes, they're being supermysterious and we should all be asking them some pretty important questions, like, you know, "Who are you guys?" But of the two opposing groups of sultry dudes on this ship, these are the guys who *weren't* trying to drown girls in the pool, so, at least for now, I think I'm going to have to go on faith that Cole and his pals can get us out of here, and explain the rest later.

Really, what other choice have I got?

Finished with my inspection, I inch myself slowly away from Natty and join Chewie, who is cajoling a group of the commandos to take off their helmets. Her pout becomes even more pronounced as, one by one, she inspects their faces and discovers that no, her boyfriend is not on board. Although, based on the ravishing good looks of every soldier here, hotness is apparently a requirement for this particular strike force.

Yow-za.

After our search is over, we still haven't come up with any more survivors. It's just twenty-two girls, including myself, and six commandos.

When the other girls finally haul their butts back from the changing room, the captain ushers us all out of the pool area into the hallway, barking at us to "Move, move, move!" I'm thrilled when the comm on his belt crackles to life, since it forces him to stop his I'm-such-a-badass-I-never-quit-shouting routine. He snatches the walkie and puts it to his mouth.

"Yes, sir. Tango Leader here."

"Tango Leader, we've located the—"

That's the last thing I hear. For, like, a while. Not because the dude on the other end of the walkie stops talking. Well, maybe he does. I don't know.

But I'm thinking my deafness probably has more to do with the explosion.

Now, when I say explosion, I mean a rock-the-entire-ship, knock-everyone-onto-their-asses kind of *KABOOM*. The explosion is a long way off, but it's strong enough to send serious shock waves from one end of the *Echidna* to the other. The girders supporting the walls collapse and block off the hallway. There's smoke in my eyes, and it stings so badly I have to squeeze them shut, tears pushing the burn away. When I open them again, I see Cole, his mouth moving frantically without making any noise. It takes me a moment to realize that he's screaming—and that I can't hear his screams because I am, at least for the moment, totally deaf from the blast. But my eyes still work, and I have the wherewithal to notice that

Cole is frantically pointing at something above our heads. Dancing in the acrid smoke are several frayed wires, sparks flying from the ends.

Natty is up on her feet looking at the sparks like a small child gawking at fireflies. Fireflies that could ignite and take off the top of her skull at any moment. "Natty!" I holler, but even I can't hear my voice. Not wanting to take any chances, I reach over and grab Natty's ankle, yanking it out from underneath her so that she falls to the ground face-first. Chipping a tooth is better than getting decapitated, I figure.

Not two seconds after I tug Natty to the floor, the sparks from the wires ignite in the fuel-laced smoke. The secondary explosions pop like fireworks in rapid succession, and the force pushes me even flatter into the floor. And here I thought the worst thing I was going to have to deal with today was the ultrasound goo during my afternoon physical.

I turn my head, and when I spot Cole about a meter away from me, eyes blinking in a way that lets me know that yes, he's still alive and kicking, I let out a breath I didn't realize I was holding. But I suck it in again when he rolls over. There's Britta, his *girlfriend*, safe and sound, wedged under the protective body shield Cole made for her with his six-pack abs.

Peachy.

I sit up and try to take stock of the situation. Natty's rubbing her lip with a pout on her face, but she's in one piece. Nearby, Ramona's struggling to her feet and yanking down her faux-leather skirt. I'm pretty sure Other Cheerleader is wailing about her nail polish. Chewie is, well, chewing on her hair. And I count nine other girls, in various states of disarray.

The rubble where the wall caved in is taller than I am, a mishmash of broken paneling, bulkheads, and smoldering comm panels. In the wreckage I make out a helmet like the one Cole had on earlier, crushed flat by the weight of the debris.

As my ears slowly regain function, I hear the captain warbling into his walkie. "Goddamn it, do you copy?" he shouts into the thing. He shakes it, as though that might make his buddy on the other end pick up. Besides him, the only commando left standing is Cole. Just two commandos, and fifteen girls.

Holy shit.

Apart from the captain's barking, and the sobs of the girls, the only other sound I can make out is a loud hissing.

Now, there are only a few things that cause hissing on a spaceship, and none of them is exactly cause for a party.

I waddle dizzily over to join the captain at the window— which, thank God, has not yet cracked, sucking us all out into the void. But, you know, the day's not over yet. My head is throbbing from the force of the explosions, and my balance is only so-so, so I brace myself against the reinforced transparent aluminum that lets us look out at the stars. But what grabs my attention isn't the pretty lights. It's the same thing that the captain's looking at. The gaping hole in the side of the ship, venting atmosphere.

We are officially leaking oxygen into space.

Why did I think Lower Merion was so bad again?

"Alpha Leader, do you copy? Alpha Leader . . . *Terrance!*" The captain is starting to lose his shit a little bit, squeezing his walkie so tightly it could pop. It takes me a moment to figure it out, but soon it hits me—the reason the captain's so shaken. It's not the gajillion casualties. It's not even the leaking O_2. The damage around the ship was blown inward, meaning it came from something *outside* the *Echidna*.

"That was your ship that blew, wasn't it?" I ask him. He looks at me, resentment in his eyes, like it's my fault or something. The glare lasts only a second, though, and then he composes himself.

"Yeah," he spits out, slapping the window with the palm of his hand. "It was our ship. Along with my commander, my squad, and the rest of your classmates."

I've heard, somewhere, that when people are faced with massive tragedy, their bodies tend to go cold. You know, "I shivered with the sudden chill that crept down my spine," "A block of ice formed in the pit of my stomach," that sort of thing. But me? When I find out that half my classmates have been blown to bits in a random space explosion, my whole body goes white hot. My cheeks burn, my forehead, even the sides of my stomach. I gulp down the lump in my throat, and even *that* feels hot. "Are you sure?" I ask the captain.

"Yeah," he says again. His gaze goes back to the stream of oxygen hissing out the window, pouring out into the atmosphere in tiny rivulets. I have a sudden urge to call Natty over to take a look. It *is* gorgeous, in a sort of holy-crap-we're-all-gonna-die sort of way.

"But how did it . . ."

The captain tosses his now useless walkie into a pile of wall debris and pulls from his pocket what must be the sweetest-looking phone I've ever seen. It unrolls like an LED readout, but snaps into place when it's extended. "Shit," he growls, punching at it with his fingers. "I'm not getting a signal."

I pull out my own phone to see if I'll have any better luck. Nope. Instead of the weak signal I usually get, there's nothing. Which makes me suspect that the ship's transmitter isn't operating at all. So much for getting in touch with my dad or Ducky and filling them in about my day of happy fun time.

I've got to admit, I'm feeling pretty sorry for myself. What I *want* to be doing is channeling my father, figuring out what he would do in such a situation. Instead the only thought that seems to be running through my brain is a pitiful *Why me?* But I'm ripped away from my pity party by the most annoying sound in the cosmos.

"Cole, *baaaay-beeee!*" It is Britta, of course, moaning from the other side of the hallway. Probably in despair over the fact that she hasn't been the center of attention for the past minute and a half. She's sitting with her back to a crushed control panel, massaging her ankle like she thinks it's going to pay for dinner afterward. "Cole, I think it's *broken*! I think I broke my *ankle*!"

Cole, who's been sifting through the debris, hesitates for a second, but then heads back over to Britta, just like she wants. I fold my arms across my chest and totally *don't* watch. What do I care if Cole hasn't even bothered to ask how *I* am yet? Why would I care about that?

I narrow my eyes and observe from behind a curtain of eyelashes as Cole takes Britta's ankle in his hands—those hands that once pulled me in close for a kiss, his breath warming my skin—and puts slight pressure on it. "Does that hurt?" he asks. Britta gives a melodramatic little squeak of agony, and sets her ankle delicately into his lap. And is it just me, or has the ankle that *he* sprained, like, fifteen minutes ago healed remarkably quickly? "I'm going to wrap it," he tells her. "That will relieve some of the pain. Hey!" he calls over his shoulder. "Is there a med kit? I need something to wrap Britta's ankle!"

"I can help!" comes a call. And then this girl named Carrie—who, even on a ship full of unwed expecting teen girls, has managed to get herself dubbed "the slutty one"— comes bounding over. She's wearing a sleeveless gray tee and a skirt so short it makes her look like the head counselor at tramp camp. "Let me just . . ." From the debris she pulls a shard of aluminum and worries at the hem of her skirt. Once she's got a tear going, she yanks all the way around until she's pulled off a swath about twenty centimeters wide. She hands the strip of material to Cole and smoothes her now 100 percent ho-approved mini-mini over her thighs. "For Britta's ankle."

"Uh," Cole says, his brain clearly unable to process such X-rated altruism. "Thanks."

Cole ogles Carrie's tuchus just a little too long as she walks away, causing Britta to cough loudly. He turns back to her and shakes his head as if to clear the image, then begins to wrap her foot. Britta preens.

God, I think while watching them, *how did I ever fall for that dinkus?* Sure, he's hot. Sure, when he holds you, the entire universe disappears.

But he's just such a *turd*.

I vow, right then and there, that when I get back home, right after I finish French kissing the soil we land on, I'm going to call Ducky, tell him to come find me, and give him a giant bear hug that'll make his eyes pop out. Because I cannot, at this moment, think of a single person I want to be around more.

There is a loud *ka-CHUNK!* sound, and a mild vibration rocks the floor. The hissing stops, and I breathe a sigh of relief. But Other Cheerleader starts whining.

"Oh, *God!*" she wails. "Another *explosion!* The whole ship is going to blow *up!*"

I am suddenly nostalgic for my brief period of deafness.

"The ship is not blowing up," I tell her, rolling my eyes at her general retardation. "That's the vacuum shield closing."

"And that's . . . good?" Carrie asks, putting her arms up to readjust her ponytail. Seriously, that girl needs to invest in a bra.

"The ship has fail-safe shielding in case of a hull breach," I say. "It'll keep the oxygen from leaking out too quickly, which should give us plenty of time to reach the escape pods."

Other Cheerleader doesn't seem as thrilled about this knowledge as I am. She sticks her hands on her hips and sneers at me. "What'd you do, like, memorize the manual?" She turns to Britta. "Where did this blubber butt even *come* from?"

From the other end of the hallway comes a meek "Excuse me," and this quiet girl, Heather, rises shakily to her feet, pushing her bangs off her forehead. "I think you meant '*From where* did this blubber butt even come?'" Other Cheerleader rounds on her with a face-melting glare, but Heather seems undaunted. "You shouldn't end a sentence with a preposition," she explains.

"Actually"—she puts a hand on her midsize baby bump and begins to rub it thoughtfully—"it might be more accurate to use the word 'whence.' It's a bit archaic but perfectly applicable in this instance. '*Whence* did this blubber butt even—'"

"Um, Elvie?" Ramona says, pointing out the window. "Did you mean *those* escape pods?"

Well, shit.

There they are, out the window. Every single escape pod on the whole damn ship is launching straight to Earth, just the way they were meant to in an emergency. . . . Except, of course, for the minor problem of us not being on them.

I'm thinking that right about now would be a good time for some leadership from our saviors.

"Well, shit," Cole says.

The pandemonium that erupts is overwhelming. The majority of the girls explode into wailing and chattering, and they clamor at the captain. The action hero does his best to get the screaming girls to calm down, but to no avail. Even Ramona looks a little shaken up. I haven't heard her make a single ironic comment in, I don't know, thirty whole seconds.

A hailstorm of überhelpful exclamations flies around the room.

"How are we going to get *home*?"

"I want to call my dad!"

"We're gonna die! We're all gonna *die*!

"I want to call my lawyer!"

"What about my baby?"

"I want to call my dad's lawyer!"

"Does your phone work? My phone's not working. How

am I supposed to blink about this if my phone's not working?"

For once Natty seems to be the sole voice of reason. "How did all the escape pods launch on their own?" she asks.

Cole squints his eyes, which is what he does when he's thinking hard about something. I've seen him do it, like, twice. "Those pods should only activate manually," he says. Shows what he knows.

"They could've been activated remotely from the bridge," I inform him.

"Wait, *what*?" Carrie screeches. And I think somehow her boobs get just a tad bigger when she's freaked out. "How could that even happen?"

"Of all the days to wear my Jimmy Choos," Other Cheerleader moans. "What was I even thinking of?"

Heather raises her hand. "Again," she says, although clearly no one has called on her. "'Of' is a preposition. So you really shouldn't end your—"

"Spare us the phonics lesson, freakazoid," Britta snaps.

"Actually," Heather squeaks, "it's more *grammar* than phonics, but I can see where you'd get—"

That's when Captain Overreaction aims his ray gun and fires a shot into the floor. The *zip-crack!* silences everyone.

"*Enough!*" he shouts at the cowed girls. "We need to get to the bridge and get our bearings. Find a way off this ship before the air runs out, or worse. Hopefully we can get a signal out from there too." All around there are slow nods. A few sniffles. The air in the room is becoming a little clearer. Finally someone has a plan. "Archer," the captain continues, "can you call up the ship schematics on that wall console?"

Cole disengages from Britta, who's clinging to him like a frightened bunny, and looks skeptically at the fried panel on the wall. The screen is shattered and the frayed circuitry behind it is visible. He taps it tentatively, and a shower of sparks flies out from the cracks, sending all the girls screaming again.

"Uh, it broke," Cole says.

The captain walks over to the panel to look for himself, although he's clearly not going to find any useful information there either. Ascertaining that, dur, the panel is not functioning, he turns away from the debris back down the hall, toward the pool. "We'll just have to get there the old-fashioned way, then, won't we?" he says. "Ladies, let's move out."

"Sir?" I holler as he passes. But he doesn't turn. "Hey, bucko!" I shout again. "Yoo-hoo!"

At *that* he turns around. You can tell just by the look on his face that he's certainly never been yoo-hoo'd at before.

"Is there something on your *mind*?" he growls. His eyebrows curl upward in annoyance. It's the first time I've ever seen anyone snarl with their eyebrows.

"*Oooh*," Britta fake-whispers to Other Cheerleader. "Hippopotabutt's in *trouble!*"

I ignore her.

"That's not the fastest way to the bridge," I tell the captain.

He pauses for a second, glancing down the length of the hall. Then, with a decisive breath, he turns back to me. "You know the way?" he asks.

I nod. "It's only a few decks up from here. We can take the back stairwell behind the pool's laundry closet."

"There's likely to be more debris blocking other areas off,"

Cole offers. Britta has her arm slung around his neck and limps next to him. It's all I can do to keep from pulling his ray gun from his hip and vaporizing both of them. Clearly Cole came all this way for her. Clearly he doesn't give a rat's ass about me. Clearly I just need to get over it.

I stand up as straight as my pregnant back will allow. "I know the layout of the *Echidna* backward and forward," I tell the captain confidently. "I'll find the way."

"Captain," Cole puts in, "we should go with your initial instinct and head back the way we came. If there's damage throughout the rest of the ship, we should be in territory we're familiar with."

"*I'm* familiar with it," I reply.

"Elvie, c'mon. This is—"

The captain holds up his hand for Cole to stop. He looks at me, and then looks at Cole. "Archer," he says finally, "you couldn't crap in a bucket if it were strapped to your ass. We will follow the lady."

So just like that I'm bumped up in rank to navigator to the bridge, leading a group of survivors in an emergency escape attempt from a reeling spaceship that, according to our pretty-boy rescuers, was until just recently controlled by aliens. My dad would be so proud. I bet even the king of disaster plans didn't have a folder for that in his crisis survival drawer.

We're just turning the first corner—the captain and me in the front, and Cole and the fab fourteen in tow—when I realize something. "Hey," I say, squinting up at the captain. He really is handsome, in a preppy catalog-model sort of way. "You got a name?"

He jerks his gaze away from his phone, which he's unsuccessfully been jabbing at for the last two minutes. "Pardon?" he replies.

"Your *name*," I repeat. "You know, '*Je m'appelle Monsieur LeDouche*,' that sort of thing?" I am going for humor, for some sort of normalcy, but the captain—surprise, surprise—does not crack a smile. "It would really help the running narrative in my head if I actually knew what to call you."

The captain pinches the bridge of his nose. When he does finally speak again, his voice is such a low grumble that I can't make out the words, but I get the gist.

"Fine," I say, shrugging my shoulders as if all my conversations go this way. "From now on I'll just call you Captain Bob. How do you like that?"

Based on his total nonresponse, I'm guessing Captain Bob likes it just fine.

Suddenly I feel a hand on my shoulder.

"Elvs, you okay?"

I don't turn around. I can hear Cole's breath as he hustles to keep pace with me, and let's just say I don't exactly feel like talking. I take a conversational cue from Captain Bob and go all stony silent.

"I didn't get a chance to check on you earlier," he says. "Did you get hurt at all in the blast? Any sign of brain damage? How's your vision?" And he begins patting me down as we walk—my head, my arms, my legs. I rip his arm away when he starts to get fresh with the Goober.

"Are you checking for internal bleeding or frisking me for a weapon?" I say.

"Jeez, Elvs," he says, "I was just worried about you. That's all." And he seems so genuinely hurt that for a second I actually feel bad for acting like such an ass monger.

But just for a second.

"Don't you have some cheerleader's ankle to be concerned about?" I snap.

"Elvs." His voice is soft. Soothing.

I catch Cole's eye then, and it all comes rushing back. God, I used to feel like I could stare into those eyes for hours, forever, just watching them stare back into mine. And right now, even though I want to hate him, the way I've been hating him for the past eight-plus months, somehow I can't. Somehow the knowledge that this might very well be my last day as a living, breathing human being makes all the hatred melt out of me.

Cole tugs on my arm, stopping my stride dead in the hallway. Then he takes my head between his hands—exactly the way he did that one beautiful afternoon—and gazes straight into my eyes. I stop breathing. Suddenly I'm not myself anymore. I'm not on a leaking spaceship. I'm not knocked up beyond all recognition. Suddenly I'm just a girl, gazing at a boy, getting goose bumps from the scent of his neck.

"I missed you," I whisper. But over the cacophony of stomping girls, I'm not sure he hears it.

Cole holds me away from him, just a little, to look at me, and—God, I love those eyes—I wait for him to say something, anything, to make me believe that this "rescue" of theirs isn't going as badly as it seems. I don't even care if he lies to me, just this once, just so I won't be so freaked.

He blinks and then raises an index finger. "How many fingers am I holding up?" he asks.

Ugh. I push the bastard away.

"I dunno," I respond, flipping him the bird. "How many am I?"

I don't need Cole, I decide as I regain my position next to Captain Bob at the head of the train, leaving the idiot to make his way back to his beloved cheerleader. I don't need anyone. Our survival is in my hands now, and God forbid I eff it up because I'm too busy freaking over someone else's boyfriend. No, I think, *absolutely. I do not need him.*

Although what I *do* sort of need, I realize as my stomach begins to gurgle-gurgle, is a bathroom. Talk about wonderful timing.

"You okay over there?" Captain Bob says, shooting a glance my way. I can't tell if he's talking about my little scene with Cole or the obvious dismayed look on my face, as I do my best to hold in what I'm sure will be one fiercely fragrant pregnant-lady fart.

"I'm fine," I manage to squeak out. "Just fine."

He curls his mouth to the side. "Good," he says. "Because I'm counting on you."

I allow myself the tiniest of smiles. *Yeah*, I think, *my dad would be pretty proud.*

"Hey," Britta calls from the back of the line. "Does anyone else smell that?"

CHAPTER SIX

IN WHICH THE PLOT GETS, LIKE, SUPERTHICK

I'm working hard at my role as human GPS, trying to get everyone to the bridge, only it's not going quite as well as I might have hoped. The damage caused by the explosion has put some serious hurt on our little space academy, and we've already had to backtrack once, after hitting up the laundry room. Talk about nasty. Stacks of dirty sports bras are foul enough when they're *not* on fire.

And then of course I lead us smack into a wall of sparking debris.

"Wow, Commander Elvie," comes a voice from behind me, and I don't have to turn around to know that it's Britta. "You are, like, so good at this. Any other giant crap piles you want to lead us straight into?"

I would like to lead a giant crap pile straight into her face.

Ramona rolls her eyes at me as we turn a corner, then jerks

her thumb in Britta's direction. "You used to go to school with that thing?" I nod. Britta is again whining about the state of her precious ankle. You'd think she broke, like, nine of them the way she's going on about it. "Rock-paper-scissors to see who gets to throw her out the window," Ramona tells me.

And we're backtracking again.

As we walk, I begin tuning into the various conversations behind me, less because I'm interested and more because I need something to think about other than, you know, our impending doom. But it turns out that most of the girls who didn't get smashed to bits are as dull as rocks. "I *knew* there was a reason you weren't returning my blinks, Coley. I just wish you'd *told* me you were leaving to become a space commando." "No, seriously, I don't get any reception." "And then Tamara was like, 'No, she didn't,' and I was like, 'Did too,' and she was like, 'You cannot get high off fermented tuna.'" "I just wonder who our teachers *really* were, you know?"

I stop switching brain dials and focus on the last conversation. A quick glance over my shoulder tells me that the two girls talking are Heather, the walking grammar lesson, and this other girl Danielle, who's svelte and sporty despite her baby bump and will probably grow up to be an underwater prenatal yoga instructor herself.

"I mean, I know they weren't aliens, that's all I'm saying," Danielle goes on. "Because that doesn't make any sense. Put aside for the moment that aliens don't exist. Even if they did, why would they want to teach calculus to a bunch of pregnant girls?"

Heather *hmmm*s on that for a second, thinking before she

responds. Finally she pipes up. "Well, that's not *all* you're say-ing, is it, since you continued speaking after that clause? Fur-thermore, you shouldn't begin a sentence with 'because.'"

Danielle continues on as though Heather hasn't said any-thing at all, which, when dealing with Heather, is probably the best course of action. "And anyway, the teachers didn't even start attacking us until *these* guys showed up, you know? So, really, I think our 'rescuers' might be the ones to look out for."

I'm starting to think this Danielle chick might be one of the few mothers on this spaceship with some brains in her head. But I don't get a lot of time to ruminate on what she's said, because it's at that moment that Ramona decides she wants to talk to me again.

"How come you decided to keep it?"

My head snaps up. She's sucking down another clove—Lord knows where she found it—and she asks the question in this, like, totally nonchalant way, but it hits me hard.

"Sorry?" I ask.

"Why'd you decide to keep your baby?" Ramona asks, tak-ing another nice long drag. "You miss the date for a reboot, or you just really into toilet training?"

I contemplate how best to answer that. It's not like the idea of "taking care of the problem" never crossed my mind. What accidentally knocked-up teen girl doesn't at least flirt with the idea of getting a fresh start? But in the end that just wasn't what I wanted to do, and it's not like I had a whole ton of time to think about it. Dad told me once that it used to be, way back in the day, that a woman could terminate an unwanted preg-nancy even several months after conception. I guess lots of people were freaked about that, and there were all sorts of laws and arguments about it. Finally with the Great Compromise it was decided that anyone who wanted to could get a termination, but only for the first two weeks after conception. These days it's possible to find out if you're preggers in as little as two hours, but a lot of girls don't know until a month or so in, and by then it's tough luck, Charlie.

"I'm not keeping it," I answer Ramona at last. "I'm giving the thing up for adoption, as soon as it pops. Already filled out the paperwork."

"Assuming we don't all asphyxiate in the next hour," she says.

"Obviously."

She nods, thoughtful, then rubs her belly, the cigarette laced between two fingers.

"You?" I ask. I can't help it.

She looks up at me and shrugs. "Officially? I'm 'keeping' it, but if you want to know, the thing's really gonna be raised by my uncle Leroy out in San Mateo County. Apparently his wife has a dried-up prune for a uterus. They've been trying to get knocked up for years. Enter the family hero." She takes another long drag on her clove. "Win-win, right? The kid gets parents who want it, and I get to play the part of the wild and crazy fun older cousin."

I smile.

"When I first found out, I freaked, though," she goes on. "I even went down to the clinic, the day after. I mean, don't get me wrong, I loved Kyran and everything. That's my boyfriend. But I didn't exactly want to look like a swollen watermelon for the next nine months."

"So," I say when Ramona stops talking. That can't possibly be the end of the story. "What changed your mind?"

"Oh." She sucks down another lungful of smoke. "One of the doctors at the clinic. You know how they have that one room, before you go in for the actual operation, where they counsel you and make sure you're mentally stable and yada, yada?" I nod like I know, even though I don't, really. "Well, the doctor I saw kinda talked me out of it, I guess. He just brought up all these other options for me. He was the one who mentioned this place, actually." She flicks the ash from her cig onto the ground, then smears it with her boot as she stomps. "Of course, now I get to thank him for all this. Dunno how he convinced me to change my mind. Probably didn't hurt that he was *dreamy* gorgeous. Usually I don't go for the dark, smoldering types. I like my boys just a little femme, like Kyr. But damn, he was smokin'."

Suddenly Ramona snaps to attention, like she's doing a double take. "Jesus, I'm such a chromer. You don't think that guy was in cahoots with our doucher teachers, do you?"

I think on that. "Yeah, probably."

"Holy hell."

"Seriously," I agree. "So what does, um, Kyran think about your whole give-the-baby-to-the-uncle plan?"

"Eh." She shrugs. "He didn't seem to care one way or the other. He was so *not* happy about the clinic, let me tell you, but when it came to raising the thing?" She pauses as we navigate another tight corner. "Anyway, he skipped town about a week before I boarded. Last I heard he was moving to Indiana."

Huh. Sounds familiar.

"Hey, does it bug you that they won't tell us the gender of our stupid babies beforehand?" Ramona asks. "Like, who cares about the element of surprise, Dr. Marsden? Just tell me if the damn thing's a boy or a girl so I know what genitals to look for."

"They wouldn't tell you either?" I ask. Dr. Marsden told me that he was "restricting gender information" from me because he thought it would be psychologically damaging to know the gender of the baby I would never form mother-child bonds with. Not that I had a burning desire to know, anyway. I had multiple opportunities to learn the Goober's sex in the five months before I got here, and I always declined.

"God, I hope we make it off this spaceship," Ramona says just as we turn another corner and get our first glance at the bridge. "If I'm going to asphyxiate in space, I'd really rather not do it next to *those* morons." She motions back toward Britta and Other Cheerleader, who are fawning over Cole's hair. Ramona stomps out the last of her cigarette as we reach the door to the bridge.

The bridge is nothing special to look at, really. Just a dull gray room with operational terminals set up at the center console and along the side walls. No captain's chair or photon torpedo launchers or anything like that. Basically it serves as the main hub of operations for the entire ship. Navigation, gravity, and O_2 levels are all controlled from the main computer, while secondary systems like communications and temperature control are run by other servers that are hardwired to the main computer. There's a small viewport that normally would have diagnostic overlays demarcating points of interest in the ship's path, while along the left side of the viewport, screens streaming feeds from cameras spread across the hull of the ship would give external views from just about every angle. Now, though, the cameras are all dead, and only the physical window shows what lies ahead, without any indication of what we're drifting toward. Students were never allowed in this area, primarily because one person with access to that main computer could do a whole heck of a lot of damage. Although the teachers liked to tell us it was off-limits because that's where Professor Wilks let off his legendary moon rockets.

While most of the girls make a beeline for the massive window on the far wall, checking out the spacescape and our leaking O_2 situation, Captain Bob directs Cole to the main communications view screen. "Tell me when you've made contact with command," he barks at Cole. "Byron will want to be notified of our situation as soon as possible."

I can see from Cole's expression that he's fighting back an "Aye, aye, Captain!" But he makes his way to the view screen without further comment. Britta, of course, follows him, simultaneously hobbling and chattering inanely in his ear. "And I was so worried that I didn't get a chance to tell you we were having a baby," she prattles on. "But I guess you sensed it? That's so amazing, that you can sense something like that. I still cannot even believe you came all this way just to rescue me!"

Meanwhile, Captain Bob heads for the main console, to check for himself what our situation is. I decide to follow him, hoping there will be something I can do to help.

Unfortunately, so does Carrie. While Captain Bob jabs his fingers at the touch screen, she drapes herself over his back, her hair in his face.

"Is there anything I can do?" she asks, her lips all pouty in this way that I'm sure she thinks is supersexy.

Captain Bob doesn't seem to have noticed that he's got a boob-shaped tumor attached to him. "It's encrypted," he growls, jabbing away at the touch screen in a futile attempt to find the right pass code. "And the code provided by control isn't working. I was hoping they wouldn't have time to lock it down. Apparently they did."

"You know," Carrie continues, trying to nudge Bob's face her way by wrenching his chin back with her hand, "you sort of remind me of my ex, Giles. He had that sensitive Mediterranean thing going for him."

"Hey, Carrie," I say, because I finally realize there *is* something I can do to help. "Why don't you turn the ho meter down a few ticks until we get out of here, okay?"

Carrie straightens up with a pout, but as she walks away, she stops and looks over her shoulder, giving Bob a choice view of her backside. "Just call if you need anything, gorgeous," she coos.

"Thanks," Captain Bob tells me softly as I join him at the console.

"No problem. You stick to the commando stuff, I can deal with twits like Carrie."

For the first time all day, I see what looks like a crack of a smile breaking through Captain Bob's mask. But just as quickly it vanishes. "Anyway, I appreciate your assistance, Miss Nara. And thank you for getting us to the bridge in one piece."

I decide to go where Cole Archer cannot. "Aye, aye, Captain," I tell him.

Freed from the distraction that is Carrie's sizeable rack,

the captain finds the encryption on the computer far easier to crack. Within moments the computer's main interface has sprung to life, and a few taps later, every console on the bridge is lit up and working again.

"*Ooooooh,*" Natty sighs from over by the window as she takes in the light display. "It looks just like *Christmas!*"

Captain Bob and I ignore her and lean in close to the console to find out exactly how boned we really are.

We are pretty supremely boned.

The bad news is that the escape pods were in fact launched from the bridge, which leaves us no exit from the ship whatsoever. It also means, of course, that someone on board this ship must have launched them, and—barring the unlikely event that our little friend the pod launcher stuck his head inside an oven or something—that person is still on board, and still probably doesn't like us very much.

The *really* bad news is that, despite the vacuum shields activating, we are still leaking oxygen. Breathable air levels are down to about 58 percent. All those explosions must have burned up a considerable amount of oxygen even before we started leaking atmo. At this rate we'll be drowning in our own air in less than forty-eight hours.

And the really, REALLY bad news? The explosions also shoved the *Echidna* into a deteriorating orbit, which means that sooner or later the ship is going to get caught in Earth's gravitational pull and crash onto the surface of the planet. Since these cruisers were built in orbital docks, they were never designed to land. Any navigational instruments will be useless once we start our descent.

The ship is going down, and we're going down with it.

"How quickly do you think your people can get a rescue ship here?" I ask the captain. "I mean, you do have people, right? A backup plan?"

In answer the captain turns to bellow at Cole. And is it just me, or do I detect a hint of panic in his voice? "Archer! What's the read on the comm panel?"

Even from here I can tell that the only thing Cole's managed to bring up on the communications panel is static. Cole is frowning at the view screen, spinning dials seemingly at random. "It should be working fine," he calls back our way, "but I can't get or send any kind of signal."

"Another encryption?" Captain Bob asks. "Or maybe the transmitter's offline."

"No, sir. There's some sort of digital noise interfering with the frequency modulator. It's scrambling all communications. Data, audio, video, everything."

"There must be a jamming device somewhere on the ship," Captain Bob mutters. "It seems we have a saboteur." He massages his temple for just a moment before turning to me. "Miss Nara, perhaps you could search for foreign energy signatures? I will help Archer find the right frequency modulation." And he makes his way to Cole across the bridge, leaving me standing alone in front of the main console.

As I'm bringing up the full layout of the ship, my ears start to tune back in to the conversations around me.

"All I'm saying," Danielle says, continuing her conversation from the hallway, "is that we can't take it on faith that the faculty were aliens. We would have noticed if they were aliens.

There would have been, like, *signs*, you know? Like, antennae or green skin or something."

"My Coley *said* our teachers were aliens," Britta shoots back, darting her eyes in the direction of Cole and Captain Bob at the communications panel. "Are you saying my boyfriend lied?"

"I'm not saying he *lied*," Danielle says, sidestepping. "Maybe he was just confused."

Other Cheerleader shakes her head. "They were definitely aliens. Last week, when they put me under for the Gatling, I swear I could see Dr. Marsden's tentacles."

"Cole wasn't confused," Britta tells Danielle. "My Coley doesn't get confused. Anyway, why the hell else would they try to drown everyone? Huh?"

"I don't know," Danielle replies. "It just seems awfully coincidental that these guys showed up right when everything started to go amuck."

Up until this point Natty has been running her fingers over the cracks in the wall with her patented dreamy gaze. But at this she looks up.

"It's because Cole and the captain are aliens too," she says matter-of-factly.

Britta is immediately right in Natty's face, teeth bared like some sort of cheerleader vampire. "Bitch, if you *ever* talk like that about my boyfriend again, I will—"

But Other Cheerleader, of all people, stops the impending girl fight by putting a hand on Britta's shoulder. Although she's clearly on Britta's side. "Gnat," she spits, with all the contempt a cheerleader can muster. Which is to say, a *lot*. "Go eat some paste, won't you?"

At that, Natty just blinks. "I left it all in the art room," she replies.

I had thought, up until now, that Cole and Captain Bob were blissfully unaware of this idiotic conversation, but apparently they've been listening too.

"Girls," Captain Bob addresses them calmly, "I understand that there is a lot of confusion right now, and I'll be happy to address all of it as soon as I can be assured we're completely safe. At the moment—"

That's when Cole, bouncing at the comm panel like a puppy anxious to get outside and pee, declares, "We're a special black ops military outfit. Gamma Force. Like, commandos and stuff. We're on the lookout to protect against alien infestation, reanimated enemy combatants, things like that." Which seems to impress the dimmer girls, but not me. Because it is the exact premise of one of Ducky's more gruesome video games, Ugolino: Brain Eater for Hire.

I smell a rat.

Captain Bob pinches the bridge of his nose, in a perfect impression of Mrs. Kwan back in English class, and offers Cole a look that could shrivel peaches. "Why don't we work on communicating with *command* at the moment, hmm?" Cole swivels around and buries his face in the comm panel.

"Ladies," Captain Bob continues, addressing the girls once more, "all you need to know at the moment is that your teachers were the bad guys, and we are the good guys." He puts up a hand to halt further inquiries. "We will discuss any other questions you may have *later*."

I resume my search of the layout of the ship, and at first

I'm so busy looking for the interference with our communication that I don't see it right away. But when I do notice it, it strikes me as particularly odd, even given our current situation.

Several of the ship's blast doors, which are meant to contain damaged portions of the ship, have been activated on the *interior* of the ship—sealing off portions of the *Echidna* that were far, far away from the explosion. Which means they must have been triggered manually.

Now, why the heck would someone do *that*?

As I squint at the screen, I also notice other anomalies— gaps in the ship's gravity, temperature, oxygen, and pressurization. Certain sections of the ship are virtually impassable, while the rest seems fine.

Cole comes strolling my way and peeks over my shoulder. "What did you find?" he asks. I guess he can tell there's something worth examining, from the way I'm squinting. But I'm not giving anything up just yet.

"I thought you were helping with the comm panel," I say.

"Yeah. Uh . . ." Cole rubs his neck. "The captain might have suggested that I would be more help if I went somewhere and scratched my ass."

"I see," I reply, then resume my squinting. I have more important things to deal with at the moment than Cole and the captain's Gilligan-Skipper relationship.

Staring at the schematic is starting to feel like looking at one of those stupid old hidden picture puzzle thingies, the kind that just look like blobs and squiggles, until suddenly they morph into a picture of an elephant or something. "The blocked portions are mainly hallways," I mutter. "And some storage, and living quarters. Nothing important."

I'm not actually talking to Cole, but he must think I am, because he replies, "Maybe that's where the guy's holed up."

I let out an exasperated huff, trying to think of what could be in those interior sections that's so important. "No," I say. "There's no way to tap into any vital systems there. He'd be like a sitting duck, no better off than we are . . ." And that's when I see the stupid elephant. It's so obvious, I can't help feeling like a chromer for not noticing it right away.

"The captain's quarters," I whisper.

"Huh?" Cole replies.

I run my finger across the layout, tracing a line through the blockaded sections. The saboteur is clearly trying to prevent us from reaching the far aft section of the ship.

"The captain's quarters," I say again. "Back in the day this school used to be a pleasure cruiser, and this section here"—I point to the far lower aft section of the ship, which has been so meticulously blocked off to us—"was where the captain had his living quarters and offices." None of our faculty actually used these rooms, as far as I know, but there *is* one thing that might make them enticing to a bastard trying to destroy a shipful of pregnant girls. "There was also," I tell Cole, finally looking up from the layout, straight into his blue-green-blue eyes, "a captain's yacht."

Cole blinks at me, then shouts at Captain Bob, over by the comm panel. "Sir!" he shouts. "I think Elvie found something!" Some of the girls turn to look at us, clearly not knowing exactly what's going on, but looking momentarily hopeful about any sort of change in our situation. Britta narrows her eyes at me as though just the fact that I'm standing next to her boyfriend makes her want to ninja attack me. Although Cole, as ever, seems oblivious. He scuttles over to relieve the captain in his role as useless-dial spinner. But not before patting me on the back and whispering, "Good job, Elvs." Like I am some sort of canine.

I roll my eyes.

"Miss Nara?" Captain Bob says as he joins me behind the main console.

Again I point out the blocked section of the ship and explain. "The captain's quarters had a small personal shuttle," I tell him. "It might not be there anymore," I continue, "because when the *Echidna* was refitted, it's entirely possible that they took it out. Assuming it is there, though, it's not connected to the main computer systems, so it couldn't have been launched from here. You'd have to do it manually." I poke around on the power grid display, looking at the systems in the aft section. Sure enough, the aft launch doors, the decompression controls, and everything else you would need to prep in order to launch a ship from back there have been powered up.

"Can you override the controls on those blast doors?" he asks me. I give it a try, but the console just buzzes.

"He's got the controls locked. We can see everything but I can't change it. Which makes me think," I say, looking up at last, "that this guy is planning on shuttling out of here, and he's trying to keep us away from his ride."

Captain Bob thinks on that. "Or," he says, "he's laying out bread crumbs, making it seem like he's trying to block off our only means of escape."

"You mean a trap?" I ask. Bob nods.

Man, this shit just got ominous.

It's at this moment that Cole, still spinning away at the comm panel, begins to shout. "Sir!" he cries. "I think I got something!"

Captain Bob rushes over, with me right behind him. The majority of the girls press in behind us, hoping for the promise of a miraculous rescue.

On the view screen there is mostly static. I can almost make out the figure of a person, if I squint hard enough. But mostly it's horizontal lines, dancing across the screen in some kind of technological mambo. The sound is on the fritz too—mostly static, with faint garbled speech straining to push its way through the noise.

But at least it's *something*.

"Home One," Captain Bob barks to the flickering image on the screen. "Home One, this is Natal Group Leader." As the picture and sound get just the tiniest bit clearer, Bob's sense of urgency seems to grow. "One, this is Natal Group Leader, do you copy?"

All Captain Bob gets in reply is a distorted voice. "*Kkkk-atal . . . stttstssst . . . please repeat . . . Natal Group . . . kzzzzzzz.*" And then, finally: "Natal Group. This is Home One. Report."

The girls behind me begin to cheer. Bob eases back in his chair just the slightest, as though he might actually be relaxing a smidge. I allow myself the tiniest twinge of hope as well. Contact with someone down on Earth. The possibility of a rescue. Maybe things are starting to take a turn for the better.

"This is Natal reporting," Captain Bob continues to the still-fuzzy picture before us. "Byron, is that you?"

"This is Byron," comes the response. "You're . . . *kzzztttt* . . . breaking . . ." The mysterious Byron begins to evaporate into the sea of static again. Bob adjusts the frequency, trying to get the image back again. And then all at once the image becomes crystal clear.

"Good to see your face, Captain," comes the static-y voice.

And now everyone's cheering. Cole is grinning ear to ear. Even Bob exhales and relaxes a bit in his seat.

Me, though? I'm not cheering. Or grinning. Or relaxed. I'm more in what you might call shock. And not because of the whole plummeting-to-Earth-in-a-giant-coffin state of emergency in which we currently find ourselves.

No, *I'm* in shock because the face on the monitor is one that I know very, very well.

CHAPTER SEVEN

IN WHICH WE LOOK BACK ON FIRST KISSES AND RANDOM CAT VIOLENCE

The afternoon of the Spring Fling, hours before Ducky arrives for our Ringwald marathon, I am holed up in my room watching *Rebel Without a Cause*. I realize I'm going to be watching flat pics all evening, but the urge has struck.

Sometimes—not always, but sometimes—I get just a little bit mom-sick. Like I miss the lady, even though I never met her. And for all Dad's strengths as a kick-ass parent, he hasn't really told me much about the chick who gave birth to me. I mean, I get that it's hard for him to talk about her, I do. But every once in a while I wish I could have just a little bit more info to latch on to. More than just wisps of who she might have been. Really, all I know for certain is that my mom wanted to see the world one day (hence the book of maps), and that she absolutely loved 1950s actor James Dean. It's not a lot to go on.

So, anyway, I guess that sort of explains why I've seen this melodramatic cheesefest, like, a thousand times. It's unfortunate that James Dean had to go and die so young, in a car crash when he was just twenty-four, because if he'd made more than three flat pics, maybe I'd feel more connected to my mom. But in a way it fits, because my mom was only twenty-six when she died. What is it they say about people who die before they grow old? Forever young, forever beautiful? That's my mom, all right.

On the bed next to me my phone begins to buzz.

I snatch it up and check the screen. UNKNOWN CALLER. That's the eighth time this week. I tap the screen, hoping I can catch my loser stalker before he has a chance to hang up. "If I were you, I'd stop the prank calls," I say into the receiver. "After the tenth one the voodoo curse kicks in, and good luck removing that badger from your ass." This time my stalker does not hang up. This time he says something.

"Hey, Elvs."

I suck in my breath. Cole Archer. Cole Archer is calling *me*?

"The mechanic savant," I say, my voice laced with annoyance. "What do you want?"

Cole doesn't seem to be bothered at all by my icy tone. He replies just the way he always does—cool and calm and utterly sure of himself. "Well, obviously, I need help with my car."

"Have you been hanging up on me for six days because you have *car trouble*?" I ask. "Just go to the auto shop."

"I didn't mean to—" For the first time ever I hear a note of hesitation in Cole's voice. "I'm sorry about the hang-ups," he says. "I kept getting, uh, distracted. But will you help me anyway? You promised you'd help me install new routers."

I trace the seams on my bed quilt with my thumb and index finger. "Yeah, there's no way I said that," I tell him.

"Oh, come on, Elvs. No one knows as much about cars as you."

Okay, I know sucking up when I hear it, but for some reason it works anyway. I sigh. I should be heading to the store soon to pick up the snacks for my marathon with Ducky, but . . . I look at the clock. I still have three hours, and it should take only about forty minutes to fix the Metric. If I can get Cole to drive me to the grocery store for snacks afterward, I'll still have plenty of time before the marathon. "My name's not Elvs," I tell him. "It's Elvie. If you want to get formal, it's Elvan. But under no circumstances, ever, is it Elvs."

Cole laughs. "I apologize profusely. Can I make it up to you by bringing you a beautiful car to work on?"

I huff in disgust. "Fine. But keep it up, and I'll start charging you."

"Fair enough. See you in five."

As soon as I hang up the phone, I'm in whirlwind girl motion. I shovel my dirty clothes into my dresser, straighten out my pillows, and kick the towering pile of books and shoes and whattheheckisthat into the closet. Then I turn my attention to the mirror. Hair a mess, sweaty after-school T-shirt with the pit stains, and the cargo shorts I don't ever wear in public. *Nice.* I've completely changed clothes, and am just beginning to run the comb through my hair, when I realize—

What on earth am I doing? Why am I trying to look cute for *Cole Archer?* Why am I trying to look cute to fix *Britta's boyfriend's car?*

I slap the comb onto the sink and race downstairs before I can preen any further. *Don't be an idiot*, I tell myself. *He's not interested in you that way. He likes girls like Britta.*

And more important, I remember, *I'm* not interested in *him*.

When the doorbell rings, I catch sight of my reflection in the window and quickly whip my hair into a ponytail before I open the door.

After I open up the garage so Cole can pull his car inside, I get right to work on the problem. Naturally the Metric is one of the models where you still need to get underneath to connect the routers to the mag sphere network. Cole is not even pretending to be interested in learning a thing. He's just standing at my dad's workbench, sucking down a glass of GuzzPop while I crawl around under his car.

"You know, you wouldn't be in this mess in the first place if you'd bothered to learn, like, the first thing about cars," I tell him, snapping one of the router lines into the right front axle.

He just shrugs and takes another slug of soda. "I wouldn't exactly call watching you work a mess."

I roll my eyes, even though he obviously can't see it. "That line ever work where you come from?" I ask.

"You know, Elvs," he says, then pauses to suck down some more soda, "you're pretty cute when you're pissy."

I squeeze myself out from under the car and stand up to work on the mag sphere. "So that's a no, then."

Cole doesn't answer, and I think maybe I've finally won this round of Stump the Doofus, when I feel it. Cole's breath on my neck. It is warm and sweet and makes me goose pimple all over. His hands are on my shoulders, a light touch but purposeful. I suck in my breath. But I don't turn around. I don't dare.

He kisses me.

Right behind the ear, at the base of my hairline. I know I'll be able to feel that spot, that kiss, forever.

"Shit," I say before he can kiss me again.

Cole pulls his hands off my shoulders. "Elvs?" he says softly.

"There's grease on my jeans," I say. "My best pair. I . . . I shouldn't have worn these ones out here. I . . . I gotta go change." And I race out of the garage, through the door to the house, not even daring to look at Cole's face as I go, because I *know* that his expression will just confirm what I am thinking.

I am the world's biggest chromer.

As soon as I get upstairs to my room, I shut the door and throw myself backward onto my bed, burying my face in the crooks of my elbows. God, what the hell is *wrong* with me? The hottest guy in school tries to make a move and I talk about *grease on my pants*. I might as well move into a nunnery now. I might as well give up on being a member of the human race altogether.

Running through my head are a billion and one thoughts, and they're all banging into one another like bumper cars. *Why did he kiss me? Does he LIKE me? Do I like him? Do I hate him? What about Britta? Did he break up with Britta? Am I hotter than Britta? Is this all because I'm wearing my shirt that shows a little bit of cleave? God, guys are so predictable. Cole is such a pig. Cole is such a dreamboat. I can still feel that kiss on my skin. I've got to wash my neck off. I will never wash my neck. Do I want to kiss Cole back? God, I want to kiss Cole all over. I never want to SEE him again. I hope he takes the hint and drives home already. I should get back down there so he doesn't drive home.*

There is a knock on my bedroom door.

I sniffle up the tears I didn't know I was crying, and wipe my face clean. "I'm changing!" I call, sitting up on the bed.

"Elvs . . ." Cole says quietly, then opens up the door and pokes his head inside.

I leap up off the bed. "I *told* you I was changing!" I screech, trying to slam the door in his face.

"But you weren't," he says. Calmly. Always calmly. "Can I come in?"

"No."

He enters the room.

"Elvs," he says again, making himself comfortable on my bed. "I shouldn't have done that."

"Don't even worry about it," I tell him. "It wasn't a big deal." But I still won't make eye contact. I'm acting like a four-year-old, but I can't help it. I open my closet door, planning on finding a new pair of jeans, but the pile of crap I shoved in earlier tumbles out and prevents me from hiding it from Cole.

"No," Cole says. "It was." He clears his throat. "I just wanted you to know that that wasn't why I came over—" He stops. "Um, Elvs? Your floor is moving," he tells me.

"Huh?" For a long second I think that Cole has lost it, that the only reason he kissed me is that he's having a stroke or something, but an instant later I see it too. The pile of heaping garbage at the bottom of my closet is indeed moving, rustling and shaking.

"Henry Chang!" I holler, kicking at the pile. "You get out of there!"

And now the pile is meowing too. With one swift ninja-kitty leap, the damn cat finally bursts out and skitters across the room, his freakishly long cat claws clattering against the hardwood floor until he finally knocks headfirst into the wall. He rights himself quickly, then gives a head shake and dives under the bed, right where Cole is sitting.

Cole bursts out laughing. "I didn't know you had a cat," he says.

"*I* don't," I reply, finally managing to shove the closet closed again. A second later I realize I didn't get a new pair of jeans out, but I give up and lean against the closet door. "It's my neighbor's. He's always getting in the basement window, and for some reason he loves my room." I can see the thing under my bed, narrow green eyes staring out at me. "It must smell like kitty nirvana up in here."

Cole smiles, then gestures to the frozen image on the television screen. "*Rebel Without a Cause*, eh?" he asks.

I raise my eyebrows. "You're a James Dean fan?"

Cole shrugs. "I wouldn't say 'fan.' I sort of know who he is. You like this stuff, huh? I could never get into it."

"It's pretty good. Crazy melodramatic, but, you know, it's . . ." I'm having trouble describing the film. How can someone like Cole Archer understand what it is to be that angsty teen? Someone no one understands? "Here." I pull my phone out and unpause the movie. "Just watch." I plop down onto the bed, achingly aware of Cole's body millimeters away from mine. We both fall silent as the TV springs to life.

On the screen James Dean's Jim Stark is on a school field trip visiting the planetarium—an old one with little lights projected onto the ceiling, before the invention of the migraine-inducing 3-D holo tech they use now, the kind that caused me to barf generously during my seventh-grade visit. Dean is broody and gorgeous, with narrow eyes and thick eyebrows and a smashingly luscious head of blond hair. I can see why my mom was so obsessed with the guy. On the ceiling above all the students, the stars are playing out their galactic theater, smashing into one another and swirling into black holes, when James Dean looks up at it all and declares, "Once you been up there, you know you've been someplace."

Cole picks up my phone and pauses the flat pic. He looks at me for a while, right in the eyes, and I'm half worried, half hopeful that he's going to try to kiss me again. But he doesn't.

"Hey, Elvs?" he says, thoughtful. "You think we could be friends? I mean, just forget about earlier, in the garage and . . . ?" He trails off.

I have plenty of friends, doofus. That's what I'm thinking. *What could I possibly need a slug-for-brains like you for?* But of course what squeaks its way out of my mouth is, "Friends?"

"Yeah," Cole replies. "We could, you know, talk and stuff."

I stand up from the bed and take a walk toward the dresser. I open a drawer like I'm looking for something inside, then close it. "Look," I finally say, turning around. "I don't know what things were like back wherever you came from, but here in Ardmore friends usually like each other."

Cole thinks that over, then nods. When he looks up at me, there's a smile on his face. "Milwaukee," he says.

"Huh?"

"I'm from Milwaukee," he tells me. His grin is growing broader, the confident Cole I'm more used to from school. "And I already know I like you."

"Well, that's one of us."

"Come on, Elvs," he pleads from the bed. And I've got to admit the guy knows how to push my buttons. His smile is just crooked enough to show that he's sure he's won me over already, but he's playing the game anyway, to make me happy. "I'd really like to get to know you."

"Why?"

Cole tilts his head. "Why what?"

"Why do you want to know me?" I ask. "I'm nothing special." When he looks like he's about to protest, I hold my hand up in front of me. "I didn't mean that in a girly, fishing way, like 'Please tell me how special I am.'" He laughs, but it's a gentle sort of laugh. "I just meant . . ." *You're rambling, Elvie. Get to the point.* "I just meant that there's a whole lot of people in the world, and before last week you'd never spoken more than four words to me."

Cole takes a deep breath and nods slowly, staring at the ground, as if I've just made a very profound point. Then he looks up at me with one of those melt-the-world, get-out-of-jail-free smiles of his.

"So now you're the boss of who I think is interesting?"

Don't smile, Elvie. *Do not smile.*

"Fine," I say, practically chewing on the insides of my

cheeks to keep from grinning. I sit down in the armchair across the room, well away from Cole and the bed. "Friends it is."

"Great," he says. He leans forward, elbows on his knees. "So, tell me about yourself."

"You're going to make an excellent shrink some day, Cole Archer. You interrogate all your friends this way?"

"No, I'm serious. I want to know more about you. Like . . . why *Rebel Without a Cause*?"

I glance at the screen, where James Dean's face is still frozen, midpout. "I don't know," I say with a shrug. "My mom always liked him."

And Cole must be more astute than I've ever given him credit for, because he tilts his head at that and says, "'Liked'?"

I sigh, leaning back in my chair. "She died," I tell him. "The day I was born. I never knew her."

"I'm sorry," Cole replies. And it's nice, that tone in his voice like he really cares. But really, what else is he going to say? "I'm really sorry, Elvs."

"Yeah, well . . ." I shrug it off, ready to change the subject.

"My mom died too." I look up at him. His face is sorrowful, serious. "When I was fifteen."

"Oh." The noise just bursts out of me. I can feel my heart, like, literally aching, for this boy I thought I knew but didn't. Clearly didn't. "I had no idea. Just, like"—I do the math—"a year ago? How awful."

"What?" Cole shakes his head. "Yeah, a little over a year. She got antibacterial-resistant TB, so . . ." He trails off. "I don't know, it just sucks, you know?"

"Yeah," I say. "I do. So you live with just your dad now?"

"Extended family."

I come over to the bed then, and we're sitting side by side for a moment, looking into each other's eyes. And I see it—I think I can really see it—how he's holding on to that same pain I am, how he's affected, just a little every day, by memories and might-have-beens about his mom. And he's leaning in, and I'm leaning in, and I know that we're going to share one hell of a kiss. One fireworks-igniting, passionate, you-know-what-I'm-thinking-about-my-dead-mom sparkler of a kiss.

Only Henry Chang seems to have other plans. He skirts out from under the bed and leaps, parkour-style, off the wall, straight toward Cole's face.

"*Aaaaghsmdkekl!*" Cole screams. Which is exactly the reaction most people have when they come face to claw with the destructo cat from hell.

"Goddammit, Henry!" I screech. I rip him off Cole, and check for damage as I toss the cat to the floor. "Oh, God, he scratched you," I say, smoothing out the cut above Cole's left eyebrow. It leaves a smear of red on my thumb. "Shit, I'm so sorry. Stay here. I'll get the Bactine."

"Elvs, it's okay," Cole calls as I race to the bathroom across the hall. "Seriously, it's no big deal. Don't worry about it."

But I'm already tearing through the medicine cabinet. Of course this would happen to me. I get the hottest boy in school up to my bedroom, and then I go and gouge his face. "You don't want it to get infected!" I shout back. I find the bandages, then toss bottle after bottle into the sink as I search for the disinfectant. With my luck Cole will end up with cat scratch fever.

Finally I find the right bottle and race back to the bedroom.

"I keep telling my dad we need to put that stupid cat down, even if he does belong to the Connors. But Dad's against murdering someone else's pets for some reason. Here," I say, sitting down on the bed to play nurse. Cole has his hand over his eyebrow, rubbing the wound. "Let me see." I pull his hand away.

There is no cut. There's not even a hint of a scrape.

My eyes dart to Cole's other eyebrow, the right one, even though I'm positive it was the left. But of course there's no injury there either.

"Wh-what . . ." I stammer. "What happened?"

Cole takes the bandages and Bactine from me and places them gently on the bedside table. "I told you, it wasn't that bad. You really need to stop worrying so much. Come on, we were chatting. Tell me . . . tell me some more about your mom. What was she like?"

My head is swimming with confusion. I can see Cole's face, as smooth as ever, not a scratch on it. Just those five tiny freckles. But there's blood smeared on my thumb, as clear as day. I shake my head, perplexed. What I know for *sure* is that there's a cute boy sitting next to me, face eager like he really does want to get to know me, and I'm not going to screw it up twice.

"She, uh . . ." I begin. I grab a tissue and wipe the blood off my hand. Then I toss it into the garbage across the room. Forgotten. I turn to Cole, giving him my full attention. "She loved exploring," I tell him. And he smiles at that. "Well, she *wanted* to explore. She had all these places planned out where she was going to go, all these adventures."

And somehow it all just tumbles out of me. I show him my

mother's book of maps. We turn the pages together slowly, taking in every line, every red dot she marked. It's strange, sharing all this with Cole. I've never even shown Ducky the maps before, even though he knows they exist. But somehow I know Cole will understand them. As we go through the maps, Cole tells me about his mom too, and about clam bakes and Brewers games in the summer and brats and Packers season tickets in the winter. It's amazing to me that all this time beneath the cocky pretty-boy bravado, Cole is just a sensitive, homesick guy. I'm thinking on this revelation, drinking in this dreamy vulnerability, when he turns the page to the next map and his eyes go wide with astonishment.

"Wow," he breathes, tracing his finger over the Antarctic ice caps. "She really planned to go here?" He ducks his head down low, inspecting the name of a ridge, one with a big fat red X on it. "Cape Crozier. I hear it's pretty heinous down there. She must've been ballsy, your mom."

I smile at that. "Yeah," I say. "I think she was." I inspect the X too. "I just wish she could have seen it, you know? Too bad I screwed it all up for her."

He nods thoughtfully at that. "I'm sure that if she could have picked between seeing the whole world and having you, she would have picked you in a heartbeat."

"That's just the thing, though, isn't it?" I say, rolling over onto my back. I fold my hands over my stomach and stare up at the ceiling. "She didn't *get* to pick." Cole doesn't say anything to that, just continues flipping pages in my mom's book. "I just . . ." I go on. "I think maybe that's why I'm so gung ho about the Ares Project. You know, the Mars terraforming program? Like, that's something that would really make my mom proud."

"There are probably easier ways to get to space, Elvs."

I turn my head and look at him. "There's nothing you feel your mom would have wanted for you?"

"My mom, she had my whole future plotted out for me. But if she could see me now, she . . ." He lets out a little snort, almost a laugh. He darts his eyes over to me. "Good thing we're not friends, huh?" he says. "Or the conversation might get serious."

And at that I have to laugh.

"Thanks for helping me with the Kia," Cole says as we walk downstairs.

"No prob," I reply, trying to sound as nonchalant as possible. "You know, you should probably get your crash sensors recalibrated too. They can be a little wonky when you use new routers."

He nods.

"And also," I continue—like, if I keep talking, he might never leave—"you should check the contacts on your secondary battery. They looked a little worn."

"How about we look at those next time I come over?" he says, turning to look at me. There's a twinkle in his eye.

So he's coming over again.

"Will I see you at the dance tonight?" he asks. The question sounds hopeful.

"Nah. I'm staying in and watching some old movies with Ducky."

"Oh. So you two are like . . ."

"No! What, Ducky? Ha! No!" I clear my throat. "We're just friends."

Speaking of Ducky, though . . . I look at the time. He's going to be here in less than an hour for our marathon.

"Could you drive me to the store real quick?" I ask Cole. "I need to pick up a few things for tonight."

"Sure," he says. "Happy to help."

"Cool. Let me just change." I may not be a fashion plate, but I refuse to go anywhere with grease-smeared jeans.

I race back to my bedroom and change in a flash, suddenly thrilled at the prospect of sitting up front in Cole's Kia. And as soon as I've squeezed my hips into my second-cutest pair of jeans, I return downstairs. "Okay, I'm ready. Sorry to make you wait," I call as I plunk down the steps. "I just needed to look presenta—"

I stop cold. Cole is not alone in my living room.

"He knocked," Cole says, "so I let him in."

Ducky is holding two grocery bags stuffed full of snacks, and for the first time since I've known him, he looks like he doesn't quite belong in my house. "Sorry I'm so early," he says. "Zeke said he'd give me a ride, and . . ." He trails off.

"No, it's fine," I say, bolting down the last few stairs. I'm trying to act like this is normal, like Cole and Ducky and I hang out awkwardly in my living room every day, but I'm sure my hands are giving me away. They're darting from my pockets to my legs to my armpits and back again. Suddenly I can't remember what I usually do with them. "Cole was just . . . He was going to drive me to the store and . . . I didn't think you were going to bring so much food."

"Elvie was helping me fix my car," Cole explains.

Ducky just shrugs, and sets the bags down on the coffee table.

"Well," Cole says, "I guess I better go." Ducky is unloading munchies and drinks out of the grocery bags, and already has a fudge-stripe cookie hanging out of his mouth. Cole glances at him, as if asking permission to leave, but Ducky just raises his eyebrows expectantly. Cole turns toward the door.

"Bye, Elvs," he says as he leaves. "Sorry again about your pants."

"Yeah," I call as the door closes behind him. "No prob. About the pants."

I join Ducky at the coffee table and dig through the last bag, looking for chocolate doughnut holes. Ducky's giving me the same eyebrows-to-the-sky expression he gave Cole as he munches on his cookie.

I plop myself down on the couch. "It's not what you're thinking," I say. "Seriously."

Ducky shakes his head at me. "Honestly, I'm just shocked it took you this long to 'fix his car.'"

"Ducky! You know that's not what . . . We didn't . . ."

But Ducky has already moved on to bigger and better things. He's on my dad's lap-pad thumbing through Molly Ringwald's oeuvre. "*Pretty in Pink* first?" he asks. "Or *Sixteen Candles*? We going chronologically?"

"You hate my face," I say, dejected.

He looks up at me and winks, wearing a bittersweet sort of smile. "Who could hate that face?" he scolds me, and plops the box of chocolate doughnut holes into my lap.

Ducky selects *Sixteen Candles*, and the pic flicks to life, the living room lights dimming automatically. As Ducky and I settle in for the evening, a calmness settles over me. Sitting with my best friend on the couch in front of the TV—this is totally me in my element. This is happy.

But still, my skin tingles when I remember Cole's kiss behind my ear, and I can't help thinking, *Once you been up there, you know you've been someplace.*

CHAPTER EIGHT

WHEREIN WE GET OUR EXPOSITION ON

"Byron," Captain Bob says to the image of his superior flickering on the view screen. My brain is fuzzy, trying to take in what I'm seeing. *Who* I'm seeing. "We're in a bad way here, sir," Captain Bob continues. "Heavy casualties among the students. Archer and I are the only . . ."

Captain Bob is recapping all our difficulties so far, and the guy on the view screen is taking it all in with an increasingly grim expression, but to me the entire exchange is just a haze of confusion. Because the guy Captain Bob is deep in conversation with, he's someone I've seen before. In fact, he's someone a *lot* of people have seen before.

The man Captain Bob is talking to is James Dean.

Those deep-set eyes, those distinctively fierce eyebrows. He's sporting a goofy thin mustache, but still it's undeniable. I'd stake my life on it. The man on the view screen is James Dean, 1950s movie heartthrob. James Byron Dean, born February 8, 1931. Died September 30, 1955. *Died.* As in, stuck in the ground 120 years ago. Way too decomposed to be looking so fine.

"Uh, Elvs?" Cole says beside me. "Are you okay?"

I know, without even the benefit of a mirror, that my face has drained completely of color.

"Elvs?"

Just then the comm emits a loud screech, and the image of James Dean vanishes.

"Dammit!" Captain Bob screams, scrambling in vain to find another frequency. "I can't reestablish contact!"

The girls fly into another panic. But I remain icily still. Cole places a hand on my shoulder and nudges me, as if he thinks I might have fallen asleep standing up.

"Elvs?" he repeats over the din of moaning girls and truly inspired expletives from Captain Bob.

Toomuchtoomuchtoomuch. My brain is in overdrive, trying to take in all of the weirdness from the past few hours. *Toomuchtoo*—I take a breath. Do what my father would tell me to. I process every fact, one at a time.

Superhunky teachers.

Who turn out to be murderous aliens.

With ray guns.

Who fight with our superhot, if slightly less butch, rescuers.

Who also have ray guns.

And talk to *James Dean* like they've just dialed up their Internet provider.

Really, there's only one conclusion.

I turn to face Cole, pushing out the words despite the

trembling all through my body. "Would you mind explaining to me," I say slowly, calmly, "why Bob was just *talking to James Dean?*"

Now it's Cole's turn to go white. Even Bob stops cursing and snaps around.

"That wasn't . . . Why would you think . . . Who?" Cole tries lamely.

"Who's James Dean?" Chewie asks, sucking on her tattered braid again. The incredulous look on her face is shared by every other girl, even Ramona. They're all staring at me now, looking at me like I'm a total chromer. And I might believe them, if I didn't know for a fact that I am right.

"*East of Eden?*" I say. "*Giant? Rebel Without a Cause?* Come *on*! James Dean!" Still nothing. And while I'm not surprised that I'm the only one with a working knowledge of twentieth-century cinema, it does momentarily make me lament the sorry state of our educational system that such basic literacy is so lacking.

"He's a movie star," I go on. "A *dead* movie star. Yet somehow this guy"—I jerk my head toward Captain Bob—"was just talking to him, live and in the flesh."

Natty sticks a finger into her mouth. I think she might be counting her teeth. "So you're saying . . . that Cole and those guys can talk to ghosts?"

"No! For crying out—" I slap my hand to my forehead. "Natty, you said it yourself. They're *aliens*."

Now they are all looking at me like I skipped my dosage. Bob is walking toward me slowly, in a way that makes me feel none too safe. But Cole surprises me and actually laughs.

"Oh, Elvie." He chuckles. "A few hours without ice cream, and suddenly you're hallucinating." This gets a few laughs from the girls, and eye rolls from Britta and Other Cheerleader. I can almost hear the cartoon steam escaping from my ears. Because I'm right, I know I am, as ridiculous as it might have seemed an hour ago. And that idiot Cole, so smug because he knows the whole thing's so insane that no one will ever believe me. I'd like to kick him right in his stupid twisted ankle.

His ankle!

"Fine," I say, wresting my arm away from the hand Cole has placed there—to try to shut me up, no doubt. "If you're such a *normal* alien-fighting space commando, how do you explain your ankle?"

"What are you talking about?" Cole says, as if he has legitimately already forgotten about the whole thing.

"When you fell off the bleachers," I say, looking to the other girls for confirmation, "you busted your ankle."

"That makes me an alien? People bust their ankles, Elvs."

"Yeah," I reply. "But they don't stop limping completely in the course of an hour and a half."

For the first time Cole pauses. "I didn't twist it that bad," he says, clearing his throat. Bob's face is turning a dark shade of red, but I'm not sure anyone notices except for me.

Natty, of all people, is the first person to log on. "You *did* hurt it pretty bad," she says. "You fell very hard, and then you said a very loud curse word."

"That's true, actually," Ramona adds thoughtfully. "I remember thinking what an idiot you were."

And for just one shining second, even Britta seems to be

on my side. "You *were* limping a lot earlier, baby," she says.

"Well, yeah, uh . . . I mean, it hurts and all," Cole stammers, losing his grip on the conversation. "But it's getting better. See?"

He walks a few steps, favoring his right ankle as he goes. "It's a little tender, but I don't see how that has anything to do with—"

"You twisted your left ankle," I tell him.

He immediately stops walking. His shoulders slump. "Right, yeah—right, left," he stammers. "I know. I was just, you know, leaning on it to show you that it's fine. I know I twisted my left ankle."

"Cole," I stop him. "It *was* your right ankle."

"Shit!" He stomps his perfectly healed right foot on the ground. "Goddammit, Elvie!"

Bob turns his attention from me to Cole and grabs him by the collar. "You have got to be the *stupidest* . . ." he starts, but he seems to get choked up on his own frustration. "If we ever get back in touch with Byron, I'm going to need a really good explanation why he insisted you be added to my squad."

But I'm not listening. I'm not sticking around to hear any more of Cole's bullshit. My former grunt buddy is an alien. Which means, by extension, that my soon-to-be-baby is an alien. And call me weak-stomached, but darn if that news doesn't suddenly give me the urge to throw up everything I've ever eaten.

"Elvs!" Cole calls after me as I race from the bridge. All around us, girls are screaming, gasping, shouting unanswerable questions. "Elvs, wait. I can explain!"

I do not wait. I'm gone.

• • •

It's not like there are a lot of places to go to be alone with your thoughts when you're on a disintegrating spaceship about to be sucked into Earth's atmosphere. But I manage to find a spot. I decide to go to a place where generations of overwhelmed girls have gone before me. The toilet.

I'm sitting on the back of the toilet, feet up on the lid, with the stall door closed, trying to settle my churning stomach, when I hear footsteps on the tile.

"Elvs," Cole says.

I do not respond. If that freak wants to get me, he's going to have to do something crazy, like crawl under the door.

"I'm sorry. I couldn't tell you. I wanted to tell you, but I . . ." He trails off.

I thumb a tear out of my eye and try to do my sniffling as quietly as possible, but Cole obviously hears it. "God, Elvs, I hate to see you cry," he says. I can see his shoes just outside the stall. He's probably got his hand on the stall door, pining-style.

I jerk out my foot and kick the door with a *whump!* and I see Cole take a startled step back. "Good thing you're not looking at me, then, huh?" I say.

He sighs.

I rub the sides of my face, elbows resting on my knees, and stare at those shoes on the other side of the stall door. I thought I knew him. I mean, I know we were only together once, but still, I somehow fooled myself into thinking I knew who he was. What food he liked, what music, what made him laugh, how sad it made him to think about his mother. But all this time . . .

"So I was right?" I say at last. "That guy on the view screen, he really is James Dean? And you really are a freaking alien? You told me you were from Milwaukee."

"Ummmm." He holds the word out superlong, like maybe if he never gets to the end of it, he won't have to explain this whole sorry situation. "Sort of."

"How the hell are you 'sort of' an alien?"

"Well." He takes a deep breath, and his feet move back, away from my line of sight under the stall door. I hear him hoist himself up onto the sink counter. He is obviously preparing himself for show-and-tell time. "I am from Milwaukee."

"Oh, really?" I snort. "So, what, all that cheese you consumed gave you invincibility or something?"

"I *am* from Milwaukee," he insists. "Born and raised. It's just that, well, I'm not technically . . . human."

And suddenly the urge to yack has returned in full force. Before I know what's happening, I find myself kneeling on the bathroom floor with my hands on the bowl of the toilet, puking. Which I realize is totally gross, but toilet seat germs are low on my list of priorities at the moment.

"Oh, God," Cole says. I can hear his footsteps coming closer, but thank goodness he doesn't try to penetrate my fortress of toilet-tude. "Elvs . . ." My name hangs on his lips so long I can practically see the ellipsis. "Are you all right?"

"Oh, yeah," I reply. I swoop back a lock of loose hair and pause for one last yack. "Just refunding my breakfast."

"Elvs."

I reach up to flush the toilet, then shift so that my back is resting against the side wall of the stall. I don't have the strength to move any more than that at the moment. From under the door I can make out Cole's legs as he situates himself cross-legged on the floor directly outside the stall. I bunch my knees up in front of me and wrap my arms around them, trying to steady my breaths.

"You all right?" he asks again.

I squeeze my eyes shut. "Tell me," I say. "I'm ready now. Tell me everything."

And just like that, Cole begins.

"I'm an Almiri," he tells me. "It's a species that came to Earth a long time ago. Like, thousands of years. They were originally from a planet on the other side of the galaxy. I'd tell you the name, but, uh, to be honest, I can't really pronounce it. They never bothered to translate it into any human language."

I nod, taking it all in. My eyes are still squeezed closed, sparks of light pricking the darkness. "So the Almiri," I say softly, "they look just like humans? Even though they're from a completely different planet?"

"Well . . ." Cole lets out a breath. "No. Not really." I can hear the soft scratching as Cole rubs his fingernails across his chin, a sure sign that he's thinking hard. "The Almiri are a . . . different sort of species. See, we can't breed on our own."

I open my eyes. There are Cole's knees, on the other side of the door, his hand resting just on top. He is so close, I could reach out and touch him. But I don't. "What does that mean?" I ask.

"It's like . . ." He scratches, thinking some more. "You know those things, what are they called? Tapeworms? They're their own species, but they can only live and grow inside another animal?"

"Are you telling me you're a freaking *tapeworm*?"

"No! Shit, that was a bad comparison. I'm bad at this. Seriously, Elvs. I got, like, a D in bio. Maybe the captain should be the one to explain this to you."

"You got me here, Cole," I tell him. "You explain it."

"But I don't . . ." He trails off, as though an idea has suddenly occurred to him. "Wait. Okay, no. I got it now." I see him shift on the floor a bit, and once he's repositioned himself, he begins his explanation again. "Okay, here it is. Yeah. The genetic makeup of the Almiri species is unparalleled, particularly within the realms of physical fitness, intellectual capacity, and aesthetic attractiveness. However, the Almiri are incapable of sexually reproducing with members of their own species. In order to propagate, a host with a sufficiently analogous genetic makeup must be procured. Once the Almiri has—"

I cut him off. "Are you, like, reading from a textbook or something?" I ask. There's no way Cole knows what half those words mean.

"Uh . . ." Suddenly his voice has turned sheepish again. I peek through the slat between the door and the stall, and see that he is holding his phone to his face. When he notices me staring at him, he flips the phone in my direction so that I can read what's on the screen.

A Brief Introduction to Almiri History.

"Are you shitting me, Cole?" I screech, scooting back against the wall to avoid further eye contact.

"What?" he mutters. "There's a lot to remember."

I slap my hand against my forehead. "I *would* have to get knocked up by the dumbest alien in the cosmos."

"Can I continue, Elvs?"

"Only if you stop calling me Elvs."

Cole sighs but carries on. "Okay, where was I? Sexual reproduction, blah, blah, blah. A host must be procured . . . All right, yeah. Here's the part that concerns you. Once the Almiri has found a viable host, he can then implant his seed in the female, so that she may carry the Almiri infant to term. The Almiri infant will have all the superficial characteristics of the host species, and in most cases the unwitting host will be unaware that the child she is carrying is not her own."

Suddenly I feel very cold all over. "Cole, put the stupid book down and just tell me straight, all right?"

"It's not a book. It's an interactive—"

"Cole!"

"Sorry."

"So I'm your 'unwitting host,' then? Is that it?"

"Well, yeah. But you're witting now."

"When I have this thing, when I finally give birth to your precious little bundle of joy, it's not even going to be mine, is it?"

The floor squeaks as Cole rubs his shoes against it, shifting his feet. "No," he says, and I'm thankful that at last he seems to be skipping the sentiment and sticking to the facts. "He'll be all Almiri. The host mother, like, *has* the baby, but it's not her child. It doesn't have any of her DNA. She's just sort of, like, the envelope. But it's not her letter."

As I think about what it means to be, as Cole so delicately put it, the container for a foreign package, I have to force the bile down. I need to listen. Even though I don't want to, I need to hear what Cole has to say.

"Anyway," he continues, "when the baby is born, it looks just like the host species. That's why I look human, because I was born to a human mom."

"In Milwaukee," I confirm.

"In Milwaukee. But I have all Almiri DNA."

"So," I say, thinking it over, "if your dad had done it with a chicken, you would've come out feathered?"

"I'm not sure if . . . No, it says here that the Almiri came to Earth because the humans were the only viable host candidate in this section of the galaxy, so I don't think the chicken thing would ever be an iss—"

"Cole, I was joking."

"Oh."

I clear my throat, stalling for time while I think things over. "So all that stuff you told me about your mom," I say slowly, "how she died, just like mine—it was, what, a lie? Just so you could get into my pants?"

"No. Elvs, I would *never*—"

"'Cause there are easier ways to get a girl to put out, you know."

"Jeez, Elvie. Who do you think I am?" I do not answer that. "My mom, she . . . Everything I told you about her was true. I grew up thinking she was my real mother, thinking I was human, thinking I was a normal kid. She had no idea about me. She . . . she loved me. And she did die when I was fifteen. And then suddenly there were all these Almiri guys, and they took me away and I had to learn to live by the Code." Even through my swirl of anger-fear-worry-resentment, I notice that Cole's voice has changed. He's not apologetic anymore. He's sort of, what's the word? Wistful? Melancholy? I settle myself against the stall and listen.

"Talk about feeling like an alien," Cole goes on. "Most of the Almiri are allowed to grow into men before they discover who they are. I was . . . I didn't get that chance. And the Almiri, they're good at lots of stuff—they're a good people, Elvie, no matter what you think—but they have no idea how to raise kids."

I bite down on the insides of my cheeks. *God*, I think, *sob story much?* I might feel sorry for Cole if it weren't for the fact that *he's an alien who took my virginity and left me with a parasitic love child*. I thump the toilet lid closed and climb up to sit on top of it.

"Look, Elvs, I know none of this is what you thought it would be. But I think if you try, you can learn to love the poor little guy. Even if he's not human, he'll be amazing, I swear. *My* mom loved me. She didn't even know I wasn't . . ." He trails off, and I let my thoughts trail with him.

There is a lot to take in right now, obviously. But before my brain careens off down the path of *holyshitholycrapholyhell*, I ask the question that has pushed itself to the forefront of my mind.

"You keep saying 'he,'" I say. "How do you know the baby's going to be a boy?"

"Almiri are always boys," Cole replies.

"Always?"

"Always. Otherwise they couldn't, you know . . ."

"Implant their seed?" I finish for him.

"Well. Yeah."

Lovely.

I hear Cole standing on the other side of the door, and when he speaks, his voice is gentle. "Elvs, why don't you come out here? I want to see you. We can't really talk like this. It isn't—"

"I prefer to stay well away from tapeworms, thank you," I tell him. I like having the stall door between us. Half a dozen centimeters of aluminum alloy might not be much distance, but right now it feels like a force field.

"Elvs . . ."

"So when were you planning on telling me all this?" I ask. "Tomorrow? On the kid's fifth birthday? When?" I gaze down at my swollen stomach, and I swear to God, if I wasn't mad about the Goober before, now I am absolutely livid. "You know, you had a really good chance to tell me this story when I let you know I was knocked up in the first place. But you didn't. You left." On the other side of the door, Cole squirms. I can tell I'm skewering the guy, that he feels downright shitty, and I guess that ought to make me happy, but it doesn't. "It's bad enough you put me in this position," I say with a sigh, "but Britta, too? Jesus, Cole, how much seed did you need to implant?"

"No," Cole replies quickly. "I didn't . . . With Britta it was . . . I didn't mean . . . It was an accident, Elvie."

"Some accident," I say with a snort. He does not reply. "I would say you're a shit of a human being. But, you know."

"I didn't mean for this to happen," he says. "Really." And I can tell by the tone in his voice that he means it. But the eight-plus-month-old fetus that's currently practicing karate on my large intestine begs to differ. "Look, it's not so bad, Elvs. I know the little guy won't *technically* be human, but . . . Almiri have lived peacefully with humans for five thousand years, virtually undiscovered. We have excellent genes. We, uh, heal well. We're always very handsome." I snort, but Cole goes on, undeterred. "No, seriously. That's how we, uh, attract our mates. And our life span is far longer than that of a human. Hundreds of years. In some cases even longer. Without ever aging."

"Shit," I spit. This is just what I need. "You're not going to tell me you're, like, a thousand years old or something, are you? God, if I did it with a *senior citizen* alien . . ." I suddenly feel like upchucking again. "You know I'm a minor. You can do some serious time for that, right?"

"Elvs, calm down." I can almost hear him rolling his eyes. "I'm nineteen. You can tell because my starkiss hasn't faded yet."

"Your *what*?" I ask. "What does tuna have to do with this?"

"No, my *starkiss*. Every Almiri is born with one. It's like a birthmark. A little pattern of freckles on the left cheek. It always fades completely after thirty or forty years. I still have mine."

"Really?" I say casually. I can picture it exactly. "I never noticed."

"Anyway," he goes on, "listen to this, Elvs. This may cheer you up." And I can hear the soft *whisk* of his fingers across the screen of his phone as he scrolls through the history once more. "Since their arrival on Earth, Almiri have contributed enormously to human society, in nearly every field of cultural and physical advancement, including politics, science, and the arts. Some of the most famous 'people' in human history were in fact Almiri. Alexander the Great, Dmitry Venevitinov, Pope Gregory V, Wolfgang Amadeus Mozart, Christopher Marlowe—"

"James Dean," I finish for him.

"Yeah," Cole replies. "He's on the list."

I think on that. My mom's favorite movie star, an alien. Well, he *was* inhumanly handsome. "So why does everyone think James Dean died in a car crash?" I ask.

Cole sighs. "Well, since we live so long, and we don't age at the normal rate, some of us—especially those who are sort of famous—have to fake an early death, so no one catches on. Can you imagine if movie stars seemed to look twenty-two forever? Byron's actually officially 'died' about five times now. He's sort of sick of it at this point, so he tries to keep a low profile. I'm probably going to have to fake my own death in a couple years, depending on how often I'm willing to move. I'm thinking tractor trailer accident."

As fascinating as this tangent is, there are other things weighing more heavily on my mind than the way in which Cole intends to fake off himself. "All right, fine," I say. "So you're an alien."

"An Almiri."

"Whatever. I guess I can deal with that." I'm gonna need some serious therapy, but just at the moment I'm busy wrapping my head around things. "And I'm guessing Captain Bob and everyone else involved in your rescue mission of crap is Almiri too."

"That's right."

"And I'm further assuming that all of us on board this

space school—me, Ramona, Natty, all of us—we're all unwitting hosts for freaking bastard alien children?"

"In a nutshell."

I clear my throat. "So that would make our teachers, what, like, Almiri gone bad?"

"It's complicated," Cole says, and he ignores my snort. "But basically your teachers are another race, similar to the Almiri. It used to be that we were all one species—the Klahnia, they were called. But when we left to come to Earth, they traveled to a different planet, and they started to evolve a little . . . *differently*. They call themselves the Jin'Kai now. They only came to Earth a few decades ago, as far as I know. And they're doing their best to wipe us out completely."

I try to wrap my head around the idea of alien ethnic cleansing. "So these Jin'Kai or whatever," I say, "they, what? Signed up for teaching positions on this space school so they could get close to all our Almiri fetuses?"

I can hear the air whistle through Cole's nose as he takes a deep breath. "Elvs," he says slowly. "They *created* this school, to lure you guys here."

Da-*fuh*?

"So what were they planning on doing with our babies?" I ask. "Were they going to . . ." I look down at the lump that's the Goober. Well, more like a parasitic freakazoid. I can't quite bring myself to put my hand on my own stomach. "Kill them?"

"Honestly, we have no idea what their plans were," Cole replies. "But given the way they freaked out when we landed on their ship, we can be pretty sure they weren't going to treat all the kids to hot fudge sundaes."

"I see." I fix my eyes on the door lock, thinking about finally exiting my little hidey-hole. Because as much as I don't want to, as much as I'd rather not face Cole ever again, like it or not I probably have to get out of here fairly soon. If I'm going to plummet to Earth in a fiery blaze, I'd rather not do it in a toilet stall.

But I take one more second to myself.

"Elvs," Cole says from the other side of the door. "There's something else I need to tell you."

"Oh?" I reply. "What, you forgot to tell me about your X-ray vision?"

"No, nothing like that. It's . . ." He rises to his feet and walks closer to the stall door. He's right on the other side now, talking to me in a hush. "The Almiri, we're . . . very particular about who we're supposed to, um, mate with. There's a Code, and the penalties for breaking it are . . ." He lets out a puff of air like he's having trouble solving a difficult trig problem. "What I'm trying to say is . . . When I said I never meant for this to happen, I was serious." He swallows audibly. "Elvs, I wasn't supposed to get involved with you. I was . . . I was only meant to be with Britta."

And if I thought this day couldn't get any shittier, well, it just has. "Wonderful," I spit. "So good to know, Cole. I hope you and Britta will be very happy togeth—"

"No." Cole cuts me off. "Elvie, that's not what I'm saying. I was *supposed* to be with Britta, but I . . . I chose you. I know you'll probably never forgive me for leaving, or for anything else, really. And I totally understand that. But." He pauses, and I can feel my whole body aching, waiting to hear what will come after that "but." "But," he goes on, "I freaked out, Elvie, when you told me you were pregnant. I knew if my superiors found out, I'd be in serious trouble. The Code isn't something they take lightly. So I panicked. I raced back to headquarters and stopped returning your phone calls, hoping that somehow no one would ever find out. But then I heard you were on board this ship with the Jin'Kai, and I . . . God, Elvie, right then I didn't care who found out about me. I *begged* to be a part of the rescue mission."

"How'd you know I was here?" I ask.

"It's, uh"—he raps his knuckles on the door—"classified."

"What in the hell does that mean? Have you been, like, spying on me?"

"No, Elvie. It's just . . . we're advanced, all right? We've got all kinds of advanced . . . stuff. To, you know, learn things. Look, it's not important how I found out. What's important is that when I did, I just . . . I needed to save you."

My heart skips a beat. Suddenly I'm not sure if I want to leap out and kiss Cole all over, or kick down the door and smash his pretty face in.

"Please don't kick me in the face, all right, Elvs?" Cole says, as if reading my mind. "And I'm not reading your mind," he states, seemingly contradicting his own statement. "I just . . . I guess I know you pretty well. Or I like to think I do anyway."

I take a deep breath then, and I make up my mind. I do not kick Cole's face in. Nor do I kiss him. I reach out a hand, slowly, and unlock the stall door. It swings open, and there's Cole on the other side, smiling at me.

"So?" he says.

For the first time in what feels like ages, I place a hand on my belly and feel around, making slow circles. Yep, there's the Goober. I always sort of thought he had an alien quality about him. I look up at Cole.

"Let's get off this spaceship," I tell him. And together we leave the bathroom.

To say that there's a bit of an uproar when we return to the bridge would be the understatement of the millennium. I can tell just from the wailing and screeching that the rest of the girls have been getting the same history lesson from Captain Bob that I got from Cole, and based on their responses, I'm thinking I should get an A-plus for keeping my shit together. Carrie is sobbing in a heap in the corner, Ramona is wrestling back Danielle, who is making a surprisingly good attempt at knocking out Captain Bob's teeth, and Chewie is practically bald on the left side of her head. But worst of all is Britta, who has splayed herself across the control panel, screeching at Captain Bob in supersonic tones.

"Get it out!" she's screaming, writhing in a panic. "Cut the alien out of me! Just chop it out! I don't want it! I don't want—" That's when Cole, pulling a trick I can only assume he learned from Captain Bob, aims his ray gun at the ceiling and shoots.

The room goes silent.

Captain Bob is the first to speak. "Thank you, Archer," he says. He looks like he's aged about forty years in the last ten minutes, the weight of this rescue mission hanging heavy on his face. He blinks a few times, gathering himself, then reaches out a hand to help Britta off the control panel. Reluctantly she accepts it, and he hoists her to her feet. Cole reaches out an arm to hug her, but—giving him a sneer I thought she reserved only for non-designer swimwear—she scuttles across the room to huddle with Other Cheerleader instead.

"Ladies," Captain Bob addresses us, "I am truly sorry about the way things have transpired today. I realize that asking for your trust, after the information I've just given you, seems somewhat ridiculous. But I can only hope that you believe me when I tell you that the survival of each and every one of you—*and* your babies—is truly important to me and Archer, and all of the Almiri. Any one of us would give our lives to save just one of you, and I think my fallen men speak to that. Our focus at the moment needs to be to get all of you off this ship, and we have a very limited window to do that. So we need to move. *Now*."

Cuddling Britta in the corner, Other Cheerleader swipes the hair out of her eyes. "What about these alien freak babies?" she says. "I want a termination. I don't *care* how far along I am. I can't bring a *thing* home to my parents. They'll totally spaz out."

"I can guarantee you that any unwanted babies will be cared for by the Almiri," Captain Bob tells us. "But these are not decisions to make now. As I said, we need to get moving, for all of our sakes. We are heading to the captain's yacht. You can go willingly, or you can go by force, but you need to *go*. Do we all understand one another?"

Around the room there are slow nods of heads. Natty is smiling in a dreamy sort of way that makes me wonder if she heard any of the captain's speech at all. But somehow, when the captain leads the way off the bridge, every one of us follows, without further complaint. Even me. Because, you know, the day couldn't possibly get any worse, now, could it?

CHAPTER NINE

IN WHICH OUR HEROINE STOPS BREATHING AND LEARNS TO FLY

I look down into the abyss. A hundred meters, give or take. The ladder bolted to the wall is narrow, with thin rungs, and the passage down would be tight even if we weren't trying to cram a bunch of swollen mommies-to-be down it.

"You can't be serious," I say, staring over the edge and imagining the gooey fate that would await me if my foot missed a rung.

"This is the fastest way down," Captain Bob replies. "You said so yourself."

And I guess I can't argue with that.

Cole seems to share my concern for free-falling pregnant girls, because he presents Captain Bob with a large coil of thin metallic cable that resembles old piano wire.

"I found this fastening cable in the depository back there," he tells Bob, gesturing to the large storage compartment we just passed. "Figured we could use it to secure the girls for the descent. It's certified for six, seven tons of resistance, easy."

"Then how's it going to hold Elvie's fat ass?" Britta says, shoving past me. Apparently that ankle of hers isn't quite as busted as she let on. "Hook me up. I'm going down first."

"No," Bob says. "Archer, you go first. If anyone loses their grip, I'd prefer they fall on you."

"Fine by me," Britta says. She gives Cole a cold stare and a face like *Come on with the cable already*. It's almost as if finding out that Cole isn't human and had been assigned by a secret society to inseminate her with a parasitic embryo has put him on her shit list for good.

Go figure.

Ramona nudges me with her elbow as Cole begins fastening the cable under each of the girls' baby bumps. "Why do you put up with that shit?" she asks me, jerking her head in Britta's direction. "You never slam that bitch back."

Cole and Britta are both several meters away, out of earshot, but still I hesitate to respond. "It's just . . ." I begin. I stare down at the bump that is the Goober. "She doesn't know," I say at last, turning back to Ramona. "She was with Cole first, and I sort of . . . I guess I kind of stole him."

"Don't tell me you feel like you *deserve* that shit," Ramona spits. "If you ask me, leaving that chrometard was the only smart move your boyfriend ever made."

"He's not my boyfriend," I reply. "Never was."

Ramona rolls her eyes. "*Anyway*"—she pokes an index finger into my stomach—"I'd say you've suffered enough for your sins, Elvie."

When we're all tied together like a string of novelty Christmas lights, Cole starts down the ladder. We all trail behind, Captain Bob coming last. It's very slow going—the sort of speed at which you might be able to squeeze peas through a drinking straw—and the metal tubing scrapes against our skin as we slide down. It's rough and surprisingly chilly and my clothes are still slightly damp from the pool, which isn't helping my comfort level any. But worst of all is the fact that I have somehow ended up right underneath Carrie.

"Jesus, Carrie," I say. "Would it have killed you to wear some underwear?"

"Oh, did I forget again?" she asks blithely. "I thought it felt colder than usual."

I swear that even from ten meters up I can hear Cole choke on his own spit.

"Explain to me why we're going down here again," Danielle says in between grunts. "I thought the captain's quarters were at the rear of the ship. So why are we heading toward the hangar? That's at the front, isn't it? We're traveling backward."

Danielle is right, of course. We are making a slight detour. Which, I might point out, was my idea. But Captain Bob agreed with me, once I explained my reasoning.

"Because," I tell her, "the hangar stretches across nearly half of the ship. So even though we're backtracking to get there, it'll be much faster, because we'll be able to bypass most of the areas that have been either damaged or tampered with."

"Yeah, but there's no air in the hangar," Chewie points out. "What do you expect us to do, snorkel?"

"And even if we can get down to the hangar floor," Ramona

adds from above me — I can hear her huffing as she pushes her belly over a rung — "how are we supposed to climb back out? There aren't any stairs at the far end."

"True," I say, up in Ramona's direction. I quickly look down again, however, after another unfortunate Carrie upskirt. "But there's no gravity in there either. So we're not exactly going to be, uh, walking it."

"Maybe we *should* have packed snorkels," Ramona says with a sigh.

We reach the bottom unscathed, if a little sweatier than I'd like, and we wriggle out of our cable harnesses. From there it's only a few short steps to the hangar entrance.

We cram into the tiny dock that normally serves as the staging area for crewmen entering the hangar deck to perform maintenance on shuttlecraft or the hangar itself. All that separates us from the long, empty space of the hangar is the narrow hatch door with one of those little turn-wheel locks. I can't see out the hatch window because I'm stuck near the back of the group, pressed up so tightly against Ramona that I can tell what kind of deodorant she didn't use this morning, but it wouldn't be much of a view anyway. The maintenance dock is a half level up from the floor of the hangar bay, so all I'd be able to see if I looked out the window is a ten-meter-long ladder down to the electromagnetic plates that line the floor. When activated, the plates serve to secure incoming shuttlecraft at both the bottom and top, eliminating the need for any mechanical locking systems, and allowing the *Echidna* to berth crafts of all sizes. So, useful, but also dangerous — 'cause I'm pretty sure those plates could fry a person to a crisp in a nanosecond. Fortunately for us, like most things at this level of the ship right now, the plates appear to have been disabled.

Once we're inside the hangar, our target will be the docking nozzle on the far end—a long, thin accordion-like sleeve that attaches to the shuttlecraft and leads to the ship's promenade/reception deck. Problem is, the nozzle hangs at least ten meters off the floor as well, and there's no ladder on that end, so in order to reach it we're going to have to make our way across the zero grav environment without floating away. Which isn't going to be a picnic, considering that the hangar is easily the length of three soccer fields. Assuming I have any sense of how long a soccer field is, which, given the number of times I ditched phys ed, is doubtful.

But I digress.

It is absolutely frigid in here, and the room is so tight, with all of us stuffed like a package of drugstore undies, that I'm already feeling slightly suffocated, but I know it will be a hundred times worse after Captain Bob wheels open the hatch and all our breathable air is sucked out at once.

"Okay. Now, we're only going to get one shot at this," Captain Bob tells us in his best authoritative-guy-in-charge voice. He is busy fussing with the length of cable we used to climb down here. "Once I open the hatch, it will be one, maybe two minutes before we can take another breath."

There is a metallic *clang* as Bob secures one end of the cable to the turn wheel on the hatch door. He yanks on the knot a few times as he continues to lay out the plan.

"Remember," he tells us, "there's virtually no atmosphere in there. No atmosphere means no maneuverability. You can't swim in zero atmo. This isn't water. This isn't even air. There will be no resistance to push off against. So you *must* hold tight to this cable. Do you all understand?" We all understand, except for possibly Carrie, who snorts at the notion of holding tight to Captain Bob's cable. "As soon as the hatch is open," he goes on, "I'll jump over to there." He points to the outer hull door, which seals the entrance to the hangar, to the right of our little hatch. "Then from there I'll push off across the hangar toward the docking nozzle. At that point I'll secure the cable, and when I give the signal, you girls will need to pull yourselves across as quickly as possible. Archer will take up the rear."

Carrie snorts again.

"When we're all across, I'll seal off the docking nozzle and open the door to the promenade. I cannot open the door until everyone is across, or the pressure will blow us all back to where we started. So we need to do this as quickly and cleanly as possible. Are there any questions before we set off?"

The severity of our situation must finally be sinking in, because for once no one has anything snarky to add.

Before he opens the hatch, Captain Bob leads us in a series of quick deep breaths, to expel as much carbon dioxide from our lungs as possible. And I'm just feeling like I might actually be able to relax and do this thing, when Cole cranes his neck across Carrie's shoulder to whisper into my ear.

"Remember," he tells me, his warm breath tingly on my cold skin, "the trick isn't to *hold* your breath. It's just to not breathe."

That's my Cole, helpful to the last.

"All right. I'm unsealing the dock now," Bob informs us. "Deep breaths, everyone." And without another word he begins turning the wheel.

Here goes nothing, I think, and I suck down a lungful of oxygen, pushing the air into the farthest depths of my chest.

The instant the seal on the hatch breaks, I can feel all the air *whoosh* out into the hangar. And cheese on a cracker, if I thought it was cold before, it's downright *arctic* now. My ears immediately pop from the pressure change, and the sudden wooziness I feel almost makes me involuntarily take a breath, but I stop myself in time. There's a low humming in my eardrums, but I try to shake my head clear as Captain Bob inches out the hatch door, holding tight to the cable.

In an instant Bob has launched himself off the hatch toward the outer hangar door. From where I'm standing I can't quite gauge the distance, but it's not too far, maybe fifteen meters or so. Once Bob expertly pivots and pushes off the hangar door, he's lined up perfectly with the docking nozzle at the other end of the hangar bay. He keeps his body stretched out as straight as a board and his arms in front of him, head down like a diver. The cable trails along behind him as he cuts his way across the length of the room.

As I watch him glide, I feel a chilly sweat form on my brow. Maybe it's just a trick of perspective, but it seems like Bob's momentum is slowing and, remembering what he said about the lack of resistance to push off in zero atmo, the length of the hangar in front of him seems to stretch out like that famous retrograde zoom shot from *Vertigo*. I can't help but wonder if he'll make it to the other side or not. I close my eyes and try to follow Cole's advice about not breathing versus holding my breath. But the more I try to focus, the more that low humming fills my ears.

I open my eyes in time to see Bob land right on the nozzle, a perfect bull's-eye. The flexible frame jiggles beneath him. Without wasting a second he attaches his end of the cable to one of the locking mechanisms meant to latch on to a shuttle's cabin door. Fortunately, the cable has a lot of give to it, and it stretches tautly but adequately across the long distance of the hangar bay.

Britta scoots out into the hangar first, gripping the cable tightly as she pulls herself toward Captain Bob, hand over hand. It's probably only been about thirty seconds since Captain Bob unsealed the hatch door, but already this whole not breathing thing is getting to be a real pain in the ass. My lungs feel like they're contracting inside my chest, and my cheeks are beginning to tingle and sting. The urge to take a breath is almost overwhelming, but I focus instead on the line of girls crawling out onto the cable. Other Cheerleader follows Britta, then Heather.

Natty's next, but she's hesitating. Her eyes are as big as saucers, taking up her entire face, and for a moment I'm worried that she's going to panic completely. But then Ramona, behind her, reaches out a hand in Natty's direction, and I can tell from the look on Nat's face that she thinks Ramona's going to slap her just like she did on the basketball courts. But she doesn't. Instead Ramona gives Natty's arm a good squeeze, and Natty nods, presses her lips together, and takes hold of the cable. I smile as she monkeys across it quickly, like a real pro. The end of the cable jangles against the turn wheel on the hatch door as she goes, the sound of metal on metal echoing in the empty chamber. Ramona shimmies out behind her, and one by one the other girls follow. In a matter of seconds it's down to just Danielle, Carrie, Cole, and me. My chest is pumping, aching for air, and my limbs are almost numb with cold. But I know I can do it. Just a few dozen seconds more, and we'll all be safely on the other side.

Danielle has just climbed out onto the cable when it happens. The cable pops loose from the turn wheel. Danielle, holding tight to her end of the cable, begins to float out into the hangar bay. The girls in front of her, noticing the sudden slack on the cable, scramble forward more quickly than before, and land on the docking nozzle easily, but Danielle is having trouble reeling herself in. She looks like she's tugging on a string of clown handkerchiefs.

But at least Danielle has something to hang on to. As Carrie, Cole, and I stand, untethered, teetering on the edge of the hatch door, peering out into the void of the hangar bay in front of us, I'm sure we are all thinking the same thing.

Shit balls.

At least, that's what I'm thinking.

Carrie tries to close the hatch door, so we can take a breath and form a plan, I guess, but Cole stops her, tugging tight on her arm. Her eyebrows are knitted together, confused and angry, but I understand Cole's reasoning. There's no more air left in this room anyway, and there's no time to reseal the hatch door and get back to the corridor before we run out of oxygen.

We have no choice. We have to cross without the cable.

This notion is just starting to sink its way into my brain-pan, when I notice the low humming again. As my ears have adjusted to the depressurization, the humming has only grown louder. And that's, well, a little unnerving.

As I watch Danielle waft closer and closer to the electro-magnetic plating on the ceiling, it hits me like a jolt. *The ceiling is humming.* The electromagnetic plates are turned on.

I gesture wildly toward Danielle, and Cole, bless him, catches on immediately. Together we push past Carrie to the front of the hatch door and try to get Bob's attention, waving our arms and pointing at the ceiling. The tingling in my cheeks is growing more intense, whether from lack of oxygen or fear, I'm not sure. Bob's eyes go wide when he realizes what Cole and I have been trying to tell him, and he frantically redoubles his efforts to reel in the cable—but there's too much slack, and he can't pull it in in time. Looking up at Danielle, then back to the girls behind him, he squares his jaw. Then, mind made up, he unfastens the cable from the locking mechanism. As he tosses it clear of the docking nozzle, Danielle's head begins to shake frantically, and she continues to waft *up, up, up* toward the ceiling—unaware, I hope, of the impending danger. I turn away so I don't have to watch, but hearing it might be worse. The low buzz is steady, terrifying, until suddenly it becomes a *buzzzzzz*FWIT! that can only be Danielle being zapped like a fly.

Carrie looks like she wants to ralph, but we have neither the time nor the oxygen that ralphing would require. We must have hit the two-minute mark by now, and my lungs feel ready to burst in my chest. My mouth is dry, and my head is dizzy. I can spot at least two crumpled floating girls in the docking nozzle at the far end of the hangar bay, probably passed out from lack of air. We need to move, and we need to move now.

With a quick yank Cole pulls Carrie forward and motions toward the main hangar door, instructing her to dive free-style, just as Captain Bob did with the cable. And, to her credit, Carrie doesn't hesitate for an instant. She leaps, boobs first, toward the door, and pivots, pushing off for the nozzle. I feel Cole's surprisingly warm, reassuring hand on my shoulder as he pushes me forward, and then I, too, dive from the hatch door.

It's an exhilarating feeling, being weightless, especially after lugging around the Goober these past several months. Every piece of me wants to float away in a different direction. I can't remember a moment in recent history when my feet have felt so relieved. The floating is awesome, like some sort of crazy dream you don't want to wake up from, but I can't afford to revel in it. I need to stay focused.

When I reach the hangar door, I'm surprised at its iciness, so cold it burns. For one terrifying moment my fingertips stick to the metal, and I worry that I will be trapped there forever, that people will find my dead, suffocated body hanging from a hangar door by my finger pads. But I manage to wrench the skin free, tugging my fingers away with ten tiny, excruciating pinches, and then I pivot, resting my ruined yellow flats against the door. I gaze straight ahead, across the long hangar bay, to the nozzle at the far end, where Captain Bob and the other girls are waiting for me. I do not pay attention to Danielle's lifeless body floating above me, or the strong smell of burned flesh that is filling my nostrils. With all my might I kick against the hangar door and launch toward the nozzle, my body as straight as a board. I pray that my aim is good. I pray that I won't miss my mark and crash into the back wall. I'm flying straight and true so far as I can tell, but as I watch the floor fly by beneath me, a noise grabs my attention, and I look up.

In front of me Carrie is having trouble. Apparently she pushed off at a bad angle, because she's definitely *not* headed for the nozzle, where Bob is waiting to grab us. If she stays on course, she's going to hit the ceiling just like Danielle, with a similarly fried-chicken fate awaiting her. And I guess she's just noticed this, because she's trying to turn in midair, grunting slightly with the effort. But without much in the way of an atmosphere to push through, there's very little to help her change direction. Her arms are flailing, trying to right herself, but even as she manages to stop her upward trajectory and straighten herself out, she can't seem to do anything for her momentum but spin uselessly like a mag sphere on ice. She's moving so slowly now, in fact, that I'm not only catching up to her, I'm about to pass her. As I float by, I turn my head and watch her struggle uselessly, kicking and clawing at the air desperately. My first instinct is to reach out and grab her, but I force myself to keep my arms steady. If I lose momentum, we'll both bite it. And in another moment it's a moot point, because I've passed her by several meters. I crane my neck, unable to look away as she struggles frantically, panic all over her face, and then she tries to breathe, and that's that.

By the time I turn around, I realize that by watching Carrie suffocate I've changed my own heading, and I'm going to miss the nozzle. Now I'm the one who's panicked, and it's all I can do not to cry out and choke to death. I'm off target by less than a meter, but "almost" won't cut it. If I try to change direction, I risk the same fate I just witnessed for Carrie. I squeeze my eyes shut, stretch my left arm out as far as I can, and pray that Bob can reach me.

There's a strong grip on my hand, and with great force I am yanked to the side. I crumple into the nozzle, and as I blink my eyes open and try to gain my bearings, I hear the flap behind me being sealed. Concentrated air rushes into the walkway, and my vision—which I hadn't realized had gone fuzzy—begins to focus. There's still no gravity, but I feel strong, warm arms wrapped around me.

When the face in front of me finally becomes clear, it is Cole. He must have shot past me while I was focused on Carrie. We are intertwined, his blue-green eyes staring into mine, and we are floating.

"Nice aim," he says.

I allow myself my first real breath, then immediately choke on the over-oxygenated air.

"Nice catch," I reply, coughing.

Captain Bob opens the hatch to the promenade, and the more-natural atmosphere breezes in. We all glide through into the large reception area and are greeted immediately by the pull of the artificial gravity. Hello, old friend. With a *thump* we all land on the ground at once, some of us more gracefully than others.

Heather, who was one of the girls who fainted from oxygen

loss, wakes up when she thumps to the ground. She rubs her eyes clear and gags a little on the air. She seems thrilled at first to be awake again and breathing. And then her face falls. She turns toward the now-sealed hatch. "Where's Danielle?" she asks.

When no one has the courage to answer, Heather figures it out. And at the sight of her choking back silent tears, even Britta has a glazed look in her eyes. I guess too much death in one day will hollow anyone out.

Cole meanwhile attempts to turn lemon powder into lemonade. "Good thing you saw that the mag locks were still online," he tells me, rubbing my shoulder.

"Yeah, good thing," I mutter. I pull back, trying to blink away the image of Danielle's lifeless floating body. But it's only replaced with Carrie's. "Otherwise someone might have gotten hurt."

Captain Bob turns then, and looks me straight in the eye. His look is so stern, at first I think he's going to shout at me. But he doesn't.

"If you hadn't warned us," he says, "then these girls here"—he sweeps his arms out to Chewie, Heather, Britta, Other Cheerleader, Natty, Ramona, and the others—"would all be dead. As would I. Now is no time for self-pity. Let's move it!" He claps his hands together loudly, which seems to snap most of the girls out of their slump. Following Bob's lead, we all head into one of the party rooms off the main promenade. We're walking a little more slowly than before, but hey, at least we're walking.

Back in the ship's cruise days, the party rooms probably made up a casino, with slot machines and a roulette wheel.

Now the rooms are home to more student-friendly video games and several of those god-awful motion-tracking dance machines. There's not much damage to this part of the ship, so we should be able to pass through quickly. From there we can make our way to the fitness gym, and then hopefully it will be smooth sailing to the captain's quarters.

"Which isn't to say," Bob says as we walk, apparently continuing on a thought that's been running silently through his head for the past few minutes, "that we should gloss over the fact that the mag locks were turned on."

"It could have been a malfunction after the blast," Cole puts in.

Bob nods slightly. "True, but it could just as likely have been—" He halts suddenly, and holds up his hand to stop us. We all obey, looking around to see what disaster is awaiting us now. But there's nothing.

"Why . . . ," I start, but Captain Bob cuts me off by slicing his hand sideways through the air. Walking slowly across the carpet, he advances on a closed closet door situated behind a row of karaoke machines. The rest of us all tiptoe in around him, as quiet as mice.

We're a meter from the closet door, and Bob has his neck craned, using his supersonic alien ears to listen for something, I guess, when Natty suddenly feels the need to pipe up. "What's in the closet?" she asks at the top of her shrill little voice.

It's too bad looks can't kill, because Bob could have single-handedly taken out every single teacher on the ship with the gaze he lays on Natty.

"Gnat, you are *such* a space case!" Britta starts up, and

soon a few of the other girls are chastising Natty too. Ramona is cracking her knuckles, probably getting ready to punch all their lights out in Nat's defense. Bob pulls out his gun, and I'd bet dollars to doughnuts that he's entertaining the notion of just gunning us all down and informing Mr. James Dean that the mission was an unavoidable failure. But then there's a clang from inside the closet, followed by a series of shuffling and rustling noises. The girls stop squabbling. Bob trains his gun on the door and motions to Cole, who whips out his ray gun too.

"Elvs," Cole whispers, "get behind me." I do as I'm told, and the rest of the girls follow suit. We're lined up like little ducks behind Bob and Cole at the closet door. Scared, confused little ducks. Bob puts his hand on the doorknob, and quickly yanks the door open. There is a flash of movement as something large tumbles out the door toward Bob, who reacts in a heartbeat, grabbing his would-be attacker and redirecting his momentum into the large Jetman console behind him. The closeted baddie crumples to the floor in a daze, Bob's and Cole's fancy ray guns right in his face.

For the third time that afternoon, I recognize a face in a surprising place.

"Hey, it's Des!" I cry.

Desi is—*was*, I guess I should say—the head of the AV club, which was most definitely the least popular activity the school had to offer, because there was only one member. As hot and smoky as he was, with his smooth-shaved head, short-trimmed beard, and bulging biceps, it was always clear to everyone that at heart Desi was a complete and utter dorkus.

The only thing he was ever good for really was fixing a broken computer or phone.

Bob leans in to Desi's face with a smug but deadly grin. "Ladies," Bob addresses us. There is venom in his voice I haven't heard before, and his eyes never leave Desi. "Our saboteur."

CHAPTER TEN

IN WHICH WE BEAR WITNESS TO LIFE, DEATH, AND MALFUNCTIONING ROBOTS

"Saboteur?" Desi repeats, staring cross-eyed up at Captain Bob as he tries to focus on the ray gun trained on his forehead. I have to admit, for an evil mastermind the guy seems fairly innocuous. Bob looks ready to squeeze the trigger at any moment, and I'm gearing myself up to witness yet another murder—what would that bring the daily tally to, a hundred and seven?—when a high-pitched squeal bursts from the closet.

"Don't hurt him! *Puh-LEEEEEEEEEZ!*" The squeal is followed, not a second later, by the squealer. It's Kate Mueller, president and sole member of Hanover's audiovisual club. She throws herself down on Desi, shielding him from Captain Bob. She cradles Desi's head and looks scornfully at all of us.

"Who is this?" Bob asks to no one in particular, pointing his gun away from Kate.

"My name is Kate. I'm a student here," Kate replies indignantly, pushing her glasses up on her nose. "And this is Des. My lover."

Okay, so this is weird for a number of reasons. First of all, Kate Mueller is officially the geekiest girl at Hanover. Seriously. They took a vote once at lunch, at Kate's insistence, and she won, hands down. She gave her award speech in binary. Kate is the last person I'd ever expect to have a "lover," unless that lover happened to be, say, an elf or a vampire. And second . . . *Desi? Lover?* Ew. Even if you ignore the fact that she's been canoodling with the man (or alien, or whatever) responsible for the deaths of more than half our classmates, that's just . . . well . . . *ew*.

Apparently over his initial shock, Bob is tightening his grip on his gun again, and it's nosing its way back up to Desi.

"Miss," he tells Kate coolly, "step away from your . . . friend."

"*Lover*," Kate corrects. If she'd known Bob for more than eight seconds, she wouldn't be so petulant, but somehow Geeky McGeekerson can't seem to see how uncomfortably focused he is on Desi. "I don't know who you are," she spits, "but I'm not going to let you hurt him."

Cole's trying to help or something, because he decides to pipe up. "Kate, was it?" he says cheerfully. But the gun he has trained lazily on her is killing the casual vibe a touch. I poke the barrel of his ray gun to the side just a few centimeters, so it's back on Desi. "Oh, um, sorry. Thanks, Elvs." I nod, and he turns back to Kate. "This guy isn't who you think he is. He's bad news. We're just trying to keep you safe. Now move aside so we can—"

"He is not *bad news*," Kate spits. "He's protecting me. He helped me hide during that attack, and kept me safe from all the explos—"

From behind us comes a sudden wail, breaking off Kate midsentence. "Kate, he's a murderer! He killed Danielle. He killed them *all*!"

And darn if that doesn't set everyone off. Soon the whole gang is wailing and screeching, and with two gun-toting aliens, a saboteur, and fourteen hormonal baby mamas in such tight quarters, I'm a little worried about our safety. Bob is clenching his jaw, eyes focused on Desi, and I know that the second Kate moves even a fraction of a millimeter, her "lover" is going to be Swiss cheese.

"Wait," I say, as something Kate said finally clicks in my brain. It makes sense, actually, about Kate and Desi. Kate *was* always blabbing on and on about the teachers quarters. I guess that's because she was up there with Desi, being all . . . *lover-ly*. Gross. "Wait!" I'm trying to be heard over the din, but it's basically impossible. I step between Bob's ray gun and its target, in what is probably one of my stupidest moves ever. But someone's got to do something.

"Miss Nara," Bob barks, "what do you think you're—"

"Bo—I mean, Captain, just wait." I turn to Kate, and the noise around me subsides slightly. "Are you saying that Desi has been with you ever since the first explosion?" She nods, and sniffles just a tiny bit. I guess all the ray gun pointing and talk of her lover being a murderer is starting to get to her. "You've both been here?" I ask. "In this closet?" She nods again, and I sigh. "I think she's telling the truth," I tell Bob. "I don't think this is our guy."

The other girls don't appear quite as ready to consider this point, however.

"Elvie, have you gone bat shit?" Ramona says. "If anyone would know how to mess with the ship's systems, it'd be the head of the AV club. Now get out of the way so the captain can fry his ass."

Bob has managed to wrench his gun around both me and Kate, and suddenly he's right up in Desi's face. "You're going to tell me exactly what encryption you used to lock us out of the main systems, and you're going to tell me now."

"He didn't encrypt anything!" Kate spits at Bob.

"I don't even know what you're talking about," Desi blurts out, more panicked than indignant. He's sweating so much that his SUDO MAKE ME A SANDWICH T-shirt's clinging to his chest.

"Guys, c'mon," I say. "This is *Desi*." Desi was never my favorite—he had an unfortunate habit of staring just a little too long while he was talking to you. But a murderer? I don't see it. "He got food poisoning from the kugel during International Foods Week and puked right in the middle of comp science."

"Oh, yeah," Nat remembers dreamily. "The noodles all over the floor looked like a minor Pollock."

"Exactly," I reply. "He's not a criminal mastermind."

"Elvs," Cole tells me, rolling his eyes like I'm being so immature. "That was probably part of the act."

"And we all know how familiar you are with putting on an

act," I respond, a little nastier than I mean to. I see Cole flinch, and I immediately feel the tiniest bit rotten. The dude *did* just save my life. If we were in China I'd, like, owe him eternal servitude or something.

Note to self: Instead of eternal servitude, vow to be less snarky.

"I didn't sabotage anything," Desi says, and I swear he's shaking a little. "Kate's telling the truth. I've been here since the attack."

Britta snorts. "Some brave alien baby snatcher you are."

"Alien?" Kate unconsciously edges away from Desi, shooting him a quizzical look. "What is she talking about, Des?" Her mouth twizzles into a knot. "You're not Canadian, are you?"

Desi looks at Bob and Cole, his expression suddenly a degree cooler. "They know?" he asks.

Bob nods. "They sussed it out," he replies flatly. Next to him Cole twists his ankle in a tight little circle, looking guilty.

"Know what?" Kate asks. She's examining her "lover" a little more closely now, eyes squinted. "Pookums, what do they know?"

"Babyface . . . ," Des begins. He reaches a hand out to touch her, but Kate is on guard now and shies away. He clears his throat, as if he's about to lay down some pretty bad news. Which, of course, he is. "Well, I probably should have told you this a long time ago, but . . . I just love you so much. I wanted to keep you safe. I'm . . . not exactly human."

Kate just sits there, eyes glazed over. She doesn't move a muscle, and for a few moments I think she might have gone catatonic. The rest of us have already absorbed the invaders-from-the-great-beyond info, so a lot of the girls are fidgeting impatiently, waiting to get things moving again.

At last Kate pipes up.

"Well, that's just great," she says flatly. "And my dad was upset when my sister married a Catholic."

There are tears in Desi's eyes now, real tears, and he's looking at Kate in this way that, like, if he weren't a crazed alien who'd posed as a teacher to kidnap a bunch of pregnant girls, might be hells romantic. "Kate," he says, "I love you more than anything. You have to believe me. I would do anything to protect you."

Kate doesn't respond, just pushes her glasses farther up on her nose. She's the only person I've ever seen wear the things besides my dad. She actually told me gleefully, our first week on board, that she didn't even need them, because, like the other 95 percent of the population, she'd had corrective eye surgery as soon as she'd hit puberty, but she thought they made her look "nerd-awesome."

Bob's trigger finger is itching, I can see it from here. "Why were you in the closet?" he asks Desi. There is not a trace of sympathy in his voice.

"I . . ." Desi is definitely shaking now, close to panic. "I had to save her. When I saw your ship, I . . . I knew what would happen to Kate, since she hadn't been processed yet. My superiors don't like to leave loose ends."

"Processed?" I ask.

But Desi doesn't get a chance to respond. Because at that moment the ship rocks violently, and from behind us the sounds of buckling metal and exploding circuitry let us know, if we didn't know it already, that there is truly no going back.

"The ship is listing into the planet's gravity faster than I'd anticipated," Bob spits out. "The hull could be breached. We've got to get away from that hangar. *Now*." And without waiting for any argument, he leans down and hoists Desi up by the armpit, his gun pressing into Desi's neck, and races down the corridor. The rest of us follow hot on his heels.

The moaning of the ship's frame takes on an ever more distressing timbre as we make our way to the Health and Wellness Center. We're almost to the automatic sliding glass doors when I notice the cool breeze on my face. It takes me a second to realize that it's not the AC kicking in; it's the air in the room being sucked around me, toward an unseen vacuum that must have opened up behind us, most likely in the hangar.

"We've got to get on the other side of those doors," I say, charging ahead of the pack to lead the way. Only, when I get there, the doors don't open. I run into them, Almiri baby bump first, before momentum sends my forehead into the glass with a thunk and I fall back on my butt.

Cue the blooper reel.

Cole has scooped me up before I can even register that I'm on the floor yet again. "You heard her. Get those doors open!" he barks. Ramona is trying to dig her fingers in between the two doors and pry them apart, while Bob, still gripping Desi tightly by the arm, looks around the area for something we can use. The other girls are hovering together.

"Um, is, like, the air getting sucked out?" Chewie asks. "'Cause I *cannot* hold my breath again."

"Y'know, someone could help me here!" Ramona shouts back at us all.

Natty has wandered over in my direction and is currently inspecting the newly raised bump on my noggin.

"I think it's going to be purple *and* orange," she coos.

"Gnat!" Ramona hollers at her. "Try to focus for once, will you?"

Natty looks over her shoulder at Ramona. "You know what would work great on that is a palette knife."

"Well, unfortunately," Ramona replies, still tugging at the gap in the door with her nails, "I didn't think to *bring* my arts and crafts kit with me for our getaw—" Ramona stops cold when she sees Natty nonchalantly wave the small, sturdy tool in her direction.

"You can keep it," Natty tells her, handing it over. "I have two more."

Ramona takes the knife and jams it between the doors. Everyone is nervously looking back and forth between Ramona and the path behind us, dreading an assumed approaching doom. Ramona scrunches up her face as she strains with the doors.

"I can help," Desi offers.

But Bob just squeezes his arm tighter and turns to Ramona. "Is it giving?" he asks. She doesn't answer, choosing instead to bully the door with a series of colorful metaphors that make even Cole blush.

"Just break the glass, idiot!" Britta yells. She never does disappoint. But if her brainless suggestion didn't surprise, the voice of reason certainly does.

"How's that gonna help us get away from the leak, dummy?" Natty says. "Really, Britta, sometimes I think you aren't paying attention at all."

Ramona gives one last tug on the palette knife, and the doors spring open. As soon as we're through, the doors slide closed behind us—not a perfect seal, but it will still buy us some time. The floor is vibrating underfoot, but the violent rocking seems to have passed, at least for the moment, and so we press on.

"How's the bump, Elvs?" Cole asks.

For a moment I think he's asking about the Goober, but then it hits me that he must mean the damage to my head. Which probably would have occurred to me right away, if not for the damage to my head.

Irony, or something.

"I'm fine," I tell him. "Takes more than a door to put me down for long."

"I always knew you were headstrong," he says with a smirk. Really? *That's* the joke you go with, Cole? Epic fail.

So how come I'm giggling?

Embarrassed for myself and for the state of comedy in general, I have no choice but to wallop Cole in the arm, which just makes his smile broaden.

Bob glances over my way as we walk. "So where to now, Miss Nara?" he asks. He's digging the barrel of his gun hard into Desi's neck, but the schlub is sweating so profusely, I'm afraid it might slip off. Poor Desi. Even with the chiseled good looks he shares with the rest of his cohorts, I cannot think of a less sexy dude.

"The fastest way from here is through the gym," I reply. "That will let us skip past all the medical suites and give us a straight shot to the gym showers. There's a dumbwaiter in the changing area, to send dirty towels to the laundry. But it also goes down to the aft crew quarters. So from there we'll be almost home free."

"The showers?" Other Cheerleader begins with a sneer. But even I notice that it lacks her usual level of disdain. "God, Elvie, if I wanted to see your dirty laundry, I would've . . ." Her face is red, and she's sweating like crazy. "You're so . . ." It's clear that all this running around has started to get to her. All of the girls look pretty run down, actually. I guess I probably am too. But I don't let myself stop to think about how sore my ankles are, or how badly my back aches, or how that lump on my forehead actually *does* hurt like a mother, 'cause if I let all the pain seep in and slow me down, I'm done for.

"Your face is ugly," she finally finishes.

"Point taken," I reply. "Regardless, that's going to be our best bet."

Bob nods at that. "Right. To the gym, then."

As we approach the big doors that open into the gym, a cacophony of noise on the other side makes the Goober inside me kick with worry.

"It's probably just the machinery malfunctioning," Ramona offers.

Um, yeah, you could say.

The gym is a *nightmare*. Like, an actual nightmare I had once where exercise equipment came to life and forced me to do Jazzercise in front of all the boys at Lower Merion until it was time for the Algebra 2 test I hadn't studied for. Normally three to five of the Treadtracks will be active at once, usually on one side of the room or the other. But now they *all* are, meaning that the entire floor is moving at high speeds back and forth in different directions, like a fun house designed by the Marquis de Sade. Most of the equipment that had been resting on stationary Treadtracks has been flung into the walls, and the friction from the tracks whirring away is generating large plumes of noxious dark smoke that fills the room. It's this smoke that makes me momentarily mistake what I see next as an illusion. But as I blink against the stinging, I realize it's no trick of the eyes.

It's a gaggle of fit-bots, once the unrelenting taskmasters of our love handles, now charging toward us with a glint in their mechanical eyes that I assume passes for crazy in the robot world.

"Feel the burn!" one threatens, in the trademark cheerful female voice shared by all the fit-bots. The mechanical monstrosity lifts a sparking StairMaster over its head and wields it like a giant club.

Another bot is flinging dumbbells of various weights and sizes at us as it charges. *"No pain, no gain!"* it buzzes, its voice box seemingly on the fritz, and then a more mechanical gender-neutral voice kicks in. *"Load exercise platitude number fourteen."*

We get the doors shut tight just as the first incoming dumb-bell slams into it, creating a sizeable dent. There's a large vending machine on the opposite wall filled with sports drinks and protein powders. Cole lifts it away from the wall with a surprising display of strength and plunks it down in front of the doors, blocking our would-be robot fitness assassins inside.

"So . . . ," Ramona muses. "Go around?"

A little extra walking never hurt anybody.

We're already well on our way through the medical corri-dor before I realize that we're missing my two favorite bloated blondes.

Now, okay, I'm not going to lie. It does, in fact, occur to me that I am the only person to notice Britta and Other Cheerleader's absence. And I do not, as it happens, like them very much. I could take their disappearance as a sudden burst of their karmic comeuppance and leave them behind.

But goddammit if I'm not just full of moral fiber or some-thing.

"Cole," I say, yanking on his arm. We're near the back of the group, scuttling the long way around toward the showers. Kate's still wailing at Captain Bob to get his dirty hands off her "lover," and quite frankly I think it's making everyone just a little nauseous. No wonder two of our own got left behind. "Britta's missing. And Other Cheer—her friend, too."

I know Britta's been giving Cole the cold shoulder for the past hour or so—ever since she found out his true identity—and there's a little part of me that almost hopes he'll be indif-ferent to their disappearance. But doggone it, he wouldn't be Cole then, would he?

"Sir!" Cole calls ahead to Captain Bob. Bob turns, his gun still expertly trained on Desi. "We have to go back. There's still two girls near the gym."

And just as quickly as we scurried down the hall, we scurry back.

Britta and Other Cheerleader aren't hard to find. They're sitting, slumped on the floor against the wall where the vending machine used to be. We can still hear the fit-bots pounding on the doors from inside. Britta is cradling her friend in this awkward sort of headlock, and let's just say Other Cheerleader should be glad today's not senior photo day, because she has looked better. Her cheeks are as red as apples and are puffed out enough that she could be stashing a few in her mouth for good measure, and, most distressing, she's holding her big fat pregnant stomach in a way that can mean only one thing.

"Oh, *shit*," Ramona says, echoing what I'm sure every single one of us girls is thinking. After all, you don't get knocked up without being fairly clear about what comes at the end of the pregnant rainbow. "You are not seriously planning on having your alien baby right *now*, are you? That has got to be, like, some terrible timing."

Other Cheerleader does not even bother to answer that. She just grits her teeth and lets out this, like, seriously freakish feral scream. Natty wails and hides behind Ramona in fear, as though she's afraid Other Cheerleader's contractions might send her into labor too. And Heather mutters under her breath, "I'm positive that wasn't a complete sentence."

Britta, for her part, shoots eye daggers up at Cole and

snaps, "You planning on *doing* something, nimrod? Or are you just going to stand there?"

Actually, it seems like Cole just plans on standing there. Captain Bob sighs, like he's cursing himself for having signed up for this mission. His grip still tight on Desi, he jerks his chin in Britta's direction. "When did the contractions start?" he asks her.

"I . . . I don't know," Britta says. She seems a little freaked out. And, okay, the girl sucks, but it's hard to blame her. Based on the preggers time line, Britta should have been the first to blow. She's farther along than any of us. So if Other Cheerleader's huffing and puffing, it only stands to reason that any minute she will be too. "Her due date's not for eight more days. I think the fit-bots freaked her out. She started shaking and . . ."

Captain Bob takes stock of the situation and makes up his mind quickly. "Archer," he instructs Cole, "pick her up."

"Pick her up?" Cole repeats.

"You think she can run on her own?" Bob asks. "Pick the girl up."

"But we can't just . . . ," Cole begins. "She's obviously . . . Don't you think we should wait until . . ."

"There's no telling how long the labor will last," Bob replies. "And we need to get moving. We can't sit around and wait for nature."

"But what if—"

"*Archer!*"

And with that, Cole scoops Other Cheerleader into his arms, and we double back to the medical corridor. Britta limps along at the back of the group, still clearly having some trouble with her ankle. But as much as Captain Bob may want to ignore Other Cheerleader's shrieking, it's becoming increasingly difficult.

Finally, Ramona's had enough. "Dude," she tells Captain Bob, her hands over her ears. Other Cheerleader's working on another set of contractions—the loudest yet. "I'm all for making a speedy exit and everything, but we gotta stop. That thing's gonna pop out of her any second, and she can't exactly shoot it out while we're running."

Captain Bob shakes his head stubbornly, but I sense a hint of doubt in his eyes. "We don't have any time to—"

"Dr. Marsden's office," I say suddenly. Bob offers me a sidelong glance. "It's on the way to the showers, about thirty meters from here. We won't even have to turn any extra corners."

"Fine," Bob grumbles.

I smell it before I see it. That familiar scent of Brut aftershave and peppermints. And suddenly I have this weird thought that maybe when we turn that corner Dr. Marsden will be sitting in his office, waiting for me with a smile. Like always. That he might even be able to help us with this whole wailing-girl-in-labor thing.

But of course he isn't. He's lying on the floor outside his office, blood dripping down the neck of his once white lab coat. He's been shot through the face.

I step delicately over the body on my way to the office door, and I try not to let it get to me, the sight of my favorite faculty member dead under my feet. Obviously the good doctor was Jin'Kai, just like everyone else on board. Obviously he wasn't as good as I thought he was. But sometimes you hope you'll be proven wrong.

By the time we plop Other Cheerleader onto the birthing table, she's practically yelping in pain. "It's coming!" she wails, thrashing her head about. "Don't let it kill me!"

The room is small—cold and white and sterile, and the entire wall between the room and the hallway is glass. Which always struck me as sort of odd—this place you go to have your girl parts examined, on view for the entire world to see—although there is a pull-down screen for privacy. The shelves that line the three other walls are filled with boxes of syringes, bandages, what have you. The birthing/exam table sits against one edge of the wall, and there are two chairs as well, along with three lap-pads strewn across the desk. I'm not sure what it says about me that this cold, clinical spot was the one place on the ship where I actually felt welcome.

Because the room is so small, Captain Bob orders most of the girls to stay outside. But he orders me into the room with a curt, "We may need someone with a brain." He tries to push Ramona out, but she insists that she wants a piece of the action, and Bob's so busy training his gun on Desi that he doesn't seem to have the wherewithal to argue. As the rest of the group mingles in the hallway, whispering and screeching and generally being the girls that they are, Captain Bob sneaks in a last word to Natty. "If any of them give you any trouble, you have my authority to sit on them." She just nods, bug-eyed.

The only people left in the room now are me, Captain Bob, Cole, Desi, Ramona, and Britta. And Other Cheerleader, of course, 'cause she's the one about to burst. Britta's squeezing Other Cheerleader's hand and shouting out things that she must think are helpful, like "Don't push too hard! You don't want its alien brain to leak all over you!" And Ramona's standing at the foot of the birthing table, like a catcher waiting for the pitch. Bob's still got his gun trained on Desi, but his focus is on the birthing table. Desi's is too. So is mine, for that matter. The girls outside have their faces plastered up against the glass wall, peering inside anxiously.

I've always thought that I'm not too shabby at the sciences. I know all about biology. Girl, boy, baby, birth. You'd think that mentally I'd be prepared for such a sight.

I am not.

Watching an *entire freaking baby* exit Other Cheerleader's bottom half is seriously the most horrifying thing I've ever witnessed. And what's worse is the way the Goober starts kicking, like he can't wait to inflict the same fate upon me. *Hold your alien horses*, I think at him as I rub my belly to calm him the shit down. *Not for, like, three weeks, dude. Or*—I think, focusing on the terror before me again—*like, never*. God, I can't look away. It's like a horror flick. It's bloody and messy and squirmy and *gross*. And at the end of it, this thing—a little creature with eyes and fingers and working knees—has actually *exited a person*, right before my very eyes.

"It's a boy!" Britta tells Other Cheerleader, gazing down at the slimy kid in Ramona's arms. She looks relieved.

"Of course it's a boy," Cole replies as he cuts the umbilical cord. He grabs a clean white towel off the counter beside him and swipes at the thing's eyes, wiping the goop away. I have to say, it does look remarkably like a human. Ten fingers, ten toes, eyes and ears and mouth in all the right places. We, all of us, lean in to take a look at it, and together—despite ourselves—we give a sort of collective "Awwwww." It is pretty darn cute. But . . .

"Didn't you say all Almiri are born with that starkiss thingie?" I ask.

"Wait, what?" Cole squints and leans in closer to the baby. But there's no cluster of freckles to be seen. Captain Bob inches nearer the baby, and, gun still in one hand, begins frantically swiping at the baby's cheek, as though that might make the distinctive Almiri birthmark appear.

It does not.

"His browridge," Captain Bob says. And I swear he shakes the baby just a little bit when he says it. I may not have taken On Your Own yet, but even I know you're not supposed to do that. "Look at his goddamn browridge."

We look.

Sure enough, there is something peculiar about the kid's brow. It protrudes just a smidge. Not in a Cro-Magnon way, but in a way where you can totally tell the kid's gonna be a macho, macho man when he grows up. Which would not be the worst thing in the world, except for the fact that, while Cole and his Almiri buddies are very pretty, they are hardly the he-man type. The only person here that fits that physical description would be . . .

"*Desi!*"

The dude is steps from the door, and he might have made it out without anyone noticing, except that Captain Bob has the reflexes of a cat. In an instant Bob is on him, ray gun aimed expertly with his right arm while he cradles the baby in his left. "Explain this," he tells Desi.

And Desi, shaking like a leaf, can only manage to get a few words out. "She's been processed," he tells us.

CHAPTER ELEVEN

IN WHICH THE PAST PORTENDS THE FUTURE, AND OUR BIOLOGY GETS ALL PHILOSOPHICAL

ok here's 1 for the record books.

Technically we're not allowed to use our phones during class hours, even if we're not in class, but I've always thought this rule was ridiculous. They really expect us to swirl around Earth and not attempt to make contact with it? In the past three months I have become an expert at blinking Ducky with my phone hidden in my pocket.

Right now, however, I don't need to go the pocket route. That's because, instead of suffering through English lit, I am currently sitting outside Dr. Marsden's office, waiting for my checkup. My due date's not for three and a half weeks, but Dr. Marsden says that as of this Monday—just three short days— the baby will technically be full term, and I should expect it to arrive anytime after that.

Color me excited.

I palm the phone, hold my hand up to face level, and—
snap!—take a pic of the view through the glass door of the
doc's office. I check the resolution quickly before I blink it off
to Ducky. Yep, it's clear. Britta McVicker, making a face like a
wounded wildebeest as Dr. M jabs her in the leg with a huge
needle. Priceless.

I have to wait only forty-nine seconds before I get a reply
from Ducky. We've been working on the Caption the Britta
Pic contest for the past six weeks or so, and I have a feeling that
today's entry will be a real winner.

britta gives birth to a mag sphere.

I'm still wiping the snot from my nose when the door to
Dr. Marsden's office opens and Britta steps out, back in her
regular clothes. That is to say, her neon-pink maternity dress
and faux-zebra Chuggz boots. I think pregnancy might have
made her go blind.

Dr. Marsden peeks his head out of the room. "Don't forget
to take those vitamins, Britta. Your baby will be here any day
now." He turns his attention to me. "Elvie. Won't you come
on inside?"

As I stand up and Britta passes me, she coughs out a
"*Slore.*" This is the particularly genius expression she and
Other Cheerleader have come up with for me recently, which
I'm assuming is supposed to mean something along the lines
of "slut whore." I would explain to them how the epithet is
a touch redundant, but then I'd just have to explain to them

what "redundant" means. I step into the office and settle onto the exam table as Dr. Marsden closes the door.

Dr. Marsden has always been my favorite faculty member. For some reason he's super-easy to talk to. It's too bad he's not an actual teacher, because then I'd have at least one class that didn't suck my balls so much. But I guess if you have to feel comfortable around only one person, it's nice for that person to be your doctor. It doesn't hurt that he's dreamy either. I actually sent a screen cap of him to Malikah when we first got here, and she said he reminded her of Jax Richter, her all-time favorite singer, of Jax Sabbath fame. I think he's *way* hunkier than Jax, though, with his thick black hair, icy blue eyes, and superhero jawline. And, okay, maybe it's gross to spend so much time thinking about how dreamy your doctor is, especially since he spends so much time all up in your girl parts, but as has been previously established, I *do* have hormones. Sometimes those sorts of thoughts sneak in.

"How's the baby been since last we saw you?" Dr. Marsden asks as he snaps on a new pair of fiber-mesh gloves. "Still kicking you like—how did you phrase it—a drunken ronin?"

I purse my lips together to stifle a smile. "Yeah," I tell him. "The kid's definitely out to avenge the death of his master. Although the rubbing trick you taught me seems to be helping a little."

"Good." He looks into my eyes with his little vision scope thingie. "Any vision changes?"

"Mine or the baby's?"

He smiles. "I'll take that as a no. How's everything else going? Grades? Friends?"

I think about that while he sticks his little lighty-up wand thing inside my ear. "Fair to middling," I reply.

He nods, then clicks the wand off. "Ears look good," he tells me as he begins attaching the electrodes to monitor my vitals. "You know, I've noticed you always schedule these appointments during your English lit class."

"Do I?" I say, raising an eyebrow. "I hadn't noticed that coincidence. Maybe that's when I'm feeling the most exam-y."

"Mmmm." He presses the stethoscope to my back. "Deep breath." I breathe. "It's funny, though, because Mr. Wilks tells me you currently have a D-minus in his class. You'd think you'd want to stick around to boost your grade a little."

I try to sigh at that, but Dr. Marsden nudges my back so that I'm sitting up straight again, and instructs me to take another deep breath.

"Look," I say when we're finally done with stethoscope time, and the doc has moved on to whacking my knee with a rubber hammer. "It's not that I don't enjoy English class." A blatant lie. "And Mr. Wilks is great and everything." He's basically Beelzebub with an English degree. "It's just that I don't understand *why* I have to spend so much time poring over *Huck Finn*, when I already know that I totally don't care. Why do *that* homework when I could be studying physics, a class that might actually get me somewhere? My time is a finite resource."

Dr. Marsden clucks his tongue. "Of course it is," he says gently. Then: "You've heard of the Wright brothers, haven't you?"

"Huh?" I ask. "Like Wilbur and Orville? Invented the airplane?"

"Precisely. Curiously enough, the brothers never would have come up with the idea had they not spent their early years working with printing presses and bicycles, learning the physics of complex machinery."

"Yes, but it was all still physics," I counter. Even so, my guard is rising. I haven't been my father's daughter for sixteen years without learning how "interesting facts" can be turned into a secret lecture. "I see where you're going with this, Doc. You're saying I should work hard in all my classes, because you never know what might be important down the line?"

"That's an interesting interpretation, Elvie," Dr. Marsden says as he checks my tonsils with his thumb and forefinger, "but I was just trying to tell you a nice story. Oh, you know what else that reminds me of? Friedrich August Kekulé von Stradonitz, who discovered the structure of the benzene ring—the key necessary to creating plastics, rubbers, and all sorts of modern technology—because of a dream about a snake eating its own tail. Just imagine. These very gloves"—he snaps the wrist of his left glove in my face with a *thwap!*—"would never have been created had Kekulé not paid attention to something that most scientists would deem utterly irrelevant."

"Yeah, yeah," I say, rolling my eyes. I have to admit I'm smiling just a twinge, though. "But the interpretation of dream imagery as signifiers in your field does not mean that reading Mark Twain is going to help me with my thermodynamics lab. Although I see your point."

"Point?" Dr. Marsden replies. "No, I don't think I was trying to make any point." He sits down in his swivel chair and tabs through my chart on his lap-pad. "You know that scientists only managed to cure cancer because one Dr. Roger Tsien thought it might be interesting to extract fluorescent proteins from jellyfish? Or that—"

"Okay!" I say, laughing. "I get it. I will work on being well-rounded."

"How about just working on a C-plus?"

"If *Huck Finn* will get me to Mars, I guess I'll read it," I tell him.

The doc scrunches his mouth to the side. "Mars, eh?" he says.

"Yeah. I've been prepping for the Ares Project since seventh grade. I want to go through the whole study program and be one of the first wave of engineers to terraform the . . ." Dr. Marsden seems to be smirking at me. "What?" I say.

"Nothing," he says, shaking his smile away. But I guess he can tell by the look on my face that his answer doesn't satisfy me, because he continues. "You've got quite a mind, Elvie. Quite a mind, indeed." He tabs through the chart again, then looks up at me. "Now." He clears his throat as he settles back into his chair. "I wanted to talk to you about your plans after the baby's birth."

I squint an eye at him. "I told you," I say. "Like a million times. I'm giving it up for adoption. Doesn't it say that on the chart?"

"Yes. Yes, of course it does," Dr. Marsden replies. "I just wanted to check with you that that's still where you're at. Sometimes, this close to the birth, some mothers change their minds. It's not unusual to suddenly feel connected to the baby at this stage of pregnancy, Elvie. I would just hate for you to make an irreversible decision because you didn't think things through."

"I've thought things through," I tell him, frowning. It's impossible *not* to think about what you want to do with a baby when you spend nine months surrounding the thing. So, yeah, I've thought about it. I've questioned my decision. But every time, I come to the same conclusion. "I don't want it. I just think someone else will be able to care for it . . . better than I can."

"That's fine if that's what you want," Dr. Marsden says. But I notice that he doesn't make a note in his chart. "I just want to be sure that you've considered all the opt—"

"Enough with the third degree, all right?" I say. And okay, yeah, maybe I snap a little bit. But *sheesh*. I take a deep breath and try to sound more rational. "I'm sixteen years old. I'm not ready to be a mom. It's not that I don't want to *someday*. It's just . . ." I always thought I would love being a mother. When I was a kid, I'd play house, just like other little girls. I'd carry around a baby doll with the bottle, the whole shebang. Wore an apron and everything. I'd be the best mom in the world. Killer, even. The kind of mom mine never got to be. I'd expose my kid to all the right music, straight out of the womb, and make sure the thing saw all the best flat pics. None of this 3-D crap that could screw up its brain. I'd teach it to fix a toaster as soon as it could hold a screwdriver. We'd be best buddies, the kid and me. Inseparable.

The funny thing is, for that first day after I found out I was knocked up, that's exactly where my brain went. Straight back to playing house—diapers, burping cloths, baby food.

Happiness and rainbows and all that crap. This thing in my stomach was like a *part* of me. And I felt, I really did, for a split second, like a mom.

But when Cole left . . . Well, it was like the world's rudest wake-up call. Suddenly it all hit me—how young I was, how inexperienced. And other stuff too, like how I had yet to see *anything* outside of the tristate area, let alone something as exotic as Mars, and how having a baby was going to make that dream pretty much impossible. How raising a kid on my own, like my dad did, might be possible, but it might not be *best*. How most of the kids at school who were born to teenage parents were absolute shit balls of human beings, and how maybe my kid deserved a better chance at life than I could give him on my own. It wasn't only because Cole was gone that I didn't want the thing. Actually, I think I'd only wanted it before because Cole was around. And I definitely owed more to the child I had helped to create than to use it as some sort of human glue to try to bind Cole and me together forever.

Once those thoughts started to creep inside my brain, well, they never really left. They started to creep inside the rest of my body too. Suddenly I felt completely disconnected from the thing inside me in this strange, disconcerting way. It didn't feel like my baby; it just felt like an object I was carrying around for someone else. I stopped even paying attention to it most of the time. I mean, sure, it's heavy. It kicks. It stretches out all my best T-shirts. But it might as well be a tumor or a heavy lunch. It's not, and never will be, my baby. And I think that's the best reason to give it up. To find someone who thinks differently.

It takes me a moment to realize that Dr. Marsden is still watching me, waiting for an answer. I look down, smoothing my hands over my maternity pants. "I plan on being a good mother," I tell him at last, "when I'm ready." Then I look up at him, so he knows I'm serious. "But right now I'm not ready."

"I understand," he replies, and he makes a note in his chart. He seems to think for a second, and opens his mouth, like he can't decide if he has something he wants to say, or something he doesn't. "Tell me, though," he says. "If this is the only child you ever have, will you still feel the same?"

"Absolutely," I say. Dr. Marsden's giving me a look like he wants me to spend more time thinking about the question than that, but I just shrug. "Look, we already know I'm fertile as hell. I did the dirty one time, and I managed to get knocked up. I think my eggs are pretty raring to be fertilized. So I'm fairly positive it won't be an issue. But . . ." He has that exasperated look he gets when I'm not taking things seriously enough. "Yeah," I tell him. "I'm sure."

"Well." He sets the chart down on the desk. "As long as you're sure." And at that he finally gives me a smile. "During your next visit we'll talk about what the actual birthing procedure will be. Your vitals are all clear, so right now I want to run a couple last-minute tests, and then I can send you back to English in time for that pop quiz I hear Mr. Wilks has been preparing."

"Joy."

"Lie back, okay? Head on the pillow."

I try to make myself comfortable on the table, the paper cover crinkling underneath me as I fidget. I watch as he pulls an enormous needle from a drawer, like the one I just saw him stick Britta with. "What tests are you doing?" I ask. "The Gatling?"

He flicks the syringe a few times and smiles at me. "For someone who doesn't care about her pregnancy," he says, "you sure know your stuff."

"I told you, I'm good at science." I prop myself up on my elbows. "So, is it the Gatling? That's usually done at the end of the third trimester, right? Do you really need to do it?"

"This is just some standard blood work," Dr. Marsden replies, sitting down in his chair and wheeling it closer to the exam table with his feet. "I will be doing the Gatling, but we'll put you under for it, and you won't feel a thing. We have to perform the test, as standard school protocol, but I'm certain it will be negative. I'm assuming you've never been on fertility meds?" I shake my head. "Then there's nothing to worry about."

The Gatling test is probably the most controversial prenatal test developed in the past two decades. With the high spike in fertility drugs came an increased number of chromosomal abnormalities, including Chromosomal Multiplasia Syndrome, a triplicate of one arm of chromosome number eight. Kids with CMS, or "chromers' disease," are severely stunted intellectually, and are born with all sorts of physical disabilities too, including, most noticeably, curled hands and feet. They have trouble breathing and swallowing, suffer from chronic pain, and usually live only into their twenties, at most. It wasn't until Dr. Joseph Gatling developed a test that the presence of the condition could be detected prenatally at all, and still it can only be detected at the end of the third trimester of pregnancy. A special exemption to the time limit for having an unwanted pregnancy "taken care of" was instituted for babies that showed signs of CMS, since the condition was considered so severe as to be almost a death sentence itself. Even so, some people—a lot of people—think that's too late. Others think it's the only humane way to deal with such a crippling condition.

"You may choose ahead of time not to hear the results, of course," the doc continues. "Some mothers do prefer that, given the emotional nature of the situation."

I think about it. "Actually, I'm not sure I'd want to know," I say. The doc sticks the needle into my arm and nods. I'm so used to blood work at this point that I barely even feel the thing, watching as the blood bubbles up into the tube. "I don't know what I'd do if I had to make a decision like that." When the tube is full, Dr. Marsden pulls it out, pressing a fiber-mesh swab into my skin to stop the bleeding. "What would you do?" I ask.

He swivels around in his chair to catalog the vial. "You really want to know?" he says, face to the wall.

"Yeah."

He turns back around to look at me. "Well, I think the question you have to ask yourself when making such a deci-sion is, which is more important to save—the individual or the group?"

Well, I wasn't expecting *that*. "Sorry?" I say.

"If you save the baby," the doc continues, "you're favor-ing the individual. But you show him mercy to the detriment of the species as a whole. Because in allowing that individual to grow, to very possibly procreate, you are paving the way for those defective genes to multiply. The species becomes weaker. And hundreds, thousands of years down the line, the species may very well die off completely." I must be frowning, because he raises his eyebrows. "You disagree?" he asks.

I shrug. The species or the individual—I'd never thought about putting it in those terms. Although I'd never thought about the dangers of mass chromer canoodling, either. That line of reasoning could be applied to almost anything. Give a generation of kids a vaccine for one ailment, and you're ensuring that all those that come after them will need the vaccine too. Allow only the healthy ones to survive, and you've created a stronger species. "I just think it's a very clinical way to think about things, that's all."

"True," he replies. "Luckily, I am certain you'll never have to worry about such things. As I said, I am one hundred percent positive that you will give birth to a perfectly healthy little baby."

I smile at that. "I'm going to hold you to that," I say.

Dr. Marsden pulls another syringe out of the drawer. "Okay, Elvie. This is the last test. Then it's back to Wilks you go. Now, brace yourself. You're definitely going to feel this one."

I squeeze my eyes shut as the needle plunges in, and suddenly my eyelids get heavy and everything goes dark.

CHAPTER TWELVE

IN WHICH THE ALIENS STOP BEING POLITE, AND START GETTING REAL

"Tell me what I want to know, or so help me . . ." For the umpteenth time Captain Bob smashes Desi hard across the face. But Desi, who's currently tied to a chair in the corner of Dr. Marsden's exam room, isn't talking. Other Cheerleader is still curled up on the delivery table, tears leaking from her eyes in this way that could probably technically be called crying, although she seems so completely vacant that I'm not sure there's any emotion behind it at all.

"That baby," Captain Bob barks, jerking his head toward Other Cheerleader's little bundle of anti-joy—the one that Britta's currently holding like it's a feral raccoon or something—"that *thing* is not Almiri. It's Jin'Kai. And I want to know why."

Desi spits blood onto the floor. "M-m-maybe," he stutters, as Captain Bob brings his ray gun closer to his nose, "maybe the dad is Jin'Kai. Maybe the girl got here by mistake."

Captain Bob closes his eyes for a brief second, exasperated, as though he's never heard such a ridiculous suggestion in his life. He turns to glance at Other Cheerleader. "Who is the father?" he asks.

Other Cheerleader smears what's left of her mascara across her face and turns to look at Britta, who nods, urging her to respond. "His name was Charlie," she says, then sniffles. "Charlie Sorley."

"Well, he's definitely Almiri," Cole tells her gently. "You sure it was him?"

"Yeah," she answers, her eyes unblinking. "Yeah." Then she sinks her chin to her knees, once again lost in her world of vacant thoughts.

Captain Bob has rounded on Desi again. His face is so close to Desi's that they're practically Eskimo kissing. "Every girl here," he says, "was implanted with an Almiri." He jabs a finger in Other Cheerleader's direction. "Including *that* one. So you tell me, and you tell me now. How did this happen? Are there more?"

I gulp.

More?

"Look," Desi says, trying to push himself away from Bob. Since his chair is flush against the wall, though, this is pretty ineffective. "I told you, I don't know anything." Beads of sweat dot his forehead. "I just work maintenance and run the AV—"

There's a sudden crackling noise, and a burst of light.

And Desi howls.

It takes me a second to realize that he's been shot. Captain Bob has blasted him with his ray gun. There's a hole, straight through his right thigh.

Outside, Kate is pounding on the locked door, screaming to be let in. The creature in Britta's arms wails.

But Desi still isn't talking.

"Flip off," he tells the captain, wincing around the words. The hole in his thigh is letting off smoke.

I've had my fill of watching Bob pound the bejesus out of Desi, and the smell of burned flesh is threatening to make me ill again, so I try as best I can to focus my attention on Dr. Marsden's computer. I'm searching for medical records on the girls, or something, *anything*, that might help fill us all in on just what the hell is happening here. I have a rock in the pit of my stomach, located right where the Goober normally kicks me, that makes me think the surprise enemy baby in Britta's arms may be just the tip of the alien iceberg.

A glance out of the corner of my eye tells me Bob's got the gun aimed at Desi's temple now. I suck in my breath as I click through Dr. M's personal files. My palms are sweaty and my fingers feel twitchy. I click on the suspiciously named PROGRAM 80 X.

"Go ahead and kill me," Desi tells the captain. There's a calmness in his voice that wasn't there before. He almost sounds like he's smiling. "I won't tell you dreck."

Bob puts his gun up. But rather than holstering the weapon, he walks to the door and yanks it open. Kate practically spills into the room, and Bob slams it shut behind her. He grabs her by the arm and presents her to Desi.

"Tell me what you've done," he says, ice in his voice. He points the gun at Kate, who promptly turns a shade of white usually reserved for vanilla yogurt. "Or it won't be you that I shoot next."

From the look on Desi's face, I'd say that Bob's scare tactic is very clearly working. But when I turn to Cole, he looks just as terrified. That's when I realize Bob might actually have lost every one of his marbles.

Fortunately for all of us, Desi immediately loses what little resolve he had. The poor schlub begins to squeal.

"All right! All right! Please, just . . . put that away." His words are spilling over one another in his rush to be heard. When Bob lowers the gun, Desi lets out a long breath. Then, his voice slow and deliberate, he starts to talk.

"We perfected a new procedure," he begins. "One that allows for the very rapid development and birthing of our young." He sounds less like a maniacal evil mastermind spilling his diabolical plans to the heroes, and more like a five-year-old explaining to his parents how he broke their favorite lamp. I'm only half-listening to Desi's speech as I open up the file on the doctor's computer. *It's not as bad as you think it is,* I tell myself. *It can't be.* "A Jin'Kai embryo, genetically pre-engineered to adapt instantly to a human host," Desi continues, "can go from inception to full term in thirteen to sixteen days." From the delivery table Other Cheerleader moans softly.

The file I open is a lot of medical gobbledygook that's hard to make out. But the phrases "genetically engineered," "accelerated development," and "re-fertilization window" make me think that this is indeed where I want to be searching.

"At this stage in the research, however," Desi says, his voice halting every few words as he swallows, "the embryos develop so rapidly that they need an environment already prepared to nourish a much older fetus. So they are inserted into a host that is already to term."

In front of me on the lap-pad is a chart, tracking each of the girls in the school over the period of their pregnancy, along with the obligatory corresponding lists of vitals and test results. The information gathered from each and every "checkup" with Dr. Marsden.

"*You son of a bitch*," Bob says in a haunted whisper. "You swapped out our offspring for your own."

My stomach flips as the Goober kicks me again. *It can't be true. I won't let it be.* A link along the side of the document reads 80 x A, and I click on it.

"A human female whose body was already housing a Klahnia," Desi says. "Can you think of an environment more suitable to handle a Jin'Kai child?"

On the lap-pad in front of me, another file pops open.

"What's a Klahnia?" Ramona asks softly.

But Desi ignores her. "Our genetic code is not so different from yours, even after thousands of years and billions of miles of separation. These girls were known to be incubating Almiri offspring, so—"

"So why not kill two birds with one stone?" Cole's voice is so harsh, so jagged and fragile, that it jolts me. "Propagate your own kind and—"

I look up from the lap-pad just in time to see Desi's eyes dart to Kate, still tangled with Bob's ray gun, but she's staring at her feet. "Rid ourselves of an enemy," Desi finishes for Cole. "Yes."

Without warning Captain Bob releases Kate from his grip, and as she slumps against the wall with tears in her eyes, he smashes Desi across the face with the butt of his gun.

"*How many?*" he shouts, his voice as hard as steel. Blood flows from Desi's broken nose. "How many of these girls have you tampered with? How many of our children have you murdered?"

I'm frantically scanning the second file now. It's another list of all the girls, except this one has only a single box next to each name. The heading at the top reads *Implementation*.

"A handful," Desi whimpers in reply. Even from the corner of my eye I can see the blood pooling in his mouth, staining his teeth. "The pregnancy needed to be nearly full-term before we could safely implant the new embryos, so only the girls who were approaching nine months have been processed."

Three names. Only three names on the new list have a check in their box. The first two are Britta and Other Cheerleader, both of whom were due to pop any day.

"Nine months," Bob says to Cole. "That explains why they were trying to save those two from the pool when we arrived. They'd already undergone this barbaric process." Bob grabs Desi by the collar. "Were there more?"

"Wait." Cole's face goes taut as he takes in the news, and from across the room I hear Britta wail.

"No," she whimpers. "*No.*" Cole tries to console her, but she shoves him away.

I tune them out. I have to. Because there's a third name on the list with a check beside it.

"Were there more?"

Elvan Nara.

I've been processed.

I feel the floor give way beneath me. *It's not mine. The baby's not mine. And it's not Cole's, either.* I don't even realize I'm shaking until I feel Cole's warm hand, steady on my shoulder. "You find something, Elvs?" he says. He peers at the lap-pad in front of me. There's a strain in his voice, and I can tell he's trying to push down whatever emotions are cropping up over the news that Britta's baby is no longer his. To hear about mine now right on top of that . . .

Without stopping to think I snap closed the second file and hide the link. "Just run-of-the-mill patient files," I tell him, trying to sound as calm as possible. I know he'll find out sooner or later. I know I have to tell him. But not now, not like this. Maybe I can hold off just a little while.

"Hey, uh, Desi's bleeding pretty bad," I say. Kate must be over her initial shock sooner than I am, because she moves to tend to Desi's wound with supplies she seems to have rummaged up from a drawer somewhere.

Bob stops her. "He bleeds until I get answers."

Cole takes out his phone and syncs it with Dr. Marsden's computer.

"What are you doing?" I ask.

"There could be useful info in these files about what the Jin'Kai have been up to," he replies. "You never know. They might want to look at them back at headquarters." I shake my head. Great, Cole, pick *now* to become smart and sensible.

"So why even come to Earth?" Ramona asks Desi. "I mean, if you guys all came from the same planet on the other side of the galaxy, why come all the way here just to mess with one another? What, your planet didn't have an ample supply of gullible teenage girls to schbadoink?"

Desi's gaze turns from Captain Bob, still threatening him with that ray gun, to Ramona. "I see your fearless leaders haven't told you everything," he says, wincing a little at the pain in his leg.

Bob releases Desi with a shove and takes a step back, glowering.

"What haven't we been told?" Ramona presses.

"The Jin'Kai arrived on Earth fifty-one years ago," Desi says, his breath worried and uneven as he speaks, "because Horon-4 could no longer sustain us."

Next to me Cole's phone has finished syncing. He slips it into his back pocket without even bothering to flip through the files, and I let out a breath I didn't know I was holding.

"Horon-4," Ramona says with a snort. She sounds like she's reading the description for some bad sci-fi flick. "That's the planet all you goons are from originally?"

"No," Desi replies. "Horon-4 was the Jin'Kai's fifth colony. Earth will be the sixth, the next in line to present a fresh crop of hosts for our young."

"First off," Ramona snaps, "I am not a crop. Second, why did you need fresh hosts?"

I've been only half-listening to this conversation, but I tune back in when I feel Cole's body go tense beside me.

"You okay?" I ask him, which is sort of funny, considering I'm the one who just discovered I have an evil-alien-swap baby inside me.

But Cole doesn't answer. He's staring at me, an odd expression on his face. It looks almost like . . . guilt?

"Elvs," he says softly. "There's something I have to tell you."

I look at him curiously, but he doesn't get a chance to say anything else before Desi starts speaking again.

"The physical resources required of the body in order to nourish a Jin'Kai through its fetal development are enormous. Once the child has come to term, the womb cannot support another fetus, Jin'Kai or otherwise."

At that, Britta shrieks. "You mean, we're gonna be *barren*? Having one of your monster babies means I can't have any babies of my own?" Britta's eyes are red and blotchy. From the table Other Cheerleader moans again.

Desi shakes his head slowly. "I'm afraid that you will indeed be unable to have any more children," he confirms.

My heart drops into my stomach. I will never be a mother. I will never have a family. I will never—

"Of course, that's true of all of the girls here," Desi continues. "The gestation of an Almiri fetus results in the same condition."

And that's it, right there—the worst piece of information I've gotten today. Not that Cole isn't human. Not that the baby

I'm carrying isn't mine. It's not even that evil alien freakazoids have swapped Cole's baby for one of their own.

It's that Cole *knew*. One look at his face tells me that much. He can barely stand to return my gaze. Cole *knew* that birthing his baby would leave me barren—without the choice to ever have children of my own—and he never told me. He's the one person I ever trusted with my whole heart, and he never even *tried* to tell me. Which makes him just as bad as any of them.

"Well, nuts to that," Ramona exclaims. "I'm not letting you guys wreck my junk for some mini E.T. Before it 'comes to term' I want a C-section. You guys have a preemie ward where you come from?"

"You can't," Bob says, still glowering. "You can't have a C-section. The fetus is adapting to survival in Earth's atmosphere up until the very end of its development, at which point it releases an enzyme into the host's system that initiates labor. This enzyme is what damages the reproductive system of the host. Removing the child before this point would be tantamount to killing it."

As this new information sinks in, a deathly quiet fills the room. But the eerie still is interrupted by the last person I ever thought would channel my innermost thoughts. Britta stuffs the Jin'Kai baby into Other Cheerleader's very hesitant arms and, with a guttural battle cry, throws herself at Cole, who grabs her by the forearms. She struggles against him, beating his chest with her fists.

"You no-good rotten alien son of a bitch! How could you

do this to me? You've ruined me! You've ruined everything!" She breaks down more and more as she screams, until she's sobbing, her fists loosened so that she's just weakly pawing at Cole now. Cole has the good sense to remain speechless, his face flushing a deep purple.

As if the room itself can no longer bear the tension, the floor and walls all shudder as the ship goes through another convulsion. The glass wall of the exam room shatters, and suddenly the entire remaining flock of terrified girls pours inside with us. The sound of creaking, contracting metal reverberates loudly through the walls and echoes down the hallway. The shudders are getting closer and closer together now.

"We have to get going," I say to no one in particular, as the girls who have just piled into the room shriek and squeal. I can't look Cole in the eyes. I may never look at him again. "It's only a matter of time before there's a critical breach somewhere and we lose all of our remaining atmosphere."

"Elvie's right," Cole says. "We need to move." He tries to help Other Cheerleader off the table, but she flinches at his touch and cowers away.

"Leave her," Bob says flatly. "We have to get the other girls out of here before the whole ship breaks apart."

Cole looks confused. "Sir?" he asks, still trying to cajole Other Cheerleader to her feet.

"Do I need to repeat myself, Archer?" Bob barks. He gestures to Other Cheerleader and Britta dismissively. "Leave the both of them, and the traitor as well."

Cole still doesn't get it, so I make it clear. "He means leave the Jin'Kai," I tell him, giving Bob a cold stare. "And save only the girls still carrying Almiri."

With that the other girls break into a confused chatter. I can see Kate trying to explain what information's just come to light, but they are too frantic with everything that's going on to be able to absorb any of it.

Cole looks disbelievingly at Captain Bob, as though he's been ordered to drown a puppy. "We can't just leave them, sir!"

"We will not jeopardize the entire mission for a couple of enemy agents, Archer. Now, follow my orders or so help me, if we survive the day, you'll wish you hadn't."

"But they're not enemy agents," Cole continues, his voice growing stronger and more defiant. "They're just girls."

"They're *incubators*!" Bob shouts.

The room goes silent. I look between Bob and Cole, who now stand toe-to-toe, each one trying to seem taller than the other. Cole turns to me, his face riddled with regret and apologies and worry. I look immediately away. If he wants some sort of validation, it's not going to come from me. But when he speaks again, his voice hardens into one of absolute resolve. I glance back up to find him looking Captain Bob right in the eye.

"I'm not going anywhere without them," he says. "*All* of them."

"Neither am I," says Ramona.

Bob blinks, but says nothing.

"Me neither," Natty adds, linking arms with Ramona.

And one by one all the other girls follow suit. Finally Cole looks to me again, and I rise, without a word, and take my place next to him, helping Other Cheerleader to her feet.

Bob just fumes as his eyes pass over each of us. When he lays his eyes on me, his shoulders drop.

"Let's get going before none of us makes it out alive," he says. "Archer, you're responsible for these girls' lives. I hope you don't screw it up like everything else you touch."

"Does this readout show the most current damage?" Bob asks, handing me his phone. I glance at the schematic for the level we're on, looking for any potential dangers that might have cropped up between our location and the linen room during the *Echidna*'s most recent contractions.

"Everything seems clear," I say as my eyes scan the offices, the garbage chute, the automated cleaning systems. *Would Bob even be talking to me if he knew what was inside me right now?* I shake my head clear. I hand him back the phone. "Straight shot," I say. "We're good to go."

"Still following your princes in shining armor?" Desi mocks. His wound is healing already, but there's still a sizeable hole through his leg, and he limps along with Kate to support him. "I would have thought you were smarter than that, Elvie."

I don't respond. Instead I work on trying to make one of my father's assessment lists in my head:

Situation:

1) Impregnated by superhunk. Am an expecting mom at
   sixteen.
2) Superhunk is from outer space. So there's that.
3) Alien love child will make me infertile.
4) Superhunk withheld this little tidbit.
5) Points 3 and 4 potentially moot because rival aliens
   have switched said alien love child with a parasite
   of their own, yielding the same results, namely, the
   aforementioned infertility.

Solution:
Um . . .
Well . . .
Shit.

I guess Bob isn't up for any Jin'Kai needling at the moment.
He rounds on Desi, his eyes flushed red. "If your kind had simply followed the *Code*," he spits, "none of this would have ever
happened. None of us would *be* here."

"What code?" Natty asks, all chipper.

Desi snorts in Bob's direction. "You Almiri and your precious Code," he says. "An archaic law best left to die on the
barren planet where it was written."

Ramona pulls another cigarette seemingly out of thin air.
"Hey, Cole," she calls down the hallway as she tries to light it.
"You want to explain what Frick and Frack here are bitching
about?"

Cole looks at Bob, who shakes his head, indicating that
Cole should remain quiet. But Cole begins anyway. "Where

we came from there were two species. The Klahnia—us—and the Pouri. The Pouri were a people a lot like you humans—males and females, standard reproduction. And the Klahnia mated with the Pouri, and produced Klahnia babies. You wouldn't be able to tell the two species apart—they looked exactly the same. At first the Klahnia didn't really understand their, whatsit, their symbiotic relationship with the Pouri. Believe it or not, it was several thousands of years before they even *knew* they were a different species. By the time they realized they were making their hosts barren, it was too late. The Pouri had been wiped out. So the Klahnia had to find new worlds with compatible species. They found six, Earth being the farthest away. Before they split into the six colonies and went their separate ways, they came up with the Code, which is, like, this super-important set of laws for how reproduction should be carried out on the new homeworlds. Klahnia mating would be very selective, and very sparse, to make sure that no Klahnia ever wiped out another host species again." I nod, despite myself. This is what Cole told me earlier, in the bathroom. I keep walking, looking straight ahead, as Cole finishes up his little history lesson. "The Code is the single most sacred tenet that holds our people together. The penalty for disregarding these rules is *very severe*."

"How severe?" Ramona asks. "Like they cut off your man parts or something?"

"*Very severe*," Cole repeats.

A chill goes down my spine. Because I remember the other thing Cole told me in the bathroom.

I chose you.

That wasn't just Cole being a doofy romantic. That was Cole blatantly disregarding the highest law of the Almiri, despite some serious freaking consequences.

But that *choice* was exactly what got me here in the first place. Cole may have risked his future to be with me, but he risked mine, too. And the difference was that *he* knew what he was risking. If I ever manage to make it safely back home—which, at this point, is seeming sort of doubtful—the only baby I'll ever be able to have isn't even human. Hell, it isn't even *his*. I'll never get to be the mother I always thought I would be.

Cole's choice has left me without one.

Ramona continues peppering Cole with questions regarding the more salacious aspects of the Code. "So you guys are told who you can, like, do it with?" she asks. "And they only let you get it on every hundred years or something?"

Cole coughs, composing himself. "It's not exactly that strict, but . . ."

"Dude, the Almiri must have *quite* the porn stash."

Ever since learning about Cole's treachery in the exam room, Britta has remained completely silent. She and Other Cheerleader are shuffling along at the back of our group, stony faced. Other Cheerleader won't even touch the baby. So now Heather's carrying it, tucked under her arm like a football. It doesn't seem to mind. Jin'Kai infants appear to be good nappers, at least.

But suddenly Britta seems to feel the need to talk.

"So what would happen to an Almiri if he broke the Code?" she asks. She says it loudly, her voice scratched from crying.

Cole does not answer.

Captain Bob stops marching to look at each of us girls as he says what he does next. "There is no greater crime for the Almiri. By following the Code the Almiri have been a great boon to mankind, and both species have thrived side by side ever since our arrival." He points his gun in Desi's direction, although most of the venom seems to have left his veins now. "Whereas these careless fools have abandoned the path, and in their recklessness they've destroyed entire worlds, and waged war on their own brothers."

"The Code allows you to hide from what you are," Desi says.

"Predators," I whisper.

A small smile crosses Desi's lips. "Exactly," he replies.

"We are not predators," Bob snaps. "We have created a mutually beneficial relationship with humans."

Ramona drops her cigarette to the floor and smashes it under her boot. "Mutually beneficial?" she says with a snort. "How? By only making some of us infertile instead of every-one, like these bozos? So that it's just our bum luck if we never get to have any kids of our own?"

"We came to a planet run by a physically and technologi-cally inferior species, and propelled your development further than you could ever have hoped to achieve in such a short time span." Bob is sounding a little like my dad when he tries to explain to Ducky why his Apple lap-pad is so much more reli-able than Ducky's old Herschel 2T. "We've given you some of your greatest thinkers. Music, literature, science—you name it. We have contributed the giants!"

"So you're saying we'd be hunkered down in caves," Ramona sneers, "counting on our fingers and toes, without you guys? Scratching pictures on walls and humming to ourselves, is that it? *That* justifies selective sterilization?"

Bob's response is calm. "Humankind has flourished with us."

"Maybe the *species* has flourished," I say suddenly. I can't hold it in anymore. "But not the poor girls you rob of any choice of what to do with their bodies. What to do with their lives." I'm practically spitting the words out now. "They're just incubators to you. You don't give a rat's ass about them. Or about us."

Captain Bob narrows his eyes at me. "I'm sorry you feel that way, Miss Nara," he says. "But at the moment you need *us* as much as we need *you*." He motions down the hallway, where the linen room stands waiting. "So I suggest we all keep walking, hmm?"

Just then Britta breaks from the back of the group and grabs Cole by the arm, stopping him dead in his tracks. I pause as well to see what the hubbub is. The rest of the group hurries on ahead after Bob.

"What the—?" he starts, but when he sees who's grabbed him, his face grows soft. "Britta, I—"

"This Code seems pretty serious," she hisses into his ear, loudly enough so that I can hear too. "So what do you think your buddy up there would do if he knew you broke it with *her*?"

With that she pushes him away and turns to look at me.

"What?" she snaps when she sees my gaping mouth. "You really thought I didn't know about you two?" She sneers, the look on her face cold and dangerous. "Bitch, *please*."

And she rejoins the group ahead, the slight limp in her stride reminding us of her wounded ankle. For a moment we remain behind, silent in her wake.

When we arrive at the linen room, it's mostly untouched by damage, although there are dozens of towels—once neatly stacked and ready to be distributed in the locker room—tossed all over the place. They got off easy, if you ask me. In the back is the object we've come all this way for—the dumbwaiter. The entire thing measures less than one and a half meters across and just as high, and it's barely a meter deep. Heavy steel doors meet horizontally in the middle.

"Looks like a tight squeeze," Bob says once he has disengaged the lock and swung the doors open. The bottom door doesn't pull all the way down when it opens, meaning that we'll have to climb up and over the fifteen-centimeter lip in order to get inside. "We'll need to go one by one. I'll go first to make sure it's operating safely. Archer, you bring up the rear."

"Naturally," Cole mutters. His eyes dart to Britta, but she hasn't said anything to anybody since her little outburst. For the moment at least, Cole's secret seems safe.

We spend the next twenty minutes loading one girl in, then sending her down, then calling the dumbwaiter back up for the next passenger. It's like waiting in line for the world's slowest roller coaster. For the first time all day, everyone is mostly quiet. It seems no one has much of anything to say.

Finally we're down to Ramona, Natty, me, and Cole. When the waiter dings its way back to our level, Cole slides the doors open, and Natty looks inside, terrified.

"Do I have to hold my breath again?" she asks.

"Just think of how you could incorporate this into your next installation," Ramona says.

Slowly Natty breaks into a grin. "I've been trying to think of a way to create a series of rotating shoehorns," she explains to me and Cole. And with that she climbs inside. Cole slams the doors shut, and we send her on her way.

Ramona offers me one of her cigarettes while we wait for the dumbwaiter to go down and come back up again. I've never really liked cigarettes. The only pleasant memory I have involving smoking was the time at Louie's Pizza Palace when Ducky rolled a combination of oregano and parmesan cheese into a napkin and tried to light it, getting a lungful of burning cheese embers for his efforts. So I mutter a soft, "No, thanks." Ramona shrugs and lights her own.

"You know, you probably shouldn't smoke," Cole tells her. "It's bad for the ba—" He stops talking as Ramona blows a puff of smoke into his face, glowering.

And so we just stand there, the three of us, in silence. Cole and I keep almost looking at each other, then jerking our eyes away at the last moment. Finally the dumbwaiter comes back up. Cole slides the doors open, and Ramona climbs inside.

"Get a room, you two," she tells us with a wink.

And she's gone.

"Well," I say, finally breaking the silence. "We're almost done, I guess. One way or another."

"Yeah," Cole replies, continuing our stellar verbal exchange. "Strange day."

I can't help but snicker at that, causing him to raise a curious eyebrow at me.

"If it's been strange for *you*, imagine how bonkers it's been for *me*," I say.

"You know," Cole says slowly, staring at the wall, "this was my very first combat mission."

That's enough to send me into a full-out fit of the giggles.

"What?" Cole says, finally turning to me. "What's so funny?"

"Nothing," I reply with a laugh. "It's just, well, *dur*." He laughs with me. I try to gain control of my breathing again, half-wishing I'd said yes to that cigarette, if only to have something to keep my hands occupied during this ridiculously awkward conversation.

"You think Britta will really tell Bob?" I ask. Cole stops smiling.

"I don't know." He looks at me, very seriously, and for the first time since the exam room I don't mind looking into those eyes. "But I do know that whatever happens, it was worth it. I mean, I'm going to have a son pretty soon, right?"

I flinch slightly at that but try to smile. Next to us the dumbwaiter dings.

"Well," Cole tells me, "looks like it's your turn." He hoists me up, one foot at a time, and gently helps me inside. He slides the top door halfway down and then stops, looking in. "Elvs, I'm sorry I got you into this. All of it. I never meant . . . I guess with you I just lost my head."

I study the faint constellation of freckles on his left cheek, the last remnants of his Almiri birthmark. Despite everything that's happened, I can't say I'm sorry to know Cole Archer.

"Kiss me," I say softly. And he smiles again, his kind eyes crinkling, and he leans in. I grab hold of his tunic and pull him in for a deep kiss. Then I put my mouth to his ear and breathe softly. "I'm sorry too," I whisper.

"Sorry for what?"

He's leaning in at such an awkward angle for our kiss that it's a cinch to yank him violently forward, smashing his head into the heavy half-closed door. He rebounds off with a CLANG! and looks at me with a puzzled and decidedly blurry expression on his face.

"Sorry! Sorry!" I squeal as I tighten my grip on his collar and yank him hard a second time, clanging his forehead and producing another resounding thunk. Now fully dizzy, Cole offers no resistance as I pull him into the dumbwaiter, then squeeze my way back out. I snatch his gun from his side and then jam the doors closed and send him on his way down to the group.

"Sorry," I whisper one more time as the steel waiter descends. Because I really am. But as much as I care about Cole Archer, I can't trust him right now. It's only a matter of time before he or Bob looks at those patient records more closely and learns the truth about the baby inside me. And even though I know Cole would defend me with his dying breath, he can't protect me from Bob or any of the other Almiri. Which is why I'm not going with them to the yacht. And I'm not going with them to Almiri headquarters. Nope, in order to make sure I'm well safe from both groups of crazy parasitic hottie pants, I'm going to have to make it on my own. I'm going to make use of what I saw on that schematic Bob asked me to look at, a detail that caught my eye and planted an idea in my brain that blossomed quickly. A detail that I never would have paid any attention to normally but that now screams out to me like a neon sign that says THIS WAY IF YOU WANT TO SAVE YOUR ASS, ELVIE!

Not twenty meters from the linen closet, there's another set of sliding doors in an adjoining corridor. But this isn't a pristine dumbwaiter for transporting linens. No, sir. I won't get off this bucket that easily.

I'm going out with the trash.

CHAPTER THIRTEEN

IN WHICH OUR HEROINE GETS IT ON, FLASHBACK-STYLE

"You're leaving already?"

I don't mean for it to come out so needy. But it does. It's just Cole and me, again, in my garage, and after installing his routers, upgrading his CPU, calibrating his mag spheres, and changing the Kuiper fluid, I've run out of things to fix on his car. It's purring like a kitten. And it's only now starting to occur to me that I like having Cole come over for more than just the joy of peering into the engine of his Kia.

"I, um . . ." He shuffles his feet, suddenly looking years younger. Like we're in middle school, even. Definitely not hot, but somehow I find it completely endearing. His eyes dart to the door of the house. "I guess I could stay a little longer."

I smile. "Want to watch a flat pic?"

"Sounds good."

• • •

We do not watch a flat pic. Instead we kiss. Cole kisses me, right there in the kitchen while I'm pouring him a glass of water. I'm just standing at the sink, glass in hand, and I hear him say, "Elvie?" And I turn, and it's—I didn't realize how close he was, how he was standing right there, right behind me. He gazes into my eyes, takes a deep breath, and without another word he kisses me.

It is only the third time I've ever been kissed in my whole life. Only the second by Cole Archer, and only the first by Cole that actually counts. Really, let's just say I've never been kissed before. Because I haven't, not like this. It is wet and warm and wonderful, and it's *Cole*.

Somehow we make it up the stairs to my room, and I'm sure our lips never leave each other's the whole time, although I guess they must, somehow. We sit on my bed and continue the kiss.

I'm not going to pretend like things just happen suddenly, like I have no idea where it's all going until it's over, in some sort of cut-to-the-fireplace flat pic cheesefest. I have every idea what's happening. Every second lasts an hour. The kissing, the *serious kissing*, the feel of Cole's hands against my back, him pushing my arms out of my cardigan sweater. I'm aware of every bit of it. And that whole time, it's both excruciating and exhilarating, both the best and most terrifying time of my entire life. As the kisses get deeper and Cole creeps a finger against the skin of my bare stomach, there are a thousand and one thoughts running through my head. There are your standard *IsthisreallyhappeningholyshitIhopeIdon'tcrap myself* sort of thoughts—the kind you'd expect in this sort of situation (not that you ever expected this situation, not really, not in your wildest dreams). And then there are the thoughts of the more nonstandard variety, such as suddenly freaking out about all that stuff from health class—pregnancy, disease, fire, brimstone—not to mention that stuff from your dad—the cow and the milk and what have you—and wondering if Cole really wants to do what you're pretty positive he wants to do, and wondering if *you* really want to do what you're pretty positive you want to do. And thoughts about how amazing Cole's lips feel on your neck, and about that weird mole above his ear you might tell him he should get checked out later, and how you're a slut if you go any further than where you are right . . . where you were a split second ago, and how no way is this happening, and how you should stop this right now, and how no way would you ever stop this, and the weird occasional wonderment about whether or not you remembered to take the garbage out this morning. And then Cole whispers into your ear how gorgeous you are, and you know that should be the sexiest thing you've ever heard, but you can't tell if he's being honest or just trying to get into your pants. But either way, it works. And you do a mental check to be sure you took your Preventra vitamin that morning, so that just in case you *did* do—I don't know, *something*—you wouldn't get knocked up or explode with warts in the down-below region, or any other unmentionable thing that the little green capsule is meant to protect against. And you did, you took it. So you look at Cole, and you just *know*—you know that this is the instant when, as much as you'd like to think that things are just sort of happening of their own accord, you need to make a decision. You need to decide if you want this, or if you don't, and take whatever consequences come either way.

So, yeah, anyway, we do it.

Sex, I mean.

In case that wasn't clear.

And it's not half bad. I mean, not that I have anything to compare it to. It feels good, obviously, although I don't exactly feel like my head's going to explode off my body the way those chicks in the movies carry on. Some of it is better than good, even—let's go with "resplendent"—and some of it not so much. Awkward and weird. Really, for all the poetry in the world on the subject, when you get right down to it, it's mostly just *boom!* penis vagina.

My favorite part—and here I risk sounding like a lovesick adolescent, but I guess I don't care—is afterward. Lying with Cole half under and half over the covers, tracing the constellation of freckles on his cheek and having him kiss the tip of my nose as we hold each other close, skin against skin. He smiles at me, in this way that I can tell he's utterly happy in that moment, and he snuggles my head into the hollow between his neck and his chin. And we lie there for a long time, enjoying the sound of each other's heartbeats.

Yeah, that's pretty nice.

"Uh, Earth to Elvie."

"Huh?" I look up. Sitting across from me at the lunch table, Malikah is waving her hand in my face.

"You alive in there?" she asks me. "Ducky's been boring us with blow-by-blow Jetman recaps for the past ten minutes, and you haven't even tried to save us once. Jennie and I are *dying* over here."

"Dude, let her space," Leo says with a laugh. "So"—he turns back to Ducky—"do you use the Fuzer Field on the Mastodon King, 'cause I read online this great strat using—not kidding—the upgraded Hydro-rush."

As Ducky and Leo and Greg continue their nerdfest, and Malikah turns to pelting Ducky in the side of the face with Tater Tots, Jennie sets a hand on top of mine. "You okay?" she asks me in a whisper.

"Yeah, I just . . ." I shake my head clear of thoughts. It's been an entire day since Cole and I slept together. Nineteen and a half hours, not that I'm counting. And I want to tell someone. *Everyone.* I want Jennie and Malikah to weigh in the way they always do with complicated boy stuff, I want Leo and Greg to make fake barfing motions the way they always do with complicated boy stuff, and I want Ducky to . . . Well, I don't know what I want Ducky to do, but it feels wrong to keep something like this from him. Something major.

Only . . . I can't tell, can I? Because I promised Cole I wouldn't make a peep until he had the chance to explain things to Britta, so that she'd hear it all from him, and not through the LMHS rumor mill. Which sounded so sensible and considerate yesterday afternoon as we snuggled under the covers. But now it's just excruciating.

"No, seriously," Ducky goes on, Leo and Greg glued to his every word. "I know it sounds idiotic, what with his resistance to ice damage, but try Hailstorm on him. When he does his Tusk-Crush, he'll get frozen in place for two seconds."

The worst part of it is that Cole is here, right now, in this lunchroom. I can see him at the table by the door, where he's sitting with Britta and all her cheerleader friends. Every time he opens his mouth, I wonder if he's going to tell her, to finally break the news that it's over, that he's found someone else. But he wouldn't do it right here in the lunchroom, would he? That seems so harsh, so un-Cole-like. No, maybe he'll do it right after school, when they're alone in the parking lot. Or when they're driving home. Or . . .

He is going to do it, right?

My stomach flips a somersault.

"Ouch!" I see the conjoined double tot skitter off the lunch table almost at the same moment that I realize I've been hit in the forehead with it. "Malikah, what the . . ."

"See something you like, eh?" she says.

"Huh?" I ask, stomach still churning.

Malikah raises her eyebrows suggestively in the direction of the door. "Someone's got a hankering for a big helping of Cole-slaw."

"*What?*" I squeal. I glance at Ducky, who is still deep in conversation with the boys. Not listening at all. "No way. I just—"

"I don't blame you," she says. "He is dreamy."

"Oh!" Jennie pipes up suddenly, popping a gum tab into her mouth. "Did you hear about him and Britta?"

Flop! My stomach's on the move again.

"No, what?" Malikah asks. "They break up?"

"Nah. You think Britta'll ever let her claws out of that one? No, it's just she started a petition for prom king and queen. *Already*. We're freaking *sophomores*."

I can't. I can't do this anymore. I need to talk to Cole. I need to make sure he was serious, that he cares about me, that he didn't just sleep with me and then plan on throwing me away like some—

"Elvie?"

It's Ducky calling my name now, his voice full of concern. And it takes me an entire second to realize that the reason everyone is staring at me is that I'm currently standing, hands gripped on the corner of the lunch table, staring at Cole Archer.

"You need to go to the nurse or something?" Jennie asks.

"I . . ." I blink. Words have completely escaped me.

And that's when I catch his eye. Across the room Cole has noticed me standing, staring. And he gives me this look—this tiny little hint of a smile that I'm sure no one else even notices but to me speaks volumes. *Soon*, the smile promises. *Soon*.

That is enough for me.

"I just have to pee," I tell the gang, snapping out of my haze.

I'm zipping up my jeans in the ladies' room when I see it.

The water in the toilet is neon blue.

Now, there are only two explanations. One, I consumed an inordinate amount of blueberry Juice Sticklers. Or two—and this is more likely, considering I hate Juice Sticklers—I am pregnant.

It kinda makes a girl wonder why she should even bother to take Preventra (the supposedly 99.999 percent foolproof pregnancy and STD prevention pill) if the *very first time* she does the dirty she gets knocked up. The added pregnancy alert fail-safe feature of the pill almost seems more like a rubbing-your-nose-in-it feature.

By God, that Cole must have some Olympic-class swimmers.

Well, I think, staring down at the irrefutable evidence of Cole's and my little dalliance, *I guess now's as good a time as any for Cole to break up with Britta, huh?*

I yank my phone out of my pocket and type a quick message to Cole before the lunch bell rings.

can u come over tonite? i want to tell u something.

It's not thirty seconds before I get a reply.

sure thing. always luv our chats.

And at that I can't help it. I smile.

I know there are a thousand and one reasons I should be freaking out right now, in the minutes after I've just discovered that I'm pregnant.

I'm too young.

It's too soon.

I've only known Cole for a few months, and been speaking to him for a few weeks.

But.

But.

Just at the moment I'm not freaking out. I'm pretty positive there will be lots of time for freaking out later. Just at the moment I'm letting myself revel in the fact that there's a tiny little life inside me. A tiny little piece of Cole.

As the bell rings I stick my phone into my pocket, flush the toilet, and head off to French class.

cole? whats going on? why wont u call me back?

It's been seven days since Cole and I slept together. Six days since I told him the news that I was pregnant.

Six days since I last heard a peep out of him.

It's Easter Sunday, and I've been sitting on my bed all morning gnawing on a gigantic milk chocolate bunny that Ducky got for me, my legs curled up to my chest, alternately trying to call Cole and looking up pics of fetuses online.

A poppy seed. Our baby is the size of a poppy seed.

Cole hasn't been to school all week. Not since I dropped the baby bomb and he raced out of my house, face ghostly pale, with some lame excuse about an orthodontist appointment. Which, given Cole's perfect teeth, I should have realized was bull honky. There are rumors that he's sick, rumors that he hooked up with a girl in Pittsburgh and skipped school to be with her, rumors that he witnessed a murder and is just lying low for a while. Yesterday I pulled my bike out of the garage to take a secret stalking trip past his house, before realizing that the dude never even told me where he lived.

I'm picking up the phone to call him again—for the thirty-third time, not that I'm counting—when I finally allow it to sink in. Maybe he doesn't, as I've been trying to convince myself, "need time to process." Maybe he's already done his processing. And maybe the outcome of all that processing was that he decided not to call me. Or see me. Again. Ever.

I put down the phone, and place a hand on my stomach, trying to feel the tiny thing growing inside of me.

I know, the way you know something in a dream—when it just *hits* you, and you understand immediately that it is absolutely true—that I will never see Cole Archer again. He's gone, for good. Which means that he didn't love me, and he won't love this baby. And that's when the tears come. Because suddenly it's crystal clear, the entire situation.

I'm pregnant.

I'm alone.

I'm screwed.

CHAPTER FOURTEEN

IN WHICH SACRIFICES ARE MADE AND PLOTS ARE FOILED

As I hurtle down the garbage chute, a lot of things should be racing through my mind. Instead my only thought is, *Way to go, Elvie.*

I am often incredibly sarcastic when addressing myself.

Really, I try to reason, I had no alternative. I didn't *want* to knock poor Cole's stupid lights out, but neither could I sit idly by and let my destiny be decided by warring factions of extra-terrestrial hotties. As far as they're concerned, I'm nothing but a disposable incubator—and especially now that I know the Goober was swapped for some evil Jin'Kai broodling, the safest place for me is on my own. Bob has shown that he's no one to trust. And Cole? When I look into his eyes, I believe that he loves me, but the fact is that he lied. If he knew I was going to be squirting out another alien's freaking fetus, what would he do then? One thing I know for sure is that when I get home,

I'm getting a termination, *STAT*. Because sixteen isn't exactly the age I planned on being when all my junk dried up and became useless. And I will not—I repeat, *not*—play mommy to some evil Jin'Kai infant baby killer.

I land with an unnerving splat in the ship's refuse reservoir. All of the garbage, waste, and trash from the entire ship travels via chutes into this one Dumpster, located along the hull on the bottom of the ship. It measures roughly twenty-five by ten meters, so that's a lotta space crap, and it's about as lovely as you'd expect. I've made a little Elvie-size crater in the muck, and various unmentionable liquids ooze and drip down on me as I try to right myself. My hand finds something slick and clammy, and as I push myself up, there is a queasy-sounding *pop-crunch*. My hand slips on the viscous substance, and I fall back, getting a nice view of the ceiling, which is dripping with garbage juice condensation. For a sickening moment I think about what it may be that I've just slipped in, but then a more pressing worry takes center stage: I can't find Cole's ray gun. It must have slipped out of my hand when I landed. A few panicked seconds later my hand slides over its smooth casing and I extricate it from under an empty carton of Chunky Chocolate Chipotle Craving Cream. I slide it safely into the back of my pants.

I pick my handholds more carefully as I attempt to lift myself up a second time. Soon I find myself standing waist-deep in shit. Or, to be more literal than figurative, shit and urine and old food and who knows what else. I'm suddenly nostalgic for when I had something in my stomach to barf. The dry heaving that follows is the worst.

I do my best to compose myself, and look around for the side hatch, which is usually only utilized if someone accidentally drops their retainer into the trash or something. Naturally it's on the opposite side of the Dumpster. I pick my way through the muck, wading slowly through things so awful that I'm sure I'll be having nightmares about them for years. Once I reach the hatch, I tap a few keys on the control panel to disengage the lock, and to my relief I hear the *hiss-pop* of the clamps releasing right away. It wouldn't have been too slick if I had escaped two groups of alien masterminds only to die in an oversize garbage can.

I step out through the hatch into the underbelly of the *Echidna*, leaving trails of Dumpster goo as I go. It's hells cold. Not freezing like the hangar but cold enough, especially now that I'm covered in unmentionable soggy garbage. Twenty decks down from where I left Cole and the rest of the group, this area of the ship is about as bare bones as you can get. Instead of finished deck floors, a series of narrow catwalks crisscross the length of the ship. They're so thin, they wobble as I walk, which is fairly unnerving, considering that they hang a good ten meters above the bottom hull. There doesn't appear to be any damage down here, and the air seems breathable, so I busy myself with preparing for my escape. Let the other girls take off with Bob and Cole. This pregnant lady is taking the classy way home: Dumpster cruising.

I can hardly hear myself think over the chattering of my teeth as I pry the front panel off the Dumpster's regulator module. The unit gauges the weight of the refuse in the Dumpster, and when it reaches, um, critical mass, it sends a signal to the United Recycling HQ in New Jersey. Then HQ bounces back a response code that tells the regulator which of the hundreds of recycling centers across the globe are open for reception, at which point the Dumpster unit automatically disengages from the ship and moseys down to the designated center to have its contents emptied, cleaned, and recycled. Not the most convenient way to travel, but hey, it beats taking the local. I figure once the Dumpster lands on Earth I can hitch a ride back home. Ideal? No. God forbid I get dropped off in Mumbai or somewhere like that. But I'd rather ride down with the trash and risk what comes than await my fate with Captain Bob's goons.

Still, it's going to be a tricky ride. The Dumpster isn't exactly designed for personnel transport, so it's unlikely that there will be enough air inside to last the thirty-six hours or so it will take to get back to the surface—not to mention the fact that the temperature will probably drop to sub-subzero. Luckily, thanks to Papa Bear's unyielding quizzing about the layout of the ship, I know that there is a maintenance locker not far from here. Once I've scrambled the regulator's sensors to make it think it's full, I'll have roughly ten minutes to grab a thermal suit and an oxygen tank before the signal bounces back from Jersey. I'm thinking I won't need any food for the trip. Despite my usual cravings, somehow I don't believe I'll be that hungry.

I fiddle around with the regulator's wiring and cross the appropriate connections. Three seconds after I press the reset button, the regulator beeps and a code flashes across the display, indicating that it has registered the Dumpster as full and is sending the signal back to Earth. With nothing left to do but grab a suit and O$_2$ tank, I trot briskly toward the locker.

I try to push thoughts of Ramona and Natty out of my head. Somehow I feel like I'm ditching the two of them more than any of the others. Assuming they get off the *Echidna* safely—and, God, I hope they do—what will happen to them? Will these Almiri jokers just let them go after their precious babies are delivered? Or will they keep them prisoner so the Almiri can protect their identities? Or maybe . . . eliminate unneeded loose ends? And what will happen to Cole if Britta really does squeal on him?

I squash the thoughts in my brain. *I can't worry about that,* I tell myself, trying not to look down as the metal of the catwalk wobbles underneath my sticky feet. I'm doing the only thing I can. I'm saving myself. And when I get back home safely, Dad and I can contact the authorities, inform them about this whole Almiri-Jin'Kai debacle. Save all the girls in one fell swoop.

The bowels of the ship echo with the irregular clanging and churning of failing systems, and the catwalk beneath my feet is making a fair amount of noise as well. So I almost don't hear the beep. I stop immediately, eyes darting around to make sure I didn't set off some kind of motion sensor. A few seconds pass, and I hear the beep again. It's coming from my back pocket.

It's my phone.

I let it slip out of my pocket and check it. Sure enough, there's a signal, albeit a fairly weak one. The screen beeps again.

YOU HAVE 31 NEW BLINKS.

I tab through to my in-box. Thirty-one new blinks from Ducky *since this morning*. My God, it was just this morning, wasn't it? When everything was normal? I scroll down and read:

> thought u'd wanna see this: gulliver/monkey_target_
> pooping/html

> hey do u remember my old jetman psswrd? have itch 2 play.

> argh did u see oscar noms today? al grant robbed again!
> sooo mad.

> what'd u think of monkey poop?

> elvie u there?

> drop ur phone in the toilet again? if so PLEASE disinfect
> this time.

> where r u?

> hellooo?????

And so on. Leave it to Ducky to realize something is wrong when we haven't communicated in forty-five minutes.

I fumble for the return tab and quickly type as I continue my way down the catwalk.

Ned help!

Thank you, SmartText, for knowing how pressing my need for Ned is at this very moment. But like an old reliable Saint Bernard, Ducky replies anyway. I open his new blink to find:

Britta's maternity look: gulliver/hippo_in_muumuu/farmfab

Dammit, Ducky. Although, I bet the vid is hilarious.

The phone's signal is still weak, but I notice that the farther along I go, the stronger it gets. Strong enough that after a few moments I can get an actual call out. I hit Ducky's speed dial tab. The phone doesn't even ring one full time before I see his goofy, wonderful face pop up on the tiny screen. Finally, contact with the outside world!

"Well where . . . oody hell ha . . . you been?" he asks, breaking up a bit from static. He's sitting at his desk in his pajamas, a bowl of cereal next to him. I can hear the tinny sounds of the original Jetman playing from his speakers. So I guess he found that password after all.

There's so much I need to tell Ducky—about the attack, about Cole, about the Almiri, the Jin'Kai, my parasitic alien baby, nearly suffocating in the hangar, how he should call my dad, help me get off this junker, mobilize the freaking army, everything. But instead of any of that, what comes out of my mouth is a sudden, and very unexpected, stream of bawling. I can't stop. I just sob and sob. I'm completely unable to form words. When I try to get them out, it sounds like I'm storing marbles in my mouth.

Ducky raises an eyebrow. "Elvie, you okay? I think you're breaking up or something. And, like, what the heck have you been doing?" His eyes drift down to examine the state of my clothes. "Mud wrestling?"

I force myself to stop crying and wipe my nose with my forearm, momentarily forgetting that it is covered in sewage. "I'm not breaking up, donktard," I respond. "I'm crying."

"I know you're crying, but you're also breaking up. What'd Britta do this time?"

"Ducky, listen very carefully to me." I make my voice as ominous as one can while picking flecks of old egg off one's upper lip. "The Hanover School is run by aliens."

"Must be an epidemic," Ducky says, attention drifting back to his video game. "I'm pretty sure my new Spanish sub is from Uranus."

"*Ducky!*" I shout at him. "Listen to me. I'm not pulling your leg. I'm not speaking in metaphor. I mean it. The Hanover School is run by a group of parasitic evil aliens, and there was an attack, and a lot of the girls are dead."

And bless whatever inner fantasy nerdiness lies behind it, but Ducky looks at me, and I know that without any further explanation he believes me.

"Jesus, Elvie, are you all right?" There's genuine concern in his voice.

"Well . . ." I think about how to answer that. "At the

moment. The *Echidna* is about to crash. I'm planning to hitch a ride back to Earth in the Dumpster."

"Holy . . ." Apparently years of video games have not prepared Ducky for this scenario. And then he asks the one question I wish he wouldn't. "Where's everyone else? Are they escaping in the Dumpster too?"

"I . . . I had to get away," I reply simply. "Look, I don't have much time to talk. I only have"—I check my watch—"seven minutes to get what I need from the maintenance closet and make it back to the Dumpster."

"Elvie, you can't . . .Won't you run out of air, or freeze, or something?"

"Thank you, Mr. Five Minutes Ago. I'm on it." And then, because I can't keep it to myself any longer, I tell him. "Ducky . . . Cole's here."

Ducky's eyes go wide, whether in disbelief or jealousy, I don't know. Funny how this seems to send him for a loop more than anything else.

"Cole *Archer*? What in the hell is he . . . *Oh my God he's an alien!*"

I love Ducky.

"I always kind of suspected he was evil," he continues.

"Cole's not evil," I correct him. "He's . . . well, it's a long story. There's good aliens and— Ducky, turn off the damn Jetman. I'm in a life-and-death situation up here!"

"Sorry," Ducky replies sheepishly as he flicks off the screen, eyes focusing on me once more. "I'm going to call your dad, okay? He'll be able to help more than me."

"Thanks. I . . ." Suddenly the thought of talking to my father is making me well up again. But I swallow the tears down. There's no more time for *that*. "Don't tell him about the aliens, though, okay? Just tell him the ship is in trouble and I'm escaping in a manner he would find incredibly ingenious. Oh, and maybe you guys can find out which recycling center the Dumpster's programmed to . . ." I trail off as I turn the corner and reach my destination.

Inside the maintenance locker room is a desk that clearly doesn't belong in such a tight space, and on top of it are several lap-pad computers, wired into the wall where the intercom panel once was. Each lap-pad's screen is scrolling through a series of various ship functions: atmosphere, door locks, what have you. And sitting on a bench next to the lockers is a device I immediately recognize as a high-tech variation on a run-of-the-mill pulse emitter, not unlike the kind used by schools, cineplexes, or other institutions that want to block external phone signals. In my attempt to escape the Hanover School for Expecting Parasitic Host Mothers, I have stumbled directly into the saboteur's center of operations.

"Elvie?" Ducky says. "What's the matter? You're making your *Oh, shit* face."

Oh, shit is right.

"Shhh, Ducky. Be quiet!" I whisper. The saboteur is nowhere in sight, but still. Ducky'd never forgive himself if I got a ray gun in the back because he was such a loudmouth. I need to get what I came here for and get out before the creep comes back.

I pick my way across the mess of wires to the lockers against the far wall. Hanging there are several thermal suits, with the oxygen tanks behind them. I pull out the first suit I can reach, set my phone and Cole's ray gun down on the bench beside me, and then step into the thin silver mesh outfit one foot at a time. The zipper strains as I yank it over the not-Goober, but it holds. The suit is huge up top and comically tight around the middle — I probably look like a giant misshapen mirror ball — but it'll do the trick for now. I flip up the hood, tuck Cole's gun down the front of the suit so that it rests rather comically between my boobs, and scoop up my phone.

Ducky is peering out into the room via my phone's cam. "What are those alien bastards up to?" he asks, pointing to the emitter on the bench in front of us.

"It blocks phone signals. That's why mine didn't work all day." I check the time on my phone. "I gotta rocket, Ducky. I only have four minutes before the Dumpster heads down planet-side."

"Well, what are you talking to me for? I've been trying to call your dad on my other line, but so far he's not answering. I'll patch you through as soon as I get him, okay?"

"Thanks."

I grab an oxygen tank and lug it up under my armpit, then turn for the door, glancing down inadvertently at the lap-pads lying on the desk. And as soon as I look at the screens, my heart sinks. I had already figured out that the saboteur had his own little makeshift mainframe down here, each computer hacked into a different ship system, screwing with it in ways I can only assume are nefarious. But the one that gets my attention is the lap-pad that *isn't* hardwired into the wall. It's running a remote program, wirelessly.

The boot-up program for the captain's yacht.

Just by glancing at it I see that our villain has control of life support, internal sensors, even the doors. The creep is herding the girls toward the yacht, just like Bob suspected.

Which is more important to save—the individual or the group? The memory pops into my brain, completely unwelcome and highly inconvenient, given the time crunch I'm facing. At the time the answer to that question seemed so cut and dried. Now . . .

I sit down at the desk and put my phone down. Tears are once again in my eyes, but they aren't tears of joy or emotional overload this time. No, these are just tears of acceptance.

"Elvie, what's the matter?" Ducky asks. "Why are you sitting down? You have to get to the Dumpster."

"I'm not going to the Dumpster," I tell him. And as soon as the words leave my mouth, I know they're true.

"What do you mean you're not going to the Dumpster?" Ducky screeches. "Elvie, you have to get out of there right now. You only have three minutes and twenty seconds. Three minutes nineteen." His voice is becoming more and more panicked. "*Elvie—*"

"Ducky, there are girls left on this ship. Lots of them. And Cole. They're planning on escaping on the captain's yacht, but this doucher has the whole ship rigged against them. They're headed straight into a trap. If I don't fix this, they'll die for sure."

"Elvie, *you'll* die for sure! Just get off the ship. If there's some bad guy up there messing with you, then you have to get away." He is practically crying. "You're a badass, Elvie, but you can't take on an evil space invader by yourself."

"Oh, yeah?" I say. "Watch me."

Just yanking the wires out of the wall works for most of the lap-pads, but in order to deactivate his overrides on the yacht, I'll have to go inside the system and reestablish manual site control. But first I need to clear a path for Captain Bob. If I can fix everything in time, the gang should be able to launch the yacht without falling into a trap. Ignoring the shrieks of outrage emanating from my phone, I focus on normalizing the environmental settings and deactivating the final few blast doors in the space between the group and their destination. I'm just disengaging the last door when I hear a loud clunking sound. The floor vibrates for a few seconds, and my phone skitters across the table before I manage to catch it.

"What was *that*?" Ducky asks.

"The Dumpster disembarking," I reply. And—quite stoically, I think, for a girl whose only way off a dying ship has just jettisoned into space—I return to my de-sabotage. I reestablish manual controls on the yacht. "Almost . . . there." A few more quick keystrokes, and . . . "Done!" The yacht, and the path to it, is safe.

"Great," Ducky says. "Now go, okay? You're freaking me out. Go join the others on this yacht thing and get the hell out of Dodge."

"Ducky," I tell him, trying to sound calm and at peace, if only for his sake, "I'm too far away now. I'll never make it before they get there and leave."

The individual or the group. I guess I've made my choice.

"Then there's got to be another way!" Ducky is pleading with me now, desperate, and I want to cry even more for knowing that all I've done by getting in touch with him is give him a front-row seat to my inevitable demise. "You've got to try! You've got to figure out *something*! Call Cole. Tell him to wait. Tell him you're coming."

I never in my wildest dreams thought Ducky would suggest that I ring up Cole. It's not a half-bad idea, actually, and it just might work, if only . . .

"I erased it," I tell Ducky, staring at my phone. Suddenly that move seems like the dumbest of all my teenage girl drama queen moments.

"Elvie, it isn't that I doubt your resolve as an independent woman, but I also know for a fact that somewhere in that jumbled brain of yours you've got the damn thing memorized. Now *think*."

And wouldn't you know it, the Duck is right.

"Stay on this line," I tell him.

I dial the number, seriously doubting that Cole brought his Nokia with him during a covert rescue mission. But it doesn't matter, because when I hit send, nothing happens. The call loading screen just spins its cute overly designed wheels.

"It won't go through," I tell Ducky when I switch back to him. "The signal is still scrambled. The saboteur doucher must have it set up so he can send signals from here but keep the rest of the ship scrambled. He must be . . ." And suddenly it all becomes remarkably clear, like, hello, freaking *lightbulb*. "Shit, Ducky. He must have been signaling his buddies this whole time. I wouldn't be surprised if there's a whole fleet of them on their way right now."

"*Very astute, Miss Nara.*"

When I hear the hard voice behind me, I tense up like I've just heard a ghost. With a surreptitious flick of my index finger I turn off my phone, disconnecting me from Ducky, the last image of his face going white as he wonders what horrible fate stands behind me. If this is really the end for old Elvie Nara, I don't want my bestie to have to witness it.

"Kindly place your hands behind your head and stand up slowly," says the voice. It's low and raspy, raw from the day's excitement, no doubt.

"So I guess this is it, then," I say as I rise.

"It is," he replies.

At first the nauseating scent that hits my nose befuddles me. The stench of brussels sprouts.

It's the goddamn cook?

But no, that's not the monster who's been making my life a living hell for the past twelve hours. Underneath the smell of vegetables is a more familiar scent, with fonder memories attached. Brut aftershave and peppermint. I stand up and turn around to face the saboteur, at last.

"Hello, Dr. Marsden."

CHAPTER FIFTEEN

WHEREIN OUR HEROINE GETS ALL HEROINIC

"Hello, Elvie," Dr. Marsden says, with the same genial smile he always wears on his face—despite the fact that he's pointing a ray gun directly at me.

My hand twitches, creeping ever so slightly closer to the ray gun stuffed down my boobs, but one look at the doc's face, and I know he's watching me like a hawk. I'd never reach the thing before he disarmed me. "I thought you were going to be Fred," I tell him, trying a different tactic. I gesture to the chef's jacket the doc has slipped on.

"Oh, this?" he says. "Just a little bit of subterfuge, along with the body you no doubt discovered outside my office. No one would spend time searching for a dead man."

"Too bad," I reply with a forced casual shrug. *Keep up the banter,* I tell myself. *The bad guys never shoot you while you're bantering.* "I had a great line all prepared if it was the cook."

Dr. Marsden cocks his head to a sharp angle. "I'd hate a good one-liner to go to waste. Please share."

"First Seafood Surprise Fridays, and now this."

His smile broadens. It's so genuine and warm that you'd never know he was a mass-murdering shithead. "You always were my favorite, Elvie. Such an agile mind."

"True," I say, all nonchalant-like. "So. You gonna put the gun down or what? We both know you're not going to shoot me."

"I'm not?"

"Not while I'm carrying your precious Jin'Kai cargo in my uterus."

For the first time Dr. Marsden's smile drops. "My, you have learned a lot, haven't you?"

"I saw the list," I reply, my confidence growing stronger with every syllable. If there's one thing I've figured out today, it's that these hottie evil alien dudes have baby fever. I've got something they want, and my only way out of here is to use it to my advantage. "I know I was 'processed.' And I'm pretty sure your bosses would be sort of pissed if you guys went to all this trouble and then zapped your incubator."

"Elvie." The doctor's tone is serious but calming, the voice he once used to make me more comfortable during exams. An unexpected shiver runs down my spine underneath my thermal suit. "I hate to break it to you, but you haven't been processed. The child you're carrying now is the one you came here with."

"I . . ." My brain is spinning. I haven't been processed yet? This should be good news, if it weren't for the ray gun trained at my forehead. "But the list . . ."

"The list showed what I wanted it to. It was important that my superiors believe you had been processed."

"Why?" I ask, truly puzzled. The doc is sabotaging our efforts to escape, while he's also hiding things from his own people. What is this guy playing at?

"*Why?*" he repeats, as though the answer is, like, über-obvious. "To protect you, of course."

"Gee, I'm touched. Are we having a special moment or something?"

The smile slowly creeps back onto his face. "I'm not going to kill you, Elvie." He does not lower his gun. "I'm sure we can find a use for you yet. So bright. And so much potential."

And okay, maybe I should just go ahead and take the compliment from the creepy dude with the gun aimed at me, but for some reason I'm not feeling so friendly. "Too bad Carrie and Danielle didn't have any potential," I spit. "Maybe you could have spared them, too."

"Sorry?" To his credit Dr. Marsden's looking genuinely confused. Although maybe they teach you that expression in evil alien medical school, I don't know.

"Carrie and Danielle. Remember them? The two girls you murdered in the hangar with your fancy little sabotage?"

"My goodness, you went through the *hangar*?" Dr. Marsden says. "I've been trying to shepherd you to the captain's quarters, not pick you off like flies. Why wouldn't you simply take the path through the ballroom? I left that wide open."

Shit. I didn't even *think* of that. "That would've been, like, a million times easier," I agree.

"A pity, I'll admit, but all things considered I'm relieved

that it's you who made it through the gauntlet." He raises an eyebrow thoughtfully. "Of course, who else but you could adapt so readily to such a terrible situation? You are a special one, Elvie Nara, there's no doubt in my mind. Hopefully someday you'll understand just how special."

"If you try to pull some lame-ass 'I'm your father' bullshit right now, I'm gonna lose it," I tell him.

His smile only broadens. "I do so envy your wit. Now, please be civil and step aside so I can return to my work, will you? We can talk more once your friends are in hand."

I might be doomed, I think, but if I can just keep the doc talking, there's a good chance I might buy the others enough time to get away safely. *Keep talking, Elvie. Keeping talking . . .* "Seriously, though, Doc," I say. "I don't understand why you're doing all this."

And to my relief he's still feeling fairly chatty. "Well, Elvie, you see, my people, the Jin'Kai, left a planet called Horon-4 more than a century ago—"

"No, I know *that* part," I say, before realizing I should probably let him prattle on as much as he wants. "I mean, you have to realize that the way things are going, you guys are going to run out of hosts eventually. Earth is the sixth colony, right? That means there's no more after this. Where do you parthenogenetic freaks go from here?"

"Ah, yes," the doc says. "Manifest Destiny with an expiration date. But as I think you've learned by now, things aren't always what they seem. Have faith that there is a plan at work. And now you must let me get back to that work."

"Maybe it's time you took a coffee break."

Not the best line in the world, admittedly, but when I see who's said it—standing behind Dr. Marsden outside the doorway—I break into a broad grin.

Dr. Marsden turns to see who it is, interrupting our expository interlude just in time to make out a Cole-shaped blur zooming at him with tremendous speed. In an instant Cole has knocked the gun from Dr. M's hand, and the two are fighting. I mean, *really* fighting, like in those old superhero flat pics where the guys just wail on each other, jumping off walls and busting out kicks and punches that have their own special sound effects. You can practically see the *FWOOSH!*es and *KAPOW!*s appearing over their heads as they pummel each other with attacks that no one should be able to inflict—or survive. It's another example of some of the tremendous differences between the Almiri, the Jin'Kai, and little old me and the rest of humanity.

Cole knocks Dr. Marsden to the ground and stands between us, a paragon of protective hunkitude. But then Dr. Marsden reaches out with one hand and flings an enormous metal trash can at Cole. Cole ducks—giving the can a clear path to my noggin. So much for Cole the Protector. There's a loud clang, and my vision goes all wobbly. I think I hear my name being called, but it sounds like I'm underwater. Am I underwater? I'm in the pool? Oh, crap, I have to save all those girls. The teachers are drowning the girls! I have to stop them. I have to . . .

I'm not in the pool. I'm flat on my back in the maintenance locker at the bottom of the *Echidna*, trying to escape from an evil band of baby-swapping aliens. And Cole is . . .

Cole! I rise from the ground, still a little shaky, and see that Dr. Marsden has Cole pressed up against the railing on the catwalk outside the locker. He's giving Cole's face a real pounding. Cole is dead on his feet, and Dr. Marsden's pushing him farther and farther over the rail, until his entire upper half is dangling over the perilous ten-meter drop. Dr. Marsden is saying something I don't understand—for all I know he's calling Cole a dirty donkey-punch enthusiast in Jin'Kai. What I *do* know is that Cole's toast if I don't do something. But what in this locker can I use as a weapon?

Um, dur, Elvie. How about the ray gun you've got crammed down your boobage?

In seconds I have the gun released from inside the sweaty confines of the thermal suit. I wrap my right hand around the butt of it, then the left, aim, and . . .

Drop it.

Seriously? My big moment and *that's* what I do?

So of course that sucks, because in addition to alerting the good doctor that I'm awake again, I've also ruined any chance of using this other really cool line I thought up to say right before I fried his alien ass.

"You know, Elvie, there are several exercises you could be doing to help with your hand-eye coordination," Dr. Marsden says, turning around to see me scrambling on all fours for the gun. He comes at me fast . . . but not as fast as Cole, who I thought was out for the count. Cole grabs the doctor by the arm, spinning him and slamming him into the rail so hard that the bar breaks away. But Cole must've gotten most of the energy sucked out of him earlier, because he can't manage to push Dr. Marsden off the catwalk. Instead, with one backhand slap, Dr. M sends Cole reeling over the edge.

"*No!*"

The scream comes from somewhere deep inside me. But rather than lose myself in the pain of watching Cole plummet to his doom, I reach out, snatch the gun off the floor, and, still kneeling, lock Dr. Marsden in my sights. He has regained possession of his own gun, and now we face each other in a standoff. My hands are trembling as I tightly grip the alien weapon.

"It's okay, Elvie," he says, smiling like a prick. "Just put the gun down. Put the gun down and you'll be fine. My brothers are already on their way. They're coming for the babies, Elvie, and after the children are delivered, we will spare your life. I can protect you, I promise. The other Jin'Kai will listen to me. But shoot me, and you sign your own death warrant. Your friends will die too. I guarantee it."

I could tell this dipshit that they're not my friends. I could tell him he just killed the love of my life, so to hell with his offer. I could bust out that new awesome one-liner I thought up specifically for him when I . . . Shoot, what was it? My head's still a little wonky.

I get woozy for a moment and my aim falters. I see Dr. Marsden ready his weapon.

"You're going to feel a sharp pain, dear, but it will last only a moment," he says bittersweetly.

That's when fate hands me a big fat overdue piece of good luck. The *Echidna* rocks hard with another convulsion, and there is a sudden buckling and a howling noise as somewhere near us along the hull atmosphere is sucked out into space with ferocious speed and intensity through a microscopic hole.

A Yeoman's Curve. Too bad the doc isn't sitting on the toilet.

The suction lasts only a moment before the edges of the hull crumple in toward each other, sealing the breach. But it's enough time that Dr. Marsden, outside the locker room on the edge of the catwalk, loses his footing and drops his gun, grabbing on to the broken rail to keep from flying away. On the floor inside the locker room, I am pulled forward, my knees scraping against metal, but I have the sense to block myself in the doorway. When Dr. Marsden regains his footing and looks up, I've got Cole's ray gun about three feet away from his chest. Now, what was that line?

Ah, screw it.

Without another word I fire three times. Dr. Marsden stumbles back, a genuinely stunned look on his face as he topples off the catwalk.

And then it's just me, alone. It's quiet. I lean my head down against the cool metal floor and begin to weep, rocking in the fetal position. I don't want any more of this. No more aliens. No more parasitic babies. No more dilapidated space cruisers. I lie there, crying, resigned to stay perfectly still until whatever happens to me happens.

And that's when I hear it.

"Elvs?"

No flipping way.

My eyes fly open. There, straining to maintain their grip on the grate of the catwalk where the rail broke away, are some seriously bruised, seriously dreamy fingers.

"Cole!" I scream. "I thought you fell! I thought you . . ." I scramble out of the locker to the edge of the catwalk. Sure enough, there he is, half dead, hanging on for dear life with one hand.

I grab hold of Cole's arm and try with all my might to pull him up, but the dude weighs a ton. I never realized he was quite so heavy.

"Cole, I can't lift you," I say, huffing with effort. "Can you get your other hand up here?"

"But what about this guy?" he asks.

"Huh?"

I peer farther over the railing until I see it. Cole's other hand has a firm grip on Dr. Marsden's ankle. The world's worst baby doc is dangling upside down, moaning softly. So . . . not dead.

Apparently marksmanship is not a skill I should boast of on my college application.

"Um, I dunno, drop him?" I suggest without much sympathy. "I mean, he is the saboteur."

"I, uh . . . Good point," Cole replies. Beautiful and stupid as ever.

And with that, Cole lets go, sending Dr. Marsden plummeting down headfirst to the solid titanium hull ten meters below. His last confused exclamation is clipped off midgasp.

SPLAT!

So . . . yeah. That happens.

I pull Cole up onto the catwalk and cradle him in my lap. "Oh, Cole," I whisper, kissing him all over. He looks like Rocky Balboa at the end of *Rocky IX*, the one where he fought

the Terminator. "Cole, baby, I'm so glad you're alive. I'm so—"
I stop talking when I see the look on Cole's face.

"Did you just call me 'Cole baby'?"

"Yeah, let's forget that ever happened."

"Agreed."

I push a sweaty lock of hair back off his forehead and
check for bruises. There are several, and some scrapes and
cuts as well. There's a deep gash on his arm where he hit the
rail. "How in orbit did you find me down here?" I ask.

"Well, there weren't that many other places you could
have gone. Unless you figured a way to tunnel behind the
convection ovens. Sorry it took me so long. I had to, um, slip
away."

"Slip away?" I ask. But I think I already know the answer.
Cole probably disobeyed a direct order from Captain Bob to
come after me, something I'm sure the doucher will relish
bringing up to his superiors if we get back to Earth.

"Elvs, I know . . . why you ran. I knew there had to be
something in those files you tried to hide from me in the
doctor's office."

I caress his hair. "I was just scared," I tell him.

"I know. I just wanted to tell you . . . I don't care. I mean,
I do care that they murdered my baby, but . . . I still love you,
Elvs. Nothing will change that."

I want to tell Cole right then about the mix-up, that for
some reason Dr. Marsden never swapped my fetus at all, that
he falsified the records for his own unknown purposes. But as
I'm about to whisper the good news into his ear, I notice that

Cole seems to have lost consciousness. Panicked, I rock his shoulders lightly, trying to wake him.

"Cole? *Cole?*"

As I cradle Cole in my arms, I swear I can *feel* him healing. His body is burning hot, and while it may be an optical illusion of the lights down here, the puffy bruises on his face seem to be, like, un-swelling right before my eyes. He turns onto his side and nuzzles his face against my thigh. I breathe a sigh of relief.

"Cole?" I ask again tentatively. He may look like he's getting better, but who knows what kind of internal damage Dr. Marsden inflicted? Even a godlike supercreature has a breaking point. When Cole doesn't answer, I nudge him more forcefully. "Cole, are you okay? Can you get up?"

A smile crosses his lips, and he peeks up at me with one eye.

"I was hoping if I didn't move you'd let me just lie here for a while."

I smack his arm lightly, but I'm smiling too. My smile quickly fades, however, because even this sweet moment can't erase the terrible reality of how screwed we are.

"We have to get back to the others," I say.

Slowly Cole sits up, rubbing the side of his face. "That's supposed to be my line."

"There are more Jin'Kai coming," I tell him, "and when they get here, we're *el finito*. Dr. M *was* luring everyone to the back of the ship, just like Bob suspected. He wanted us all in one spot so his buddies could scoop us up, nice and neat."

"Dr. M?" Cole asks, his face twizzled in confusion once again. "Bob?"

There's no time for explanation. I hoist myself to my feet and head to the maintenance locker, to look at the doctor's computer hookups again. I need to make sure I didn't miss any booby traps before. "We've got to warn them. Even if they launch the yacht before the Jin'Kai get here, they'll never manage to outrun—"

Thunk! The ship vibrates gently.

"What was *that*?" Cole asks as he enters the room behind me. "Don't tell me the ship's flying apart again?"

"No," I say with a sigh. "Worse. Our new friends have officially arrived."

I pick up Dr. Marsden's pulse emitter and smash it on the ground.

"Where's your communicator?" I ask Cole. "We need to get in touch with the captain. *Now.*"

"Um." Cole scratches the back of his neck. "I kinda ditched it when I came after you."

"What? Why?"

"The captain was very . . . detailed in his description of what he'd do to me if I followed you, Elvs. I figured it was better to have radio silence."

I check each of the lap-pads on the desk again, just for the slightest hope that I can tap into the intercom. But no deal. I guess announcing the results of yesterday's intramural volleyball matches was not high on Dr. Marsden's list of priorities once he came down here. But I refuse—*refuse*—to let some alien baby snatcher win after I've already killed him. I am not giving up.

"Then we're going to have to hurry," I say. "If they can't get to the yacht before the Jin'Kai find them, then they're going to need all the help they can get."

"Elvs, we're too far away. There's no way we can—"

"We don't have to jump through Dr. Marsden's hoops anymore," I tell him. "I already opened all the blast doors that aren't shielding us from the hull breaches, and I've got the lifts running again. We'll be there faster than it takes to . . ." I trail off. Hidden behind a window on one of the lap-pads is a surveillance camera display. But it isn't Bob and the girls that it's been keeping tabs on.

"No. Flipping. Way."

Cole squints at me. "What? What is it?"

"Cole, let's get going. We've got to pick something up on the way."

Riding the lift back up from the bottom of the ship is fast—so fast, that we make it to the lido deck in exactly thirty-three seconds. Nothing like an elevator to put twelve-plus hours of climbing through wreckage into perspective. By now Cole's wounds and bruises are almost completely healed. At worst he looks like he slept on the wrong side of the bed. I, on the other hand, am beet red, dripping sweat and garbage juice in my now totally unnecessary thermal suit, my hair matted to my head.

"And I thought I'd never find an outfit for the junior prom," I mumble.

"What?" Cole asks.

"Nothing."

When the elevator opens, we make our way past a series of exterior blast doors that are sealing the open side of the hull. There's scoring and burn damage all around the place.

"This is where our ship was docked," Cole says.

"I know," I say, and I try to add a bit of sympathy to my tone for his fallen compatriots, but honestly, at this moment, I have other things on my mind. Like what's behind the door to the utility closet, not three meters to the right of the scorched hull where the Almiri ship exploded, sucking more than half of Cole's buddies out into space. I jerk on the door handle, but it's locked or stuck or something.

But I can hear whispers.

"Hello!" I scream, banging on the door. "Open up!"

"Elvs, what are you doing?" Cole asks, looking around— making sure we don't have any unexpected company, I guess.

I bang on the door again. "Let me in there!"

Finally I hear a tiny voice from inside. "Who's that?"

"It's Elvie," I answer. "Elvie Nara?"

"Who?" the voice asks.

Then another voice chimes in. "It's that girl who fell on her butt in gym this morning."

My reputation precedes me. "Open the door, will you?"

There's a click as the person on the other side of the door undoes the lock, and at last the door swings open . . . revealing twenty-two completely unharmed girls, packed into the closet like sardines.

Cole is looking more confused than usual. "Elvie, what the . . ."

"I saw them on Dr. Marsden's setup. These are the girls

from the On Your Own class. The half of my classmates you haven't met yet."

"But . . ." Cole blinks. "They were with the commander when our ship exploded. They all died."

"Who's the commander?" asks a very not-dead girl named Amy, notable only because of the spread of red freckles on her cheeks. "Is he that dreamsicle Terrance who told us to hide in here until he came back? How come he left all these guns?" Resting against the wall of the closet, beside a huddle of crouched sophomores, is a pile of Almiri guns, pistols and rifles both. I guess the captain left them so the girls could defend themselves if need be.

"It's a really, really long story," I tell her. "I'll explain on the way, but right now we have to go. We're getting off the ship."

"Wait, we're leaving? Did something bad happen?"

"*I will explain on the way*," I say. "Bring the guns."

"What should we do with our babies?" a girl named Sara asks.

"Babies?" Cole's up on his toes, anxious. "Some of you delivered?"

Amy laughs. "No, silly." She twirls a strand of strawberry hair around her finger. "Our babies, for class?"

And sure enough, as I crane my head farther into the closet, I see that each and every girl is cradling a sack of flour, holding it close and careful like it was a newborn child.

I nearly bit it a dozen times today, and they've been nursing *flour sacks with diapers on*?

"Leave the cake mix," I tell them.

"But it's fifty percent of our grade!"

I grab Amy's flour baby and tear it open, spilling semolina all over the floor. The girls all scream in horror.

They'll get over it. I grab a rifle from the pile and motion for the rest of them to get up.

"Time to move it or lose it," I say, the butt of the rifle resting on my hip. I catch Cole smirking at me. "What?" I ask angrily.

"You're pretty awesome, Elvs," he tells me.

It takes us a little more than five minutes to get down to the aft section of the ship, right near the captain's quarters. I can tell we're getting close because of the gunfire. Or ray gun blast-o's, or whatever you want to call it. It's loud.

Shit, as they say, is going *down*.

Cole and the other girls and I creep along one of the side hallways, getting as close as we can without being spotted by the Jin'Kai. Even when we come across the one lookout they've placed in our path, Cole—in a nice twist—points his ray gun in the right direction and neatly takes the guy out with a shot to the throat before he even notices us.

Cole and I peek our heads around the corner as the sound of shooting grows louder.

We're currently standing in the doorway of one of the side entrances to the captain's quarters, which leads down, via a ramp along the wall, to a luxurious sitting room, decorated like a parlor on a nineteenth-century ocean liner. Another ramp on the far side winds around the opposite wall and, along with our ramp, leads down to the sunken sitting area filled with plush velvet sofas and armchairs, meant for entertaining smaller parties of well-to-do passengers. There's even an ornate bar to one side, probably made out of real mahogany. Superclassy.

Or at least it *was* superclassy, before, you know, all the holes and burn marks and stuff.

Bob is ducking for cover behind the bar, single-handedly holding back what appears to be an entire squad of Jin'Kai goontroopers. It's unclear how much longer he can hold them off with only a pistol. From this angle I can't see any of the girls, but I'm assuming Bob has them in the main quarters behind him, through a door that leads to the captain's stateroom and, farther along, the loading bay and small hangar that houses the infamous captain's yacht.

"All right, girls," I say, turning to face the On Your Own class before we storm the scene. "Remember what Cole told you. Stay low. Don't die."

"You guys should be motivational speakers," Amy tells me.

I'm about to motion for the troops to *movemovemove*, when Cole grabs my elbow.

"Elvs," he whispers, "are you sure this is a good idea?"

"It's a terrible idea," I reply. "But it's the only one I have. Now let's GO!"

I don't know much of anything about the Jin'Kai, other than the fact that they are apparently miserable bastards who hold very little value in human (or Almiri) life. But one thing that's fairly clear is that they are highly militaristic. Which is why I think it's so impressive how completely unprepared they are to suddenly find themselves flanked by two dozen pregnant teenagers, ray guns blazing. We rain down laser-y hell on them, their cover useless. They return fire as they retreat through the rear entry that sits at the back center of the room, but they don't manage to strike anything other than one girl's funky perm. Which is really not such a crime, if you ask me.

"We're not hitting anything!" Sara cries out as she blasts away indiscriminately into the room, taking out a very expensive-looking chaise longue. And she's right on that count. It's clear that I'm the only one in the group who has logged any hours on Jetman.

"Just aim for their faces!" I scream as I let the blast-o's fly. The nice thing about these fancy Almiri weapons is that they don't have any kickback when you fire them.

"No," Cole cries. "Aim down! Shoot at their feet!"

"Wait, why?" I ask. Who's he to question my commando skills?

"This lot can't hit anything they're aiming for!" he replies over the din. "If they aim low, chances are they'll hit something by mistake!"

"Hey!" Amy shouts, offended. But just as she does, she wings one of the retreating Jin'Kai in the knee and he crumples to the ground, where Bob has a clear shot to put him down for good. "*Hey!*" she says again, more brightly. "It worked!"

The Jin'Kai have fallen back completely out of the room in an attempt to regroup. What they don't know is that I brought one of Dr. M's handy dandy lap-pads with me, which I use to remotely seal the door behind them. For the moment, at least, all of us "good guys" are in the captain's quarters, and the baddies are not. We scurry down into the room, where Bob greets us.

"Nice work, Archer!" he says, clasping Cole by the forearm. "I didn't think you had it in you."

"Don't thank me," Cole says. "This was all Elvie. She found and neutralized the saboteur and all his booby traps, rescued the other girls, and hatched this little bit of battlefield strategy."

Captain Bob looks at me with the sort of blank stare you'd give an opossum you just found out could play the ukulele.

"Not bad for an incubator, huh?" I say.

The shocked expression on Bob's face is replaced by a strange, warm smile. I can only assume that it's equal parts glad to see me, impressed with me, and feeling like an absolute shit for his behavior earlier.

But what do I know from smiles?

"Not bad at all, Elvie," he tells me. "But we're not out of this yet." And just like that he's back in captain mode, all seriousness and hard angles. "That door won't hold them for long, and there's at least another full squad on board. And . . ."

"And what?" I ask. It's not a good sign when the steely hero types trail off like that.

"They aren't from around here," he finishes.

Cole's eyes go wide. "You don't mean . . . Devastators?"

"What the hell are Devastators?"

"They're Jin'Kai, but not born from human mothers," Cole explains. "They're from a previous Jin'Kai colony world. The host species there was a little more . . . Well, you know the poster you had in your bedroom of that old flat pic, *Alien vs. Predator*?"

"Wait, are they like the Alien or the Predator?"

"Kinda both."

"And you call them *Devastators?*" I thought these guys were supposed to be creative supergeniuses.

"Why don't we talk about it on the yacht," Cole says.

As if on cue, there's a tremendous crash from behind the door I closed on the Jin'Kai, as though something seriously bad and burly is trying to bust through. The metal frame begins to buckle in. We take that as our sign to hightail it the hell out of there, running toward the captain's main quarters at top speed.

I have never been so happy to see my Hanover classmates.

"You're alive!" Ramona shrieks, giving me a big bear hug before she realizes what she's done. I have to admit, I'm just as thrilled to see her. Our new gang squeezes into the captain's quarters—which were clearly not built to house thirty-six pregnant girls, one newborn Jin'Kai baby, two Almiri sharpshooters, and the head of Hanover's now defunct AV club. But everyone seems too happy to be alive and reunited to notice the cramped space.

"I was wondering when you were going to get back," Natty says, patting me on the shoulder in a weird sort of halfhug. "Ooh, and I love your new outfit. Very avant-garde."

Another crash from the sitting room lets me know that the Jin'Kai have broken through the door. Blaster fire starts zipping through the doorway, thankfully missing everyone. Other Cheerleader's baby, which Heather has strapped to her chest in a makeshift sling made of an old velvet slipcover, begins to wail, frantic screams piercing through the sound of gunfire. Bob slams shut the door we've just entered, but this door, in keeping with the décor outside, is made of wood. Even as Bob and Cole hurry to hoist a massive ornate desk in front of the door to block the entrance, the door begins to visibly splinter with shots from the other side, and as strong as our two Almiri heroes are, I'm afraid they'll never get the desk in place in time. Desi scoops Kate up in his arms and races her down the hall toward the loading dock to the captain's yacht, limping as he goes. Ramona and I are just beginning to corral girls in that direction as well, when I notice Other Cheerleader. She is struggling with Heather, pulling the howling baby away from its sling.

"Give me that thing!" she shrieks at Heather.

"You told me to *carry* him!" Heather insists. "What are you doing? He's upset!"

"*Give* it to me! It's *mine*!" And with one final tug she frees the baby and barrels not toward the safety of the yacht but *toward the flipping splintering door*.

"What the hell are you doing?" Britta shrieks as her BFF rushes toward the enemy. "Are you a total chromer?" As uncomfortable as it is to know that Britta and I are having the exact same thought at the exact same time, I'm more concerned about just what is happening. Other Cheerleader's eyes are about two sizes too wide as she stares in our direction, one hand on the doorknob and the other around her bundle of evil alien joy.

"Don't you see?" she shouts, but she doesn't seem to really be looking at anyone in particular. "We should just surrender. We have their babies. That's what they want!" And with that she tugs open the door and disappears down the hallway. The gunfire on the other end stops momentarily, as if even the Jin'Kai are confused by this turn of events.

Britta tries to run after her, but in a moment of true stupidity I decide to risk my neck for Little Miss McSicker and tackle her to the ground.

"Stay put!" I scream into her ear. "You can't help her!" Britta lets out a feeble moan as she watches her friend go.

I can hear Other Cheerleader shouting as she approaches the Jin'Kai, but from my angle on the floor I can't see anything but the open door. Britta, though, she can see it—I can tell just by the look on her face as she watches helplessly.

"Don't shoot! Don't shoot!" Other Cheerleader wails. "I have one of your babies! I just had the baby! Don't shoot! Here, here you go. Just let me live, God, please. Oh, thank you, thank you. Here he is. I just . . . What the fuck is wrong with your face?"

There's a terrifying roar, like a lion screaming into a bullhorn.

And a sickening *fttt* sound.

Then a thunk.

Britta's face instantly turns the color of sour milk, and I can feel every muscle in her body go taut underneath me. "She doesn't have a head anymore," she says flatly. "They cut off her head."

A shot rings through the door and catches Bob in the knee, knocking him to the ground. The Jin'Kai are rushing the door again now, the sound of boots and something else—footsteps with a much heavier gait—stomping along side by side, and it's obvious that there's no way Cole can close the door and barricade it by himself in time to save us. Bob, seeming to sense this, grabs something small and oval-shaped out of his vest. Something with a button on it. No, not just a button.

A detonator.

"Get them onto that yacht," he orders Cole.

And without hesitation Cole leaves his post at the door and begins pushing girls toward the back passageway to our getaway ship. But I just lie there, Britta still wedged underneath me. Looking at Bob.

He rises up to his feet, wincing at the pain in his shattered knee. When he sees me, he winks.

"Go on, Elvie," he says. "You haven't saved Archer's ass yet."

I never even learned his real name.

Bob limps out into the sitting room, gun blazing. I pull Britta to her feet and run toward the passageway. There's a sizzling sound of laser hitting flesh, and I hear Bob cry out. And then the explosion. The grenade fills the sitting room with napalm or something equally pleasant, the force of the blast so strong that, even from a room away, Britta and I are knocked right back to the ground. The door frame crumbles, and on the other side come inhuman screams, which must be the Jin'Kai and Devastators, on fire.

"Elvie, let's go!"

It's Cole, snapping me out of my daze. I get to my feet again and run after him. We, all of us, race down the passageway, around the corner, and toward the hatch to the yacht. I shove my way through the throng of girls already packed into the tiny ship, to get to the cockpit console. The yacht is decorated like some kinky 1970s sex pad, complete with leopard prints and water bed. I push my way through the curtain of hanging beads to take my place in the captain's chair, a pair of fuzzy dice hanging above my head.

No one seems to have any problem with my being there.

Cole plops himself down next to me in the copilot chair as I fire up the controls. "Everything good to go?" he asks.

"Just need to do a system check, and then we're out of here. Undo the docking clamps. It's those switches to your left. Cole," I say, pausing for just the briefest of milliseconds. "How are we going to outrun their ship?"

"We'll worry about that when we have to, Elvs. Just get us out of here, okay?"

"I might be able to help with that," Desi says from the back. We all look at him incredulously. "I know the specs for their transport. We can outrun her if we dip down into the ionosphere and run a counter-rotational course back to the surface."

We just stare at him blankly.

"I want Kate to be safe," he says. "Nothing else matters. Nothing."

Overwhelmed, Kate immediately starts sucking face with Desi. And I'm back to flipping switches.

"Um, don't you need to open that thing?" Ramona asks, pointing to the hangar door in front of the cockpit window. "Unless you're planning on smashing through it?"

"Thank you, Ramona." I whistle through my teeth as I find the button for the hangar door. Then I begin the start-up sequence.

Power.

Life support.

Engines.

. . . Engines . . .

ENGINES.

That's when I let loose with a string of curses that would make even the saltiest astronaut blush.

"What's wrong?" Cole asks.

"The engines are dead." There's no use whispering about it. We're screwed.

"Can't you reroute power from another system?" Desi asks over the din of the *"We're gonna die!"*s from the Greek chorus behind us. He peers over my shoulder at the console, Kate still glued to his side.

"It's not the power; it's the actual engines," I say, reading the diagnostic on the screen. "They're total dinosaurs. The manifolds are all cracked. The fuel lines aren't even *there*. They must have been removed or disintegrated or something." It's not fair. Not after all this, after the pool, the explosion, the hangar. After Bob just . . . "I'm sorry," I say. "This yacht isn't going anywhere."

"They're going to get through that rubble any minute!" Kate screeches.

Thank you, Queen Obvious.

Beside me Cole takes a deep breath. "We need to think of something," he says. "Come on, Elvs. You know every centimeter of this ship."

Think, Elvie. *Thinkthinkthink.* "But we've *exhausted* every centimeter of this—" And then, suddenly, I have it.

I pull out my phone from the front of my thermal suit.

"What the hell are you doing?" Britta asks.

I answer calmly as I flick the digits with my thumb. "I need to make a phone call."

Each clunk of Jin'Kai boots stomping up the passageway sends a tiny tremor down my spine. Our enemies are walking slowly, no doubt anticipating a volley of gunfire. But when the chatter echoes out from inside the yacht, they all stop. I hold my breath.

"What are we going to *doooo?*" comes the nasal whine. "They're going to kill us and wear us like coats or something!"

The Jin'Kai exchange a few hushed words in their alien tongue, and then begin moving even more carefully toward the small ship.

"I'm too *young* to die!" a slightly higher-pitched voice chimes in. "I can't believe this is happening. I've never even kissed a *boy!*" A little more, just a little more . . .

"What are you *talking* about?" The first voice responds. "You're *pregnant.*"

"Well, yeah, but I never *kissed* him. It's, like, totally different. Nail polish, hair products, boys, boys, boys."

I roll my eyes.

The Jin'Kai are very close now. From where I'm crouched I can't see anything, but I can smell them all right. A sharp, pungent stench pierces my nose. It's like nothing I've ever come in contact with before—wretchedly sour, the scent so thick it seems to line the inside of my nose and mouth as I breathe, creeping its way down my throat and burning through my lung tissue. I can hear their skin *slick-slick* as they walk, and their breathing is raspy, unsettling, inhuman.

These must be the Devastators. I *really* don't want to meet those guys.

The yammering from the cockpit reaches a fever pitch as the two arguing voices vie for glass-shattering supremacy, and the Jin'Kai and Devastators rush up the ramp into the yacht, barking commands at their would-be captives. I can't help but smirk as the last of the Jin'Kai walks up the yacht's ramp, expecting to find a gaggle of frightened girls . . . .

Only to find my phone propped up on the cockpit console.

"Hi, fellas." I hear Ducky greet them through the tinny phone speaker. I can almost see him putting down his giant bowl of cereal, smirking at these freakish baddies, who've been taken in by a teenage boy chattering to himself in falsetto. "Wow, what is up with your faces?"

"Okay. Now!" I say, and with a solid kick the metal door of the ship's outer baggage compartment, where we've been hiding, pops open, and we all jump out into the loading bay. I tap the controls on Dr. Marsden's lap-pad and with a *shunka-shunka!* all the yacht's external security doors slam shut and lock.

We make our way back up the passageway amid the racket of the Jin'Kai futilely blasting away at the thick titanium doors.

"You're sure they can't get out of there?" Natty asks as we run.

"Sure they can," I reply. "If they keep at it for, I dunno, the next ten hours." The yacht's security doors were designed to protect the captain and VIPs from the most extreme attacks. I'm certain they can withstand considerably more punishment than even the Jin'Kai guns can dole out. And since I disabled the controls inside the ship, there's no way for them to get out . . . at least not before the *Echidna* breaks apart.

Which, by the looks of things, is going to be soon. The ship is groaning and creaking as we make our way through the newly accessible direct passageway, back toward the hangar bay where the Jin'Kai ship is docked. What wasn't sparking and hissing before is doing so now. Suddenly the ship jolts sharply. We're thrown into the wall.

"The ship's artificial gravity is going screwy," I say, picking myself off the floor. I offer a hand to Heather, still visibly shaken after the incident with Other Cheerleader. "We're getting pulled farther into the Earth's atmosphere. At this rate the ship will be down in less than an hour."

"Then wasn't it nice of our friends to prep their ship for our departure?" Cole asks as we head into the open door of the waiting Jin'Kai vessel.

I can't help but agree.

The only Jin'Kai on board is the pilot, who doesn't even see the shot that kills him.

"Nice shooting!" I declare, looking around to see who blasted him.

Meekly, Amy stuffs her ray gun into her back pocket. "I think I could get the hang of this," she tells me.

I situate myself at the control panel, but immediately notice the problem. "Shit!" I cry. "I have no idea how to fly this thing!" The layout of the controls is, quite literally, alien. I can't tell which button powers up the fusion cells and which one microwaves frozen burritos.

"Here," comes a voice from behind me. "Let me."

It's Desi, who takes his place at the control panel with a sort of calm dignity I've never seen from him before. "Like I said, I know these specs inside and out."

And for once I am more than happy to let someone else take the controls.

The Jin'Kai ship lifts off the platform and heads out the hangar door that I've remotely activated, and we pull away from the *Echidna* moments before it starts to buckle and collapse in the Earth's lower atmosphere. It burns a trail in the sky like an enormous shooting star as it hurtles toward the ground, the Jin'Kai still trapped helplessly inside the captain's yacht with no one but Ducky for company.

I hope he's telling them his best knock-knock jokes.

"We made it, girls!" Cole shouts, and everyone goes nuts. Like, bonkers. You'd think we'd just escaped from evil alien baby snatchers or something.

"Where are we going now?" Ramona asks.

"Headquarters, to start," Cole answers, "In Pennsylvania. The Poconos, to be precise."

"The Poconos?" Ramona snorts. "What, do all the Almiri go around masquerading as superhot ski instructors?"

"It's better cover than you might think," Cole says sheepishly. "Look, you've all been through a lot, and most of it was done to you without your knowledge. I don't think that's right." He looks me straight in the eye as he speaks. "If we're all going to live together, each one of you, individually, has to decide what's best for you. We're going home, all of us. And the choices that were taken from you, I'm going to see that you get those choices back to make for yourselves."

I love that dumbass alien.

Desi is busy tapping something into the computer, and maybe I'm paranoid, but I still don't totally trust the guy. I catch Cole's eye and motion to Desi.

"What are you doing there, Des?" I ask. Cole's hand reaches slowly to his holstered gun.

"Syncing with the *Echidna*'s bio-rhythms monitor," Desi says, finishing his typing with a flourish. He looks up at me, grinning. "Tragically, every person at the Hanover School—faculty, students, 'guests'—was killed as the ship fell to Earth."

The import of what Desi has done is not lost on anyone. If the Jin'Kai think we're all dead, they won't come looking for us.

"Why would you do that?" Cole asks, still suspicious. "Why the sudden change of heart?"

"There's nothing sudden about my change of heart," he says, wrapping an arm around Kate's waist. She swoons at his gesture.

"Oh, pookie-kins!" she coos, covering the side of his face with smooches.

"I've helped you escape with your young, Almiri," Desi says, addressing Cole. "All I ask is that I'm allowed to remain—*safely*—by Kate's side."

"But she's not even carrying a Jin'Kai baby," Chewie says through a wad of hair. "She's still got an Almiri in her."

"My concern is with the mommy," Desi says, and they both dissolve into a nauseating display of PDA that starts the girls all fawning about how romantic they are. Desi comes up for air long enough to ask Cole: "You think it can be arranged?"

"I guess I can find out," Cole replies, as if Desi just asked to borrow his dad's car. The girls cheer.

As Cole settles back into his chair, I can't help studying his face. He is the same beautiful, wonderful Cole I've always known, and yet there's something different about him now. He seems stronger, older. And it might be just my imagination, but I think the constellation of freckles on his left cheek is beginning to fade, ever so slightly.

"Cole?" I whisper. "I have to tell you something."

He turns to me.

"The Goober," I begin, clearing my throat. "It's . . . yours." I put a hand on my stomach. "It's still yours. Dr. Marsden told me, on the catwalk. It wasn't swapped."

The look on Cole's face as he takes in the news is pure happiness. Despite everything that's happened to him, everything that could have happened, he is happy in this moment. "Oh, Elvs!" he breathes, and he reaches toward me for a kiss, that look still splayed across his face. It's an exquisite sort of look.

Which is why I can hardly believe what I'm about to say to him.

"I'm not going to the Poconos."

"But the baby . . . ," he begins.

I pause. "I'm not sure what I'm going to do yet, Cole." He blinks, and I can tell there's so much he wants to say to me, but he doesn't. He lets me continue. "I'll tell you when I decide, but for now . . . I'm not going with you. I don't care if you have to lie or fight or argue or what, but I'm not going." I watch through the view screen as Earth grows closer and closer, welcoming us back from the longest, strangest day of my life. "I am going home."

Cole thinks about that, and nods slowly. Then, without a word of response, he punches up the comm.

"Home One, this is Archer. Do you read?"

A crackling noise comes over the comm, followed by that unmistakable voice.

"Loud and clear, Archer," James Dean says. "What frequency are you on?"

"Shit," Cole says, before switching to a secure frequency. "Home One, this is Archer . . . again. Do you read?"

"Good to hear your voice, kid," Dean says. "What's your status?"

Cole looks back at all of us crammed around the console, and smiles.

"Byron, do we have a story for you."

CHAPTER SIXTEEN

IN WHICH EVERYTHING WRAPS UP NICELY WITH ABSOLUTELY NO LOOSE ENDS

The first thing I do when we land is literally kiss the soil.

The second thing I do is retch a little bit. Because it's been a long day, and because, well, dirt tastes gross.

Dad and Ducky are already here, waiting for me. Which is kinda nuts since we had to land way out in the middle of farm country, a good four-hour drive from home. I'm pretty sure Dad didn't even remember to put up the parking brake. He hugs me so tight, I would remind him not to block my airways if, you know, my airways weren't blocked.

"Dearheart," he sighs. "I missed you so much."

I squeeze him back. "I missed you too, Dad."

Ducky is next. He walks over shyly at first, as though he almost isn't sure he recognizes me. I reach out a hand and, ever so gently, tug on his earlobe.

That's when he loses it.

"Good to have you back," he says, falling into an enormous bear hug.

"God, you cry like a girl," I tell him. But I'm crying too.

I say my good-byes to the others quickly. Most are easy, but saying good-bye to Ramona and Natty gives me a little extra phlegm in the chest.

"Make sure those Almiri bastards take good care of you," I instruct Natty. "Don't let them give you any shit."

She nods as she sniffles into my shoulder. "I won't," she replies. She looks up and gets this naughty little grin on her face. "You think maybe I could convince them to pose for a series of nudes?"

"That's one art class I might actually show up for," Ramona says.

I make to hug Ramona, but she punches me in the shoulder instead. "I . . . ," I begin, but she stops me.

"Here," she says, and she hands me a brand-new pack of cigarettes. Seriously, I don't know where she keeps those things. "You might need them," she tells me. "For the baby. You know, in case you decide to keep it."

I must inadvertently raise an eyebrow at that, because she just snorts. "They're medicated," she replies. "See?" I look at the label. Sure enough, Ramona is right — Immunity-Boosting Mist Sticks: 100 percent tar and nicotine free. It's right there on the box. "Jeez, you think I'm some kind of chromer or something?"

"I . . ."

She tucks the cigarettes into my pants pocket and punches me in the other shoulder. "I know you have to make up your own mind," she says. She's quiet, so no one else can hear. "But if you ask me, you'd make one hell of a mom. Even if the thing has antennae."

And with that she strolls off to the van that Cole has procured to take those that want to go to the Poconos. Every girl—besides me, that is—has agreed to go and at least find out more about the Almiri. Even Britta, though I don't know why. Maybe she's hoping they'll "deal" with her little Jin'Kai issue. She's slouched by the door of the van. I wave to her, a meager olive branch, perhaps, after all we've been through, but a heartfelt one. Britta's look, however, makes the skin on the back of my neck prickle, and then she turns away, her arms wrapped almost protectively over her stomach.

Cole is standing awkwardly beside me, shuffling his feet, so I give him a tight hug. "Are you worried?" I whisper, and I don't clarify, but I think he understands what I don't say. *Are you worried that Britta will rat you out about the Code? Are you worried what will happen to you when they discover you let me go? Are you worried what I'll do with this baby?*

"You just worry about you," he replies. "Whatever happens to me . . ." He stares at the ground. "I think I probably deserve it."

I give him a quick kiss then, right on his starkiss. "I'll be in touch," I say. "I promise."

He squeezes my hand tightly as I climb into the front seat of my dad's car. And I think he wants to say something else, but he doesn't.

As Dad pulls onto the street, I decide to break the silence. You know, bring us all back to what's truly important. "Can we make a stop on the way home?" I ask. "I need a new phone. Mine sort of maybe exploded."

Four days later—my due date looming ever closer—Ducky and I are in my room playing Jetman. Ducky claims he read a study that video games are good for calming the nerves of pregnant women, but I'm pretty sure he made that up. To our everlasting surprise, Ducky's normally douchy stepdad seemed more than agreeable to the idea of Ducky playing hooky from school to hang out with me nearly full-time. Zeke even convinced Ducky's mom to write him two weeks' worth of sick notes. Ducky says it's the most pleasant case of pneumonia he's ever experienced.

"So . . . ," Ducky starts, and just from his tone I know he's going to ask me another in a long line of questions about my experience with the Almiri and Jin'Kai. It's like he was given a front-row seat to his utmost nerd fantasy. He's been asking questions nonstop since the car ride home. He hands me the tub of peach yogurt, as if that's going to soften the interrogation. "These Almiri guys, they live to be, like, hundreds of years old?"

"So it seems," I say as I pour the yogurt generously over my bowl of black olives.

"And they're all, like, completely famous."

"Not all of them. Just some, I think. Like, apparently Mozart was an Almiri. And James Dean, obvi."

Ducky scratches his chin quickly before returning his hand to the controller.

"That's so messed up, faking your own death and then getting to be famous *again* doing something else if you want to. Are the bad ones, the Jin . . ."

"Jin'Kai."

"Right, are any of the Jin'Kai famous too?"

"I don't think so. They haven't been on Earth nearly as long. And they seem to be trying to lay low, you know, while they conquer the world. So they're probably not auditioning for America's Next Top Botanist or anything."

"But they're all superpretty like Cole?" The moment the words are out of his mouth, he scrunches up his face. "You know what I mean."

"Mmm," I say, trying to find the most succinct way to describe it so that hopefully Ducky will stop with the twenty questions. "The Jin'Kai are hot too, but kinda, like, burlier than the Almiri. More Jax Richter, less Hansel Wintergarden."

"Those dudes I saw on your phone up there were *not* good-looking, Elvie."

"The Devastators? I never got a good look at them."

Ducky shivers. "Lucky you."

"I think the definition of 'studmuffin' is different on the planet where they come from."

Ducky raises an eyebrow. "Wait, so is Hansel Wintergarden . . ."

"Not to my knowledge," I say as I pull a tornado kick out of nowhere for a double critical bonus hit. "Can you imagine the horror of getting stuck on a spaceship with him while he's singing 'Baby, Let's Go to the Prom with All Our Friends'? I follow up my tornado kick with a nuke-fist to the face, and Ducky throws down his controller in mock disgust.

"No more pregnancy handicaps," he tells me. "You are trouncing me, and it's not fun anymore."

"Suck it up, Pence," I reply. "And stop trying to distract me with your stupid questions."

Ducky thinks about that. "Just one more," he promises. I groan, focusing on the screen, but Ducky is undeterred. "How do the Almiri pick who to impregnate?" he asks. "Is there some sort of system, or what? Who tells them who they can sleep with? And how come the Almiri and Jin'Kai always have to be dudes? That's just patently unfair. Why can't there be a whole army of redheaded bombshells out there who need *me* for a good roll in the hay? And why did they—"

"Ducky!" I shout with a laugh. "Just give it a rest, all right? Isn't the fact that I survived a big alien throw-down in space enough for you?"

Ducky smiles at that. He picks up one of the yogurt-laden olives before thinking better of it and putting it back in the bowl. "Fine," he says, "I'm done."

"Thank you," I reply. And then I blast his avatar to smithereens.

We've just started our rematch when I finally decide to tell him. "Cole called this morning," I say slowly. I glance sideways to see how Ducky will respond to the news, but I'm having trouble reading his expression.

Today was the first I'd heard from Cole since I got back, so there was quite a bit of catching up to do. Apparently he told Byron—aka James Dean—that I miscarried on the *Echidna* during all the excitement, to explain my absence from the Poconos pregnancy party. "The girls all seem to be doing well," I continue. "Cole said that Ramona's old boyfriend Kyran was there. I guess she gave him quite an ass-whooping." Ducky smiles. "And Natty's going to start some sort of weekly art review going up there. Seems she's fitting in pretty well. No word about Britta, though."

"Yeah, Cole didn't mention her to me, either," Ducky replies with a shrug, and I'm so startled that I drop my controller. Ducky doesn't miss a beat, giving my avatar a roundhouse kick to the face.

KO!

"You talked to Cole?" I ask, incredulous. "When? How? Why?"

Another shrug from the master shrugger. "He gave me his number when we picked you up. Figured it would be good to have, I dunno, like, an emergency contact or something."

I am not at all sure if I like the idea of Cole and Ducky talking behind my back. Between the two of them, they know just about every secret I have. If they pooled their info, I could really be done for.

"So . . . you talked with Cole . . . ." The words taste funny in my mouth.

"Only once or twice. It's not like we're PIPs or anything. He was just checking in. He was curious."

"*About?*" I prod.

"About whether you'd made a decision yet."

"He could ask me himself."

"That's what I told him." Ducky looks up from the screen for just a split second. "Anyway," he says, more serious, "have you?"

I shake my head. "Nope." The days are ticking away, and I know I need to make up my mind soon, but . . . Have an Almiri or terminate the pregnancy? The pros and cons of each choice have been swirling around in my brain nonstop, and I'm no closer to deciding anything. I reach for the yogurt and take a deep scoop.

"If you could," Ducky asks, back to plugging away at the game, "would you change it? Would you go back in time and do things differently? You know, with Cole? Would you not . . ."

I close my eyes and think that through. If I had known, in that moment, that that one tiny decision would change my whole life, would I have decided differently? Would I have chosen not to do the dirty with Cole? I want to say yes. But honestly, I don't know. Try as I might to do otherwise, I might make the same choice again.

"You'll make the right decision, you know," Ducky says. He looks at the TV when he says it, not at me, but I know he means it. "Whatever you do will be the right thing."

"Thanks, Duck."

There is a soft knock on my bedroom door. "Dearheart?"

I look up from the game. "Come on in, Dad." He steps into the room. "You want to join us? You can sub for Ducky."

Dad laughs. "No, just wanted to see how you two were doing up here. I was setting up the new filing cabinet, and I needed a break." He rubs his shoulder.

"New filing cabinet?" Ducky asks.

"I needed one with extra drawers," Dad says with a nod. "Can you believe I only had *one* crisis folder on alien invasions?"

Before I can respond to that, the front doorbell rings downstairs.

"That must be the new crew of construction workers," Dad says. I'd have thought, with the whole daughter-in-a-space-emergency thing, that maybe he'd give up on his plans for the solar deck, but it's been going full-throttle. The sawing and banging outside the window has really put a damper on my afternoon naps. "I got a call yesterday that my normal crew was all reassigned. Can you believe that, right in the middle of the job? Anyways. Donald, would you mind letting them inside? Tell them I'll be there in just a second?"

"Sure thing, Mr. Nara," he replies. As he gets up, he pauses the game and looks at me. "No cheating while I'm gone," he says, and leaves the room.

After Ducky's footsteps fade down the stairs, Dad pulls something out of his pocket. An LED. "I wanted to give you this," he says, handing it to me.

I put down the yogurt and take it. Slowly I read the words on the page.

It is an official doctor's note, claiming that, after administration of the Gatling test, the fetus I am carrying has been determined to have CMS. My all-access pass to a legal late-stage termination with a certified physician. "How did you . . ." I ask.

"It doesn't matter," he replies, sitting down on the edge of my bed. "And before you say anything, I know you haven't made up your mind yet, and I'm not trying to force you one way or the other. I think you know what my opinion is, but in the end it doesn't matter. I just want you to have everything you need for whatever decision you make."

I snuffle back a sudden wave of tears. "Thanks, Dad," I whisper. My mind is roller-coastering out of control again, with the same thoughts that have been banging around in there ever since I learned about my situation. Do I really want to give up a baby, even if it isn't mine? Do I really want to *have* a baby, especially if it isn't mine? If I have this Almiri, that's it for me. I can never have a child of my own after that. Period. And could it really be considered a termination? I mean, there was no fertilization of any egg going on here. The thing is a parasite inside me. Cole's parasite . . .

Dad reaches across the space between us, to where I'm sitting curled in the armchair in front of the TV, and tucks a loose strand of hair behind my ear. "What are you thinking?" he asks gently.

I sigh. "I'm thinking . . ." One thing I know for sure is, if I *do* have this baby—and I don't know at all that I will—there's no way I'd *ever* let it be raised by James Dean and his merry band of babe magnets in the Poconos. The brief conversation I had with Cole in the bathroom of the *Echidna* was enough to convince me of that. This kid, even if it weren't mine, would need a more fair and balanced view of the human race than you can get from the top of North Knob. "All I keep thinking," I tell my dad, "is how, if I have this baby, I'll never go to Mars." I am definitely crying now. I swipe at a tear before it can escape down my cheek. "I mean, I don't want to be selfish, but . . . That's what I've wanted *forever*. How can I give up my whole life for a baby? For *someone else's* baby? For a *parasite*?" Dad presses his thumb against the line of my nose, blotting out another tear. "There's no way I'll be able to get into the Ares

Project, because I'll have this *thing* with me, slowing me down every step of the way. And I'll never get to see the world, the universe, anything. I'll end up . . ." Yep, it's turning into a sob fest. "I'll be just like Mom."

My father cocks his head to the side, curious. "Like Mom?" he asks.

"How . . ." I do my best to gather the words to explain. "How she marked all those places she wanted to go in her stupid book of maps"—I swing an arm in the direction of the book, propped up as always on my bookshelf—"and she never got to go to any of them because she . . . because she had me."

"Elvie." Dad waits until I'm looking into his eyes, and then he gives me the most soulful look I've ever seen. "Dearheart. Is that what you think?"

Sniffle. "What do you mean?"

"I suppose it's my fault. Talking about your mother—well, you know that it's very difficult for me. Very painful. I guess I just figured that if I buried the memories, they wouldn't sting so much. But I never meant to rob you of your mother. For that I am truly sorry."

Dad stands up and kisses my forehead gently. Then he walks to the bookshelf and takes down Mom's book of maps. He sits back gingerly on the bed and turns a page to show me.

It's my favorite map. Antarctica. I don't even have to look at it to know exactly where it is marked in red, right over Cape Crozier.

"Your mother fed penguins, right here," he tells me with a wistful smile. His finger lands directly on the dot that marks Cape Crozier. "They walked right up to her and ate out of her hand." He laughs to himself. "She must've told me the story a dozen times. Her group nearly died of starvation on the trek there, but she still hid a package of granola just for those damn birds."

"Dad?" I say, confused. "But . . ."

He turns to another page. Peru. "Your mother rode a burro all the way up the Inca trail." Another map. He points to a dot off the coast of New Zealand. "And here's where she solar surfed for the first time." He flips to another page, but before he can continue on, I rest a hand across the book. He looks up at me. "Your mother was a remarkable woman, Elvie. Olivia did a lot of things in her few short years on Earth."

"But . . . I thought the book was . . . Why did she keep all these maps? I thought they were places she wanted to see."

"They were places she *loved*," Dad replies. "Your mother was quite the explorer. I should've told you more about her, I know I should have. I always thought it'd be easier to do when you were older." He looks at my baby bump and laughs weakly. "I guess you're old enough now."

Inside me the Goober kicks. It's the first time I've felt his presence in I don't know how many days, and the feeling is strange, jarring.

"Dearheart," my dad continues. "Your mom kept this book of maps for you. She was so excited that . . ." I think for a second that I hear his voice break, but he swallows it down and begins again. "She was so happy when she found out she was having a little girl. She said she wanted to share the world with you." He closes the book of maps and places it in my lap. "I guess in some small way she did."

I look at the book in my hands. Feel its weight. All the places in the world my mother adored and wanted to share with me. All that love, in one book.

"If you want to go to Mars," Dad tells me, "one little baby won't stop you. It will take longer, it will be much more difficult. But there are other paths besides the Ares Project. If that's what you want, Elvie Nara, I won't *let* you fail." With that he stands up slowly, gives me another kiss on the forehead, and walks to the door. "I've got to go talk to the new construction crew," he says. "Show them some of the gremlins to watch out for."

And he leaves me alone with my thoughts.

I spend a long time with that book. I don't open it, just run my hands across its cover. Thinking about the places I've never been. Thinking about my mother. Thinking about the baby inside me.

I don't know anything about the Goober, not really. I don't know what he'll look like, act like, want to eat. He'll be a completely foreign creature to me, without a single strand of my DNA.

What I do know, though, is that he could grow up to be someone amazing. Important. Because all those famous Almiri that Cole listed in the bathroom that day on the *Echidna*—Mozart, Marlowe, Alexander the Great—he was right about them. There *was* something incredible about each of them, and they contributed so much to human society. Now that someone's given me the chance to adopt baby Mozart— whether I asked for it or not—can I really turn that down? How can I deny the world a child who may one day grow up to cure

CMS? Or compose the next great symphony? Or develop a brave new political philosophy?

And if *I* raise the baby, I can make it more than simply the sum of the great genes it was born with. I can teach it the things that make human beings so wonderful—the joy of blowing bubbles on a sunny day, the opportunity to go to school, to have a family. The unconditional love of a real, true parent who already knows that great things lie in store for him, and can help him prepare for them. If I raise this baby, it will be mine, DNA or not. And I can prove once and for all that Dr. Marsden was wrong. When it comes to caring for the species or caring for the individual, sometimes you don't have to choose.

I look at that book of maps for a long time, thinking. Then I pick up the LED my father gave me and look at that, too.

My mind made up at last, I wrestle my phone out of my pocket and open a new message box.

keeping it

I send the blink to Cole and set my phone on the bed. Then, my heart a thousand times lighter for having made my decision at last, I flop back into my chair.

I am having this baby. And I will share the world with him.

As I'm crossing to the bathroom to wash my face, I hear my dad deep in conversation with one of the new construction workers. He's essentially giving him a lesson on the history of the fusion boom, as if he needed or wanted it. I can only imagine the amount of eye rolling that's transpiring.

"So you see, that's why you can't use those cheap new filters on these old vents," Dad's telling the guy. "You need to go with good old reliable coral. The new junk will just disintegrate because these old systems have such a variable rate of flow. You get what you pay for, that's what I always say."

"Mmmm," I hear the construction worker reply, thoughtful. "We can do that, sure, no problem. Whatever you want."

I pause, right at the top of the stairs, my feet frozen to the carpet. There is something about that voice, the way it is both smooth and dangerous at the same time, like dark chocolate with a hint of chili powder. Very man's man.

And much too sultry for a replacement construction worker.

I tiptoe to the edge of the top stair and tilt my head down to get a look into the living room. Sure enough, there is my father talking to a burly man in a sleeveless tee. The dude has his back to me, though, so I can't make out anything more than his full head of thick, lustrous hair.

Until, glancing around the room, he shifts just enough so that I get a good sideways look at his face.

Deep, dazzling brown eyes. Sharp cheekbones. Chiseled chin. Like a young Marlon Brando but with a sexy five o'clock shadow.

Holy.

Shit.

Without another thought in my brain, I dash to my bedroom and shut the door. Somehow the Jin'Kai have found out I am very much alive and still pregnant. Somehow they have come to get me. I have got to get out of here.

I whip my phone out of my pocket and send Ducky a blink.

construx workrs r jinki.

It's not until after I push send that I realize my blink may be completely inscrutable. But no time to deal with that now. I cram my phone back into my pocket and cross the room to the window, which I yank up with a startling *whoosh!* Then, on my hands and knees and swollen belly, the Goober and I make our way quickly but delicately out across the half-finished solar deck. If I can just make it to the garage, maybe I can get to Dad's car and get out of here. They're bound to take off after me if I go, which should leave Dad and Ducky in the clear. Of course, that means I should probably figure out somewhere to, you know, *go*.

I immediately find myself with a splinter in my palm, but there's no time to think about that now. The planks are sturdy but hardly meant for a human to walk on yet—especially a human-and-a-half like me. The boards creak under my weight as I shuffle my way farther to the edge of the deck. Then, with a deep breath, I ease my body over the edge and begin lowering myself backward off the deck, feet first, then knees, then—*WHOMP!*—belly, my hands gripped tightly around the supporting beam underneath.

And that's where I am, dangling with my ass in the breeze, gathering the nerve to brace myself on the beam and then shimmy the last ten or so feet to the ground, when I hear my father's voice again.

"And here's where you'll find the—*Elvie, what in God's name are you doing?*"

I look down, and standing below me are my father and six brooding hulksters in construction caps and carpenter jeans. So this is how it's all gonna end, captured like a fish on a line by six walking clichés.

"Hello, Elvie," the lead construction guy says, locking eyes with me. "Seems you're just as crafty as Marsden said."

Before my father can say a word, the Jin'Kai bruiser knocks him to the edge of the driveway and pulls a small, smooth oval disc from his back pocket, which I realize must be a weapon. He trains it on me. I close my eyes and wait for the shot.

It never comes, because just at that moment the garage door bursts off its hinges, and my dad's shiny classic Toyota comes crashing through, with none other than Ducky at the wheel. The Jin'Kai turn around just in time to see Ducky blast right through them. They go flying like bowling pins in every direction. The car screeches to a halt, and Ducky kicks open the driver side door and looks up at me.

"Come with me if you want to—"

"Stop right there," I command him, shimmying down to the ground as quickly as I'm able. I will not allow Ducky to indulge his sci-fi geekiness while we're still in a life-and-death situation. The Goober shifts uncomfortably as I touch down.

Ducky shrugs as he exits the car, clearly proud of his little action-hero moment. He helps my father to his feet.

"What in blue blazes . . . ," Dad begins, totally befuddled.

"Aliens, Dad," I tell him. "Folder three."

With that he snaps into crisis mode. "Right!" he shouts.

He moves Ducky out of the way and slides into the driver's seat. "I'll take the wheel, thank you, Donald," he says, taking a moment to assess the damage to the front of his car. "Good Lord, son. I just had this thing restored."

I've made my way to the passenger seat and am opening the door when Ducky grabs my arm.

"Uh-uh," he says. "Not with the package you're carrying." And he ushers me to the backseat before piling in next to my dad.

"But—" I protest.

"He's quite right, dearheart," my dad chimes in. "The backseat will be safer. Now, let's *vámanos!*"

Dad peels rubber as we zoom out of the driveway and turn down the street. I twist around in my seat and see that the Jin'Kai are recovering. They've picked themselves off the pavement and are running down the driveway after us, but once they realize they can't catch up, they turn toward the van that's parked outside the house.

"They're coming after us!" I cry.

"Not to worry, sweetie. This baby can hit one twenty if need be."

"I don't doubt your driving or your car, Dad," I say, twisting again to look nervously down the road. "I'm worried about traffic."

We're heading down the road toward Bryn Mawr, and the late afternoon traffic is already in high gear. Or no gear, as it were. Nothing is moving, and thanks to a few goofy traffic lights that haven't worked properly in more than a hundred years, only one car is getting through the intersection at a time. Clearly this will not do.

"Hold on!" Dad yells. He veers out of his lane, and to my astonishment/horror he hops up onto the sidewalk. Fortunately there's no one walking on it, or we might have a few new hood ornaments. There are several honks of indignation from those stuck at the light as Dad blows through the intersection and starts over the low bridge that crosses the creek. Another car is coming from the opposite direction, and Dad has to swerve quickly to avoid clipping it. We're going so fast that we actually hop off the road and seem to be flying for about two seconds before we touch back down lightly and continue on our way.

"How about that suspension, eh?" Dad says, beaming with pride. "Just like I always say. You get what you pay f—"

"Uh, Mr. Nara," Ducky says, looking out the back. "We've got company." Sure enough, the Jin'Kai van is coming over the bridge, flying off the road just like we did, and landing just as smoothly.

Cole, I think. *We need Cole.* If I can just get in touch with him and let him know where we are . . . I reach for my phone, but it's gone. I must have dropped it when I was crawling out onto the deck. So that's *two* phones the Jin'Kai have cost me now.

"Ducky, I lost my—" A sudden pang makes me stop. Well, perhaps more than a pang. It feels like my stomach and my liver have suddenly decided to switch places. Let's call it a *pong.* I yelp, and Ducky turns to look at me with concern.

"What's the matter?" he asks.

"Nothing, I just—*Oof.*" Another one. "I'm fine. It's just indigestion or somethi—*agh!*"

Ducky's eyes go as wide as saucers. "Elvie," he says. "You're going into labor."

Shit balls. What is it about these alien pod babies that they love to pop out at the worst possible times?

"It's all right, dearheart," Dad assures me. "Folder three, scenario four: going into labor during a high-speed chase with extra-terrestrials. We'll be at Bryn Mawr Hospital in four minutes flat." He makes a sharp right-hand turn against the light at the intersection as angry motorists honk at him. The Jin'Kai get momentarily stalled behind the ensuing jam. "I've got the route memorized."

"No," Ducky says firmly. "Turn around."

"Turn around—why?"

"We're not going to Bryn Mawr. We need to get to Lankenau."

"But folder three—" Dad starts.

"Just do it," Ducky says firmly. He's so authoritative that Dad does the unthinkable and deviates from his plan. "Elvie, we've got this," Ducky assures me. And somehow, in this one second, I believe him. "Just do your breathing exercises." He leans over the backseat and grabs my hand. "Come on. That's it. *Hoo-hoo-hoo, hee-hee-hee. Hoo-hoo-hoo . . .*"

"Keep that up," I warn him, wincing around another contraction, "and I'm going to hit you right in your 'hoo-hoo.'" But I squeeze his hand tightly and begin my Lamaze breathing.

Dad zigzags down some back roads until we're rerouted and heading toward Lankenau Medical Center, right on the edge of the west city line. We rapidly approach the intersection of Wynnewood and Lancaster, a busy shopping area with left-hand turns so wiggy that they always back up traffic for blocks. To make matters even worse, on the east side of the street as we approach the shopping center is the Sunset Towers senior citizens apartment complex. The blue-hairs who live there always pull out of that driveway like they're putting their lives in God's hands. Sure enough, as my dad speeds down the road, one such little old lady flies out in front of us in her enormous old Hyundai without even looking. I scream for my dad to watch out. He zips around her deftly, and we hit a bump in the road. Suddenly the hood of the car—which must have been pretty banged up when Ducky crashed through the garage—flies open, blocking the windshield and our view completely.

"Shit!" Ducky screams.

My father has a somewhat different reaction.

"*All right!*" he hoots. And just like that he's got his head stuck out the window, driving like a madman.

"Prepare for any situation, Elvie!" he hollers, his words getting lost in the wind.

There's a screeching noise behind us. I turn and gape. The Jin'Kai are right on our tail. "Hold on. I'll lose 'em!" Dad shouts, ducking past a pickup truck whose driver has a few choice words for us as we cut him off. Dad continues that way for several blocks, weaving around minivans and all-terrain SUVs, bobbing and darting with his head still out the window and his arms stretched to the wheel. For some reason the Jin'Kai are not shooting at us. I'm guessing that they must not want to call more attention to themselves than they already have, because Dad's big ol' noggin would probably make for some fun ray gun target practice right about now.

"This is like the *best* game of JetKart ever!" Ducky squeals gleefully.

We're flying straightaway down the avenue now. The traffic is heavy but the path is direct, and Dad weaves between lanes deftly, his head still stuck out the window. He's actually *enjoying* this.

"What are we going to do?" I ask. I can feel the perspiration dripping down my forehead. "We can't just go to the hospital. They'll be right behind us. We need—"

Ducky squeezes my hand even tighter and offers me a reassuring smile. "It's okay," he says. "Don't worry about anything. I've got it covered."

Ducky's got it covered? I guess stranger things have happened. I try to focus on my breathing and trust that, somehow, my bestie can mastermind a plan to foil an entire Jin'Kai strike force.

We screech into the hospital complex. The hospital itself sits almost a quarter mile in from the road, with several car paths winding up and around the hill it's situated on, making for some wicked nausea-inducing hairpin turns as Dad whips around to the ER ambulance entrance. Ducky and Dad are out in a flash, flinging open the door to the backseat, where I'm sitting in a puddle of my own fluids. No time to contemplate how disgusting *that* is. They lift me out of the seat, supporting me on both sides, and an orderly races out of the sliding doors of the hospital pushing a wheelchair.

"My daughter's in labor!" Dad cries. He and Ducky plop me into the wheelchair and spin me around toward the door. I can just make out the Jin'Kai van bursting over the horizon, heading straight for us. I grab Ducky's sleeve.

"Ducky, they're here!" I grunt out through the contractions. Ducky just trots by my side as the orderly wheels me into the ER.

"Elvie, I *told* you . . ." And then he points, straight ahead, as we pass through the sliding doors.

Leaning against the reception desk, like he doesn't have a care in the world, is Cole. He's tabbing through a chart as if he were a flipping doctor or something. When he sees me, a goofy grin crosses his face.

"Hey there, good-lookin'."

My heart does about fourteen somersaults, which syncopate nicely with the rapidly increasing contractions.

"Cole, the Jin'Kai—"

"It's okay, Elvs," he assures me, making his way to us. He brushes some matted hair off my forehead. "Ducky told me everything."

I turn to Ducky, incredulous, and he shrugs with a sheepish grin.

Our reunion is interrupted by the six faux construction workers who run into the ER behind us. I try to leap out of my wheelchair, but Ducky puts a hand on my shoulder.

The Jin'Kai stop cold when they see Cole. He walks calmly toward them and goes toe-to-toe with the lead baddie, the one who nearly zapped me while I hung midair from the deck.

"I think you guys are turned around," Cole says. "The new construction is over in the east wing."

The Jin'Kai edges closer to Cole and whispers menacingly, "Get out of our way, Almiri. We're here for the girl."

"And here I thought you came for the cherry blossoms."

"Don't make a scene," the Jin'Kai growls, "or we'll be

forced to kill you *and* the girl. You're outnumbered."

Cole scratches his chin. "Well, math was never my strongest subject," he says. "But it seems to me"—he looks to either side of the ER—"that you may want to count again."

The Jin'Kai look around the room, and so do I, and that's when I notice it. The two dreamy blond doctors talking next to the vending machines. The lithe strong-armed male nurse writing in a chart and his two equally hot-tastic buddies standing by the elevator bank. Even my orderly, now that I stop to take notice, is a fox. I realize the situation at the same time as the Jin'Kai—the entire ER is populated by Almiri, who are now not so subtly tracking the construction workers with their eyes.

"How did they all get here?" I whisper to Ducky.

"Elvie, they've *been* here," he tells me. "Round the clock since you've been back."

Cole leans in to the lead Jin'Kai, that smug grin of triumph plastered on his face. "Now, about not making a scene . . ."

Before the Jin'Kai can back out of the sliding doors, a team of security guards that look like they stepped out of a bachelorette party catalog step into place behind them, weapons already drawn. But even as the head baddie and his cohorts are placed in restraints, the guy finds it in him to smirk.

"When all is said and done," he says with disdain, "you may wish you'd lost here today."

"This is our home now, Jin'Kai," Cole replies very seriously. "Our planet. We don't have room for noobs."

The security guards drag the Jin'Kai away, and Cole returns to my side, his face immediately lightening.

"Hey, babe," he says. "Was that badass or what?"

"Very," I grunt. "And I'd love to celebrate with you, but right now we're kinda—*oof!*—*having a baby.*"

Cole kisses me on the forehead, and he, Ducky, and my dad follow along as the orderly pushes my wheelchair into the delivery room.

I'm not gonna pretend like labor is all cream and peaches. It's disgusting and loud and painful, every second of it. But I've got Cole—who's right at my side, squeezing my hand—and Ducky, and Dad, and one seriously pretty doctor to get me through it, so I guess things could be worse.

"All right, Miss Nara," the doctor tells me, "it looks like the little guy's just about ready to come out. Have you thought of a name for him yet?"

"Oliver," I tell him, "after my mom."

"Your mom's name was Oliver?" Cole asks.

"Sweetie," I say in between contractions. "You are very pretty. But you're dumb as a brick."

Cole gives my hand an extra tight squeeze and brings his face down close to my ear. "I love you, Miss Elvie Nara," he whispers.

And maybe it's just the rush of the moment, or the total incoherence of having a *living being trying to escape my body*, but I look at Cole, right in those enchanting eyes, and I tell him, "I love you, too."

"You do?" he asks, all incredulous.

"Yeah. I mean, I think so. I mean, yeah. I do."

And Cole laughs at that, and then gives me a kiss, right on the mouth. It is wet and warm and wonderful.

"*Ewwww*," Ducky exclaims from his post down by Dr. Handsome.

"What?" I cry, wrenching away from Cole and trying to hoist myself up on my elbows to see. "What's going on? Is something wrong with the baby?"

"Oh, I didn't mean 'eww' the baby," Ducky says. Quite frankly, I never imagined my best friend would ever be that up-close-and-personal with my girl parts, but once you've nearly lost your life and your bowels in the span of fifteen minutes, privacy doesn't seem to matter so much. "Everything on this end is perfectly *delightful*. I meant 'eww' stop kissing."

"Thanks a lot, Duck."

"Any time."

"Does this mean . . . ," Cole asks, squeezing my hand a little harder. "Does this mean we can, you know, get back together again? I mean, since you're having my baby and everything?"

"I'm having *my* baby," I remind him. "And one step at a time, all right?"

He smiles. "All right."

"Okay, Miss Nara. This is it," the doctor announces. "I need you to push. *Push!*"

And I do.

It is in this moment—finally pushing the goddamn Goober out of his hiding place in my uterus—that I look at the faces in front of me. Cole. Ducky. My dad. All of them watching, waiting, to meet my new baby. And, even through the mind-searing, body-splitting pain, I smile. I am pretty lucky, I think.

"Push again, dearheart!" Dad cries.

Cole squeezes my hand so tightly that I momentarily can't feel the pain in my groin.

And Ducky, he looks at me and says, "I just want you to know, Elvie, that this is, like, the *most* intense horror movie I have ever seen."

Yeah. Pretty lucky.

Push.

Push.

"A little harder!" the doctor says. "I can just make out the head!"

And as I *push, push, push,* my three fellows lean in to look.

Push.

Push.

"Yes!" Cole pumps the air. "There's the starkiss! He's beautiful, Elvie. Such a gorgeous little face." My dad is grinning from ear to ear. Ducky high-fives the doctor. I would join the party too, but you know, I'm a little busy, what with two thirds of a baby still inside me.

"Almost there, Miss Nara!"

Push.

Push.

PUSH.

And I flop back onto the bed in relief as I feel little Oliver leaving me completely. My bones have turned to jelly. It's official. I'm a mom.

I look up, smiling, my entire body overcome with exhaustion. "Can I see him?" I ask the doctor, who is cradling my little bundle of joy in his arms.

That's when I notice their faces. The doctor. Cole. Ducky.

Even my dad. They all look completely bewildered.

"What's the matter?" I ask. Suddenly I'm afraid that Dr. Marsden was messing with my head when he told me that I hadn't been processed. "It's Jin'Kai, isn't it?"

"No, Elvie. It's not that." Cole seems positively dumbstruck. "It's . . ." His voice turns to a nervous whisper as the doctor hands me my baby.

"It's a *girl*."

WHEN YOU THOUGHT THINGS
COULDN'T GET ANY WEIRDER . . .
DON'T MISS THE NEXT CHAPTER OF
THE EVER-EXPANDING UNIVERSE.

BOOK TWO OF THE EVER-EXPANDING UNIVERSE

A STRANGER THING

MARTIN LEICHT & ISLA NEAL

"WHO KNEW SCIENCE FICTION
ABOUT UNWED MOTHERHOOD
COULD BE SO VERY HYSTERICAL?"
—KIRKUS REVIEWS

IN WHICH OUR HEROINE IS LICKED BY A BEAR

"Everything's okay, Elvs. Seriously, like, no worries."

Easy enough for Cole to say—he didn't just push a *person the size of a watermelon* out of his private parts. Nor does he currently find himself under the piercing gaze of several suddenly constipated-looking Alien McHotHotts.

Now, I know I was preoccupied and everything, but I am *certain* that there were only five people in the room as I grunted, strained, and (let's be perfectly frank here) farted the Goober out of my womb and into the world. Besides me, there was Cole (my baby daddy), Dad (my dad), Ducky (world's best bestie), and one smokin' Almiri doctor. And baby makes six. Or so I thought. Now I realize that several others were either waiting in the wings the entire time, or standing elsewhere out of sight. And now that my little bundle of joy is lying in my arms, they have all stepped forward, each one looking grimmer than the last.

"It's female?" one of the dudes asks the doc gravely.

The doctor nods, stunned. And everybody in the room—even my own father—is staring at me and my newborn like we just snuck a jumbo-size combo meal past the ticket guy into the movie theater.

"I'm confused," Ducky says, scratching his head. "I thought Almiri were always male."

"I was under a similar impression, Donald," my father says beside him. "Fascinating."

Maybe "fascinating" isn't the word I would use, but yeah, I'm a little perplexed myself. From everything Cole's told me about his race (or species, or whatever you want to call an extraterrestrial group that traveled to Earth thousands of years ago to use human women as hosts for their offspring), I took it as fact that the Almiri only have one gender—a gender that requires a dongle. And yet . . . looking down at the gooey infant in my arms, it's hard to argue that she most definitely has a full array of girl parts.

"Take it," one of the Almiri snaps. "And secure the host and the father for questioning."

No sooner are the words out of his mouth than all of the Almiri burst into a flurry of panicky action. One of the fellows standing in my peripheral vision rushes forward and snatches the Baby-Formerly-Known-as-Goober away from me before I can even react.

"Hey!" I shout, reaching clumsily to grab my baby back, but the thief is already moving toward the exit. Another Almiri falls into step behind him.

"What do you think you're doing?" I hear Cole demand.

"*Ibrida*," the baby-napper says . . . to which Cole (who, I should mention, can barely speak English most days, let alone whatever language *that* was) responds with a completely blank stare. "It's a mule," the guy says—as though that clarifies anything. His voice is even but strained. "Did you know about this?"

"Know about what?" Cole asks. "What are you talking about?"

"What's going—ahhh!" I turn at the sudden sharp pain and see the doctor remove the syringe from my arm. "No, please, I . . . ," I begin, but words are failing me. *They have my baby. They took my baby.*

I turn my head—which, holy *crap*, just got forty pounds heavier on my neck—to see if I can catch another glimpse of my daughter. Instead, I see only the second Almiri, who turns to Cole with a disgusted look on his face. "You just can't help finding shit to step in, can you, Archer?"

"I don't even . . . Hey, come back here with my kid!"

That's when whatever night-night cocktail the doc has fed me begins to set in, so the Almiri at the door blocking Cole's path and clasping him by the arms, trying to immobilize him, goes kinda fuzzy. Little swirlies dance in my field of vision, mixing in with the sight of Cole head-butting his restrainer—but *that* can't be right, I think. The guy was his friend just moments ago, when they arrested the Jin'Kai heavies who chased us here in the first place. I'm pretty sure the head-buttee crashes to the floor, but there's three more of him who take his place. And then I *know* the happy mommy juice is really starting to get to me, because I see two more Almiri move in beside Dad and

Ducky, and calmly but forcibly escort them out of the room. And that shit just doesn't make any sense.

"It's all right, Elvie!" I hear Cole call, his voice growing fainter. "Don't worry about anything! I'm here!"

The rest is all purple unicorns and gold stars singing show tunes, until everything goes black.

The first thing I wonder, as I come to, is whether or not the handcuffs shackling me to the hospital bed will be covered by my health insurance. My *second* thought, obviously, is what the flip am I doing handcuffed to a hospital bed? And where in the hell am I? This certainly doesn't look like a recovery room at Lankenau Medical Center.

The haze quickly lifts, and I shuffle through a few blurry memories, mostly overheard snippets of conversation.

". . . did we have any indication . . . ?"

". . . Archer doesn't seem to have a clue . . ."

". . . never met a bigger numbskull . . ."

". . . wreck was not salvageable . . ."

". . . decrypted full records from the ship . . ."

". . . last time this happened . . ."

". . . what Byron has to say when we get there . . ."

". . . have you seen my lip balm . . . ?"

None of which is helping me solve Elvie Nara and the Case of the Mystery Room. There are no monitors, nursebots, or any other medical gear keeping track of vitals or anything like that. As far as I can tell, the room consists of four white walls, a door, and a bed.

And me, of course.

"Hello?" I call out. There is no response for, like, a while, and I start to worry that I'm in some sort of soundproof room, or that maybe I'm just hallucinating the whole weird scene. Creepy dead silence, that's all I get. But right when I'm really about to panic, the door slides open and in walks the same doctor from the delivery room, carrying a slender lap-pad and a scowl.

"Hey, are you my OB/GYN?" He scrolls through something on his lap-pad and does not respond. "What's with the cuffs?" I try again. "You guys afraid that I'll Hulk out on you?" I'm trying to play it light, hoping my gay spirits will take the edge off the fact that they're treating me like a Jin'Kai POW, instead of, you know, their old pal Elvie. But the doc doesn't seem to want to play along. "How long have I been here?" By the way my stomach's growling I'm guessing it's been at least a day, if not longer.

At last the doc looks up. "You're feeling normal? No discomfort or odd sensations?"

"I'm hungry." Understatement of the millennium. "Where is every—"

"I'll see about getting you some food. In the meantime, Alan here is going to take you upstairs for a little while."

Before I can ask if Alan is the doc's imaginary six-foot white rabbit, the dude comes walking through the door.

Most of the Almiri are young-looking, but this guy's stiff demeanor makes him look even younger, like he's fresh out of the Almiri Acadamy for Impregnating Unsuspecting Earth Girls. He's bland as toast, too. Standard-issue haircut, no scars or wacky tattoos to help place him in a lineup. As Ducky might put it, if Alan were on *Star Trek*, he'd be wearing a red shirt and an expiration date.

Alan glances at me. "Uh, what am I supposed to do, wheel her?" he asks.

"She can walk," the doc replies. "We can undo the cuffs for now, I think."

The doc strolls over and jabs a code into the handcuffs, quickly ridding me of my shackles. I rub my wrists like they're terribly sore, but it's mainly just an effort to garner a smidgen of sympathy.

My captors do not seem to notice.

"Hey, guys?" I say as they help me to my feet. "Two questions for you. First, where's my baby? And second, could I get something to wear besides this gown? My butt's, like, flapping in the wind."

"There's a robe in the closet," the doc replies. And with that, he walks out the door, leaving me alone with Alan.

"He didn't answer my first question," I say. "That was kind of the important one."

"Come on," Alan says, clearly anxious to be rid of me. "Byron's waiting."

I sit quietly in the middle of the room where Alan has deposited me, tugging nervously at the trim of my not-quite-long-enough terrycloth robe. It solves the butt-on-display-to-the-world problem I was having, but I'm still flaunting enough leg to make a burlesque dancer blush. If I was feeling particularly whimsical, I might enjoy conjuring the image of the Almiri prancing around in these robes that, at best, are going to cover them to mid-thigh.

I can hear several voices coming through the adjoining side door keep rising and falling—some sort of group powwow. The volume occasionally reaches a decibel that indicates that nobody inside is feeling very polite.

Alan didn't leave anyone to guard me while I wait. Well, I should say, he didn't leave any *person*. I am currently surrounded by a literal menagerie of assorted animals. And we're not just talking goldfish and kittens and parakeets, your typical household pets. Oh no. There are two large flamingos crowding me on the faux leather chair that's busy sticking to my thighs. Seated across from me on the ornate stone desk are the three smallest monkeys I've ever seen, fighting over a banana that's bigger than they are. Behind me, two foxes and a badger are wrestling with one another, and a peacock fans its feathers in a defensive stance as it tries to convince the meerkat to look elsewhere for a playmate.

And then, of course, there's the bear.

It's probably not a real big one, by bear standards, but honestly, when you're sitting three feet away from a bear—any bear—it seems like the most gigundous thing in the entire universe. This particular *Ursus whateverus* has been blocking the main doorway, licking its own cinnamon fur, for the past ten minutes, oblivious to anything else in the room.

I look away (because everyone knows it's rude to stare at animals that can eat you) and find myself studying an oddly familiar oil painting hanging over the mantel of the fireplace. I know I've seen the thing before somewhere, but I can't place it. Old-school mustachioed dude with a chin dimple, sporting a seriously ugly orange-and-green headscarf.

Lots of terrible thoughts are running through my mind at the moment, and only a few of them are bear-related. Obviously, my Almiri hosts are not quite as benevolent as they once appeared. The fact that my baby turned out to be a girl must either have them confused, scared, or both. They've done something with the baby, something with Cole, something with my dad and Ducky. And they're clearly planning something for *me*. A sane person would sit quietly and pray to come out of this whole situation in one piece.

I have never been accused of being a particularly sane person.

I rise to my feet with thoughts of bursting into the side room, all bravado and bluster, and shouting that I'm tired of being shoved around by different factions of extraterrestrials who think they're entitled to mess with my reproductive organs, and that I'm sick of waiting in this zoo, and if they're going to interrogate me or torture me or whatever, could they please just get it over with already? But I don't get that far, because that's when Cinnamon finally realizes I'm in the room. He flops forward onto all fours with a harrumph and plods toward me.

"Okay, okay!" I shout. My mind is racing. Which are the sorts of bears you're supposed to try to scare off, and which are the ones you're supposed to play dead with? Shit. "I'm sitting," I tell it, more gently. And I plop back down on the chair. "See how well I'm sitting? Like nobody's business. So heel. Or mush. Or . . . go away."

Cinnamon does not go away. He shuffles over to me, and I realize with a great amount of uneasiness that even on all fours he's looking *down* on me. He starts nuzzling my shoulder, and his head is so huge that he practically pushes me off the chair into a pile of something one of the birds has left behind. His fur is rough and scratchy, prickling my neck. Less "teddy bear" and more "roadhouse creeper." I want to grab the thing's jumbo noggin and shove him away, but I have this overwhelming desire to keep all my limbs attached to my body, so I just grip the edge of the seat until my fingers turn white, and try to look nonchalant. Like I get nuzzled by bears all the time.

"I'm just sitting," I mutter. Cinnamon continues to get his nuzzle on. The giant furball is now licking my neck and the side of my face, long leathery slurps that leave trails of sticky bear saliva on my skin. "Not going to let a big-ass bear licking half my face off get in the way of a good sit," I squeak out in between slurps. "Why don't you try sitting too?"

The door to the side room opens up, and the muffled voices from within are suddenly clear.

"You cannot expect us to go along with this," comes a strident voice. It's angry. Pissed, even. "It goes against every protocol!"

Then I hear another voice, calmer and steadier than the rest.

"I've made my decision, gentlemen." I look past the furball assaulting my personal space to see a tall, slender figure in a red jacket standing with his back to me in the doorway. "I do not make it lightly, nor should you take it as a point of debate."

That's when another angry voice chimes in. "The Council will never stand for such a blatant disregard for procedure!"

The figure in the doorway shifts casually. "The Council

will have their say, of course. But so long as I'm the commander of this station, I will make the call."

"But—"

"Thank you, gentlemen, that will be all for now," the man in the doorway interrupts. "Alan, please see that the arrangements are being made. There's a good lad." And with that, he turns and steps inside to join me, closing the door behind him. And the moment he enters the room, he owns it.

Byron.

That's what the Almiri call him. Their leader. I've seen him before, of course—on the communication view screen back on the *Echidna*, when we were trying to avoid being blown to smithereens. But I've seen him elsewhere, too. *East of Eden. Giant. Rebel Without a Cause.* No matter what the leader of this group of parasitic alien life-forms chooses to call himself, I will always think of him as James Dean, my mother's favorite 1950s flat-pic dreamboat.

"Drusilla!" he booms to the gargantuan mound of fluff that's currently using my face as a tasting menu. "Get down off of Elvie, please. That's a good girl." And just like that, the licking stops. Drusilla backs away from me, giving me one last sneeze as a parting gift before retreating to her master.

I've got to say the guy looks pretty good for a dude who's supposedly been dead for 120 years. He pets Drusilla on the head as he makes his way over to his desk. He's followed by two dogs, a black-and-white long-haired Newfoundland and a large husky. Drusilla grumbles at the dogs as they pass, and the husky scurries away, tail between its legs. The Newfoundland, though, despite weighing approximately as much as one bear poop, defiantly nips at Drusilla before wandering right up to me and putting his head in my lap.

"Boatswain likes you," Byron says as he flops down in his big swivel chair. "That's a good sign. Poor Thunder here"—he rubs the timid husky under the chin—"has always been a little shier with new people. Haven't you, girl?"

I scratch Boatswain behind the ear, because it seems like the most normal thing I can do. Bears, peacocks, *James Dean talking to me about his pets*—those are the things that I'm not quite ready to process yet. "Dogs seem to have a thing for me," I say, kneading the bed of Boatswain's floppy ears a little harder, until he lets out a satisfied whine.

"Amazing creatures, aren't they?" Byron replies, putting his feet up on the desk. He looks very much like he did when he was James Dean in *Rebel Without a Cause*, perhaps a bit older but not by much. He's even wearing a red windbreaker and some antique-looking jeans, which should seem ridiculous and sad, but somehow he pulls it off effortlessly. Utterly assured of himself, cool, and in charge of the whole room without even trying—that's James Dean, all right. "*The poor dog*," he goes on, leaning back in his chair with his eyes closed, as though reciting words he's said many times before. "*In life the firmest friend, the first to welcome, foremost to defend.*"

"Uh," I say. "Yeah. Sure."

Byron's eyes pop open, and he smiles warmly. "It's nice to meet you at last, Elvie Nara." He seems awfully friendly for someone who's kidnapped me and taken my newborn child. "I've heard only good things."

I nod and clear my throat. "Look," I start, as much of an edge to my voice as I dare use with a guy who has a pet bear, "you're a very busy alien, I'm sure." His smile shifts sideways a little, amused. "So I'm not going to waste your time with the totally appropriate amount of indignation that I should feel right now."

"That's awfully understanding of you."

I fold my arms across my chest, ignoring Boatswain's whines for more scratching. "Why don't you just cut to the chase and tell me what the hell is going on?"

Byron's eyes brighten, like I just complimented his haircut. I cannot detect even an ounce of the cruelty that someone like, say, Dr. Marsden had when he had me at gunpoint back on the *Echidna*. By contrast, this Byron guy doesn't seem to find the whole situation all that serious. Like hospital bed abductions are as common as artificial grass.

"Elvie, everything's going to be fine, don't worry. You haven't done anything wrong. Your baby is in perfect health, and your father and friend are safe and in our care."

It's his casual tone that's more disconcerting to me than anything else. I was kind of expecting a villainous speech. Boatswain starts licking the sweat from my palm. As interrogations go, I have to admit, this is all pretty chill. Everything, as Byron says, seems to be going fine.

"What was all that shouting about? Me?"

Byron waves me off dismissively. "Don't worry about all that. Some of the lads have their knickers in a bunch over this whole Ares mess."

"Ares?" I ask, confused. "The Ares Project?" The Ares Project is the multitrillion-dollar government program whose purpose is the wide-scale terraforming of the surface of Mars for human habitation, the first such attempt of its kind. The idea that the Almiri are behind it in some way probably shouldn't shock me as much as it does—since I'm well aware of how technologically advanced they are, and how they've made a habit of getting their hands into every major scientific break-through of the past several thousand years. It's more of the fact that Byron's dropping the information so nonchalantly that has me baffled. After all, aren't I some sort of prisoner here?

"A bit of an issue with some cyberterrorism, nothing that should slow matters down terribly, but enough of a breach that some folks are nervous." Byron leans forward in his chair. "Cole told me how keen you were on being a part of the proj-ect someday. You don't know how happy that would make—"

"Cole," I say. "What have you done with Cole?"

Byron's face turns slightly more serious, but it's undercut by his tickling one of the miniature monkeys with his index finger. Seriously, the thing is the size of a Ping-Pong ball.

"Cole has broken our cardinal law," he says simply, "and will have to be dealt with accordingly."

I can feel the color leave my face. "What do you mean, 'dealt with'?"

"Don't worry. It's not—"

"Don't *worry*?" I screech out. He might as well tell me not to blink. "Don't WORRY?" Drusilla lurches to her feet at my sudden outcry, like there's some threat she needs to deal with, but one low growl from Boatswain and she backs off. "Please don't hurt him." My voice is shaky, and I am *this close* to crying, but I use every ounce of strength to hold it together. Boatswain drops his head into my lap.

Again, Byron's pretty chillaxed about the whole scene. "Ah," he says calmly. "The drama of young love." And he closes his eyes once more. *"I tell thee, minstrel, I must weep, or else this heavy heart will burst; for it hath been by sorrow nursed, and ached in sleepless silence."* He opens his eyes once more and gives me a bittersweet smile.

"Cole told me all about your Code, or whatever," I say, petting Boatswain with both hands in an effort to calm myself. "I know that what he did was bad. I mean, I know *you guys* think it was bad." Cole was not supposed to sleep with me. The Almiri have superstrict rules about which human ladies are meant to be knocked up and how frequently an Almiri can do the deed, in order to avoid overpopulation and the eventual destruction of both our species, since Almiri pregnancies lead to sterility in their human hosts. Cole was originally sent to Ardmore, PA, to knock up übercheerleader-mega-skank Britta McVicker, but he disobeyed orders because, as he put it, he "fell for me."

Also, he's sort of a chromer.

"But it wasn't his fault," I go on. "I, like, totally seduced him. He tried to resist, but . . . what's going to happen to him?" I whisper around the lump forming in my throat.

"You've learned quite a bit about us the past few weeks, Elvie," Byron says. And perhaps I'm misreading things, but there seems to be some sympathy in his voice. "And seeing that this is the case, I hope that you can appreciate the reason for the Code, and why our adherence to it is so important. I can't overemphasize what a big deal it is." The monkey lets out a miniature cheep of insistence until Byron returns to tickling him. "Like, humongous big."

"But Cole didn't *mean*—"

Byron cuts me off. "I've tried to shield Cole from repercussions with regards to your situation, as best I could. It was no easy task, mind you. The fact that Cole violated protocol and had relations with a second host—someone who clearly had not been vetted for hosting—was not only foolish but dangerous. For both our species." He clears his throat. "However, in light of the heroism Cole displayed on the *Echidna*, I felt compelled to petition for some degree of leniency for the boy. It was not the most popular sentiment, I can assure you, but I was able to arrange a sort of . . . tenuous probation for young Mr. Archer. Which might have been the end of it, were it not for his unfortunate behavior at the hospital. At this point, my hands are tied. One simply does not head-butt a superior and walk away, even under the cheeriest of circumstances."

So Cole *did* head-butt that dude. At least I wasn't hallucinating.

Byron shakes his head in a mannered gesture of regret. "He will be punished, Elvie, but I swear on my life, he will not be harmed."

"Oh, well, if you swear on your *life*," I reply. Still, I am relieved by the news. But . . . "That doesn't explain why you've taken me or my dad. Or Ducky. And where is my baby girl?" I shove Boatswain away, suddenly very frustrated. The dog whines piteously.

Byron stands up, and Boatswain and Thunder snap to attention and move into flanking position beside him as he walks to the front of the desk. He sits on the edge and looks down on me, much like a hip teacher from a bad sitcom about to dole out "serious life lessons." Byron temples his fingers in front of his mouth and considers me with an intense gaze.

"Elvie, do you know how incredible your baby is?" he begins. "I mean, all babies are incredible. Life, I mean, wow, right? Whether it's human or Almiri or, I dunno, whales . . . it's just a miracle. But *your* baby . . . she's even more special."

"Because she's a chick," I say.

"Because she's a chick," he confirms. "Almiri do not have baby girls." He reaches across his desk for a round red tin and pops open the top. "Biscuit?"

I seem to have lost my appetite. "So, my daughter's, like, a miracle squared?"

Byron sets the tin on the desk and rests one hand on each of the heads of his two dogs. It's a measured and self-conscious pose. I can totally picture him practicing in front of the mirror for dramatic situations just like this. Then he lapses into that annoying closed-eye reciting thing again. "*What a whirlwind is her head, and what a whirlpool full of depth and danger is all the rest about her.*" He opens his eyes again. "No," he says, and the ice that's suddenly in his voice startles me a bit. "Not a miracle. On the contrary, the child is a great danger."

"A danger?" I ask, baffled. "To who?"

"All of us," Byron says. And just as quickly he snaps back into levity. "Seriously, you should try one of these biscuits." He plucks one from the tin. "They're delish."

I'm not even sure I manage to shake my head. *Dangerous?* How can one baby girl be a danger to anyone, let alone a guy who's well over a hundred years old and has two Academy Award nominations on his resume?

"What's an *ibrida*?" I ask. Byron chokes on his biscuit, trying his best to hide a double take.

"Where'd you hear that word?" he asks pointedly.

"At the hospital, when your goons decided to go all batshit crazy on me."

Byron tries to smile casually. "That's not really important at the moment," he says, and it's the first time I don't buy the acting job. His eyes shift to the biscuit tin for a split second, before he looks back up at me. "I know you are somewhat aware of the history of the Almiri, Elvie, but let me explain it to you a little more fully, so that you'll understand." He nudges Thunder's nose away from the biscuit tin. "We came to the Earth nearly five thousand years ago. Humans were one of six viable host species in the entire galaxy, and they were remarkable creatures. We sought to make them more remarkable. You are familiar, to some extent, with Greek mythology?"

"Sure," I say, bracing myself for yet another history lesson. The Almiri seem to love them. "Zeus, Athena, all that crap."

"Exactly," Byron says. "Those were us."

"Excuse me?" I say, eyebrows up. "Sorry, but not for one second do I believe that you guys are *gods*."

"No, of course not," Byron replies. "You misunderstood my meaning." Beside him, Boatswain manages to sneak a biscuit from the tin unnoticed, but I decide to let this go unmentioned. "When we first arrived on Earth, we couldn't blend in as we do now, so of course our appearance was strange to humans. They had stories of deities already in their society, and whenever anyone happened to spy one of us, they simply slotted us into those appointed roles. Burning bushes, talking clouds, showers of gold, these were ways for them to describe what was beyond their understanding. Thunder, no. You *just* ate." Thunder glares at Boatswain, who's licking the crumbs stealthily off his doggy gums. "Soon," Byron continues, oblivious, "we Almiri had our first children, and they appeared to be human. Their abilities, however, made them stand out."

"Lemme guess," I interject. I'm wondering when this is going to lead to a smidgen of information about my baby. About my dad and Ducky. About Cole. "Achilles, Hercules, Perseus . . ."

"They were the first Earthborn Almiri," Byron confirms. *"Thy Godlike crime was to be kind, to render with thy precepts less the sum of human wretchedness, and strengthen Man with his own mind."* He's doing that closed-eye thing again. Boatswain sneaks another cookie. I clear my throat, and Byron's eyes fly open. "Where was I? Oh yes. Over time, successive generations appeared as human, and it became easier and easier to simply disappear into human society."

"This is all fascinating, really," I lie. "But can we skip along? You were explaining how my baby was going to bring about the apocalypse."